THE END
OF THE
HOUSE
OF
ALARD

CATHOLIC WOMEN
WRITERS

THE END OF THE HOUSE OF ALARD

Sheila Kaye-Smith

WITH AN INTRODUCTION BY
BONNIE LANDER JOHNSON AND
JULIA MESZAROS

The Catholic University of America Press
WASHINGTON, D.C.

First published in 1923
by E. P. Dutton & Company.
Introductions Copyright © 2022
The Catholic University of America Press
All rights reserved
The paper used in this publication meets
the requirements of American National Standards
for Information Science— Permanence of
Paper for Printed Library Materials,
ANSI Z39.48-1992.

∞

Library of Congress Cataloging-in-Publication Data
Names: Kaye-Smith, Sheila, 1887–1956, author. |
Lander, Bonnie, 1977– writer of introduction. |
Meszaros, Julia T. (Julia Theresa), 1983–
writer of introduction.
Title: The end of the House of Alard /
Sheila Kaye-Smith ; with an introduction by Bonnie
Lander Johnson and Julia Meszaros.
Description: Washington, D.C. : The Catholic University
of America Press, 2022.
Identifiers: LCCN 2022016674 (print) |
LCCN 2022016675 (ebook) |
ISBN 9780813235622 (paperback) |
ISBN 9780813235639 (ebook)
Subjects: LCGFT: Novels.
Classification: LCC PR6021.A8 E65 2022 (print) |
LCC PR6021.A8 (ebook) |
DDC 823/.912—dc23/eng/20220425
LC record available at https://lccn.loc.gov/2022016674
LC ebook record available at https://lccn.loc.gov/2022016675

*"We only know that the
last sad squires ride slowly
towards the sea,
And a new people takes
the land...."*

—G. K. CHESTERTON

CONTENTS

THE END
OF THE
HOUSE
OF
ALARD

INTRODUCTION TO
THE CATHOLIC WOMEN
WRITERS SERIES

The Catholic Literary Revival was concentrated primarily in Britain, France, and America. Spanning the hundred years between the late nineteenth century and the late twentieth century, the movement saw an unprecedented quantity of writing by and about Catholics emerging after a protracted absence of Catholic faith and culture from the public sphere. In Britain the catalysts for this flourishing of poetry, prose fiction, and nonfiction were the beginning of the Oxford Movement, John Henry Newman's conversion to Rome, and the re-establishment of the Catholic hierarchy after three hundred years of persecution. In France, amid continuing anti-clericalism following the revolution, Catholic literature flourished alongside new religious orders and lay spiritual communities. And in America, European immigrants arriving in the nineteenth century were entering a society marked by a long history of anti-Catholicism. They utilized literature to explore a dimension of human thought and experience that was still largely absent from the American imagination.

The Catholic Literary Revival is exemplified by the work of Hilaire Belloc, Robert Hugh Benson, Georges Bernanos,

Léon Bloy, G. K. Chesterton, Graham Greene, Gerard Manley Hopkins, Jacques Maritain, Thomas Merton, Charles Péguy, Walker Percy, J. R. R. Tolkien, and Evelyn Waugh. The works of all of these writers have been consistently in print, in modern editions, throughout the last century and up to the present day. The Revival's most numerous members, however, were women, and although some of these women remain well known—Muriel Spark, Antonia White, Kate O'Brien, Flannery O'Connor, Dorothy Day—many have been almost entirely forgotten. These include Mary Beckett, Kathleen Coyle, Enid Dinnis, Anna Hanson Dorsey, Alice Thomas Ellis, Eleanor Farjeon, Rumer Godden, Caroline Gordon, Clotilde Graves, Caryll Houselander, Sheila Kaye-Smith, Jane Lane, Marie Belloc Lowndes, Alice Meynell, Kathleen Raine, Pearl Mary Teresa Richards, Edith Sitwell, Gladys Bronwyn Stern, Josephine Ward, and Maisie Ward.

There are various reasons why each of these writers fell out of print. Broadly, we can point to changes in the commercial publishing world after World War II as well as changes within the Church itself and in the English-speaking universities that redefined the literary canon in the last decades of the twentieth century. Yet it remains puzzling that a body of writing so creative, so attuned to its historical moment, and so unique in its perspective on the human condition should have fallen into obscurity for so long.

This series brings together the English-language prose work of Catholic women from the nineteenth and twentieth centuries, work that retains its literary excellence and its accessibility to a broad range of readers. Although the series includes some short stories and nonfiction, it concentrates primarily on the novel. The novel was modernity's chief literary innovation. It grew out of several prose traditions, especially the spiritual autobiography, and yet it has been called both a Protestant and a secular form. The novel usually concentrates on the personal lives of a small cast of characters drawn from a range of social demographics; its demand for psychological realism and the nuances of lives lived in the material world mean its vision is usually more earthly than spiritual. The novel is able to contain and explore religious concerns, especially the roles of providence and personal conscience, and many great novels depict elements of religious experience. Yet these novels nonetheless tend to remain worldly, secular or materialist in structure and vision. This is no surprise, for the novel is ultimately resistant to "the pressures put upon it by many writers to transcend the limits" of the secular world.[1]

However, many of the writers in this series used the novel as an opportunity to rethink the form and its capacity to express a uniquely Catholic perspective. In doing so, they not only developed and advanced the form itself but also brought an ancient faith to bear on life in the modern world. There is a certain paradox here: Catholic writers effectively helped to push the novel into newer, and therefore more "modern" forms, even though they did so in pursuit of a truth that sometimes required a rejection or questioning of modernity's broader cultural movements.

The novel has often been characterized, especially in its

---

1. George Levine, *Realism, Ethics and Secularism: Essays on Victorian Literature and Science* (Cambridge: Cambridge University Press, 2011), 210. See also Deirdre Shauna Lynch, "Gothic Fiction and 'Belief in Every Kind of Prodigy,'" in *The Routledge Companion to Literature and Religion*, ed. Mark Knight (Oxfordshire: Routledge, 2016), 252–62, 252.

early-eighteenth-century form, as primarily concerned with female experience and the domestic sphere. Although prominent counter-examples to this thesis exist, such as in the work of Fielding and Dickens, the genre nonetheless frequently explores the internal lives of female characters and their negotiation of personal relationships within the more limited geographical settings of a single house, village, or city. But the novel is also a genre well suited to the exploration of social and political change. Unlike drama or epic, it can provide a voice for those who do not possess great social power, who must navigate moral challenges, often on their own and in direct conflict with the culture around them, and who, in doing so, offer criticisms of the society in which they find themselves. In this respect, the novel offered a perfect vehicle for exploring the challenges faced by a Catholic in modern society.

The historical period in which the Catholic Literary Revival emerged witnessed a complex renegotiation of almost all European social institutions, from the aristocracy and the family to party politics and the role of the state. There were Catholic writers among the many voices calling for change as well as among the many questioning its validity. Many of the novels in this series are concerned with distinguishing between stale social conventions that confine, suppress, or limit human capacities and timeless spiritual traditions that are morally and doctrinally true and authentic. Indeed, Catholic writers of the period drew on their faith to interrogate their society while also exploring how modern Catholics could live faithfully in a rapidly changing world.

The nineteenth and twentieth centuries were religiously tumultuous; they were often defined, even at the time, as an age of both faith and doubt. Writers and artists of every stripe examined the role of institutional religion in public life and the personal consequences of lives lived with faith or without it. The period has been described as the beginning of a modern secular society, but it also witnessed powerful resistance to secularization; writers from Austen to Eliot, Wilde to Waugh identified religious belief as newly urgent and necessary. A nonreligious or strictly materialist worldview was for many an increasingly dangerous proposition. In 1935, T. S. Eliot criticized writers who failed to resist the drift toward secularism: "the whole of modern literature is corrupted by what I call Secularism.... [I]t is simply unaware of, simply cannot understand the meaning of, the primacy of the supernatural over the natural life ... something which I assume to be our primary concern."[2] Indeed, the period saw many conversions to Catholicism, notably among writers and artists, all of whom helped to shape in new and dynamic ways the "Catholic imagination."

This term can be broadly defined as a vision of the world in which the drama of salvation is played out in the mundane experiences of the everyday, in which the visible and created things of the world, the development of individual character and community identity, and the adventure of human relationships—all these are phenomena through which readers can touch spiritual realities. The Catholic imagination is that state of awareness through which the seemingly abstract doctrines of Church teaching are played out in a person's day-to-day experiences and moral actions, to the point

2. T. S. Eliot, "Religion and Literature," in *Selected Prose*, ed. Frank Kermode (New York: Harcourt Brace Jovanovich, 1975), 97–106, 104–5.

that some of the smallest human endeavors become nothing less than matters of life and death. From a technical point of view, the novel was uniquely suited to exploring these varied levels of human experience. Its innovations in voice and point of view, in narrative time and the role of description and world-making in constructing human interiority, predispose it to the dramatization of both earthly and cosmic dimensions and moral or spiritual battles both social and personal.

The neglected female representatives of the Catholic literary revival cast a distinct and important light on the Catholic imagination. Typically writing from within more introspective, domestic and romantic contexts, they often root Catholic experience in the everyday, revealing its relevance in and to the lives of ordinary men and women. This less socio-political touch may be one reason for their fall from the public eye, but it is also what makes them so uniquely relevant to contemporary life. As politico-cultural and religious institutions continue to drift into separate spheres of public influence, Christians today often struggle to grasp how faith should or does inform their day-to-day lives. Through fiction, the authors in this series provide a bridge over the divide between religious belief and everyday experience.

If the women writers involved in the Catholic literary revival often wrote from a more domestic or interpersonal angle, they were by no means unaware or uncritical of the social, cultural, political, and ecclesial developments of their time. Indeed, their more marginal role in Anglo-American society often allowed them to adopt a uniquely perceptive outsider's view. For many of the women in this series it was precisely their Catholic faith that empowered them to adopt a prominent voice. Inspired by the rich intellectual tradition of the

Church and the prominent female saints throughout history, these writers made important contributions to Catholic thought on human dignity and the sacramental potential of the ordinary.

A large number of writers in this series were converts from Anglicanism or from no religion at all. Their imaginations were therefore shaped by a radical change in perspective. Becoming Catholic meant accepting a place outside of the British and American establishment, but it also meant they could often see their society with clear eyes for the first time. Many of the writers in this series also experienced personal suffering to an inordinate degree. Catholic teaching on the salvific nature of suffering provided them with means by which to understand the role that their loss played in the small drama of their own life as much as the bigger cosmic drama in which we are all players. Caryll Houselander, for example, understood personal suffering to be a means by which Christians could "give birth to Christ" in the lives of others. Like many writers, she understood that the novel is itself a vehicle for understanding suffering. Houselander turned to the novel after decades of writing spiritual prose. She did so because she no longer wanted to "preach" to her fellows; she wanted instead to "take sinners by the hand" and walk in their lives for a time. The wounds experienced by our writers, when combined with the existential awakening of a conversion to faith, shaped their particular view of human experience and divine truth. Faced with the emotional and spiritual reality of deep suffering, convert novelists often saw in Catholicism what they saw in the novel itself: a space able to contain all the mysteries of human experience.

Benedict XVI said that "the only really effective apologia for Christianity comes down to two arguments, namely, the *saints* the Church has produced and the *art* which has grown in her womb."[3] We should not, therefore, underestimate the importance of artists for defending the credibility of the Christian faith. This pertains also to the Catholic women writers of this series. Few of these writers will go on to be canonized; indeed some of them may not have been particularly saintly, but through their interventions in literary tradition, these women powerfully reshaped the literary and religious landscape.

For the Catholic reader, the writing in this series provides a fictional exploration of the moral and spiritual adventure offered by Catholic life. It also offers a way of holding together themes that have become increasingly partisan in the Church today. Most of the women in this series were writing at a time when the Church was grappling to define its relationship to an increasingly secular world. They were innovators who raised questions that would eventually be posed at the Second Vatican Council, but they were also loyal to many of the traditions and doctrines that disappeared after the Council. Their vision incorporates both a rigorous personal morality and a concern for social justice; an awareness of God's grandeur and an appreciation of his presence in the ordinary; and the importance of both piety and charitable works.

For the non-Catholic reader, the writing in this series offers a crucial but overlooked vision of modernity. It provides

3. Joseph Cardinal Ratzinger (with Vittorio Messori), *The Ratzinger Report: An Exclusive Interview on the State of the Church*, trans. Salvator Attanasio and Graham Harrison (San Francisco, Calif.: Ignatius Press, 1985), 129.

insight into a unique form of female experience but also a unique means of understanding how the Catholic faith is played out in the everyday. For those interested in the history of the novel, these writers demonstrate some of the ways in which the genre is able to explore and express the highest and most timeless spiritual realities, often through the application of the most avant-garde novelistic techniques.

Bonnie Lander Johnson and Julia Meszaros

FURTHER READING

Tom Woodman. *Faithful Fictions*. Washington, D.C.: The Catholic University of America Press, 2022.

James Emmett Ryan. *Faithful Passages*. Madison: University of Wisconsin Press, 2013.

INTRODUCTION TO

The End of the House of Alard

The End of the House of Alard was a UK and US bestseller in 1923. The novel was just one of over fifty books written by Sheila Kaye-Smith, and yet—with the exception of Virago's late-20th-century editions of *Susan Spray* and *Joanna Godden*—few of Kaye-Smith's titles have been in print since her death in 1956.

Like many of the writers in this series, Sheila Kaye-Smith was a woman both at the center of her community and an outsider. She was a wife but not a mother. She was a Catholic convert whose husband had once been an Anglican priest. And she was a woman of Sussex, where she was surrounded by rural people who belonged to ancient social groups, from yeomen to gentry; groups to which she herself, as a writer and daughter of a doctor, did not belong. However, with the personal blessing of the Pope, she oversaw the establishment and running of a Catholic parish church in East Sussex, while also earning much of the household income from writing after her husband gave up his Anglican parish stipend to be a Catholic layman.

Many of Kaye-Smith's characters possess this same quality: at once outside of, and figures of authority within, their social world. Indeed, it is often the case that the outsider in a Kaye-Smith novel possesses a personal and moral strength through which he or she is able to rescue or redeem those who have been trapped too long by social convention. *The End of the House of Alard* is especially concerned with the human search for that crucial distinction between restrictive social conventions that stifle human flourishing and the abiding and authentic spiritual traditions from which people gain liberty and true goodness. Set in rural Sussex in the decades that saw the rapid decline of England's aristocratic families, Kaye-Smith is able to frame this distinction in both class and religious terms.

THE AUTHOR

Emily Sheila Kaye-Smith was born on February 4, 1887, at 9 Dane Road, St. Leonards-on-Sea, a suburb of Hastings on the East Sussex coast. The house was a newly built Edwardian family home, and still stands (divided into flats) on the corner of Dane and Brittany Streets in what is now one of St. Leonards' smartest areas, just a few blocks from the seafront. It was then a modest and suitable home for a widowed country doctor, his new wife (herself a widow), and a growing family. Sheila had two older sisters, one from her father's previous marriage and one from her mother's. She was the first child of the new marriage, and one younger sister, Mona, also born in the Dane Road house, arrived two years after Sheila.

While the girls were too young for lengthy travel, the Kaye-Smith parents spent their summer holidays alone on the continent. The sisters would stay on the Sussex farm of a family friend. These rural summers were the most important and formative experiences for the young Sheila, who would go on to become one of the most famous "Sussex writers." Almost all of her fiction is set in rural Sussex, primarily in the border territories between East Sussex and Kent. Her writing is steeped in farming lore, local landscape and legend, and the peoples and dialects of the region. Although Sheila would spend some of her adult years living in London and enjoying a full urban social life within both the literary and the Anglo-Catholic milieux of the capitol, she never lost her passion for Sussex.

In 1896, when she was nine years old, Sheila went to the local school for girls, St. Leonards Ladies College. There she made her first great friend, Pansy, a skilled classicist and mathematician who would go on to win a scholarship at Girton College, Cambridge. Dr. Kaye-Smith had hoped that Sheila might do the same; but by the time she finished school, Sheila had already spent two years writing fiction and had decided to become an author. Instead of moving away to university, she continued living in her parents' house, where she could work and from where she could visit the Sussex farmhouses in which her fiction is set. Her first novel, *The Tramping Methodist*, was published in 1908. Sheila went on to write almost one novel each year until the Great War began, when she became involved in making bandages for the wounded. Then in 1918, at the end of the war, her old school friend Pansy died and Sheila entered a period of introspection. Still living at home with her parents, she wrote some of her finest and most famous novels. She also began to think more seriously about religion.

Her parents were low-church Protestants, but just before she was confirmed in 1902, Sheila attended a High-Anglican church in Devon and fell in love with the beauty of its ceremonial life. In *Three Ways Home*, Sheila writes that

Here for the first time I saw the Church. Hitherto—ever since the instinctive religion of childhood had passed—religion had been a strictly personal affair, governed by rules of conduct. Now for the first time I saw myself as one of the company, approaching God, not merely to win His favour by our good behaviour. But to do Him honour and to give Him praise and to receive in exchange those gifts which I had vaguely sensed as a child but had never apprehended until now.[1]

The High-Anglican tradition had a home in London and, most notoriously, in Oxford. But it was also well-established in rural Sussex, where churches like Christ Church in St. Leonards attracted a large congregation of rural and semi-rural families who embraced catholic liturgy, morals, and doctrine, but who remained wary of Roman Catholicism.

The Anglo-Catholic movement believed—and still believes—that its mission was to bring the Church of England back to its catholic foundation. In 1925, Kaye-Smith wrote a book that outlined the movement's contemporary position almost a century after it first emerged in Oxford.[2] She describes a movement that both accepted the Reformation and quarreled with it. On the one hand, it recognized the Reformation's intention of locating an older form of universal Christianity before the Eastern and Western churches split, and of returning the church in England to Christian practices that were thought to predate Roman "innovations." And yet, the movement disagreed with how the Church of En-

---

1. Sheila Kaye-Smith, *Three Ways Home* (New York: Harper & Brothers, 1937), 44.

2. Sheila Kaye-Smith, *Anglo-Catholicism* (London: Chapman & Hall, 1925).

gland had proceeded to alter its doctrines and practices after the Henrician controversy. It sought to return the Church of England to its true catholic identity; more than this, as it developed, the movement perceived the catholic party within the Church of England as uniquely able to unite all Christians—Eastern, Roman, and Protestant—into a fully unified and universal Church. In this way, it was grounded in neither the Roman nor Eastern traditions but in its hope for a future universality, which Anglo-Catholicism itself sought to bring about.[3]

This was an ambitious goal. While Anglo-Catholicism's hopes for bringing about a fully universal Church may not have been realized, the movement certainly did bring significant changes to the Church of England. The Anglican Church in which Newman, Pusey and Keble initially found themselves was mostly sober in worship. The Anglo-Catholic movement reintroduced at the parish level a significant degree of high ceremony and "catholic" sacramentalism. By the time Kaye-Smith wrote her book in 1925, it had become commonplace for many Anglican parish churches, even those professedly moderate, to use candles and vestments, confession, and regular communion—practices that priests in the early days of the movement were sometimes imprisoned for refusing to give up.

But the movement's belief that it possessed a true catholicity even beyond that which could be claimed by the Roman and Orthodox Churches was a tenuous position to maintain. It submitted only tentatively to the authority of Church of England bishops and did not recognize any other Church

3. Kaye-Smith, *Anglo-Catholicism*, 189.

authority, even while it modelled its liturgy and practice upon the Church of Rome. It believed it held the full, universal catholic truth, but it was also an avant-garde and self-governed movement within the national Church. In practice, this fragile position produced a niche form of nationalism; Anglo-Catholics were passionately invested in the idea of England and its early religious history. One result of this, and of the movement's difficult relationship with ecclesial authority, was its rather precise interest in the internal workings of its own community, especially its liturgical practice.

Sheila Kaye-Smith and other converts from Anglo-Catholicism describe the movement's attention to liturgical detail as an over-investment in external forms. But it was precisely this desire for ritual splendor that initially attracted Kaye-Smith to Anglo-Catholicism. As a young woman, she had been to the Roman Catholic Church in St. Leonards and found it unimpressive, preferring instead the Anglo-Catholic Christ Church, where she could enjoy the beauty of catholic devotion, together with those qualities she had come to assume as her birthright: ancient rural traditions, an establishment clergy, and a feeling of belonging. But, she says, "though I did not know it, my whole idea of religion was sentimental."[4] It would be unfair to accuse Sheila of cultural elitism, because her novels everywhere attest to her belief in the danger of class hierarchies. But the anti-Catholic prejudice in England ran deep. Like many Anglo-Catholics before her, Sheila had to work through these instinctive barriers to Catholic communion and, in doing so, realize that what she had perceived as an insurmountable distinction between one religious iden-

4. Kaye-Smith, *Three Ways Home*, 103.

tity and another, was in fact but a mere step across a small but crucially important threshold.

Sheila Kaye-Smith made that step only once she had married, and she was married very late in life. Having lived through her twenties and thirties as a single woman and writer, Sheila had few romantic entanglements. Then, in January 1924, her younger sister Mona died of a heart attack after suffering influenza. Mona's death caused Sheila to question her own future. During this same month, the *Woman's Pictorial* magazine commissioned a series of articles from Sheila asking, "What Makes A Woman A Success?" The second of these articles addressed success in marriage. With no first-hand experience herself, Sheila had nonetheless written about numerous married characters, not all of whom enjoyed success or happiness. But around this time, Sheila decided that she would marry the first man who asked her, whether or not she loved him. That man was Theodore Penrose Fry, a curate at the High Anglican Christ Church in St. Leonards, where Sheila was a parishioner. They announced their engagement in June that year and were married in St. Paul's, the largest church in St. Leonards, on October 16th, 1924. The marriage was to be a very happy one.

Sometime between January and June, Penrose had to retire from his curacy at Christ Church because the rector insisted on the celibacy of his clergy. Instead, Penrose was given a position as assistant priest at St. James Norlands Church in West London, and the couple moved into a flat in Holland Park. One of their wedding presents was a cat. They named him John Henry after John Henry Newman—who had, by the time the Frys arrived in the capital, been dead almost thirty-five years. In London, the Frys became even more fully involved in Anglo-Catholicism. The Chestertons had converted to Roman Catholicism just two years earlier, in 1922, and the Frys stepped into their position as unofficial leaders of the catholic wing of the Church of England. Sheila found herself in the role of spokeswoman for a religious movement. Together with a small band of passionate Anglo-Catholics, she travelled the country giving talks. But public speaking did not come naturally to her, and she soon returned to her writing.

Sheila was now the wife of a clergyman, but this new position did not diminish her literary output. She says in *Three Ways Home* that "the clergyman's wife is in some ways the most maligned woman of the community. In novels she is nearly always represented as stupid, domineering, interfering, a gossip, a busybody and uncharitable—always uncharitable."[5] The clergyman's wife in *Alard* fits this same character type. And yet Kaye-Smith felt that it was almost always an untrue representation of the real clergymen's wives she met both in London and Sussex, who were instead generous, kind, charitable and hard-working. Her own friends expressed the commonly held expectation that she would give up her work to join in her husband's parish duties. But this was not the case. Except for her short-lived role on the Anglo-Catholic lecture circuit, married life provided Kaye-Smith with almost more time to write than she had when single.

However, both at St. James and at Penrose's subsequent church, St. Stephens, neither of the Frys were very content. Sheila missed Sussex, and they were both growing increas-

5. Kaye-Smith, *Three Ways Home*, 154.

ingly disillusioned with Anglo-Catholicism. In 1928, they travelled to Sicily. Sheila writes in *Three Ways Home* that they believed they might witness in the south of Italy the Catholic Church "at its most repulsive" and so be cured of their misgivings about Anglo-Catholicism. But the opposite occurred. There, she found that she was "disturbed by the holiness of Rome ... by the fact that I was cut off from it. This surely was the heart and blackness of schism. I was cut off from the Altar of the Saints ... just as I was cut off from the altar of the people—the people of Palermo, Preston, Peking, every part of the world where the Catholic Church draws together all classes, colours and races."[6] They saw in Sicily a Church for everyone: beautiful and historical but also universal.

Conversion was challenging for the Frys. Like many other Anglo-Catholics before them, most notoriously Newman himself, going to Rome would mean relinquishing Penrose's clerical identity, their parish, their broader Christian community and Penrose's income. Sheila remembers that when they first began to talk seriously about conversion, she asked Penrose the question that "any Anglo-Catholic would have asked: 'What about your Orders?' The answer he gave was what any Catholic would have given: 'That goes with the rest. If one accepts the Church, everything else follows.'"[7]

Around this time, the Frys—like Caryll Houselander and others in this series—developed a devotion to St. Teresa, the Little Flower. They visited her convent in Lisieux and, at home, prayed countless novenas in her name. In 1929, just one year after their journey to Sicily, Penrose retired from his

---

6. Kaye-Smith, *Three Ways Home*, 186.
7. Kaye-Smith, *Three Ways Home*, 191.

curacy. The Frys began to receive instruction in the Catholic faith from Father Charles C. Martindale, SJ, who was in Rye at the time, not far from Sheila's childhood home, and who had read all of Sheila's novels. It was Father Martindale who, a decade earlier, had read her 1917 novel about the American Civil War, *The Challenge to Sirius,* and declared in his review that its author was a Catholic at heart and would one day convert. Just before Christmas in 1929, the Frys were received into the Roman Catholic Church by Father Martindale at the Farm Street Jesuit church in London.

Now homeless, with Penrose unemployed, the Frys used Sheila's money to purchase a home in Little Doucegrove on the Kent and East Sussex borders. The farm they bought had been the setting of Sheila's 1910 novel, *Spell Land.* Sheila had come home—first to Rome and now to the Sussex country-side. But the nearest Catholic church was nine miles away in Rye. The Bishop of Southwark granted them permission to build a small chapel on their new property, though he doubted the success of it. In January 1930, the Frys traveled to Rome, where they were given a personal audience with Pope Pius XI, who blessed their venture. It would be some years before the Frys could build a new church, but on their return from Rome they converted their hayloft to a small chapel—and on December 7th, 1930, the second Sunday of Advent, a Mass was said by a local priest, Father Dudley, to a congregation of 28 people. The parish had no permanent clergy assigned to it, and so the entire management of its administrative and pastoral activities fell to the Frys. Now, as a lay woman married to a lay man, Sheila found that she was more involved in the Church than she had been as a clergyman's wife.

By the mid-1930s, the Sunday masses at the Little Douce-grove chapel had become so popular they were proving perilous; the hayloft was not strong enough for a large congregation. Sheila and Penrose commissioned architects and builders to begin construction of St. Teresa's, a simple brick chapel that still stands on the rise overlooking the woods between Clayhill and Broad Oak, surrounded by gravestones and oak trees. In a small ceremony on 6th August 1935, Sheila cut the first clod of earth from one of the Frys' fields, and the land was blessed. Four months later the building was finished, and on the Feast of the Immaculate Conception, St. Teresa's held its first Mass. Two local priests celebrated, and over one hundred people attended; the sisters of the Little Flower at Lisieux sent prayer cards from France to everyone in the congregation. Sheila was almost fifty years old. No children had been born of her marriage. But she had published over thirty books, and with the money from her work she had planted a Catholic church in the soil of her homeland.

The Frys lived at Little Doucegrove for another two decades, writing, walking the fields and the seafront, and praying in the chapel they built. Then on January 14th, 1956, Sheila died from a cerebral hemorrhage. She was buried in the churchyard of St. Teresa's. Penrose sold the house to Rumer Godden, herself a novelist and Catholic convert, and dedicated as the Frys had been to the Sussex countryside. Fifteen years later, Penrose died in a Hampshire nursing home. His body was brought back to the chapel.

St. Teresa's is now in the Diocese of Arundel and Brighton, within the parish of Our Lady Immaculate & St. Michael, Battle. It offers two Masses on Sundays, and its statue of St. Teresa looks out benignly at the congregation. It is a thriving rural parish, its older members still knowledgeable about Sheila. But even those who never met her continue each Sunday to fulfil the request that is etched in stone on the north side of the porch: "Pray for the soul of Emily Sheila Fry, writer and novelist." Outside the church, the twinned graves of Sheila and Penrose face the Sussex landscape that shaped Sheila's life and writing. On her grave is written: "She hath considered a field and bought it, with the fruit of her hand, she hath planted a vineyard from it."

THE NOVEL

Sheila Kaye-Smith began writing *The End of the House of Alard* in 1922, after the death of her father. It documents the choices made by the final generation of the aristocratic Alard family and the ways in which they, both willingly and reluctantly, bring the long line of their ancestral blood to a complete and sudden end. Each sibling plays his or her role in this dynastic death, either through a rebellious choice of spouse or a radical choice of religious allegiance. For some of them, the end of the Alard line is as painful to enact as it is for the generation above to witness; for others, it is welcomed as a necessary modernization or a true realignment toward religious integrity and universal human truth. Some of the siblings yearn for individual liberty; others have it forced upon them. But none of them can find it under the burden of the Alard name and its crumbling estate.

It is difficult to account for Kaye-Smith's fall from popularity in the last fifty years. While she was alive, her novels met with both literary and commercial success, and it is clear that they retain their literary strength today. We could point to changes in the commercial fiction market after the Second World War. But in fact, many Kaye-Smith novels address the very concerns emerging in the middle of the twentieth century: the end of the old social order, the search for spiritual meaning amid personal suffering and radical social change, the changing situation of women in society, the shifting relationship between rural and urban economies. Certainly, post-war readers looking back at the start of the century professed a growing interest in the period's avant-garde literary movements. Especially in the burgeoning literary departments of English-speaking universities, students looking to understand the first decades of the twentieth century focused primarily on Modernist, Decadent, and Surrealist literature. When compared to this body of writing, Kaye-Smith appears thoroughly mainstream. At a time when the dominant literary figures were seeking controversy, Kaye-Smith was exploring the abiding human search for meaning in subtle and profound narratives of significant literary merit that were nonetheless accessible to all readers. She may not have revolutionized the novel form like her modernist peers, but she was certainly more widely read than them.

The End of the House of Alard presents an ensemble cast in a form reminiscent of large-scale 19th-century novels such as George Eliot's *Middlemarch*, in which each member of the fictional community is given a distinct role to play while embodying different perspectives on a central moral question. In Kaye-Smith's novel, that question could be defined as: How do we navigate various traditions, both social and religious, in order to find our human purpose? How do we distinguish between purely socially constructed traditions that restrict human flourishing, and those that are authentic and time-less and have the potential to reveal to individuals their true identities? For the first act of this novel, these questions are posed within a socio-political context, as they were for so many 19th-century novels of social conscience. But the question of religious faith begins to emerge at a crucial point in the narrative, demonstrating that, for Kaye-Smith, the only real way to answer the novel's questions is to push them into the cosmic sphere. Although she may not be a card-carrying literary modernist, Kaye-Smith nonetheless occupies a his-torical ground somewhere between the Victorian novel, with its ensemble cast and its burning questions about social jus-tice, and the emerging modern novel with its focus on the individual in a world increasingly drained of cosmic reality. To both of these moments in the history of the novel, Kaye-Smith brings a unique vision of faith at work in the world, one both consoling and radical. That she manages this while still writing in the tone of commercially popular fiction is quite extraordinary.

Kaye-Smith wrote *The End of the House of Alard* when she was still an Anglo-Catholic, and it needs to be read in that context. The "catholic" parish in the novel remains within the Anglican diocese. However, it is depicted in ways that will be recognizably Catholic to readers today, and the novel's char-acters perceive it much like how they would have perceived a Roman Catholic parish. It is impoverished and excluded from establishment privilege; its ornaments and furnishings, made by parishioners, are sentimental or gaudy; it is open to everyone regardless of social standing; its moral teaching re-

mains firm against changing cultural attitudes to divorce; and
it is ordered toward the worship of God rather than the social
life of the parish. In many ways, the novel documents Kaye-
Smith's own project of working through what it means to belong to a Church whose moral and doctrinal tenets remain
abject from the perspective of the English establishment.
However, more important than the distinctions between Catholicism and Anglo-Catholicism is the novel's concern with
the human need for faith.

Alard was published shortly after *Joanna Godden*, a novel
about a female Sussex farmer. Ever afterwards, *Joanna Godden*
was "sighed over" as the last novel Sheila wrote "before religion spoilt" her as a novelist. (Actually, *Joanna Godden* "is full
of clues to the author's religious position." It contains a sym-
pathetic portrayal of a monk and several allusions to Catholic customs. And "Joanna's morality—her attitude toward
divorce and illegitimacy—is definitely Catholic and Christian."[8]) Kaye-Smith believed that *Joanna Godden's* religious
elements would not have escaped critics' notice had she published the novel after *Alard*. Instead, *Alard* was the first novel
to appear after its author was known publicly to have become
an observant Christian, and the novel subsequently met with
critical disdain for its explicit religious content. As one friend
told Sheila, "Now, whatever you may write for the rest of your
life, you will always be suspected of religious propaganda."
This proved to be true. Kaye-Smith's subsequent novels were
identified as works of proselytization and mostly dismissed
by reviewers. Even those of her later novels that contained no
explicit Catholic materials were assumed to be "propaganda"

8. Kaye-Smith, *Three Ways Home*, 131.

by default; negative traits in her characters were interpreted as a message that, if only the character had the author's religion, they might have been happier. And yet, despite these negative reviews, *Alard* was the first of Kaye-Smith's best-sellers. Whatever her critics felt, readers wanted to read good novels that were not afraid of looking at religion and its importance to the human condition.

Kaye-Smith did sometimes wonder if religion should ever be made the subject of a novel. And yet, "how can one leave it out?... It exists as a powerful and universal force. It may be suppressed, inhibited or misdirected, after the manner of other instincts, but it is still there, colouring and directing human life for good or evil, according to whether it is or is not given healthy expression. To ignore it gives a lop-sided view of the world." In an observation that holds perhaps even truer today than it did when she wrote it eighty years ago, Kaye-Smith argues that "the number of people without religion in fiction is out of all proportion to the number in fact."[9]

She says that "in the course of nearly twenty years' experience I have come to the conclusion that in England we are not quite normal on the subject of religion," but that

This is not surprising if you apply to the general public those psychological theories which are with monotonous frequency applied to the individual, and if you accept the hypothesis that religion is a fundamental human instinct, the suppression of which may be attended by quite as many disastrous consequences as the suppression of any other. Four hundred years ago the Catholic religion was forcibly suppressed in this country. Without the slightest attempt to change or educate public opinion it was entirely swept

9. Kaye-Smith, *Three Ways Home*, 132–33.

away. The system established in its place bore so little resemblance to it in the popular mind that it was looked upon as a game, until fines, imprisonment, torture and death for those who refused to play it established it in sober earnest. Is it to be wondered that so gigantic a repression should create an equally gigantic neurosis? The attitude of many people today toward Catholicism, in fact to any kind of religion, is not unlike that of the inhibited type of spinster towards sex. They giggle nervously or become angry and excited if it creeps into the conversation.[10]

Kaye-Smith saw clearly that religion provides the fiction-writer with "nearly as many good situations as the sex-instinct—there are endless combinations, permutations, frustrations and deviations which the novelist can use, and its effect on character (either by its growth or by its thwarting) makes something new in the way of psychological interest." The struggles and concerns that religious belief or non-belief bring to Kaye-Smith's characters were recognized as true and human by her readers, but they have remained consistently underexplored by novelists to this day.

In fact, Kaye-Smith's craft as a writer did change around the time she wrote *Alard*. Her critics interpreted this change as the result of her marriage or her "finding religion." Kaye-Smith herself believes the change was a natural result of growing up. She was thirty. Her parents had died. The war had come and gone. She was married, and happily so. And she had allowed herself to freely embrace her desire for God. In *Three Ways Home*, she argues that her early success as a young novelist was due to her very active imagination. She had almost no direct experience of human love or suffering.

---

10. Kaye-Smith, *Three Ways Home*, 157–58.

Instead, she drew on material from other writers, from the Sussex landscape around her, and from her own imagination. She describes an artistic process that occurred in her subconscious but which, for this reason, produced quite romantic or sentimental literature. As she grew older, she began instead to write more from her conscious mind, from her observations and experiences. The result was novels of greater realism; novels that certainly proved more popular with the public, but that did not fit the profile the publishing world had come to expect from her. More importantly, she observes that, when she was younger, her entire human happiness depended on her literary success. This early success did indeed bring her happiness. But, she says, "the majority of human beings do not turn to God because they have not enough happiness but because happiness is not enough."[11] Literary success was not enough to make her life full.

The End of the House of Alard is a novel about the human need for purpose, for a truth by which to live and for which to die. It is a novel about faith and idolatry, love and death, freedom and bondage, nature and grace. Put another way, it is about how human beings cannot escape the great challenge of salvation, of breaking free from false, manmade gods in order to unite instead with the divine love of Christ. The novel's characters span a breadth of options on this spectrum, and their various outlooks on life, though indicative of the options open to an Anglican of the 1920s, continue to reflect those available to us today.

11. Kaye-Smith, *Three Ways Home*, 115.

Old and New Order

Sir John, head of the Alard estate, evokes the Biblical figure of Adam. He represents—and actively strives to promote— the "old order," a term that is not just socio-cultural but also theological. Sir John stands for a dated and morally compromised social class, but also for the wider human choice of self-assertion over surrender to God. He lives by pride, self-centeredness, and self-assertion—sins which cause both his own and his family's demise. His stance towards Peter's quest for a spouse, his behavior in the matter of Mary's divorce, or towards his son George's faith all confirm that he has only contempt for questions of truth and goodness. Instead, he has made an idol of "the house of Alard," and himself its high priest. In this role, he subordinates all other goods to Alard interests and demands his family members' total submission.

Sir John's willful disdain for God has nothing glamorous about it, and fails even to result in worldly success. Like his wife and daughter Doris, he in fact lives by nothing more than social convention and a pragmatic utilitarianism, which reduces even his children to mere instruments in the Alard mission and justifies any sacrifice to the family name. Sir John's profound dismissal of the reality of God also translates into a denial, or even disdain for the reality of the world. He refuses to confront the collapse of his estate and, even more significantly, the individual personalities and needs of his children. Unable to see or respect his own children for who they are, he provokes them into total dependency (Doris), joyless conformism (George, Peter), apathetic indifference (Mary) or rebellion (Jenny, Gervase).

Yet all of Sir John's children, despite their efforts to please him, are a disappointment to him, precisely because his desires are ultimately self-serving. In this way, his particular contempt for Doris, his most devoted child, is ironic but also apt. In giving him precisely the subservience he demands, she reveals to him in ways he cannot abide how erroneous and misdirected his desires truly are. Like Adam, he has passed on to his children the effects of his sin, including an obscured vision of reality and a false loyalty that stand in the way of faith and moral goodness.

Sir John's relentless attempts at self-assertion fail on every level. His stubborn unwillingness to surrender to reality leads to constant unhappy battles, even hatred, and comes at the cost of communion—a theme that pervades this novel. Although he seems to be putting the family first, he is unable to truly encounter any of his family members; ultimately, he does not know them at all. His error produces the devastating and dehumanizing effects that idol worship has always produced: he himself is a cold and unhappy man, lacking any meaningful relationships.

The archetypal death of the unrepentant sinner, Sir John's death is subtly contrasted with that of Christ: he dies surrounded by women, with the cocks crowing on three farms. But, contrary to Christ, who forges a bond between the beloved disciple and his mother even from the cross, Sir John, in his final hours, no longer knows anyone and his last words are words of anger. Jenny notes that his body is at peace in death, yet the narrative implies that his soul is in turmoil—a stark contrast with Christ's death, which involves a stricken body but a peaceful soul.

The fate of the squire's descendants (like that of the descendants of Adam) is determined by whether they choose to remain faithful to the false god of Alard, with whom they have a natural bond via their upbringing and natural instincts; or whether they have the wisdom and courage to cast off the shackles of the old order. The narrative is here clearly inspired by the Biblical theme that "whoever loves father or mother more than me is not worthy of me" (Mt 10:37). Kaye-Smith demonstrates that the choices Christianity presents us with are no ethereal abstractions, but embody themselves repeatedly within the day-to-day reality of every human life.

Idolatry

Several characters serve to illustrate the bitter existential consequences of betraying God for an idol. This theme is played out most completely and tragically in the figure of Peter. In Peter, the family's idolatry is made explicit: Alard is his "first love." The estate is described as "the First and Last Things of his life, the very rock on which it stood." Mistaken for the true God, it "feels ancient, like an eternity." However, as Peter later comes to realize, Alard lacks truth and hence coherence. Like any idol, "it had an awkward habit of splitting up into its component parts, into individuals, every separate one of which hurt and vexed."

As heir of the estate but desiring a marriage that appears to threaten the estate, Peter's true loyalty is tested most acutely. In one sense, his conflict stands for the decision of every Christian. He must decide whether he is willing to forego his natural inheritance and seeming material security for the sake of a higher good, a truer love. As his father's son or a descendant of Adam, Peter does not recognize things for what they are and therefore misdiagnoses his options. Marrying Stella, whose religious faith he does not understand, is his chance of heaven, his salvation. Yet to Peter, mired in the sins of his father, it appears unreasonable, risky, willful. Following social and familial convention and accepting the role intended for him seems to him more sensible, more secure, more likely to bring happiness, more selfless even, than to marry his beloved. It is the house of Alard that he associates with eternity, and not Stella's love, which he has known only for a year. He cannot see that the inverse is true—true because Stella's love is rooted in God's own, eternal love, which gives it a faithfulness that makes it more secure than his Alard family bonds can ever be; whereas the morally ambiguous Alard estate is part of the passing, finite world. Tragically, Peter's heart tells him of the idolatry taking place, but his mind is too inculcated with the family dogma for him to break free.

In the spirit of Catholic Christianity, Kaye-Smith does not portray his choice as one between natural desires on the one hand and supernatural love on the other. Peter is not called to reject his erotic love for Stella and sacrifice it to a supernatural, purely spiritual cause. Rather, it is Peter's two natural desires—the desire to continue the family heritage and the desire to marry Stella—that are in conflict. His salvation lies in discerning which of these loves or desires is more truthful, more worthy and capable of being perfected by supernatural love. Peter's vocation, like most vocations, would in this way involve an intermingling of (true and righteous) human love with divine love: a union of both *eros* and *agape*.

Like other Catholic writers of the twentieth century, Kaye-

Smith locates a decisive key for discerning between our conflicting desires in the category of the "ordinary." One of the
novel's key themes is that God speaks to us through ordinary
means, just as Catholicism is there for everyone; that is, for ordinary men and women. Among other things, Peter's down-
fall is rooted in the fact that, as Stella later observes, he did
not trust his desire for "ordinary things like love and marriage"
and instead sacrificed them "to things like family pride and the
love of a place." Had Peter honored the ordinary, he would not
have "inherited only the things which are shaken"—the estate
of Alard—but received his divine inheritance, the kingdom of
God. Stella recognizes this and feels pity for him for having
"belonged to the new but [...] stood by the old [order]," such
that he "failed the spirit of life."

The figure of Peter illustrates Kaye-Smith's observation
that our knowledge and judgment of reality suffers the further we are removed from God. This is equally true of Doris and Mary. Like Peter and her father, Doris has put her
faith in the house of Alard. She, too, is in denial about the
true state of Alard and is prepared to sacrifice anything to
her false god. Unlike the true surrender of Christian faith,
her surrender to her father's idol results not in communion
with her family (or even her father) but in the same isolation
wrought by Peter's and Sir John's idolatry. She has forgone
her prospect of marriage as well as any other aspirations in
life, only to be taken for granted, overlooked, despised even.
The estate's eventual dissolution shocks her and drives her
into despair. She cannot accept the fact that she has put her
faith into something flawed and temporal, lacking ultimate
significance.

Mary, by contrast, had in her youth attempted the seeming stroke of genius that Peter so desires. She married for love *and* money—that is, she sought to fulfil her own desires while also appeasing the Alard god. But her plan failed; an idol cannot be toppled quite so comfortably. So it is no surprise that Alard, and the manipulation of her father, return to threaten her again. Mary's attempted emancipation from Alard lacked any real objective, let alone a transcendent reference point. She replaced the Alard idol with comfort and pleasure; with nothing more than that most subjective and fickle of realities: human emotion uprooted from divine love. Unable or unwilling to submit to the Good, let alone God, Mary resigns herself to aimless apathy, drifting through life. She has emancipated herself from the Alard god to the point of disregarding social convention altogether. She envies those who have real faith and expresses a vague notion of truth: "I must say that if I had any religion myself, I'd like a religion which at least was religion and not soup." But Mary has numbed her true self, living distractedly and on the surface for too long to grasp any sure reality. As is evident in her stance towards her divorce case, Mary's notion of truth is reduced to a kind of personal authenticity, to an acknowledgement of the blunt facts: "it's what's true that I mind people knowing."

George Alard is also struggling to break away from the family. Like Mary's marriage, his ministry in the parish of the Alard estate is a half-way house. Too cowardly to cast off the shackles of the Alard idol, he struggles to forge a genuine relationship with the true God. But he cannot serve two masters. Where Mary's ignorance of the transcendent God leads to an amorality that makes her "neither good nor bad,"

George's ignorance of the transcendent leads to an almost puritanical moralism. Encouraged by his wife Rose, he has reduced the Christian faith to a materialistic, humanistic, and spiritless enterprise. Yet, in George's case, his sense of his impending death and his Christian ministry provoke a quest for his own identity, especially when the latter is painfully ridiculed by his father, the rival priest of Alard. As is the case for other characters, George's search for himself and his true vocation directly overlaps with his search for God. It is what allows George to overcome conventions and self-importance and to surrender, almost unconsciously, to his divine savior.

In all of the above figures, Kaye-Smith uses the social world and its bonds and struggles to illustrate the interior, spiritual drama of the soul. She makes evident the concrete and dramatic consequences of everyday forms of idolatry. Sir John, Peter, Doris, and Mary are alone, aimless and unhappy, often desperate. George overcomes his pride just in time. Jenny, Gervase, and Stella, on the other hand, are figures of true love or true faith. Importantly, however, none of their fates are portrayed as idyllic or easy, and the lives of Gervase and Stella demonstrate the formidable challenges posed by Christianity: as the novel concludes, "Christianity is a hard faith."

Living in Reality

The two youngest Alard children, Jenny and Gervase, are unlikely heirs and so have been largely neglected by their parents. But this has also meant that they are less infected by their parents' idolatry. Significantly less enthralled by Alard than Mary, Peter, or George, the younger siblings have been allowed to live in reality. Instead of the false, superficial bonds imposed on them by the family name, Jenny and Gervase know and accept themselves and one another in ways that are essential to their ability to open up to other relationships, such as with Godfrey and Stella. Both of them recognize the futility and relative irrelevance of their family's desperate attempts to save the estate and support each other in the pursuit of genuine truth and love.

Jenny's temperament and experiences direct her hunger for reality towards natural—as opposed to supernatural or spiritual—truth. It is on this level that her break with Alard takes place. Jenny is attracted to Godfrey's natural goodness and his upright way of life. Like Peter, Godfrey is not especially religious, yet unlike Peter's love for Stella, Godfrey's love for Jenny is firmly rooted in the Good. He is a genuinely good man who embodies natural human values like honesty, dignity, honor. He therefore treats Jenny with the respect Peter fails to show Stella and, despite his deep attachment to his ancestral home, would not hesitate to let even this go for her sake.

Jenny and Godfrey embody the idea that human beings have access to truth and goodness even apart from God—a conviction firmly held by Catholic Christianity. We are wired in such a way that the Good attracts us: human reason is persuaded by it, just as human desire is fulfilled by it. Jenny's deep and overwhelming attraction to Godfrey is thus clearly based on more than his good looks. Less enslaved to Alard than some of her siblings and on a wider quest for truth, Jenny's loves and desires are rightly ordered, and she is able to distinguish between lesser or even false goods and objective

Good. She intuitively recognizes Godfrey's goodness and the purity of his love for what it is. Both her and Godfrey have healthy, natural loyalties towards their family, home, and land, but are nonetheless willing to leave these behind for the sake of the higher love that grows between them. Jenny is "someone who knew what she wanted and had got it, whom the family had not bound fast and swallowed up."

However, it is not easy for Jenny to honor her love for Godfrey, and indeed she might not have had the necessary courage without the support of her brother's more divine faith. In this sense, Jenny's natural love is already perfected by grace. This is because (true) love requires what, with Saint Paul, can be described as a dying to self—perhaps the novel's most central theme. This idea has its roots in the Gospel's inversion of the values of "the world"; that is, in the paradox taught by Jesus that he who loses his life will find it. God is present in the world but he is not of the world. God can thus be encountered in worldly things but, given the fallenness of the world, these things can also come between us and God.

True love requires at least a willingness to renounce one's lesser attachments: in Jenny's case, her childhood home, her social circle, and way of life, but also her family's hopes and expectations for her. She knows that the choice of her life is between these attachments, which constitute who she has been as a child, and the true love and goodness embodied by Godfrey. At the moment of her marriage, Jenny realizes that "Jenny Alard is dead." Kaye-Smith depicts how the dying to self that is needed for a true communion with the Good is an ongoing process. Jenny's new life, though good and happy, is not an easy life and requires continuous self-renunciation and self-sacrifice. Already having let go of many things dear to her, she must now embrace many things difficult for her: a more physically demanding life, a lack of privacy, and a lack of time with her husband. True love and true happiness— that is, life in the real world—is never idyllic or unambiguous. In fact, it can be hard. In this finite world, it will be fully tasted only in fleeting moments. Without some kind of death to self, it will not be tasted at all.

Nature and Grace

The themes governing Jenny's story are deepened and pushed further in the stories of Stella and Gervase. In both of these characters, the relationship between nature and grace is worked out most fully. Jenny's quest for a more real and truthful way of living does not venture beyond the realm of nature, so she and Godfrey can only follow Gervase so far; theirs is a worldly happiness. Gervase's pursuit of a more divine love and happiness lies beyond the horizon of their comprehension.

Gervase, the youngest of the Alard children, has always been the most independent. His decision to forego an Oxford education and instead train in a car workshop goes almost unnoticed by his family. And yet it is the beginning of an even deeper process of "unselfing" than that undergone by Jenny. Gervase's work at the garage puts him entirely out of his familiar social realm. In his co-workers, rough men entirely unlike him, he is forced to confront the human "other." In this way, his new role constitutes an important step towards weaning himself of the delusional and morally corrupting comforts of life on the estate. The tough manual labor necessitates a highly self-disciplined, more bodily, and less comfortable way of being than what he is used to. He is subject to the elements—the weather and the rhythm of day and night. His long car rides to work are times of solitude and self-reflection. In all of this, the illusions and false pretenses of Alard are fully exposed and Gervase is increasingly drawn into reality—that of the world around him and, eventually, the reality of God.

Stella is the central medium on his path towards a life of grace. Gervase's attraction to her is, initially, simply an attraction to her lively natural beauty and authenticity. Yet, his spiritual openness enables him, unlike Peter, to recognize Stella for who she is: "he was to find that her religion was the deepest, the most vital and most interesting part of her—in it alone did the whole Stella come alive." Gervase recognizes and is drawn toward Stella's faith, the very faith that perplexes Peter. Although genuine, Peter's love for Stella is exposed as inadequate: his false god prevented him from truly knowing—and therefore loving—the object of his desire.

It is worth noting that Gervase had long been prejudiced against religion, viewing it as part of the social fabric he was looking to escape. For instance, he had always thought of the Catholic view on marriage and divorce "as a fad and a convention, a collection of moral and intellectual lumber." But his dismissal of religion is based on the way in which its agents, such as George and Rose, have robbed it of its divine core and its claim to truth by reducing it to gentlemanly good manners and spiritless aesthetics. Divorced from truth, beauty and goodness become distorted and fail to persuade—an observation as relevant today as it was in the 1920s.

In Stella's Catholicism, Gervase encounters a faith that is more true and hence more bold, that has precisely "something ungentlemanly about [it]." Even gentleman-vicar George feels a similar pull toward the worship at his rival parish. Yet where Mary's apathy and, initially at least, George's moralism prevent them from exploring the Catholic faith, Gervase's inner freedom has prepared him for receiving it. Debating with Stella the matter of Mary's divorce, Stella's faith shows itself to Gervase "almost shockingly as an adventure and a power"; Gervase notices that "she carried in her heart a force which might one day both make and break it."

Here, thought Gervase, was a faith which did not depend on the beauty of externals for its appeal—a faith, moreover, which was not afraid to make itself hard to men, which threw up round itself massive barriers of hardship, and yet within these was warm and sweet and friendly—which was furthermore a complete adventure, a taking of infinite risks, a gateway on unknown dangers … "I'm afraid Christianity's a hard faith, my dear," he said as he took her hand—"the closer you get to the Gospel the harder it is. You've no idea what a shock the Gospels gave me when I read them again last year, not having looked at them since I was a kid. I was expecting something rather meek-and-mild, with a gentle, womanly Saviour, and all sorts of kind and good-natured sentiments. Instead of which I find that the Kingdom of Heaven is for the violent, while the Lion of Judah roars in the Temple courts … He built His Church upon a Rock, and sometimes we hit that Rock mighty hard."

If Gervase's conversion rests on discovering the "hardness" of Christianity, it is equally rooted in the way in which true Christianity resonates with the intuitive faith of his childhood self. The conventional, spiritless form of Anglicanism to which he had been exposed dulled his spiritual senses and the religious imagination of his childhood. Stella's more dramatic, demanding faith is able to bring this experience back to life and puts into practice the Biblical idea that we must come to God as children—a focus evocative of St. Teresa of Lisieux, among others.

One way in which Stella's Catholic faith keeps alive and nurtures the imaginative world of the child in us is through its sacramentality. Catholic Christianity does not merely dwell in lofty ideals or refined aestheticism but is rooted in the material, ordinary realities of everyday life, which have the power to reveal and manifest the divine. This is not the immanentist materialism of George and Rose's concern with committees, donations, and charitable works. Instead, it is one which flows directly from the Incarnation—a materialism wherein humble, simple, even broken things like bread, wine, or the human body become vessels of God.

Stella's entire person reflects this truth. Her personality, her faith and love, express themselves in simple, concrete, material acts and loyalties: she is her father's chauffeur and pharmacist, a dedicated cook and hostess, and deeply sensitized to the material landscape around her. It had been her desire that her and Peter's love be "well rooted in the earth." Luce's parish church, similarly, has nothing of the imposing, luxurious beauty of George's church. Its beauty consists in an aesthetic that is as messy and inviting as an ordinary person's parlor. In this way it manifests the Catholic faith Luce preaches, which intends to be a home for everyone.

Dying to Self

It is ironic, perhaps, that while the Catholic faith comes to us in and through natural things, it also asks us to detach from natural things and desires. Both Stella and Gervase take on the challenge of surrendering to God instead of self. As Kaye-Smith consistently underlines, this path is not easy. Even Stella, whose faith is so steady and whose love is so pure, experiences turmoil when faced with this challenge:

> She was no longer herself—she was two selves—the self that loved Peter and the self that loved God. She was Stella Mount at prayer in Vinehall church—Stella Mount curled up on Peter's knees ... long ago, at Starvecrow—Stella Mount receiving her soul again in absolution ... Stella Mount loving, loving, with a heart full of fiery sweetness.... Well, aren't they a part of the same thing—love of man and love of God? Yes, they are—but today there is schism in the body.

Grace wants to perfect nature. But not all of our desires can be fulfilled. Stella's love for Peter and Gervase's love for Stella must remain unfulfilled because they are at odds with reality. The refusal to accept this fact would separate both Stella and Gervase from God. Instead, they allow themselves to be changed, to let go of their worldly attachments and to fully surrender to God's will instead. Dying to self typically consists in renouncing one's disordered attachments and vices, and sometimes even more: Stella's love for Peter and Gervase's love for Stella are intrinsically good and yet, given the circumstances, those loves risk undermining the higher love which unites them with Christ.

Both Gervase and Stella illustrate how the process of dy-

ing to the "old man" (Sir John/St. Paul's "old self") and putting on the "new man" (Christ)—or of being broken in order
to rise again—is complicated and at times painfully lonely. In liberating himself from family expectations and social
conventions, Gervase appears to be asserting himself. Peter's
choice not to marry Stella may seem more selfless and more
conscious of the needs of others (his immediate family, the
community occupying Alard land, previous Alard generations). And yet the reverse is true. Even more confusing is
the fact that Gervase's dying to self brings him great suffering
and plunges him into a deep loneliness:

He felt rather forlorn as the lorry's lights swept up the Vinehall road. During the last few months he had been stripped of
so many things—his devotion to Stella, his comradeship with
Jenny—he knew that he could never be to her what he had been
before she married—and now his family and his home. And all
he had to look forward to was a further, more complete stripping,
even of the clothes he wore, so that in all the world he would own
nothing.

Stella, similarly, undergoes great suffering; a test of faith
and the experience of being stripped in the cruelest way of
what she loves most on earth. But unlike the truly unbearable loneliness Peter experiences as a result of surrendering
to a false god, her and Gervase's loneliness is only temporary,
even superficial. It is situated in the context of a larger reality of communion that can accommodate even the unfulfilled
worldly loves. Gervase is conscious that by becoming a priest,
he "shall be able to help [Stella] more" and that "it isn't every
man who's given the power to do so much for the woman
he loves." Stella's agony of love, on the other hand, may help

atone for Peter's sins, thus facilitating her reunion with Peter in heaven.

Like other Catholic novelists, such as her contemporary Evelyn Waugh in *Brideshead Revisited*, Kaye-Smith is here giving expression to the fundamental Catholic belief that holiness is inseparable from suffering. But as Caryll Houselander observes, the saint's distinctiveness lies in his willingness to accept suffering where it comes. And so, while Peter, Gervase and Stella all suffer, only Gervase's and Stella's suffering will sanctify them. All three made acts of total surrender and entered into a kind of bondage. But, geared towards avoiding suffering, Peter's bondage to Alard enslaves him, whereas Gervase's and Stella's submission to the God of love frees them for new life. Gervase and Stella are "born again" into a new and greater freedom, into the peaceful certainty of being held in divine love. As Stella notes in the midst of her own ordeal, "[Gervase] was free—he had made the ultimate surrender and was free ... he had passed beyond her.... His soul had escaped like a bird from the snare, but hers was still struggling and bound."

Importantly, the stripping of the self does not necessarily imply a wholesale dismissal of one's old loves and loyalties. Gervase's worldly attachments to Stella and to his family are neither irrelevant nor bad but given their true and proper place: Gervase's acceptance of the fact that Stella does not reciprocate his romantic feelings allows him to sublimate or "translate" his natural love for Stella into a supernatural love for her and God. This results in his ongoing faithfulness to Stella as a friend: "his love for her was not dead—that was the whole point; like Enoch, it was translated.... God had taken it." Through Gervase's death to self, his relationship with Stella is not denied or undone but taken to a higher, purer level which will also be more fruitful.

Likewise, while emancipating himself from family pressures, Gervase does not turn against his family or become indifferent to their suffering. Instead, by renouncing his inheritance and putting an end to the estate, he offers his family the opportunity to liberate itself from its enslavement to a false god and to take personal responsibility for their lives—albeit one they tragically seem to refuse. Gervase becomes "another Christ," whose freedom is the precondition for the liberation of his family, yet who is rejected by his own.

Holiness

Kaye-Smith offers important reflections on the role temperament plays in a person's spiritual life or vocation. As Stella observes, Gervase is "naturally spiritual" where she is "spiritually natural." This comparison is evocative of the Mary and Martha narrative in Luke 10:38–42, in which Jesus visits the house of the two sisters where Mary sits and listens to Jesus speak while Martha busies herself with the domestic demands of the occasion. Following Jesus's words in the text, Mary's choice has classically been deemed "the better part," facilitating union with God more directly and immediately. Yet both responses to Jesus are valid and form the basis of distinct religious observances, the contemplative and active. Gervase and Stella echo the different roles of Mary and Martha. His greater individualism and his "natural" hunger for God help him in transcending his earthly desires for higher goods. He sublimates his earthly love for Stella into a divine love, trades his manual work for the spiritual work of prayer, his physical childhood home on the Alard estate for a spiritual home in a monastery, his biological family for the ecclesial family of the Church. And he achieves all this with relative ease. Gervase's temperament has helped him in turning potential revolt into surrender, and his choice to work at the garage indicates that he has an early and intuitive understanding of the need to strip himself of all comfort and illusion. Stella is baffled at how quickly he has found the love and peace of God.

Instead, Stella intuitively seeks, and meets, God in the natural world—in the people and landscape surrounding her. Her "disposition is eminently practical," and it is through practical acts of service that she expresses her love. Her passionate love of the world (including Peter himself) presents both a source of and a challenge to her faith: "Why should God want her to give up for His sake the loveliest thing that He had made?... Why should He want her to *burn*?"

Martha and Mary are both saints, however, and Stella's surrender is perhaps all the more heroic for her attachment to the world, which makes her dying to self more counterintuitive and more painful. Stella undergoes a genuine "dark night of the soul," experiencing the torturous inability to doubt God even while feeling wholly let down by God. Stella, too, becomes a Christ-figure: like Christ, she, the innocent victim of Peter's unfaithfulness, is an embodiment of pure love who is made to suffer for the sin of her beloved. Like Christ's, her suffering is all-encompassing. Not only must she undergo personal disappointment, emotional betrayal, and an unjust exclusion from her home, but she is made a scapegoat for Peter's fate. Stella is stripped of everything and is, in this way, forced to die to self.

Like Houselander's *The Dry Wood*, Kaye-Smith's novel offers a meditation on the Catholic theme of the economy of salvation. Is it possible, Kaye-Smith seems to suggest, that the suffering of the innocent has redemptive power? Do those who are dealt the hardest challenges in this life, yet who nonetheless persevere, grow in holiness to the extent that they can atone not only for their own but also for the sins of others? Is Stella's ordeal her divinely given opportunity to truly love Peter to the point of atoning for his sins and thus of saving his soul? As Gervase puts it, "He takes your love out of the world unspoilt by sin. Your love is with him now, pleading for him, striving for him, because it is part of a much greater Love, which holds him infinitely dearer than even you can hold him."

Kaye-Smith does not give any definite answers to these difficult questions, but Stella's story is suggestive of a Christian mysticism, which calls us to join our love to Christ's own love and thereby to aid Him in his work of salvation. This again highlights the need for human love to be perfected by divine grace: only a love that participates in God's infinite love could persevere in the way asked of Stella. As Gervase had come to learn, we alone are "not big enough."

Just as it is a study of idolatry as opposed to true faith, *The End of the House of Alard* is also a study of the different forms of love. As Gervase observes, "religion is the fulfilment of love." Stella's love, unlike Peter's, has the quality of fidelity precisely because it is perfected by grace. Love's true foundation becomes apparent only when it is put to the test. Where

Peter's (and also Mary's) love fails under duress, Stella's love remains both faithful and rightly ordered. Rooted in the love of God, her love of Peter overrides loyalty to family customs and expectations but refuses to become complicit in Peter's moral weakness. Gervase shares a similar sense of love's sacred quality, of the need to honor love at all costs: where Peter had "sacrificed his uttermost human need"—the need for love—to the "monster" of Alard, Gervase refuses "to let his love be spoilt by family pride ... love must come before everything else."

Kaye-Smith's novel illustrates how placing the love of God above all else comes at a great price. One of its core observations is that the life of faith and love, the pursuit of holiness, is uncomfortably distinct from the pursuit of worldly happiness. This does not mean that the true lover or saint is unhappy. Both Gervase and Stella seek happiness and are guided by their instinctive human desire for joy. But there is a clear sense that, having cleared their love of all self-interest, of all worldly hopes and aspirations, such happiness will not be what they had once thought or hoped. The saint must be open to the idea that the life of grace to which he is called may not correspond with personal preferences.

The truth is not comfortable and true love is not easy: as Stella and Gervase come to learn, Christianity is a "faith which makes such demands on us." Indeed, it may even put to us the painful choice between happiness in this world and happiness in the next. As Gervase himself argues, were Stella to betray God for her own worldly happiness she would most likely have experienced great happiness in this world: "we're made so that the supernatural in us may regret the natural,

I doubt if the natural in us so easily regrets the supernatural. Your tragedy would have been that you would have regretted nothing. You would have been perfectly happy, contented, comfortable, respectable, and damned."

The End of the House of Alard was written six years before Kaye-Smith's conversion. The novel makes clear that she had long been on the road to Rome. But when she finally made that last step it altered, subtly but powerfully, her relationship to all that she held most dear, including the Sussex landscape around her and her identity as a writer. She wrote in her memoir *Three Ways Home,*

As for my writing—I have to learn a new method, just as I have much that is new in my Catholic faith.... Actually the change in my writing has been more fundamental than the change in my religion, but it is less obvious because there is here no change in externals. I will still write about Sussex, but even Sussex has suffered a change, and my feeling for it has become more detached and external, and yet more detailed and intimate. I am not unlike a person who, having for years played the piano by ear, is now for the first time learning to read music. It is a slow process, and, one is even handicapped by one's earlier capacity ... one would probably do better if one had never played at all.[12]

Much of Kaye-Smith's later writing did indeed become more recognizably "Catholic" in the sense that it engaged closely with questions and events specific to the Catholic Church, both in her own time and its history. But she also began to write more frequently in different modes; short story, nonfiction, memoir. She wrote about the saints and about other writers, and about the world around her.

---

12. Kaye-Smith, *Three Ways Home,* 218.

Sheila's conversion to Catholicism so changed her internal landscape that she perceived her world and her abilities as a woman and a writer in new ways. Certainly, her efforts as a laywoman became more pronounced in these years; evidently, through her establishment of the parish. Not only did Kaye-Smith discover that her technical habits as a writer needed to be reappraised after conversion, but it would appear that her life, and the life of the Church, became a more urgent source of spiritual reality; whereas before her conversion, she lived more fully for and through her writing alone. And yet, *The End of the House of Alard* continues to stand as a fully Catholic novel, perhaps in ways that Kaye-Smith herself did not recognize.

In *Three Ways Home*, she observes that

the parallel between Catholicism and marriage is a fairly close one. The convert does not necessarily live happily ever afterwards, any more than the bride and groom; but it is his own fault, and not the fault of the system, if he does not live a very much fuller, richer and better life than he lived before. He will find in Catholicism as in marriage a stabilizing effect, also a more adult, objective attitude toward life, which for that very reason becomes in the eyes of the world less romantic and less exciting. Dreams are no longer necessary for happiness, and poetry has ceased to be explicit in words, but is, rather, implicit in things. Just as the evidence of a happy marriage does not lie in the couple's exclamation of rapture or the embraces they give each other—especially in public—so in a happy Catholicism there are fewer shouts of joy, more acts of penance, less outward bustle and protestation, more turning away of the soul to her own quiet home.[13]

---

13. Kaye-Smith, *Three Ways Home*, 201–2.

PART I

CONSTER MANOR

CONSTER MANOR

§1

THERE ARE Alards buried in Winchelsea church—they lie in the south aisle on their altar tombs, with lions at their feet. At least one of them went to the Crusades and lies there cross-legged—the first Gervase Alard, Admiral of the Cinque Ports and Bailiff of Winchelsea, a man of mighty stature.

Those were the days just after the Great Storm, when the sea swallowed up the first parish of St. Thomas à Becket, and King Edward laid out a new town on the hoke above Buke-nie. The Alards then were powerful on the marsh, rivals of De Icklesham and fighters of the Abbot of Fécamps. They were ship-owners, too, and sent out to sea *St. Peter*, *Nostre Dame* and *La Nave Dieu*. Stephen Alard held half a knight's fee in the manors of Stonelink, Broomhill and Coghurst, while William Alard lost thirty sailors, thirty sergeants-at-arms, and anchors and ropes, in Gascony.

In the fifteenth century the family had begun to dwindle—its power was passing into the hands of the Oxen-bridges, who, when the heiress of the main line married an

Oxenbridge, adopted the Alard arms, the lion within a border charged with scallop shells. Thus the trunk ended, but a branch of the William Alards had settled early in the sixteenth century at Conster Manor, near the village of Leasan, about eight miles from Winchelsea. Their shield was argent, three bars gules, on a canton azure a leopard's head or.

Peter Alard re-built Conster in Queen Elizabeth's day, making it what it is now, a stone house with three hipped gables and a huge red sprawl of roof. It stands on the hill between Brede Eye and Horns Cross, looking down into the valley of the river Tillingham, with Doucegrove Farm, Glasseye Farm and Starvecrow Farm standing against the woods beyond.

The Alards became baronets under Charles the First, for the Stephen Alard of that day was a gentleman of the bedchamber, and melted down the Alard plate in the King's lost cause. Cromwell deprived the family of their lands, but they came back at the Restoration, slightly Frenchified and intermarried with the Papist. They were nearly in trouble again when Dutch William was King, for Gervase Alard, a son in orders, became a non-juror and was expelled from the family living of Leasan, though a charge of sedition brought against him collapsed from lack of substance.

Hitherto, though ancient and honourable, the Alards had never been rich, but during the eighteenth century, successful dealings with the East India Company brought them wealth. It was then that they began to buy land. They were no longer content to look across the stream at Doucegrove, Glasseye and Starvecrow, in the hands of yeomen, but one by one these farms must needs become part of their estate.

They also bought all the fine woodlands of the Furnace, the farms of Winterland and Ellenwhorne at the Ewhurst end of the Tillingham valley, and Barline, Float and Dinglesden on the marshes towards Rye. They were now big landowners, but their land-hunger was still unsatisfied—Sir William, the Victorian baronet, bought grazings as far away as Stonelink, so that when his son John succeeded him the Alards of Conster owned most of the land between Rye and Ewhurst, the Kent Ditch and the Brede river.

John Alard was about thirty years old when he began to reign. He had spent most of his grown-up life in London— the London of gas and crinolines, Disraeli and Nellie Farren, Tattersalls and Caves of Harmony. He had passed for a buck in Victorian society, with its corruption hidden under outward decorum, its romance smothered under ugly riches in stuffy drawing-rooms. But when the call came to him he valiantly settled down. In Grosvenor Square they spoke of him behind their fans as a young man who had sown his wild oats and was now an eligible husband for the innocent Lucy Kenyon with her sloping shoulders and vacant eyes. He married her as his duty and begat sons and daughters.

He also bought more land, and under him the Alard estates crept over the Brede River and up Snailham hill towards Guestling Thorn. But that was only at the beginning of his squireship. One or two investments turned out badly, and he was forced to a standstill. Then came the bad days of the landowners. Lower and lower dropped the price of land and the price of wheat, hop-substitutes became an electioneering cry in the Rye division of Sussex and the noble gardens by the river Tillingham went fallow. Then came Lloyd George's

Land Act—the rush to the market, the impossibility of sale. Finally the European war of 1914 swept away the little of the Alard substance that was left. They found themselves in possession of a huge ramshackle estate, heavily mortgaged, crushingly taxed.

Sir John had four sons—Hugh, Peter, George and Gervase—and three daughters, Doris, Mary and Janet. Hugh and Peter both went out to fight, and Hugh never came back. George, following a tradition which had ruled in the family since the days of the non-juring Gervase, held the living of Leasan. Gervase at the outbreak of hostilities was only in his second term at Winchester, being nearly eighteen years younger than his brother George.

Of the girls, only Mary was married, though Doris hinted at a number of suitors rejected because of their unworthiness to mate with Alard. Jenny was ten years younger than Mary—she and Gervase came apart from the rest of the family, children of middle age and the last of love.

§2

A few days before Christmas in the year 1918, most of the Alards were gathered together in the drawing-room at Conster, to welcome Peter the heir. He had been demobilised a month after the Armistice and was now expected home, to take on himself the work of the estate in the place of his brother Hugh. The Alards employed an agent, and there were also bailiffs on one or two of the farms, but the heir's presence was badly needed in these difficult days. Sir John held the authority, and the keenness of his interest was in no wise diminished by his age; but he was an old man, nearly seventy-five, and honourably afflicted with the gout. He could only seldom ride on his grey horse from farm to farm, snarling at the bailiff or the stockman, winking at the chicken girl—even to drive out in his heavy Wolsey car gave him chills. So most days he sat at home, and the work was done by him indeed, but as it were by current conducted through the wires of obedient sons and servants.

This afternoon he sat by the fire in the last patch of sunlight, which his wife hankered to have shut off from the damasked armchair.

"It really is a shame to run any risks with that beautiful colour," she murmured from the sofa. "You know it hasn't been back from Hampton's a week, and it's such very expensive stuff."

"Why did you choose it?" snarled Sir John.

"Well, it was the best—we've always had the best."

"Next time you can try the second best as a new experience."

"Your father really is hopeless," said Lady Alard in a loud whisper to her daughter Doris.

"Sh-sh-sh," said Doris, equally loud.

"Very poor as an aside, both of you," said Sir John.

The Reverend George Alard coughed as a preliminary to changing the conversation.

"Our Christmas roses are better than ever this year," he intoned.

His wife alone supported him.

"They'll come in beautifully for the Christmas decorations—I hope there's enough to go round the font."

"I'd thought of them on the screen, my dear."

"Oh no! Christmas roses are so appropriate to the font, and besides"—archly—"Sir John will let us have some flowers out of the greenhouse for the screen."

"I'm damned if I will."

Rose Alard flushed at the insult to her husband's cloth which she held to lie in the oath; nonetheless she stuck to her coaxing.

"Oh, but you always have, Sir John."

"Have I? Well, as I've just told my wife, there's nothing like a new experience. I don't keep three gardeners just to decorate Leasan church, and the flowers happen to be rather scarce this year. I want them for the house."

"Isn't he terrible?" Lady Alard's whispered moan to Doris once more filled the room.

Jenny laughed.

"What are you laughing at, Jenny?"

"Oh, I dunno."

She was laughing because she wondered if there was anything she could say which would not lead to a squabble.

"Perhaps Gervase will come by the same train as Peter," she ventured.

"Gervase never let us know when to expect him," said her mother. "He's very thoughtless. Now perhaps Appleby will have to make the journey twice."

"It won't kill Appleby if he does—he hasn't had the car out all this week."

"But Gervase is very thoughtless," said Mrs. George Alard.

At that moment a slide of wheels was heard in the drive, and the faint sounds of a car coming to anchor.

"Peter!" cried Lady Alard.

"He's been quick," said Doris.

George pulled out his watch to be sure about the time, and Jenny ran to the door.

§3

The drawing-room was just as it had always been.... The same heavy dignity of line in the old walls and oak-ribbed ceiling spoilt by undue crowding of pictures and furniture. Hothouse flowers stood about in pots and filled vases innumerable ... a water-colour portrait of himself as a child faced him as he came into the room.

"Peter, my darling!"

His mother's arms were stretched out to him from the sofa—she did not rise, and he knelt down beside her for a moment, letting her enfold him and furiously creating for himself the illusion of a mother he had never known. The illusion seemed to dissipate in a faint scent of lavender water.

"How strange you look out of uniform—I suppose that's a new suit."

"Well, I could scarcely have got into my pre-war clothes. I weigh thirteen stone."

"Quite the heavy Squire," said Sir John. "Come here and let's have a look at you."

Peter went over and stood before his father's chair—rather like a little boy. As it happened, he was a man of thirty-six, tallish, well-built, with a dark, florid face, dark hair and a small dark moustache. In contrast, his eyes were of an astounding blue—Saxon eyes, the eyes of Alards who had gone to the Crusades, melted down their plate for the White King, refused to take the oath of allegiance to Dutch William; eyes which for long generations had looked out on the marshes of Winchelsea, and had seen the mouth of the Rother swept in spate from Romney sands to Rye.

"Um," said Sir John.

"Having a bad turn again, Sir?"

"Getting over it—I'll be about tomorrow."

"That's right, and how's Mother?"

"I'm better today, dear. But Dr. Mount said he really was frightened last week—I've never had such an attack."

"Why didn't anyone tell me? I could have come down earlier."

"I wanted to have you sent for, dear, but the children wouldn't let me."

The children, as represented by George Alard and his wife, threw a baffled glance at Peter, seeking to convey that the "attack" had been the usual kind of indigestion which Lady Alard liked to ennoble by the name of Angina Pectoris.

Meanwhile, Wills the butler and a young footman were bringing in the tea. Jenny poured it out, the exertion being considered too great for her mother. Peter's eyes rested on her favourably; she was the one thing in the room, barring the beautiful, delicate flowers, that gave him any real pleasure to look at. She was a large, graceful creature, with a creamy skin, wide, pale mouth, and her mother's eyes of speckled brown. Her big, beautifully shaped hands moved with a slow grace among the teacups. In contrast with her, Doris looked raddled (though she really was moderate and skillful in the make-up of her face and hair) and Rose looked blowsy. He felt glad of Jenny's youth—soft, slow, asleep.

"Where's Mary?" he asked suddenly, "I thought she was coming down."

"Not till New Year's eve. Julian can't come with her, and naturally he didn't want her to be away for Christmas."

"And how is the great Julian?"

"I don't know—Mary didn't say. She hardly ever tells us anything in her letters."

The door opened and the butler announced—

"Dr. Mount has come to see her ladyship."

"Oh, Dr. Mount" ... cried Peter, springing up.

"He's waiting in the morning room, my lady."

"Show him in here—you'd like him to come in, wouldn't you, Mother?"

"Yes, of course, dear, but I expect he'll have had his tea."

"He can have another. Anyhow, I'd like to see him—I missed him last leave."

He crossed over to the window. Outside in the drive, a small green Singer car stood empty.

"Did Stella drive him over? She would never stay outside."

"I can't see anyone—Hello, doctor glad you've come—have some tea."

Dr. Mount came into the room. He was a short, healthy little man, dressed in country tweeds, and with the flat whiskers of an old-time squire. He seemed genuinely delighted to see Peter.

"Back from the wars? Well, you've had some luck. They say it'll be more than a year before everyone's demobbed."

"You look splendid, doesn't he, Lady Alard?"

"Yes—Peter always was healthy, you know."

"I must say he hasn't given me much trouble. I'd be a poor man if everyone was like him. How's the wound, Peter? I don't suppose you even think of it now."

"I can't say I do—it never was much. Didn't Stella drive you over?"

"No—there's a lot of medicine to make up, so I left her busy in the dispensary."

"What a useful daughter to have," sighed Lady Alard. "She can do everything—drive the car, make up medicines—"

"Work in the garden and cook me a thundering good dinner besides!" The little doctor beamed. "I expect she'll be over here before long, she'll be wanting to see Peter. She'd have come today if there han't been such a lot to do."

Peter put down his teacup and walked over again to the window. Rose Alard and her husband exchanged another of those meaning looks which they found a useful conversational currency.

§4

Jenny soon wearied of the drawing-room, even when freshened by Dr. Mount. She always found a stifling quality in Conster's public rooms, with their misleading show of wealth, and escaped as early as she could to the old schoolroom at the back of the house, looking steeply up through firs at the wooded slope of Brede Eye.

This evening the room was nearly dark, for the firs shut out the dregs of twilight and the moon that looked over the hill. She could just see the outlines of the familiar furniture, the square table on which she and Gervase had scrawled abusive remarks in the intervals of their lessons, the rocking chair, where the ghost of Nurse sometimes still seemed to sit and sway, the bookcase full of children's books—"Fifty-two Stories for Girls" and "Fifty-two Stories for Boys," the "Girls of

St. Wode's" and "With Wallace at Bannockburn"—all those faded gilded rows which she still surreptitiously enjoyed.

Now she had an indefinite feeling that someone was in the room, but had scarcely realised it when a shape drew itself up against the window square, making her start and gasp.

"It's only me," said an apologetic voice.

"Gervase!"

She switched on the light and saw her brother standing by the table.

"When did you come?"

"Oh, twenty minutes ago. I heard you all gassing away in the drawing-room, so thought I'd come up here till you'd finished with Peter."

"How sociable and brotherly of you! You might have come in and said how d'you do. You haven't seen him for a year."

"I thought I'd be an anticlimax—spoil the Warrior's Return and all that. I'll go down in a minute."

"How was it you and Peter didn't arrive together? There hasn't been another train since."

"I expect Peter came by Ashford, didn't he? I came down on the other line and got out at Robertsbridge. I thought I'd like the walk."

"What about your luggage?"

"I left that at Robertsbridge."

"Really, Gervase, you are the most unpractical person I ever struck. This means we'll have to send over tomorrow and fetch it—and Appleby has something better to do than tear about the country after your traps."

"I'll fetch 'em myself in Henry Ford. Don't be angry with

me, Jenny. Please remember I've come home and expect to be treated kindly."

He came round the table to her and offered her his cheek. He was taller than she was, more coltish and less compact, but they were both alike in being their mother's children, Kenyons rather than Alards. Their eyes were soft and golden-brown instead of clear Saxon-blue, their skins were pale and their mouths wide.

Jenny hugged him. She was very fond of Gervase, who seemed specially to belong to her at the end of the long, straggled family.

"I'm so glad you've come," she murmured—"come for good. Though I suppose you'll be off to a crammer's before long."

"I daresay I shall, but don't let's worry about that now. I'm here till February, anyway. Who's at home?"

"Everybody except Mary, and she's coming after Christmas."

"I wish she'd come before. I like old Mary, and I haven't seen her for an age. Is Julian coming too?"

"I don't suppose so. He and Father have had a dreadful row."

"What about?"

"He wouldn't lend us any of the money he profiteered out of those collapsible huts."

"Well, I call it rather cheek of Father to have asked him."

"It was to be on a mortgage of course; but I quite see it wouldn't have been much of an investment for Julian. However, Father seems to think it was his duty as a son-in-law to have let us have it. We're nearly on the rocks, you know."

"So I've been told a dozen times, but the place looks much the same as ever."

"That's because Father and Mother can't get out of their grooves, and there are so few economies which seem worthwhile. I believe we need nearly fifty thousand to clear the estate."

"But it's silly to do nothing."

"I don't see what we can do. But I never could understand about mortgages."

"Nor could I. The only thing I can make out is that our grandfather was a pretty awful fool."

"He couldn't read the future. He couldn't tell the price of land was going down with a bump, and that there would be a European war. I believe we'd have been all right if it hadn't been for the war."

"No, we shouldn't—we were going downhill before that. The war only hurried things on."

"Well, certainly it didn't do for us what it did for Julian— Seventy thousand pounds that man's made out of blood."

"Then I really do think he might let us have some of it. What's Mary's opinion?"

Jenny shrugged.

"Oh, I dunno. He's had a row with her too."

"What?—about the same thing?"

"No—about a man she's friends with. It's ridiculous, really, for he's years and years older than she is—a retired naval officer—and awfully nice; I lunched with them both once in town. But it pleases Julian to be jealous, and I believe poor Mary's had a hideous time."

"Lord! What upheavals since I was home last! Why doesn't anyone ever write and tell me about these things?"

"Because we're all too worried and too lazy. But you've heard everything now—and you really must come down and see Peter."

"I'm coming in a moment. But tell me first—has he changed at all? It's more than a year since I saw him."

"I don't think he's changed much, except that he's got stouter."

"I wonder what he'll do with himself now he's home. Is there really a rumor, or have I only dreamed, that he's keen on Stella Mount?"

"Oh, I believe he's keen enough. But she hasn't got a penny. Father will be sick if he marries her."

She switched off the light, and the window changed from a deep, undetailed blue to a pallid, star-pricked grey, swept across by the tossing branches of trees.

§5

At Conster Manor, dinner was always eaten in state. Lady Alard took hers apart in her sitting-room, and sometimes Doris had it with her. On his "bad days," Sir John was wont to find Doris a convenient butt, and as she was incapable either of warding off or receiving gracefully the arrows of his wrathful wit, she preserved her dignity by a totally unappreciated devotion to her mother. Tonight, however, she could hardly be absent, in view of Peter's return, and could only hope that the presence of the heir would distract her father from his obvious facilities.

George and Rose had stayed to dinner in honour of the occasion, or rather had come back from a visit to Leasan Vicarage for the purpose of changing their clothes. Rose always resented having to wear evening dress when "just dining with the family." At the Rectory, she wore last year's summer gown, and it seemed a wicked waste to have to put on one of her only two dance frocks when invited to Conster. But it was a subject on which Sir John had decided views.

"Got a cold in your chest, Rose?" he had inquired, when once she came in her parsonage voile and fichu, and on another occasion had coarsely remarked: "I like to see a woman's shoulders. Why don't you show your shoulders, Rose? In my young days, every woman showed her shoulders if she'd got any she wasn't ashamed of. But nowadays the women run either to bone or muscle—so perhaps you're right."

Most of the Alard silver was on the table—ribbed, ponderous stuff of eighteenth century date, later than the last of the lost causes in which so much had been melted down. Some fine Georgian and Queen Anne glass and a Spode dinner-service completed the magnificence, which did not, however, extend to the dinner itself. Good cooks were hard to find and ruinously expensive, requiring also their acolytes; so the soup in the Spode tureen might have appeared on the dinner-table of a seaside boarding-house, the fish was represented by greasily fried plaice, followed by a leg of one of the Conster lambs, reduced by the black magic of the kitchen to the flavor and consistency of the worst New Zealand mutton.

Peter noted that things had "gone down," and had evidently been down for a considerable time, judging by the placidity with which (barring a few grumbles from Sir John) the dinner was received and eaten. The wine, however, was good—evidently the pre-war cellar existed. He began to wonder for the hundredth time what he had better do to tighten the Alard finances—eating bad dinners off costly plate seemed a poor economy. Also, why were a butler and two footmen necessary to wait on the family party? The latter were hard-breathing young men, recently promoted from the plough, and probably cheap enough, but why should his people keep up this useless and shoddy state when their dear lands were in danger? Suppose that, in order to keep their footmen and their silver and their flowers, they had to sell Ellenwhorne or Glasseye—or, perhaps, even Starvecrow....

After the dessert of apples from Conster orchard and a dish of ancient nuts which had remained untasted and unchanged since the last dinner-party, the women and Gervase left the table for the drawing-room. Gervase had never sought to emphasise his man's estate by sitting over his wine—he always went out like this with the women, and evidently meant to go on doing so now he had left school. George, on the other hand, remained, though he rather aggressively drank nothing but water.

"It's not that I consider there is anything wrong in drinking wine," he explained broad-mindedly to Sir John and Peter, "but I feel I must set an example."

"To whom?" thundered Sir John.

"To my parishioners."

"Well, then, since you're not setting it to us, you can clear out and join the ladies. I won't see you sit there despising my port, which is the only good port there's been in the Rye division since '16—besides, I want a private talk with Peter."

The big clergyman rose obediently and left the room, his feelings finding only a moment's expression at the door, when he turned round and tried (not very successfully) to tell Peter by a look that Sir John must not be allowed to drink too much port in his gouty condition.

"He's a fool," said his father just before he had shut the door. "I don't know what the church is coming to. In my young days, the Parson drank his bottle with the best of 'em. He didn't go about being an example. Bah! Who's going to follow Georgie's example?"

"Who, indeed?" said Peter, who had two separate contempts for parsons and his brother George, now strengthened by combination.

"Well, pass me the port, anyhow. Look here, I want to talk to you—first time I've got you alone. What are you going to do now you're back?"

"I don't know, Sir. I've scarcely had time to think."

"You're the heir now, remember. I'd rather you stayed here. You weren't thinking of going back into Lightfoot's, were you?"

"I don't see myself in the city again. Anyhow, I'd sooner be at Conster."

"That's right. That's your place now. How would you like to be Agent?"

"I'd like it very much, Sir. But can it be done? What about Greening?"

"He's an old fool, and has been muddling things badly the last year or two. He doesn't want to stay. I've been talking to him about putting you in, and he seemed glad."

"I'd be glad too, Sir."

"You ought to know more about the estate than you do. It'll be yours before long—I'm seventy-five, you know. When Hugh was alive, I thought perhaps a business career was best for you, so kept you out of things. You'll have to learn a lot."

"I love the place, Sir— I'm dead keen."

"Yes, I remember you always wanted.... Of course I'll put you into Starvecrow."

"Starvecrow!"

"Don't repeat my words. The Agent has always lived at Starvecrow, and there are quite enough of us here in the house. Besides, there's another thing. How old are you?"

"Thirty-six."

"Time you married, ain't it?"

"I suppose it is."

"I was thirty, myself, when I married, but thirty-six is rather late. How is it you haven't married earlier?"

"Oh, I dunno—the war I suppose."

"The war seems to have had the opposite effect on most people. But my children don't seem a marrying lot. Doris ... Hugh ... there's Mary, of course, and George, but I don't congratulate either of 'em. Julian's a mean blackguard, and Rose—" Sir John defined Rose in terms most unsuitable to a clergyman's wife.

"You really must think about it now," he continued— "you're the heir; and of course you know—we want money."

Peter did not speak.

"We want money abominably," said Sir John, "in fact, I don't know how we're to carry on much longer without it. I don't want to have to sell land—indeed, it's practically impossible, all trussed up as we are. Starvecrow could go, of course, but it's useful for grazing and timber."

"You're not thinking of selling Starvecrow?"

"I don't want to—we've had it nearly two hundred years;

it was the first farm that Giles Alard bought. But it's also the only farm we've got in this district that isn't tied—there's a mortgage on the grazings down by the stream, but the house is free, with seventy acres."

"It would be a shame to let it go."

Peter was digging into the salt-cellar with his dessert knife.

"Well, I rely on you to help me keep it. Manage the estate well and marry money."

"You're damn cynical, Sir. Got any especial—er—money in your mind?"

"No, no—of course not. But you ought to get married at your age, and you might as well marry for the family's advantage as well as your own."

Peter was silent.

"Oh, I know there's a lot to be said against getting married, but in your position—heir to a title and a big estate—it's really a duty. I married directly my father died. But don't you wait for that—you're getting on."

"But who am I to marry? There's not such a lot of rich girls round here."

"You'll soon find one if you make up your mind to it. My plan is, first, make up your mind to get married, and then look for the girl—not the other way round, which is what most men do, and leads to all kinds of trouble. Of course, I know it isn't always convenient. But what's your special objection? Any entanglement? Don't be afraid to tell me. I know there's often a little woman in the way."

Peter squirmed at his father's Victorian ideas of dissipation, with their "little women." He'd be talking of "French dancers" next....

"I haven't any entanglement, Sir."

"Then you take my words to heart. I don't ask you to marry for money, but marry where money is, as Shakespeare or somebody said."

§6

Peter found a refreshing solitude in the early hours of the next day. His mother and Doris breakfasted upstairs, his father had characteristically kept his promise to "be about tomorrow," and had actually ridden out before Peter appeared in the morning room at nine. Jenny, who was a lazy young woman, did not come down till he had finished, and Gervase, in one of those spasms of eccentricity which made Peter sometimes a little ashamed of him, had gone without breakfast altogether, and driven off in the Ford lorry to fetch his luggage, sustained by an apple.

The morning room was full of early sunlight—dim as yet, for the mists were still rising from the Tillingham valley and shredding slowly into the sky. The woods and farms beyond the river were hidden in the same soft cloud. Peter opened the window, and felt the December rasp in the air. Oh, it was good to be back in this place, and one with it now, the heir.... No longer the second son who must live away from home and make his money in business.... He stifled the disloyalty to his dead brother. Poor old Hugh, who was so solemn and so solid and so upright.... But Hugh had never loved the place as he did—he had never been both transported and abased by his honour of inheritance.

As soon as he had eaten his breakfast, Peter went out, at his heels a small brown spaniel who, for some reason, had not gone with the other dogs after Sir John. They went down the garden, over the half-melted frost of the sloping lawns, through the untidy shrubbery of fir, larch and laurel, to the wooden fence that shut off Conster from the marshes of the Tillingham. The river here had none of the pretensions with which it circled Rye, but was little more than a meadow-stream, rather full and angry with winter. Beyond it, just before the woods began, lay Beckley Furnace with its idle mill.

And away against the woods lay Starvecrow ... just as he had dreamed of it so many times in France, among the blasted fields. "Starvecrow"—he found himself repeating the name aloud, but not as it was written on the map, rather as it was written on the lips of the people to whom its spirit belonged—"Starvy-crow ... Starvy-crow."

It was a stone house built about the same time as Conster, but without the compliment to Gloriana implied in three gables. It lacked the grace of Conster—the grace both of its building and of its planting. It stood foursquare and forth-right upon the slope, with a great descent of wavy, red-brown roof towards the mouth of the valley, a shelter from the winds that came up the Tillingham from the sea. It seemed preeminently a home, sheltered, secure, with a multitude of chimneys standing out against the background of the woods. From one of them rose a straight column of blue smoke, unwavering in the still, frost-thickened air.

Peter crossed the stream by the bridge, then turned up Starvecrow's ancient drive. There was no garden, merely an orchard with a planting of flowers under the windows. Peter did not ring, but walked straight in at the side door. The estate office had for long years been at Starvecrow, a low farmhouse room in which the office furniture looked incongruous and upstart.

"I'll change all this," thought Peter to himself—"I'll have a gate-legged table and Jacobean chairs."

The room was empty, but the agent's wife had heard him come in.

"That you, Mr. Alard? I thought you'd be over. Mr. Greening's gone to Winterland this morning. They were complaining about their roof. He said he'd be back before lunch."

Peter shook hands with Mrs. Greening and received rather abstractedly her congratulations on his return. He was wondering if she knew he was to supplant them at Starvecrow.

She did, for she referred to it the next minute, and to his relief did not seem to resent the change.

"We're getting old people, and for some time I've been wanting to move into the town. It'll be a good thing to have you here, Mr. Alard—bring all the tenants more in touch with the family. Not that Sir John doesn't do a really amazing amount of work...."

She rambled on, then suddenly apologised for having to leave him—a grandchild staying in the house was ill.

"Shall you wait for Mr. Greening? I'm afraid he won't be in for an hour at least."

"I'll wait for a bit anyway. I've some letters to write."

He went into the office and sat down. The big ugly roll-top desk was littered with papers—memoranda, bills, estimates, plans of farms, lists of stock-prices. He cleared a space, seized a couple of sheets of the estate notepaper, and began to write.

"My loveliest Stella," he wrote.

§7

He had nearly covered the two sheets when the rattle of a car sounded in the drive below. He looked up eagerly and went to the window, but it was only Gervase lurching over the ruts in the Ford, just scraping past the wall as he swung round outside the house, just avoiding a collision with an outstanding poplar, after the usual manner of his driving.

The next minute he was in the office.

"Hullo! They told me you were over here. I've just fetched my luggage from Robertsbridge."

He sat down on the writing-table and lit a cigarette. Peter hastily covered up his letter. Why did Gervase come bothering him now?

"I wanted to speak to you," continued his brother. "You'll be the best one to back me up against Father."

"What is it now?" asked Peter discouragingly.

"An idea came to me while I was driving over. I often get ideas when I drive, and this struck me as rather a good one. I think it would be just waste for me to go to a crammer's and then to Oxford. I don't want to go in for the church or the bar or schoolmastering or anything like that, and I don't see why the family should drop thousands on my education just because I happen to be an Alard. I want to go in for engineering in some way and you don't need any 'Varsity for that. I could go into some sort of a shop...."

"Well, if the way you drive a car is any indication—"

"I can drive perfectly well when I think about it. Besides, that won't be my job. I want to learn something in the way of construction and all that. I always was keen, and it strikes me now that I'd much better go in for that sort of thing than something which won't pay for years. There may be some sort of a premium to fork out, but it'll be nothing compared to what it would cost to send me to Oxford."

"You talk as if we were paupers," growled Peter.

"Well, so we are, aren't we?" said Gervase brightly. "Jenny was talking to me about it last night. She says we pay thousands a year in interest on mortgages, and as for paying them off and selling the land, which is the only thing that can help us...."

"I don't see that it's your job, anyway."

"But I could help. Really it seems a silly waste to send me to Oxford when I don't want to go."

"You need Oxford more than any man I know. If you went there you might pick up some notions of what's done, and get more like other people."

"I shouldn't get more like other people, only more like other Oxford men."

Peter scowled. He intensely disapproved of the kid's verbal nimbleness, which his more weighty, more reputable argument could only lumber after.

"You've got to remember you're a gentleman's son," he remarked in a voice which suggested sitting down just as Gervase's had suggested a skip and a jump.

"Well, lots of them go in for engineering. We're in such a groove. I daresay you think this is just a sudden idea of mine—"

"You've just told me it is."

"I know, but I've been thinking for ages that I didn't want to go to Oxford. If I took up engineering, I could go into a shop at Ashford.... But I'll have to talk to Father about it. I expect he'll be frightfully upset—the only Alard who hasn't been to the 'Varsity and all that ... but, on the other hand, he's never bothered about me so much as about you and George, because there's no chance of my coming into the estate."

"I wouldn't be too sure," gibed Peter.

"Yes, of course, you might both die just to spite me—but it wouldn't be sporting of you. I don't want to be Sir Gervase Alard, Bart.—I'd much rather be Alard and Co., Motor-engineers."

"You damn well shan't be that."

"Well, it's a long time ahead, anyway. But do back me up against Father about not going to Oxford. It really ought to help us a lot if I don't go—a son at the 'Varsity's a dreadful expense, and when that son's me, it's a waste into the bargain."

"Well, I'll see about it. My idea is that you need Oxford more than—hullo, who's that?"

"Dr. Mount," said Gervase, looking out of the window.

Peter rose and looked out, too, in time to see the doctor's car turning in the sweep. This morning he himself was not at the wheel, but was driven by what looked like a warm bundle of furs with a pair of bright eyes looking out between collar and cap.

Peter opened the window.

"Stella!" he cried.

§8

A minute later, Stella Mount was in the room. Gervase had not seen her for several years; during the greater part of the war, she had been away from home, first at a munition factory, then as an auxiliary driver to the Army Service Corps. When last they had met, the gulf between the schoolboy of fourteen and the girl of twenty had yawned much wider than between the youth of eighteen and the young woman of twenty-four. Stella looked, if anything, younger than she had looked four years ago, and he was also of an age to appreciate her beauty, which he had scarcely noticed on the earlier occasions.

In strict point of fact, Stella was not so much beautiful as pretty, for there was nothing classic in her little heart-shaped face, with its wide cheekbones, pointed chin and puckish nose. On the other hand, there was nothing of that fragile, conventional quality which prettiness is understood to mean. Everything about Stella was healthy, warm and living—her plump little figure, the glow on her cheeks, the shine of her grey eyes between their lashes, like pools among reeds, the decision of her chin and brows, the glossy, tumbling masses of her hair, all spoke of strength and vigour, a health that was almost hardy.

She came into the room like a flame, and Gervase felt his heart warming. Then he remembered that she was Peter's—Jenny had said so, though she had not blessed Peter's possession.

"How d'you do, Stella?" he said, "It's ages since we met. Do you know who I am?"

"Of course I do. You haven't altered much, except in height. You've left Winchester for good now, haven't you?"

"Yes—and I've just been arguing with Peter about what I'm to do with myself now I'm home."

"How very practical of you! I hope Peter was helpful."

"Not in the least."

He could feel Peter's eyes upon him, telling him to get out of the way and leave him alone with his bright flame....

"Well, I must push off—they may be wanting the Ford at home."

He shook hands with Stella, nodded to Peter, and went out.

For a moment Peter and Stella faced each other in silence. Then Peter came slowly up to her and took her in his arms, hiding his face in her neck.

"O Stella—O my beauty!..."

She did not speak, but her arms crept round him. They could scarcely meet behind his broad back—she loved this feeling of girth which she could not compass, combined as it was with a queer tender sense of his helplessness, of his dependence on her—

"O Peter," she whispered—"my little Peter...."

"I was writing to you, darling, when you came."

"And I was on my way to see you at Conster. Father was going there after he'd called on little Joey Greening. I wouldn't come yesterday—I thought your family would be all over you, and I didn't like...."

She broke off the sentence and he made no effort to trim the ragged end. Her reference to his family brought back into his thoughts the conversation he had had with his father over the wine. She had always felt his family as a cloud, as a barrier between them, and it would be difficult to tell her that now he was the heir, now he was home from the war, instead of being removed the cloud would be heavier and the barrier stronger.

"I'm so glad you came here"—he breathed into her hair—"that our first meeting's at Starvecrow."

"Yes—I'm glad, too."

Peter sat down in the leather-covered office chair, holding Stella on his knee.

"Child—they're going to give me Starvecrow."

"O Peter!"...

"Yes—Greening wants to leave, and my father's making me agent in his place."

"How lovely! Shall you come and live here?"

"Yes."

The monosyllable came gruffly because of the much more that he wanted to say. It was a shame to have such reserves spoil their first meeting.

"I'm so awfully, wonderfully glad, Peter darling."

She hid her soft, glowing face in his neck—she was lying on his breast like a child, but deliciously heavy, her feet swung off the floor.

"Stella—my sweetheart—beautiful...."

His love for her gave him a sweet wildness of heart, and he who was usually slow of tongue, became almost voluble—

"Oh, I've longed for this—I've thought of this, dreamed of this.... And you're lovelier than ever, you dear.... Stella, sweetheart, let me look into your eyes—close to—like that ... your eyelashes turn back like the petals of a flower.... O you wonderful, beautiful thing.... And it's so lovely we should have met here instead of at home—the dearest person in the dearest place.... Stella at Starvecrow."

"Starvycrow," she repeated gently.

For a moment he felt almost angry that she should have used his name—his private music. But his anger melted into his love. She used his name because she, alone in all the world, felt his feelings and thought his thoughts. Perhaps she did not love Starvecrow quite as he did, but she must love it very nearly as much, or she would not call it by its secret name. They sat in silence, her head upon his shoulder, his arms about her, gathering her up on his knees. On the hearth a log fire softly hummed and sighed. Ages seemed to flow over them, the swift eternities of love.... Then suddenly a voice called "Stella!" from the drive.

She started up, and the next moment was on her feet, pushing away her hair under her cap, buttoning her high collar over her chin.

"How quick Father's been! I feel as if I'd only just come."

"You must come again."

"I'm coming to dinner on Christmas day, you know."

"That doesn't count. I want you here."

"And I want to be here with you—always."

The last word was murmured against his lips as he kissed her at the door. He was not quite sure if he had heard it. During the rest of the morning, he sometimes feared not— sometimes hoped not.

§9

"It will be a green Christmas," said Dr. Mount.

Stella made no answer. The little car sped through the lanes at the back of Benenden. They had driven far—to the very edge of the doctor's wide-flung practice, by Hawkhurst and Skullsgate, beyond the Kent Ditch. They had called at both the Nineveh farms—Great Nineveh and Little Nineveh—and had now turned south again. The delicate blue sky was drifted over with low pinkish clouds, which seemed to sail very close to the field where their shadows moved; the shadows swooped down the lane with the little car, rushing before it into Sussex. Stella loved racing the sky.

On her face, on her neck, she could still feel cold places where Peter had kissed her. It was wonderful and beautiful, she thought, that she should carry the ghosts of his kisses through Sussex and Kent. And now she would not have so long to be content with ghosts—there would not be those terrible intervals of separation. She would see Peter again soon, and the time would come—must come—when they would be together always. "Together always" was the fulfilment of Stella's dream. "They married and were together always" sounded better in her ears than "they married and lived happy ever after." No more partings, no more ghosts of kisses, much as she loved those ghosts, but always the dear, warm bodily presence—Peter working, Peter resting, Peter sleepy, Peter hungry, Peter talking, Peter silent—Peter always.

"It will be a green Christmas," repeated Dr. Mount.

"Er—did you speak, Father dear?"

"Yes, I said it would be a gr— but never mind, I'm sure your thoughts are more interesting than anything I could say."

Stella blushed. She and her father had a convention of silence between them in regard to Peter. He knew all about him, of course, but they both pretended that he didn't; because Stella felt she had no right to tell him until Peter had definitely asked her to be his wife. And he had not asked her yet. When they had first fallen in love, Hugh Alard was still alive and the second son's prospects were uncertain; then when Hugh was killed and Peter became the heir, there was still the war, and she knew that her stolid, Saxon Peter dis-

approved of war weddings and grass widows who so often
became widows indeed. He had told her then he could not
marry her till after the war, and she had treated that negative
statement as the beginning of a troth between them. She had
never questioned or pressed him—it was not her way—she
had simply taken him for granted. She had felt that he could
not, any more than she, be satisfied with less than "together
always."

But now she felt that something definite must happen
soon, and their tacit understanding become open and glorious.
His family would disapprove, she knew, though they liked her
personally and owed a great deal to her father. But Stella, outside and unaware, made light of Conster's opposition. Peter
was thirty-six and had five hundred a year of his own, so in
her opinion could afford to snap his fingers at Alard tyranny.
Besides, she felt sure the family would "come round"—they
would be disappointed at first, but naturally they wouldn't expect Peter to give up his love-choice simply because she had
no money. She would be glad when things were open and acknowledged, for though her secret was a very dear one, she
was sometimes worried by her own shifts to keep it, and hurt
by Peter's. It hurt her that he should have to pretend not to
care about her when they met in public—but not so much as
it would have hurt her if he hadn't done it so badly.

"Well, now he's back, I suppose Peter will take the eldest
son's place," said Dr. Mount, "and help his father manage the
property."

"Yes—he told me this morning that Sir John wants
him to be agent instead of Mr. Greening, and he's to live at
Starvecrow."

"At Starvecrow! You'll like that—I mean, it's nice to think Peter won't have to go back and work in London. I always felt he belonged here more than Hugh."

"Yes, I don't think Hugh cared for the place very much, but Peter always did. It always seemed hard lines that he should be the second son."

"Poor Hugh," said Dr. Mount—"he was very like Peter in many ways—sober and solid and kind-hearted; but he hadn't Peter's imagination."

"Peter's very sensitive," said Stella—"in spite of his being such a big, heavy thing."

Then she smiled, and said in her heart—"Peter's mine."

§10

Christmas was celebrated at Conster in the manner peculiar to houses where there is no religion and no child. Tradition compelled the various members of the family to give each other presents which they did not want, and to eat more food than was good for them; it also compelled them to pack unwillingly into the Wolsey car and drive to Leasan church, where they listened in quite comprehensible boredom to a sermon by brother George. Peter was able to break free from this last superstition, and took himself off to the office at Starvecrow—his family's vague feeling of unrest at his defection being compensated by the thought that there really wouldn't have been room for him in the car.

But Starvecrow was dim and sodden on this green Christmas day, full of a muggy cloud drifting up from the Tillingham, and Peter was still sore from the amenities of the Christmas breakfast table—that ghastly effort to be festive because it was Christmas morning, that farce of exchanging presents—all those empty rites of a lost childhood and a lost faith. He hated Christmas.

Also, he wanted Stella, and she was not to be had. She too had gone to church—which he would not have minded, if she had not had the alternative of being with him here at Starvecrow. He did not at all object to religion in women as long as they kept it in its proper place. But Stella did not keep hers in its proper place—she let it interfere with her daily life—with his ... and she had not gone to church at Leasan, which was sanctified to Peter by the family patronage and the family vault, but to Vinehall, where they did not even have the decencies of Dearly Beloved Brethren, but embarrassing mysteries which he felt instinctively to be childish and in bad taste.

In Stella's home this Christmas there would be both religion and children, the latter being represented by her father and herself. Last night when he called at Hollingrove— Dr. Mount's cottage on the road between Leasan and Vinehall—to ask her to meet him here today at Starvecrow, he had found her decorating a Christmas tree, to be put in the church, of all places. She had asked him to stop and go with her and her father to the Midnight Mass—"Do come, Peter—we're going to make such a lovely noise at the Gloria in Excelsis. Father Luce has given the boys trays to bang this year." But Peter had declined, partly because he disapproved of tray-banging as a means of giving glory to God, but mostly because he was hurt that Stella should prefer going to church to being with him at Starvecrow.

She had made a grave mistake, if only she'd known it—

leaving him here by himself today, with his time free to think about her, and memories of her dark side still fresh in his mind. For Stella had her dark side, like the moon, though generally you saw as little of it as the moon's. In nearly all ways she was Peter's satisfaction. He loved her with body and mind, indeed with a sort of spiritual yearning. He loved her for her beauty, her sense, her warmth, her affectionate disposition which expressed itself naturally in love, her freedom from affectation, and also from any pretensions to wit or cleverness, and other things which he distrusted. But for two things he loved her not—her religion and her attitude towards his family.

Hitherto, neither had troubled him much. Their meetings had been so few that they had had but little talk of anything save love. He had merely realised that, though she held the country round Vinehall and Leasan as dear as even his idolatry demanded, she was very little impressed with the importance of the family to whom that country belonged. But up in London that had scarcely mattered. He had also realised that Stella, as she put it, "tried to be good." At first, he had thought her wanton—her ready reception of his advances, her ardent affection, her unguarded manner, had made him think she was like the many young women filling London in those years, escaped from quiet homes into a new atmosphere of freedom and amourousness, making the most of what might be short-lived opportunities. But he was glad when he discovered his mistake. Peter approved of virtue in women, though he had occasionally taken advantage of its absence. He certainly would never have married a woman who was not virtuous, and he soon discovered that he wanted to marry Stella.

But in those days, everything flowed like a stream—nothing was firm, nothing stood still. Things were different now—they could flow no longer; they must be established; it was now that Peter realised how much greater these two drawbacks were than they had seemed at first. Stella's religion did not consist merely in preserving his treasure whole till he was ready to claim it, but in queer ways of denial and squander, exacting laws, embarrassing consecrations. And her attitude towards the family gave him almost a feeling of insult—she was so casual, so unaware... she did not seem to trouble herself with its requirements and prohibitions. She did not seem to realise that the House of Alard was the biggest thing on earth—so big that it could crush her and Peter, their hope and romance, into dust. But she would soon find out what it was—whether they married or not, she would find out.

Sometimes—for instance, today—he was almost savagely glad when he thought how sure she was to find out. Sometimes he was angry with her for her attitude towards the family, and for all that she took for granted in his. He knew that she expected him to marry her whatever happened—with a naivety which occasionally charmed but more often irritated him. She imagined that if his father refused to let them live at Starvecrow, he would take her and live with her in some cottage on five hundred a year ... and watch the place go to ruin without him. She would be sorry not to have Starvecrow, but she would not care about anything else—she would not fret in the least about the estate or the outraged feelings of those who looked to him to help them. She would not even have cared if his father had had it in his power—which he had not—to prevent her ever becoming Lady Alard. Stella

did not care two pins about being Lady Alard—all she wanted was to be Mrs. Peter. He had loved her for her disinterest-
edness, but now he realised that it had its drawbacks. He saw
that his choice had fallen on a woman who was not a good
choice for Alard not merely because she had no money, but
because she had no pride. He could not picture her at Conster—lady of the Manor. He could picture her at Starvecrow,
but not at Conster.

... He bowed his head upon the table—it felt heavy with
his thought. Stella was the sweetest, loveliest thing in life,
and sometimes he felt that her winning was worth any sacrifice, and that he would pay her price not only with his own
renunciation but with all the hopes of his house. But some
immovable, fundamental part of him showed her to him as
an infatuation, a witchlight, leading him away from the just
claims of his people and his land, urging him to a cruel betrayal of those who trusted to him for rescue.

After all, he had known her only a year. In a sense, of
course, he had known her from her childhood, when she had
first come with her father to Vinehall, but he had not loved
her till he had met her in London a year ago. Only a year....
To Peter's conservative soul, a year was nothing. For nearly
two hundred years the Alards had owned Starvecrow, and
they had been at Conster for three hundred more. Was he
going to sacrifice those century-old associations for the passion of a short year? He had loved her only a year, and these
places he had loved all his life—and not his life only, but the
lives of those who had come before him, forefathers whose
spirit lived in him, with love for the land which was his and
theirs.

§11

The Christmas tension at the Manor was relieved at dinner time by the arrival of George Alard and his wife, Dr. Mount and Stella, and a young man supposed to be in love with Jenny. A family newly settled at the Furnace had also been invited and, though it had always been the custom at Conster to invite one or two outside people to the Christmas dinner, Rose Alard considered that this year's hospitality had gone too far.

"It's all very well to have Dr. Mount and Stella," she said to Doris, "but who are these Hursts? They haven't been at the Furnace six months."

"They're very rich, I believe," said Doris.

"They may be—but no one knows how they made their money. I expect it was in trade," and Rose sniffed, as if she smelt it.

"There's a young man, I think; perhaps he'll marry Jenny—he's too young for me."

"But Jenny's engaged to Jim Parish, isn't she?"

"Not that it counts—he hasn't got a bean, or any prospects either. We don't talk of them as engaged."

"Is she in love with him?"

"How can I possibly tell?" snapped Doris, who had had a trying afternoon with her mother, and had also been given "The Christian Year" for the second time as a present from Rose.

"Well, don't bite my head off. I'm sure I hope she isn't, and that she'll captivate this young Hurst, whoever he is. Then it won't be so bad having them here, though otherwise I should feel inclined to protest; for poor George is worn out after four services and two sermons, and it's rather hard to expect him to talk to strangers—especially on Christmas day."

Doris swallowed her resentment audibly—she would not condescend to quarrel with Rose, whom she looked upon much as Rose herself looked upon the Hursts, George having married rather meanly in the suburb of his first curacy.

When the Hursts arrived, they consisted of agreeable, vulgar parents, a smart, modern-looking daughter and a good-looking son. Unfortunately, the son was soon deprived of his excuse as a possible husband for Jenny by his mother's ready reference to "Billy's feeonsay"—but it struck both Rose and Doris separately and simultaneously that it would do just as well if the daughter Dolly married Peter. She really was an extraordinarily attractive girl, with her thick golden hair cut square upon her ears like a mediaeval page's. She was clever, too—had read all the new books and even met some of the new authors. Never, thought Rose and Doris, had wealth been so attractively baited or "trade" been so effectively disguised. It was a pity Peter was in such bad form tonight, sitting there beside her, half-silent, almost sullen.

Peter knew that Dolly Hurst was attractive, he knew that she was clever, he knew that she was rich, he knew that she had come out of the gutter—and he guessed that his people had asked her to Conster tonight in hopes that through him her riches might save the house of Alard. All this knowledge crowned by such a guess had the effect of striking him dumb, and by the time Wills and the footmen had ushered in with much ceremony a huge, burnt turkey, his neighbour had almost entirely given up her efforts to "draw him out," and had turned in despair to George Alard on her right.

Peter sat gazing unhappily at Stella. She was next to Gervase, and was evidently amusing him, to judge by the laughter which came across the table. That was so like Stella ... she could always make you laugh. She wasn't a bit clever, but she saw and said things in a funny way. She was looking devilish pretty tonight, too—her hair was done in such a pretty way, low over her forehead and ears, and her little head was round and shining like a bun ... the little darling ... and how well that blue frock became her—showing her dear, lovely neck ... yes, he thought he'd seen it before, but it looked as good as new. Stella was never tumbled—except just after he had kissed her ... the little sweet.

He was reacting from his thoughts of her that morning—he felt a little ashamed of them. After all, why shouldn't she have gone to church if she wanted to? Wasn't it better than having no religion at all, like many of the hard young women of his class who shocked his war-born agnosticism with theirs?—or than having a religion which involved the whole solar system and a diet of nuts? And as for her treatment of his family—surely her indifference was better than the eager subservience more usually found—reverence for a title, an estate, and a place in the charmed exclusiveness of the "County." No, he would be a fool if he sacrificed Stella for any person or thing whatsoever. He had her to consider, too. She loved him, and he knew that, though no troth had yet passed between them, she considered herself bound to the future. What would she say if she knew he did not consider himself so bound?... Well, he must bind himself—or let her go free.

He longed to talk to her, but his opportunity dragged. To his restlessness, it seemed as if the others were trying to keep them apart. There was Gervase, silly fool, going out with the women as usual and sitting beside her in the drawing-room—there was George, sillier fool, keeping the men back in the dining-room while he told Mr. Hurst exactly why he had not gone for an army chaplain. Then directly they had joined the ladies, both Doris and Rose shot up simultaneously from beside Dolly Hurst and disposed of themselves—one beside Lady Alard, the other beside Stella. He had to sit down and try again to be intelligent. It was worse than ever, for he was watching all the time for Miss Hurst to empty her coffee-cup—then he would go and put it down on the Sheraton table, which was not so far from Stella, and after that he would sit down beside Stella no matter how aggressively Rose was sitting on her other side.

The coffee cup was emptied in the middle of a discussion on the relative reputations of Wells and Galsworthy. Peter immediately forgot what he was saying....

"Let me put your cup down for you."

He did not wait for a reply, but the next minute he was on the other side of the room. He realised that he had been incredibly silly and rude, but it was too late to atone, for Jim Parish, Jenny's ineligible young man, had sat down in the chair he had left.

Stella was talking to Rose, but she turned round when Peter came up and made room beside her on the sofa. Rose felt annoyed—she thought Stella's manner was "encouraging," and began to say something about the sofa being too cramped for three. However, at that moment Lady Alard called her to come and hear about Mrs. Hurst's experiences in London on Armistice Day, and she had regretfully to leave the two ineligibles together, with the further complication that the third ineligible was sitting beside Dolly Hurst—and though Jim Parish was supposed to be in love with Jenny, everyone knew he was just as much in need of a rich wife as Peter.

"Stella," said Peter in a low voice—"I'm sorry."

"Sorry! What for, my dear?"

He realised that of course she did not know what he had been thinking of her that morning.

"Everything," he mumbled, apologizing vaguely for the future as well as the past.

Stella had thought that perhaps this evening "something would happen." At Conster—on Christmas night ... the combination seemed imperative. But Peter did not, as she had hoped, draw her out of that crowded, overheated room into some quiet corner of the house or under the cold, dark curtains of the night. Peter could not quite decide against the family—he must give it time to plead. He leaned back on the sofa, his eyes half-closed, tired and silent, yet with a curious peace at his heart.

"You're tired, boy," said Stella—"what have you been doing today?"

"I've had a hateful day—and I was tired—dog tired; but I'm not tired any longer now—now I'm with you."

"Oh, Peter, am I restful?"

"Yes, my dear."

Stella was satisfied. She felt that was enough—she did not ask anything more of the night.

§12

It was Gervase, not Peter, who lay awake that night, thinking of Stella Mount. He had been glad when he was told to take her in to dinner, and the meal which had been so unspeakably trying to his brother had passed delightfully for him. On his other side sat Doris, deep in conversation with Charles Hurst, so he did not have to bother about her—he could talk to Stella, who was so easy to talk to....

Afterwards, in the drawing-room, he had not felt so easy. He knew that he must not monopolize Stella, for she was Peter's. So, when he heard the men crossing the hall, he made some excuse and left her, to see Rose sit down by her side directly Peter came in. He was glad when poor old Peter had managed to get near her at last ... though he hadn't seemed to make much of his opportunities. He had sat beside her, stupid and silent, scarcely speaking a word all the evening through.

Upstairs in bed, in his little misshapen room under the north gable, where he had slept ever since the night-nursery was given up, Gervase shut his eyes and thought of Stella. She came before the darkness of his closed eyes in her shining blue dress—a dress like midnight.... She was the first woman he had really noticed since in far-back childish days he had had an infatuation for his rather dull daily governess—his "beautiful Miss Turner" as he had called her, and thought of her still.... But Stella was different—she was less of a cloud and a goddess, more of a breathing person. He wondered—was he falling in love? It was silly to fall in love with Stella, who was six years older than he ... though people said that when boys fell in love it was generally with women older than themselves. But he mustn't do it. Stella was Peter's.... Was she?... Or was it merely true that he wanted to take her and she wanted to be taken?

He did not think there was any engagement, any promise. Circumstances might finally keep them apart. Rose, Doris, Jenny, his father and mother—the whole family—did not want Peter to marry Stella Mount, whose face was her fortune. It was the same everlasting need of money that was making the same people, except Jenny of course, shrug at poor Jim Parish, whose people in their turn shrugged at portionless Jenny. Money—money ... that was what the Squires wanted—what they must have if their names were to remain in the old places.

Gervase felt rather angry with Peter. He was angry to think that he who had the power was divided as to the will. How was it possible that he could stumble at such a choice? What was money, position, land or inheritance compared to simple, solid happiness?... He buried his face in the pillow, and a kind of horror seized him at the cruel ways of things. It was as if a bogey was in the room—the kind that used to be there when he was a child, but no longer visible in the heeling shadows round the nightlight, rather an invisible sickness, the fetish of the Alards dancing in triumph over Stella and Peter.

It was strange that he should be so hurt by what was, after all, not his tragedy—he was not really in love with Stella, only felt that, given freedom for her and a few more years for him, he could have been and would have been. And he was not so much hurt as frightened. He was afraid because life seemed to him at once so trivial and so gross. The things over

which people agonized were, after all, small shoddy things—
earth and halfpence; to see them have such power to crush
hopes and deform lives was like seeing a noble tree eaten up
by insects. In time he too would be eaten up.... No, no! He
must save himself, somehow. He must find happiness somewhere. But how?

When he tried to think, he was afraid. He remembered
what he used to do in the old days when he was so dreadfully
afraid in this room. He used to draw up his knees to his chin
and pray—pray frantically in his fear. That was before he had
heard about the Ninety-nine Just Sheep being left for the one
that was lost; directly he had heard that story he had given up
saying his prayers, for fear he should be a Just Sheep, when
he would so much rather be the lost one, because the shepherd loved it and had carried it in his arms.... He must have
been a queer sort of kid. Now all that was gone—religion ...
the school chapel, confirmation classes, manly Christians, the
Bishop's sleeves ... he could scarcely realise those dim delicate
raptures he had had as a child—his passionate interest in that
dear Friend and God walking the earth ... all the wonderful
things he had pondered in his heart. Religion was so different after you were grown up. It became an affair of earth and
halfpence like everything else.

Stella's religion still seemed to have some colour left in it,
some life, some youth. It was more like his childhood's faith
than anything he had met so far. She had told him tonight
that there were two Christmas trees in church, one each side
of the Altar, all bright with the glass balls and birds that had
made his childhood's Christmas trees seem almost supernatural.... Yggdrasils decked for the eternal Yule ... he was

falling asleep.... He was sorry for Stella. She had told him, too, about the Christmas Crib, the little straw house she had built in the church for Mary and Joseph and the Baby, for the ox and the ass and the shepherds and their dogs and the lambs they could not leave behind.... She had told him that she never thought of Christ as being born in Bethlehem, but in the barn at the back of the Plough Inn at Udimore.... He saw the long road running into the sunrise, wet and shining, red with an angry morning. Someone was coming along it carrying a lamb ... was it the lost sheep, or just one of the lambs the shepherds could not leave behind?... all along the road, the trees were hung with glass balls and many-coloured birds. He could feel Stella beside him, though he could not see her. She was trying to make him come with her to the inn. She was saying, "Come, Peter—oh, do come, Peter," and he seemed to be Peter going with her. Then suddenly he knew he was not Peter, and the earth roared and the trees flew up into the sky, which shook and flamed.... He must be falling asleep.

§13

Gervase's feelings towards Alard being what they were, anybody might wonder he should think of giving up Oxford for the family's sake. Indeed, he almost changed his mind in the throes of that wakeful, resentful night, and resolved to take his expensive way to Christ's or Balliol. But by morning, he had come to see himself more clearly and to laugh at his own pretences. He wasn't "giving up" Oxford—he didn't want to go there—he had always shrunk from the thought of Oxford life, with its patterns and conventions—and then at the end of it he would still be his father's youngest son, drawing a youngest son's allowance from depleted coffers. He would far rather learn his job as an engineer and win an early independence. Going to his work every morning, meeting all sorts of men, rough and smooth, no longer feeling irrevocably shut up in a class, a cult, a tradition … in that way, he might really win freedom and defy the house of Alard. "My name's Gervase Alard," he said to himself, "and I'm damned if Gervase shall be sacrificed to Alard, for he's the most important of the two."

If only he could persuade his father to see as he saw—not quite, of course, but near enough to let him make a start. Peter had not seen very well; still, he had nearly agreed when the argument was broken up. Sir John must be found in a propitious hour.

The next day provided none such, for Christmas had—not unexpectedly—brought a return of the Squire's twinges, but these passed off with unusual quickness, and on Innocents' Day his indomitable pluck mounted him once again on his grey horse to ride round the farms. Gervase found him finishing his breakfast when he came down for his own, and seeing by whip and gaiters what was planned, he realised that a favourable time had come. So he rushed into his request while he was helping himself to bacon.

To his surprise, his father heard him without interruption.

"Have you any bent for engineering?" he asked at the end.

"Oh, yes, Sir. I can drive any sort of car and mess about with their insides. I always was keen."

"You've been keen on a good many things if I remember right, but not always proficient. All my sons have been to Oxford."

"But think what a lot it 'ud cost you, Sir, to send me."

"I expect it 'ud cost me nearly as much to make an engineer of you."

"Oh, no, Sir—you'll only have to plank down about a hundred to start with, and in time they'll pay me some sort of a screw. And if I go into a shop at Ashford I can live at home and cost you nothing."

"You think you'll cost nothing to keep at home? What 'ull you live on, you damned fool?"

"Oh, relatively I meant, Sir. And if I get, say, fifteen bob a week, as I shall in time....

"It'll be a proud day for me, of course."

"Things have changed since the war, and lots of chaps who'd have gone up to the 'Varsity now go straight into works—there's Hugh's friend, Tom Daubernon, opened a garage at Colchester...."

"That will be your ambition in life—to open a garage?"

"No, Sir—Alard and Co., motor engineers and armament makers—That's my job, and not so bad either. Think of Krupps."

Sir John laughed half angrily.

"You impudent rascal! Have it your own way after all, it'll suit me better to pay down a hundred for you to cover yourself with oil and grease than a thousand for you to get drunk two nights a week at Oxford" ... a remark which affected Gervase in much the same way as the remark on "little women" had affected Peter.

The conversation was given a more romantic colour when Sir John retailed it to Peter on the edge of the big ploughed field by Glasseye Farm. Peter was going out after duck on the

Tillingham marshes—he had that particularly solitary look of a man who is out alone with a gun.

"I must say I think the boy has behaved extremely well," said his father—"it must have cost him a lot to give up Oxford. He thinks more of our position than I imagined."

"I don't see that it'll add much to the dignity of our position to have him in a workshop."

"It mayn't add much to our dignity—but he's only the youngest son. And what we want more than dignity is money."

"Gervase giving up Oxford won't save you more than a few hundred, and what's that when it'll take fifty thousand to pay off the mortgages?"

"You're a sulky dog, Peter," said Sir John. "If you'd only do as well as your brother, perhaps you could pull us out of this."

"What d'you mean, Sir?"

"Gervase has done his best and given up the only thing he had to give up—Oxford. If you could sink your personal wishes for the family's sake...."

Peter turned crimson and his pale Saxon eyes darkened curiously.

"D'you know what I mean?" continued his father.

"You mean marry a rich woman ... you want me to marry Dolly Hurst."

For a moment Sir John was silent, then he said in an unexpectedly controlled voice—

"Well, what's wrong with Dolly Hurst?"

"Nothing that I know of ... but then I know nothing ... and I don't care."

"I'm told," continued the baronet, still calmly, "that you have already formed an attachment."

"Who told you?"

"Never mind who. The point is, I understand there is such an attachment."

Peter sought for words and found none. While he was still seeking, Sir John shook the reins, and the grey horse moved off heavily up the side of the field.

§14

On the spur of the hill below Barline stands that queer edifice known as Mocksteeple. It has from the distance a decided look of a steeple, its tarred cone being visible for many miles down the river Tillingham. It was built early in the eighteenth century by an eccentric Sir Giles Alard, brother of non-juring Gervase and buyer of Starvecrow. A man of gallantries, he required a spot at which to meet his lady friends, and raised up Mocksteeple for their accommodation—displaying a fine cynicism both towards the neighbours' opinion—for his tryst was a landmark to all the district—and towards the ladies themselves, whose comforts could have been but meagrely supplied in its bare, funnel-shaped interior.

Today it had sunk to a store-house and was full of hop-poles when Peter approached it from the marshes and sat down to eat his sandwiches, in the sunshine that, even on a December day, had power to draw a smell of tar from its walls. At his feet squatted the spaniel Breezy, with sentimental eyes fixed on Peter's gun and the brace of duck that lay beside it. Peter's boots and leggings were caked with mud, and his hands were cold as they fumbled with his sandwiches. It was not a good day to have lunch out of doors, even in that tar-smelling sunshine, but anything was better than facing the family round the table at Conster—their questions, their comments, their inane remarks....

It was queer how individually and separately his family irritated him, whereas collectively they were terrible with banners. His father, his mother, Doris, Jenny, George, Gervase—so much tyranny, so much annoyance ... the Family—a war-cry, a consecration. It was probably because the Family did not merely stand for those at Conster now, but for Alards dead and gone, from the first Gervase to the last, a whole communion of saints.... If Conster had to be sold, or stripped to its bare bones, it would not be only the family now sitting at luncheon that would rise and upbraid him, but all those who slept in Leasan churchyard and in the south aisle at Winchelsea.

Beside him, facing them all, would stand only one small woman. Would her presence be enough to support him when all those forefathers were dishonoured, all those dear places reproached him?—Glasseye, Barline, Dinglesden, Snailham, Ellenwhorne, Starvecrow ... torn away from the central heart and become separate spoil ... just for Stella, whom he had loved only a year.

Leaning against the wall of the Mocksteeple, Peter seemed to hear the voice of the old ruffian who had built it speaking to him out of the tar, deriding him because he would take love for life and house it in a Manor, whereas love is best when taken for a week and housed in any convenient spot. But Peter had never been able to take love for a week. Even when he had had adventures, he had taken them seriously—those independent, experience-hunting young women of his own class who had filled the place in his life which "little women" and "French dancers" had filled in his father's. They had always found old Peter embarrassingly faithful when they changed their minds.

Now, at last, he had found love, true love, in which he could stay all his life—a shelter, a house, a home like Starve-crow. He would be a fool to renounce it—and there was Stella to be thought of, too; he did not doubt her love for him; she would not change. Their friendship had started in the troublesome times of war, and he had given her to understand that he could not marry till the war was over. Those unsettled conditions which had just the opposite effect on most men, making them jump into marriage, snatch their happiness from under the cannon wheels, had made Peter shrink from raising a permanent relation in the midst of so much chaos. Marriage, in his eyes, was settling down, a state to be entered into deliberately, with much background.... And Stella had agreed, with her lips at least, though what her heart had said was another matter.

But now the war was over, he was at home, the background was ready—she would expect.... Already he was conscious of a sharp sense of treachery. At the beginning of their love, Hugh had been alive and the Alard fortunes no direct concern of Peter's—he had expected to go back into business and marry Stella on fifteen hundred a year. But ever since Hugh's death, he had realised that things would be different—and he had not told her. Naturally she would think his prospects improved and he had not undeceived her, though on his last leave, nine months ago, he had guessed the bad way things were going. He had not behaved well to her, and it was now his duty to put matters right at once, to tell her of his choice ...

if he meant to choose.... Good God! he didn't even know yet what he ought to do—even what he wanted to do. If he lost Stella, he lost joy, warmth, laughter, love, the last of youth—if he lost Alard, he lost the First and Last Things of his life, the very rock on which it stood. There was much in Stella which jarred him, which made him doubt the possibility of running in easy yoke with her, which made him fear that choosing her might lead to failure and regret. But also there was much in Alard which fell short of perfection—it had an awkward habit of splitting up into its component parts, into individuals, every separate one of which hurt and vexed. That way, too, might lead to emptiness. It seemed that, whichever choice he made, he failed somebody and ran the risk of a vain sacrifice.

But he must decide. He must not hold Stella now if he did not mean to hold her forever. He saw that his choice must be made at once, for her sake, not in some dim, drifting future as he had at first imagined. He was not going to marry the Hurst girl—he almost hated her—and to marry a girl for her money was like prostitution, even though the money was to save not him but his. But if he was not going to marry Stella, he must act immediately. He had no right to keep her half bound, now that the time had come to take her entirely. Oh, Stella!...

Breezy the spaniel came walking over Peter's legs, and licked his hands in which his face was hidden.

§15

That night Peter wrote to Stella:—

My own dear—

I've been thinking about you all today—I've been thinking about you terribly. I took my gun out this morning after duck, but I had a rotten day because I was thinking of you all the time. I had lunch down by the Mocksteeple, and Stella, I wanted you so that I could have cried. Then afterwards when I was at home I wanted you. I went in to Lambard and we cut some pales, but all the time I was thinking of you. And now I can think no longer—I must write and tell you what I've thought.

Child, I want to marry you. You've known that for a long time, haven't you? But I wanted to wait till the end of the war. I don't believe in marrying a girl and then going out and getting killed, though that is what a lot of chaps did. Well, anyhow the war's over. So will you marry me, Stella child? But I must tell you this. My people will be dead against it, because they're looking to me to save the family by making a rich marriage. It sounds dreadful, but it's not really so bad as it sounds, because if we don't pick up somehow we shall probably go smash and lose almost everything, including Starvecrow. But I don't care. I love you better than anything in the world. Only I must prepare you for having to marry me quietly somewhere and living with me in London for a bit. My father won't have me as agent, I'm quite sure, if I do this, but perhaps he'll come round after a time. Anyhow Stella, darling, if we have each other, the rest won't matter, will it? What does it matter even if we have to sell our land and go out of Conster? They've got no real claim on me. Let Jenny marry somebody rich, or Doris—it's not too late. But I don't see why I should sacrifice my life to the family, and yours too, darling child. For I couldn't do this if I didn't believe that you love me as much as I love you.

I think this is the longest letter than I have ever written

to you, but then it is so important. Dearest, we must meet and talk things over. The Greenings are going into Hastings on Tuesday to look at a house, so will you come to me at Starvecrow?

My kisses, you sweet, and all my love.

PETER

It was nearly midnight when he had finished writing at the table in his bedroom. He folded up the letter and slipped it under the blotting paper, before getting into bed and sleeping soundly.

But the next morning he tore it to pieces.

§16

On the last day of the old year, Mary Pembroke came down to Conster Manor, arriving expensively with a great deal of luggage. Her beauty was altogether of a more sophisticated kind than Jenny's and more exotic than Doris's—which, though at thirty-eight extinct in the realm of nature, still lived in the realm of art. Mary was thirty-one, tall and supple, with an arresting fineness about her, and a vibrant, ardent quality.

The family was a little restless as they surrounded her in the drawing-room at tea. She had that same element of unexpectedness as Gervase, but with the difference that Gervase was as yet raw and young and under control. Mary gave an impression of being more grown-up than anyone, even than Lady Alard and Sir John; life with her was altogether a more acute affair.

Only Lady Alard enquired after the absent Julian.

"I wonder he didn't come down with you," she murmured.

"I sent him a very special invitation."

"Bah!" said Sir John.

"Why do you say 'Bah,' dear?"

"Doris, tell your mother why I said 'Bah.'"

"Oh, Father, how do I know?"

"You must be very stupid, then. I give leave to any one of you to explain why I said 'Bah,'" and Sir John stumped out of the room.

"Really, your father is impossible," sighed Lady Alard.

Mary did not talk much—her tongue skimmed the surface of Christmas: the dances they had been to, the people they had had to dinner. She looked fagged and anxious—strung. At her first opportunity, she went upstairs to take off her travelling clothes and dress for dinner. Of dressing and undressing, Mary made always a lovely ceremony—very different from Jenny's hasty scuffle and Doris's veiled mysteries. She lingered over it as over a thing she loved; and Jenny loved to watch her—all the careful, charming details, the graceful acts and poses, the sweet scents. Mary moved like the priest of her own beauty, with her dressing table for altar and her maid for acolyte—the latter an olive-skinned French girl, who with a topknot of black hair gave a touch of chinoiserie to the proceedings.

When Mary had slipped off her travelling dress, and wrapped in a Mandarin's coat of black and rose and gold, had let Gisèle unpin her hair, she sent the girl away.

"Je prendrai mon bain à sept heures—vous reviendrez."

She leaned back in her armchair, her delicate bare ankles crossed, her feet in their brocade mules resting on the fender, and gazed into the fire. Jenny moved about the room for a few moments, looking at brushes and boxes and jars. She had always been more Mary's friend than Doris, whose attitude had that peculiar savour of the elder, unmarried sister towards the younger married one. But Jenny with Mary was not the same as Jenny with Gervase—her youth easily took colour from its surroundings, and with Mary she was less frank, more hushed, more unquiet. When she had done looking at her things, she came and sat down opposite her on the other side of the fire.

"Well—how's life?" asked Mary.

"Oh, pretty dull."

"What, no excitements? How's Jim?"

"Oh, just the same as usual. He hangs about, but he knows it's no good, and so do I—and he knows that I know it's no good, and I know that he knows that I know—" and Jenny laughed wryly.

"Hasn't he any prospects?"

"None whatever—at least none that are called prospects in our set, though I expect they'd sound pretty fine to anyone else. He'll have Cock Marling when his father dies."

"You shouldn't have fallen in love with a landed proprietor, Jen."

"Oh, well, it's done now and I can't help it."

"You don't sound infatuated."

"I'm not, but I'm in love right enough. It's all the hanging about and uncertainty that makes me sound bored—in self-defence one has to grow a thick skin."

Mary did not speak for a moment, but seemed to slip through the firelight into a dream.

"Yes," she said at last—"a thick skin or a hard heart. If the average woman's heart could be looked at under a microscope,

I expect it would be seen to be covered with little spikes and scales and callouses—a regular hard heart. Or perhaps it would be inflamed and tender.... I believe inflammation is a defence, against disease—or poison. But after all, nothing's much good—the enemy always gets his knife in somehow."

She turned away her eyes from Jenny, and the younger sister felt abashed—and just because she was abashed and awkward and shy, for that very reason, she blurted out—

"How's Julian?"

"Oh, quite well, thank you. I persuaded him not to come down because he and father always get on so badly."

"It's a pity they do."

"A very great pity. But I can't help it. I did my best to persuade him to advance the money, but he's not a man who'll lend without good security, even to a relation. I'm sorry, because if he would stand by the family, I shouldn't feel I'd been quite such a fool to marry him."

Though the fiction of Mary being happily married was kept up only by Lady Alard, it gave Jenny a faint shock to hear her sister speak openly of failure. Her feelings of awkwardness and shyness returned, and a deep colour stained her cheeks. What should you say?—should you take any notice?... It was your sister.

"Mary, have you ... are you ... I mean, is it really quite hopeless?"

"Oh, quite," said Mary.

"Then what are you going to do?"

"I don't know—I haven't thought."

Jenny crossed and uncrossed her large feet—she looked at her sister's little mules, motionless upon the fender.

"Is he—I mean, does he—treat you badly?"

Mary laughed.

"Oh, no—husbands in our class don't, as a rule, unless they're qualifying for statutory cruelty. Julian isn't cruel—he's very kind indeed—probably most people would say he was a model husband. I simply can't endure him, that's all."

"Incompatibility of temperament."

"That's a very fine name for it, but I daresay it's the right one. Julian and I are two different sorts of people, and we've found it out—at least I have. Also, he's disappointed because we've been married seven years and I haven't had a child—and he lets me see he's disappointed. And now he's begun to be jealous—that's put the lid on."

She leaned back in her chair, her hands folded on her lap, without movement and yet, it seemed, without rest. Her body was alert and strung, and her motionlessness was that of a taut bowstring or a watching animal. As Jenny's eyes swept over her, taking in both her vitality and her immaculacy, a new conjecture seized her, a sudden question.

"Mary—are you … are you in love?—with someone else, I mean."

"No—what makes you think so?"

"It's how you look."

"Jen, you're not old enough yet to know how a woman looks when she's in love. Your own face in the glass won't tell you."

"It's not your face—it's the way you behave—the way you dress. You seem to worship yourself …."

"So you think I must be in love—you can't conceive that my efforts to be beautiful should be inspired by anything but the wish to please some man! Jen, you're like all men, but,

I'd hoped, only a few women—you can't imagine a woman wanting to be beautiful for her own sake. Oh, my dear, it's just because I'm not in love that I must please myself. If I was in love, I shouldn't bother half so much—I'd know I pleased somebody else, which one can do with much less trouble than one can please oneself. I shouldn't bother about my own exactions any more. The day you see me with untidy hair and an unpowdered skin, you'll know I'm in love with somebody who loves me, and haven't got to please myself anymore."

"But, Mary ... there's Charles. Don't you love Charles?"

"No, I don't. I know it's very silly of me not to love the man my husband's jealous of, but such is the fact. Nobody but Julian would have made a row about Charles—he's just a pleasant, well-bred, oldish man, who's simple enough to be restful. He's more than twenty years older than I am, which I know isn't everything, but counts for a good deal. I liked going about with him because he's so remote from all the fatigue and fret and worry of that side of life. It was almost like going about with another woman, except that one had the advantage of a man's protection and point of view."

"Does he love you?"

"I don't think so for a moment. In fact, I'm quite sure he doesn't. He likes taking out a pretty woman, and we've enough differences to make us interesting to each other, but there the matter ends. As it happens, I'm much too fond of him to fall in love with him. It's not a thing I'd ever do with a man I liked as a friend. I know what love is, you see, and not so long ago."

"Who was that?"

"Julian," said Mary dryly.

A feeling of panic and hopelessness came over Jenny.
"Oh, God ... then one can never know."

§17

Gervase's scheme of going into a workshop materialised more
quickly than his family, knowing his rather inconsequent nature, had expected. The very day after he had obtained his
father's consent, he drove into Ashford and interviewed the
manager of Messrs. Gillingham and Golightly, motor engineers in the station road. After some discussion, it was arranged that he should be taken into the works as pupil on the
payment of a premium of seventy-five pounds to cover three
years instruction, during which time he was to receive a salary
starting at five shillings a week and rising to fifteen.

The sarcasm that greeted his first return on Saturday afternoon with his five shillings in his pocket was equalled only
by his own pride. Here, at last, was money of his own, genuinely earned and worked for—money that was not Alard's,
that was undimmed by earth, having no connection with the
land either through agriculture or landlordism. Gervase felt
free for at least an hour.

"We can launch out a bit now," said Sir John at luncheon—"Gervase has come to our rescue and is supporting
us in our hour of need. Which shall we pay off first, Peter?
Stonelink or Dinglesden?..."

Peter scowled—he seemed to find his father's pleasantry
more offensive than Gervase, who merely laughed and jin-
gled the coins in his pocket.

The youngest Alard threw himself with zest into his new
life. It certainly was a life which required enthusiasm to make

it worth living. Every morning at nine he had to be at the works, driving himself in the Ford farm-lorry, which had been given over to his use on its supplanting by a more recent make. He often was not back till seven or eight at night, worn out, but with that same swelling sense of triumph with which he had returned from his first day's work. He was still living at home, still dependent on his people for food and clothing if not for pocket money, but his feet were set on a road which would take him away from Conster, out of the Alard shadow. Thank God! he was the youngest son, or they wouldn't have let him go. He enjoyed the hardness of the way—the mortification of those early risings, with the blue, star-pricked sky and the deadly cold—the rattling drive in the Ford through all weathers—the arrival at the works, the dirt, the din, the grease, the breaking of his nails, his filthy overalls, his fellow workmen with their unfamiliar oaths and class-grievances, the pottering over bolts and screws, the foreman's impatience with his natural carelessness—the exhausted drive home over the darkness of the Kent road ... Gable Hook, Tenterden, Newenden, Northiam, Beckley, going by in a flash of red windows—the arrival at Conster almost too tired to eat—the welcome haven of bed and the all too short sweet sleep.

Those January days in their zeal and discipline were like the first days of faith—life ceased to be an objectless round, a slavery to circumstances. Generally, when he was at home, he was acutely sensitive to the fret of Conster, to the ceaseless fermentation of those lives, so much in conflict and yet so combined—he had always found his holidays depressing and been glad to go back to school. Now, though he still lived in the house, he did not belong to it—its ambitions and its strife did not concern him, though he was too observant and sensitive not to be affected by what was going on.

He saw enough to realise that the two main points of tension were Mary and Peter. Mary was still at Conster, though he understood that Julian had written asking her to come home—February was near, and she stayed on, though she spoke of going back. As for Peter, he had become sulky and self-absorbed. He would not go for walks on Sundays, or shooting on Saturday afternoons—he had all the painful, struggling manner of a plain man with a secret—a straight-forward man in the knots of a decision. Gervase was sorry for him, but a little angry too. Over his more monotonous jobs at the works, in his rare wakeful moments, but most of all in his long familiar-contemptible drives to and from Ashford, he still thought of Stella. His feeling for her remained much the same as it had been at Christmas—a loving absorption, a warm worship. He could not bear that she should suffer—she was so very much alive that he felt her suffering must be sharper than other people's. He could guess by his own feelings a little of what she suffered in her love for Peter—and once he got further than a guess.

During those weeks, he had never met her anywhere, either at Conster or outside it; but one Saturday at noon, as he was coming away from the shop, he met her surprisingly on foot in the station road. He pulled up and spoke to her, and she told him she was on her way to the station in hopes of an early train. The Singer had broken down with magneto trouble and she had been obliged to leave it for repair—meantime, her father wanted her back early, as there was always a lot of dispensary work to do on a Saturday afternoon.

"Well, if you don't mind a ride in a dying Ford...."

He hardly dared listen to her answer; he tried to read it as it came into her eyes while he spoke.

"Of course I don't mind. I should love it—and it's really most frightfully good of you."

So she climbed up beside him, and soon her round bright eyes were looking at him from between her fur cap and huge fur collar, as they had looked that first morning at Starvecrow.... He felt the love rising in his throat ... tender and silly ... he could not speak; and he soon found that she would rather he didn't. Not only was the Ford's death-rattle rather loud, but she seemed to find the same encouragement to thought as he in that long monotonous jolt through the Weald of Kent. He did not have to lift himself far out of the stream of his thoughts when he looked at her or spoke, but hers were evidently very far away. With a strange mixture of melancholy and satisfaction, he realised that he must count for little in her life—practically nothing at all. Even if she were not Peter's claim, she could never be his—not only on account of her age, six years older than he, but because the fact that she loved Peter showed that it was unlikely she could ever love Gervase, Peter's contrast.... In his heart was a sweet ache of sorrow, the thrill which comes with the first love-pain.

But as they ran down into Sussex, across the floods that sheeted the Rother levels, and saw the first outposts of Alard—Monking and Horns Cross Farms with the ragged line of Moat Wood—his heart suddenly grew cold. In one of his sidelong glances at Stella, he saw a tear hanging on the dark stamen of an eyelash ... he looked again as soon as he dared, and saw another on her cheek. Was it the cold?...

"Stella, are you cold?" he asked, fearing her answer.

"No, thank you, Gervase."

He dared not ask, "Why are you crying?" Also, there was
no need—he knew. The sweetness had gone out of his sorrow, he no longer felt that luxurious creep of pain—instead
his heart was heavy, and dragged at his breast. It was faint
with anger.

When they came to the Throws, where the road to Vinehall turns out of the road to Leasan, he asked her if she
wouldn't come up to Conster for tea—"and I'll drive you
home afterwards." But again she said in her gentle voice, "No
thank you, Gervase." He wished she wouldn't say it like that.

§18

What did Peter mean?

That was the question Stella had asked herself at intervals
during the past month, that she had been asking herself all
the way from Ashford to Vinehall, and was still asking when
Gervase set her down on the doorstep of Hollingrove and
drove away. What did Peter mean?

She would not believe that he meant nothing—that their
friendship had been just one of those war-time flirtations
which must fade in the light of peace. It had lasted too long,
for one thing—it had lasted a year. For a whole year they
had loved each other, written to each other almost every day,
hungered for meetings, and met with kisses and passionate
playful words. It is true that he had never spoken to her of
marriage except negatively, but she knew his views and had
submitted if not agreed. All that was over now—he was no
longer a soldier, holding his life on an uncertain lease; and
more, he was now the heir—their prospects had improved

from the material and practical point of view. He might, like so many men, have found it difficult to get back into business, recover his pre-war footing in the world; but there need be no concern for that now he was not only the heir, but his father's agent, already established with home and income, and his home that dearest of all places, Starvecrow....

She would not believe that he had been playing with her, that he had only taken her to pass the time, and now was looking for some decent pretext for letting her go. He was not that sort of man at all. Peter was loyal and honest right through. Besides, she saw no sign that his love had grown cold. She was sure that he loved her as much as ever, but more painfully, more doubtingly. Their meetings had lately been given over to a sorrowful silence. He had held her in his arms in silent, straining tenderness. He would not talk, he would not smile. What did he mean?

Probably his family was making trouble. She had been only once to Conster since she had dined there on Christmas Day, and it had struck her then that Doris and Lady Alard had both seemed a little unfriendly. Everyone in Leasan and Vinehall said that the Squire's son would have to marry money if he meant to keep the property going. She had often heard people say that—but till now she had scarcely thought of it. The idea had seemed impossible, almost grotesque. But now it did not seem quite impossible—Peter's behaviour, his family's behaviour, all pointed to its being a factor in the situation; and since she could not refuse to see that something was keeping him silent when he ought to speak, it was easier to believe in a difficulty of this kind than in any commonplace cooling or change. Once she had thought that, nothing, not even Alard, could come between them—now she must alter her faith to the extent of believing that nothing could come between them except Alard.

She could not help being a little angry with Peter for this discovery. It seemed to her a shameful thing that money should count against love. As for herself, she did not dare think what she would not sacrifice for love—for Peter, if occasion arose. And he, apparently, would not sacrifice for her one acre of Conster, one tile of Starvecrow.... Was it the difference between men and women which made the difference here? If she was a man, would she be able to see the importance of Peter's family, the importance of keeping his property together, even at the expense of happiness and faith? She wondered.... Meanwhile she was angry.

She wished he would have things out with her, try to explain. That he did not was probably due to the mixture of that male cowardice which dreads a "scene" with that male stupidity which imagines that nothing has been noticed which it has not chosen to reveal. But if he didn't tell her soon, she would ask him herself. She knew that such a step was not consistent with feminine dignity, either ancient or modern. According to tradition, she should have drooped to the masculine whim: according to fashion, she should have asserted her indifference to it. But she could do neither. She could not bear her own uncertainty any longer—this fear of her hopes. Oh, she had planned so materially and wildly! She had planned the very furnishing of Starvecrow—which room was to be which—the dining-room, the best bedroom, the spare bedroom, Peter's study ... cream distemper on the walls, and for each room different colours ... and a kitchen furnished with natural oak and copper pots and pans....

The tears which up till now had only teased the back of her eyes, brimmed over at the thought of the kitchen. The dark January afternoon, clear under a sky full of unshed rain, was swallowed up in mist as Stella wept for her kitchen and copper pans.

She was still on the doorstep, where she had stood to see the last of Gervase, and even now that she was crying she did not turn into the house. The iron-black road was empty between its draggled hedges, and she found a certain kinship in the winter twilight, with its sharpness, its sighing of low, rain-burdened winds. After a few moments, she dried her eyes and went down the steps to the gate. Thanks to Gervase, she had come home nearly an hour earlier than she need— she would go and sit for a few minutes in church. She found church a very good place for thinking her love affairs into their right proportion with all time.

The village of Vinehall was not like the village of Leas-an, which straggled for nearly a mile each side of the high road. It was a large village, all pressed together like a little town. Above it soared the spire of Vinehall church, which, like many Sussex churches, stood in a farmyard. Its lovely im-age lay in the farmyard pond, streaked over with green scum and the little eddies that followed the ducks.

Stella carefully shut out a pursuing hen and went in by the tower door. The church was full of heavy darkness. The after-noon sun had left it a quarter of an hour ago, showing only its pale retreat through the slats of the clerestory windows, white overhead, and night lay already in the aisles. She groped her way to the east end, where the white star of a lamp flickered against a pillar guarding a shrine. She flopped down on the worn stones at the foot of the pillar, sitting back on her heels, her hands lying loosely and meekly in her lap.

She had no sense of loneliness or fear in the dark—the white lamp spoke to her of a presence which she could feel throughout the dark and empty church, a presence of living quiet, of glowing peace. Outside she could hear the fowls clucking in the yard, with every now and then the shrill gobble-gobble of a turkey. She loved these homely sounds, which for years had been the accompaniment of her prayers— her prayers which had no words, but seemed to move in her heart like flames. Oh, it was good to be here, to have this place to come to, this Presence to seek.

Now that she was here, she could no longer feel angry with Peter, however stupid, obstinate and earthy he was. Poor Peter—choosing it for himself as well as for her ... she could not be angry with him, because she knew that if he pulled catastrophe down upon them, he of the two would suffer the most. Unlike her, he had no refuge, no Presence to seek, no unseen world that could become real at a thought.... His gods were dead Squires who had laid up wealth to be his poverty. Her God was a God who had beggared Himself, that she through His poverty might become rich.

This beggar and lover and prisoner, her God, was with her here in the darkness, telling her that if she too wished to be a lover, she too must become a beggar and a prisoner. She would be Peter's beggar, Peter's slave. She would not let him go from her without pleading, without fighting, but if he really must go, if this half-known monster, Alard, was really strong enough to take him, he should not go wounded by her detaining clutch as well as by its claws. He should not go shamed and reproached, but with good-will. If he really must go, and she could no longer hold him, she would make his going easy.... He should go in peace.... Poor Peter.

§19

At the end of January, Mary left Conster. She could not in any spirit of decorum put off her return longer—her husband had wired to her to come home.

"Poor Julian," said Lady Alard—"he must be missing you dreadfully. I really think you ought to go back, Mary, since he can't manage to come here."

Mary agreed without elaboration, and her lovely hats and shoes with the tea-gowns and dinner-frocks, which had divided the family into camps of admiration and disapproval, were packed away by the careful, brisk Gisèle. The next day she was driven over to Ashford, with Jenny and Peter to see her off.

There had been no intimate talks between the sisters since the first night of her coming. Jenny was shy, and typically English in her dislike of the exposure of anything which seemed as if it ought to be hidden, and Mary either felt this attitude in her sister or else shrank from disillusioning her youth still further. They had arrived a little too early for the train, and stood together uneasily on the platform, while Gisèle bought the tickets and superintended the luggage.

"I wish you didn't have to go," said Jenny politely.

"So do I—but it couldn't be helped after that telegram."

"Julian sounded rather annoyed—I hope he won't make a fuss when you get back."

"I'm not going back."

There was a heavy silence. Neither Peter nor Jenny thought they had quite understood.

"Wh-what do you mean?" stammered Jenny at last—"not going back to Chart? Isn't Julian there?"

"Of course he's there. That's why I'm not going back. Gisèle is taking the tickets to London."

"But"—It was Peter who said 'But,' and had apparently nothing else to say.

"Do you mean that you're leaving him?" faltered Jenny.

"I'm not going to live with him anymore. I've had enough."

"But why didn't you tell us?—tell the parents?"

"I'd rather not bring the family into it. It's my own choice, though Julian is sure to think you've been influencing me. I didn't make up my mind till I got his telegram; then I saw quite plainly that I couldn't go back to him."

"You're not going to that other fellow—what's his name—Commander Smith?" cried Peter, finding his tongue rather jerkily.

"Oh, no. As I've told Jenny, making a mess of things with one man doesn't necessarily encourage me to try my luck with another. Besides, I'm not fond of Charles—in that way. I shall probably stay at my Club for a bit, and then go abroad.... I don't know.... All I know is that I'm not going back to Julian."

"Shall you—can you—divorce him?"

"No. He hasn't been cruel or unfaithful, nor has he deserted me. I'm deserting him. It's simply that I can't live with him—he gets on my nerves—I can't put up with either his love or his jealousy. I couldn't bear the thought even of having dinner with him tonight.... And yet—" the calm voice suddenly broke—"and yet I married for love...."

Both the brother and sister were silent. Peter saw Gisèle coming up with a porter and the luggage, and went off like a coward to meet them. Jenny remained uneasily with Mary.

"I'm sorry to have had to do this," continued the elder sister—"it'll upset the parents, I know. They don't like Julian, but they'll like a scandal still less."

"Do you think he'll make a row?"

"I'm sure of it. For one thing, he'll never think for a minute I haven't left him for someone else—for Charles. He won't be able to imagine that I've left a comfortable home and a rich husband without any counter attraction except my freedom. By the way, I shall be rather badly off—I'll have only my settlements, and they won't bring in much."

"Oh, Mary do you really think you're wise?"

"Not wise, perhaps—nor good." She pulled down her veil. "I feel that a better or a worse woman would have made a neater job of this. The worse would have found an easier way— the better would have stuck to the rough. But I—oh, I'm neither—I'm neither good nor bad. All I know is that I can't go back to Julian, to put up with his fussing and his love and his suspicion—and, worse still, with my own shame because I don't love him any more—because I've allowed myself to be driven out of love by tricks—by manner—by outside things."

"—London train—Headcorn, Tonbridge and London train—"

The porter's shouting was a welcome interruption, though it made Jenny realise with a blank feeling of anxiety and impotence that any time for persuasion was at an end.

"Do you want us to tell Father and Mother?" she asked as Mary got into the train.

"You needn't if you'd rather not. I'll write to them tonight."

She leaned back in the carriage, soft, elegant, perfumed, a

little unreal, and yet conveying somehow a sense of desperate choice and mortal straits.

Peter and Jenny scarcely spoke till they were back in the car driving homewards. Then Jenny said with a little gasp—

"Isn't it dreadful?"

"What?—her going away?"

"No, the fact that she married Julian for love."

Peter said nothing.

"If she'd married out of vanity, or greed, or to please the family, it would have been better—one would have understood what's happened now. But she married him for love."

Peter still said nothing.

§20

He sat waiting at Starvecrow on an early day in February. Outside the rain kept the Feast of the Purification, washing down the gutters of Starvecrow's mighty roof, lapping the edges of the pond into the yard, and further away transforming all the valley of the Tillingham into a lake—huge sheets and spreads of water, out of which the hills of Barline and Brede Eye stood like a coast. All the air was fresh and washed and tinkling with rain.

The fire was piled high with great logs and posts, burning with a blue flame, for they had been pulled out of the barns of Starvecrow, which like many in the district were built of ships timbers with the salt still in them. The sound of the fire was as loud as the sound of the rain. Both made a sorrowful music together in Peter's head.

He sat with his hands folded together under his chin, his large light blue eyes staring without seeing into the grey dripping world framed by the window. The clock in the passage struck three. Stella would not come till a quarter past. He had arranged things purposely so that he should be alone for a bit at Starvecrow before meeting her, strengthening himself with the old loyalties to fight the brief, sweet faithfulness of a year.

He felt almost physically sick at the thought of what lay before him, but he had made up his mind to go through with it—it had got to be done; and it must be done in this way. Oh, how he had longed to send Stella a letter, telling her that they must never see each other again, begging her to go away and spare him! But he knew that was a coward's escape—the least he owed her was an explanation face to face.... What a brute he had been to her! He had no right to have won her love if he did not mean to keep it—and though, when he had first sought her, he had thought himself free to do so, he had behaved badly in not telling her of the new difficulties created by his becoming the heir. It was not that he had meant to hide things from her, but he had simply shelved them in his own mind, hoping that "something would turn up," that Alard's plight would not be as bad as he had feared. Now he saw that it was infinitely worse, and he was driven to a definite choice between his people and Stella. If he married Stella, he would have failed Alard—if he stood by Alard, he would have failed Stella. It was a cruel choice—between the two things in the world that he loved best. But he must make it now—he could not keep Stella hanging on indefinitely any longer. Already he could see how uncertainty, anxiety, and disappointment were telling on her. She was looking worn and dim. She had expected him, on his return home after the wars, to proclaim their love publicly, and he was still keeping it hidden, though the reasons he had first given her for doing so were at an end. She was wondering why he didn't speak—she was hesitating whether she should speak herself.... He guessed her struggle, and knew he must put an end to it.

Besides, now at last his choice was made. He no longer had any uncertainty, any coil of argument to encumber him. Mary's words on the Ashford platform had finally settled his difficulty—"And yet I married for love." Seven years ago, Mary had loved this man from whom she was now escaping, the very sight of whom in her home she could not bear. Love was as uncertain as everything else—it came and it was gone. Mary had once loved Julian as Peter now loved Stella—and look at her!... Oh, you could never be sure. And there was so much in Stella he was not sure of—and she might change—he might change; only places never changed—were always the same. Starvecrow would always be to him, whether at eighteen, thirty-eight or eighty, the same Starvecrow.... How could he fail the centuries behind him for what might not live more than a few years? How could he fail the faithful place for that which had change for its essence and death for its end?

Far away he could hear the purring of a car—it drew nearer, and Peter, clenching his hands, found the palms damp. All his skin was hot and moist—oh, God, what had he to face? The scene that was coming would be dreadful—he'd never get through it unless Stella helped him, and he'd no right to expect help from her. Here she was, driving in at the gate ... outside the door ... inside the room at last.

§21

He sought refuge in custom, and going up to her, laid his hands on her shoulders and kissed her gravely. Then he began to loosen the fur buttons of her big collar, but she put up her hand and stopped him.

"No—I'll keep it on. I can't stop long. Father's waiting for me at Barline."

"It's good of you to come—there's something I've got to say."

"You want to tell me we must end it."

He had not expected her to help him so quickly. Then he suddenly realised that his letter had probably told her a lot—his trouble must have crept between the lines—into the lines ... he wasn't good at hiding things.

"Oh, Stella."

He stood a few paces from her, and noticed—now that his thoughts were less furiously concentrated on himself—that she was white, that all the warm, rich colour in her cheeks was gone. He pulled forward one of the office chairs, and she sank into it. He sat down opposite her, and took her hand, which she did not withdraw.

"Oh, Stella, my darling ... my precious child.... It's all no use. I've hoped and I've tried, but it's no good—I must let you go."

"Why?"

The word came almost sharply—she wasn't going to help him, then, so much.

"Darling, I know I'm a cad. I ought never to have told you I loved you, knowing that ... at least when Hugh died,

I should have told you straight out how things were. But I couldn't—I let myself drift, hoping matters would improve ... and then there was the war...."

"Peter, I wish you would tell me things straight out— now's better than never. And honestly I can't understand why you're not going to marry me."

He was a little shocked. Tradition taught him that Stella would try to save her face, and he had half expected her to say that she had never thought of marrying him. After all, he had never definitely asked her, and she might claim that this was only one of those passionate friendships which had become so common during the war. If she had done so, he would have conceded her the consolation without argument—a girl ought to try and save her face; but Stella apparently did not care about her face at all.

"Why aren't you going to marry me? You've never given me any real reason."

"Surely you know"—his voice was a little cold.

"How can I know? I see you the heir of a huge estate, living in a big house with apparently lots of money. You tell me again and again that you love me—I'm your equal in birth and education. Why on earth should I know that you can't marry me?"

"Stella, we're in an awful mess—all the family. The estate is mortgaged almost up to the last acre—we can hardly manage to pay the yearly interest, and owing to the slump in land we can't sell."

Stella stared at him woodenly.

"Can't you understand?"

"No"—she said slowly—"I can't. I've heard that the war

has hit you—It's hit all the big landowners; but you're—good heavens! you're not poor. Think of the servants you keep, and the motor-cars—"

"Oh, that's my hopeless parents, who won't give up anything they've been accustomed to, and who say that it's not worth while making ourselves uncomfortable in small things when only something colossal can save us. If we moved into the Lodge tomorrow and lived on five hundred a year it would still take us more than a lifetime to scrape up enough to free the land."

"Then what do you propose to do?"

"Well, don't you see, if I live at home I can manage somehow to keep down expenses, so that the interest on the mortgages gets paid—and when Greening's gone and I'm agent I can do a lot to improve the estate, and send the value up so that we can sell some of the outlying farms over by Stonelink and Guestling—that'll bring in ready money, and then perhaps I'll be able to pay off some of the mortgages."

"But couldn't you do all that if you married me?"

"No, because for one thing I shouldn't be allowed to try. Father wouldn't have me for agent."

"Why?"

"Oh, Stella darling, don't make it so difficult for me. It's so hard for me to tell you ... can't you see that my people want to get money above all things—lots of it? If I marry you, it'll be the end of all their hopes."

"They want you to marry money."

"They want us all to marry money. Oh, don't think I'm going to do it—I couldn't marry anyone I didn't love. But I feel I've got my duty to them as well as to you ... and it's not only to them ... oh, Stella sweetheart, don't cry!"

"I—I can't help it. Oh, Peter, it all sounds so—so dreadful, so sordid and so—so cruel, to you as well as to me."

He longed to take her in his arms, but dared not, partly for fear of his own weakness, partly for fear she would repulse him.

"Darling—I'm not explaining well; it's so difficult. And I know it's sordid, but not so sordid as you think. It's simply that I feel I must stand by my family now—and I don't mean just my people, you know; I mean all the Alards ... all that ever were. I can't let the place be sold up, as it will have to be if I don't save it. Think of it ... and the first part to be sold would have to be Starvecrow, because it's the only free, unmortgaged land we've got. Oh, Stella, think of selling Starvycrow!"

She took away her hands and looked at him through her streaming tears.

"Oh, don't look at me like that—don't reproach me. What I'm doing is only half selfish—the other half is unselfish, it's sacrifice."

"But, Peter, what does it matter if the land is sold? What good is the land doing you?—what good will it ever do you, if it comes to that? Why should we suffer for the land?"

"I thought you'd have understood that better."

"I don't understand at all."

"Not that I must stand by my people?"

"I don't understand why your people can't be happy without owning all the land in three parishes."

"Oh, my dear...."

He tried to take her hand, but this time she pulled it away.

"It's no good, Peter. I understand your selfish reason better

than your unselfish one. I fail to see why you should sacrifice
me and yourself to your family and their land. I can see much
better how you can't bear the thought of losing Starvecrow.
I know how you love it, because I love it too—but much as
I love it, I never could sacrifice you to it, my dear, nor any
human soul."

"I know—I know. I'm a beast, Stella—but it's like this ...
human beings change—even you may change—but places are
always the same."

"What do you mean?"

"Well, I love you now—but how do I know ... Mary married for love."

"What's Mary got to do with it?"

"She's shown me that one can never be sure, even with
love."

"You mean to say you're not sure if you'd be happy with
me?"

"Darling, I'm as sure as I can ever be with any human
being. But one never can be quite sure, that's the terrible
thing. And oh, it would be so ghastly if you changed—or I
changed—and I had left the unchanging place for you."

Stella rose quietly to her feet.

"I understand now, Peter."

For a moment she stood motionless and silent, her mouth
set, her eyes shining out beyond him. He wondered if she was
praying.

"Stella—don't hate me."

"I don't hate you—I love you. But I quite understand that
you don't love me. Your last words have shown me that. And
your not loving me explains it all. If you really loved me, all

these difficulties, all these ambitions, would be like—like chaff. But you don't love me, at least not much; and I don't want you, if you only love me a little. I'm relieved, in a way— I think you'd be doing a dreadful thing if you gave me up while you really loved me. But you don't really love me, so you're quite right to give me up and stand by your family and Starvecrow. Oh, I know you love me enough to have married me if everything had been easy...."

"Stella, don't—it isn't that I don't love you; it's only that I can't feel sure of the future with you—I mean, there are so many things about you I can't understand—your way of looking at life and things...."

"Oh, I know, my dear—don't trouble to explain to me. And don't think I'm angry, Peter—only sick—sick—sick. I don't want to argue with you anymore—it's over. And I'll make things as easy for you as I can, and for myself too. I'll go away—I'll have to. I couldn't bear meeting you after this— or seeing Starvecrow...."

She went to the door, and he hoped she would go straight out, but on the threshold she suddenly turned—

"I'm not angry, Peter—I'm not angry. I was, but I'm not now.... I'm only miserable. But I'll be all right ... if I go away. And some day we'll be friends again...."

The door crashed behind her. She was gone.

INTERLUDE

INTERLUDE

May 29, 1919.   Conster Manor,
                                                Leasan,
                                                Sussex.

My dear Stella,

I hope you won't think it awful cheek of me to write to
you, but I've been thinking of doing so for a long time—ever
since you left, in fact. I felt so very sorry that just after I'd begun to know you again you should go away. You see, I'm rather odd-man-out in the family, for though Jenny and I have
always been pals, she's frightfully preoccupied with things
just now, and I get back so late and start off again so early next morning that I see very little of people at home. The
same fact makes it difficult for me to keep up with the people
I knew at school—I can't have them at Conster, anyway. And
at the works—oh, Gee! I can't think where they come from.
Either they're of quite a bit different class, which I can get on
with, though I don't think I could ever make a friend of it, or
else they're a type of man I've never struck before, the kind
that's always talking of horses and girls, and the way he talks
it's rather difficult to tell t'other from which. So may I—now

it's coming out!—may I write to you now and then? It would make such a difference to me, and you needn't answer—at least, not so often as I write. I'd never dare ask you this to your face, but I can write things I can't say. So please let me— it would be such a relief, and I'd be so grateful. I don't pretend for a minute that it'll be entertaining for you—I'll simply be getting things off my chest. You see, I do such a frightful lot of thinking on the way to and from Ashford and you've done a lot of thinking too—I'm sure of it—so perhaps you'll understand my thoughts, though I can tell you some of 'em are precious silly. This letter is a pretty fair specimen of what you'd have to expect, so if you don't like it, squash me at once, for I'd hate to be a nuisance to you.

I hope you're still liking the clinic. Your father told us about it last Sunday. I expect he's given you all the Leasan and Vinehall news. He'll have told you about Dolly Hurst's wedding, anyhow. It was a simply terrible affair. I had to go, because they heartlessly chose a Saturday afternoon, and I was nearly stifled with the show. The church reeked of flowers and money and Israelites. In spite of my decided views on the filthiness of lucre, I can't help thinking it a waste that a rich Gentile should marry a rich Jew when there are plenty of poor Gentiles in the neighbourhood. However, the bride-groom looks a decent fellow, and not so violently a son of Abraham. He had three sisters who were bridesmaids, and all treats, as we say at the shop. Forgive these vulgar musings on a solemn subject, but the occasion provokes them—and any-how write and tell me if I may write again.

Yours in hope and fear,

GERVASE ALARD

June 3.   15, Mortimer Street,
                                          Birmingham.

My dear Gervase,

Very many thanks for your letter. Of course go on writ-ing—I shall love hearing from you, though please don't think I'm clever and "do a lot of thinking"—because I don't. And I'm glad you say you won't be exacting in the way of answers, for I'm frightfully busy here. I have to be at the clinic at nine every morning, and often don't get away till after six. I do all the dispensary work, weigh babies, etc.—it's all most amus-ing, and I love it, and would be ever so happy if I felt Father was getting on all right without me.

Now you might help me here and tell me what you think of Miss Gregory. Father of course makes out that he's per-fectly satisfied, but I feel that may be only because he doesn't want me to worry or think I ought to come back. So you tell me if you think she's a dud, though of course I don't expect you'll have much opportunity for finding out.

Yes, Father told me about the Hurst wedding, and I had a letter too from Mrs. George Alard. It seems to have been a regular Durbar. I'm rather surprised they found it possible to get married in church, the bridegroom not being a Christian. But perhaps he's Jewish only by race. I hope so, because Mrs. George said Peter seemed very much smitten with his sister, who was chief bridesmaid. Of course, this may be only her imagination. I wonder if you noticed anything. I suppose Pe-ter's living at Starvecrow now. I hope so much he'll be able to do all he wanted for the estate.

Excuse more, but I'm frightfully busy this week, as there

are one or two cases of smallpox in the city and a lot of vacci-
nation being done.

Yours,

STELLA MOUNT

§2

Nov. 16.   Hollingrove,

Vinehall,

Sussex.

My dear Little Girl,

When we were together in the summer you told me you
had quite "got over" Peter Alard, and I was so glad. All the
same I want to send you the enclosed newspaper cutting before you have a chance of hearing the news from any other
source—I feel it might still be a shock. I wish I had been less
of a dull fellow and had my suspicions beforehand—then I
might have prepared you—but I assure you I never thought
of it. He met her for the first time at her brother's wedding to
Miss Hurst in May—she was one of the bridesmaids, and I'm
told now that she stayed at Conster for a fortnight while we
were away in August. She was down again this last week and
I met her once or twice—she seems a very nice girl, quiet and
well-bred and decidedly above the average in brains, I should
think. Lady Alard told me she is writing a book. I was asked
up to dinner last night, and Sir John announced the engagement, and this morning it was in the *Times*, so I'm writing
off to you at once. My darling, you know how sorry I am that
things did not turn out as we had both so fondly hoped. But
I think that what has happened may be a comfort to you
in many ways, as you were so afraid he would marry Dol-

ly Hurst to please his family and we both agreed she could never make him happy. Miss Asher seems much more likely to be the kind of wife he wants—she is not so cold and intellectual, but seems warm-hearted and friendly, though as I've told you she's decidedly clever. Peter seemed extremely happy when I congratulated him—it's so nice to think that I can tell you this, and that your love was always of a kind which wanted his happiness more than its own. But I'm afraid this will be a blow to you, dear; in spite of what you have told me, and I heard Mass this morning with a special intention for you. I will write again in a day or two and tell you how the Elphicks are getting on, and the rest of the news, but I must stop now as I hear Miss Gregory trying to crank up the car. It's funny how she never seems able to manage it when the engine's cold, while a little bit of a thing like you never failed to get it started. Goodbye, my darling, and God bless you.

Your loving father,

HORACE J. MOUNT

Cutting from the *Times* of Nov. 16, 1919:

Mr. P. J. Alard and Miss V. L. I. Asher.

A marriage has been arranged and will shortly take place between Peter John Alard, eldest son of Sir John and Lady Alard of Conster Manor, Leasan, Sussex, and Vera Lorna Isabel, daughter of Mr. and Mrs. Lewis Asher of 91, Orme Square, Bayswater.

Nov. 20.   15, Mortimer Street,
                                               Birmingham.

Dearest Father,

Thank you so much for writing to me the way you did, because in spite of what I said at Grasmere I think it would have been rather a shock if I'd seen it in the paper. Of course I have "got over" Peter in a way, but, oh, dear, it always gives one rather a pang to see one's old love marrying—you remember all the lovely things he said to you, and you wonder if he's now saying just the same to the other girl.

I'm afraid this sounds rather cynical and sad, and a bit selfish, because I had definitely broken off with Peter, and since he can't have really and truly loved me, I ought to be glad he's found someone he can really and truly love. Oh, I do hope he really and truly loves her, but one's always afraid in a case like this when there's money. It may have influenced him unconsciously, though I'm quite sure he wouldn't have married her if he hadn't been fond of her as well. Still, "fond of" isn't enough—oh, it would be dreadful to think he'd given me up and then married another woman whom he didn't love even as much as he loved me. But do believe me, Father dear, I'm being sensible. Yesterday I went to confession and this morning I went to the Altar, and I feel ever so much better than I did at first. Of course, after what I said, it seems ridiculous to mind so much, but it's only when a thing is utterly finished that one realises how one has been stupidly hoping against hope the whole time.

I had a letter from Gervase yesterday, telling me a lot about Vera Lorna Isabel. I think she sounds nice, though rather brainy for old Peter. She and Dolly Hurst were both in a sort of literary set up in London and have met lots of authors and authoresses. Gervase says she has read them some of her book, and it's frightfully clever, but he doesn't think she'll finish it now she's engaged. I still hear regularly from Gervase; he writes once a week and I write once a fortnight, which sounds unfair, but you know how busy I am though, for the matter of that, so is he. I think he's an awfully nice boy, and I admire him for breaking free from the family tradition and striking out a line of his own.

Really Miss Gregory's an awful ass if she can't crank up the car—I never knew a car start easier, even on a cold morning. Father, when Peter's safely married I think I'll come home. I can't bear being away from you, and I know nobody looks after you as well as I do (said she modestly). It'll be quite all right—I came away partly for Peter's sake as well as my own—I thought it would help the thing to die easier— but really I'd be a hopeless fool if I could never bear to meet him again, and whatever would become of you without me? How good of you to hear Mass for me. How is Father Luce? Please give him my love, though I don't suppose he wants it. Does he talk any more now? I wish he'd be a more entertaining companion for you on Sunday evenings,

Lots of love and kisses and thanks and bless-yous from

STELLA

PART II

LEASAN
PARSONAGE

LEASAN PARSONAGE

§1

FEBRUARY was nearly over when Peter came back from his Algerian honeymoon, and found Starvecrow waiting to receive him. It was the mild end of a rainy day, with the air full of yellow sunshine, which was reflected in the floods of the Tillingham marshes. The house was faintly bloomed with it, and its windows shone like golden pools. Peter caught his first glimpse from the top of Brede Eye hill, and his heart grew warm in the chill English dusk as no African sun had made it. "Look!" he said to Vera, and pointed over the top of Conster's firs at the grey and golden house with its smoking chimneys—for the first time the smoke of his own fires was going up from Starvecrow.

The car—the splendid Sunbeam which Vera's parents had given as their wedding present—swept down into the valley, over the Tillingham bridge, and up Starvecrow's twisting drive, reflecting the rushing hazels and apple-trees in the mirror of its polished sides. Without noise or jar it stopped outside the porch—"Wait for the man, dear," said Vera, but

Peter was out, staring enraptured at his own front door. He had a foolish, ridiculous feeling that he wanted to carry her across the threshold, but was deterred by the appearance of a smart parlourmaid, also by Vera's obvious unpreparedness for so primitive an entrance.

So he contented himself with kissing her in the delightful drawing-room that led out of the hall. A large wood-fire burned in the open fireplace, and bright cretonnes were in rather sophisticated contrast to oak beams and pure white walls. The house had been thoroughly overhauled, and amazing treasures had come to light in the way of Tudor fireplaces and old oak. It seemed to Peter that it was now more like a small country house than the farmhouse of his love and memory, but certainly these things were more appropriate than the Greenings' rather ramshackle furniture, Victorian wallpapers and blackleaded grates.

"Isn't it lovely?" breathed Vera, crouching down by the fire and warming her delicate hands.

"Yes, it is," said Peter—"and so are you."

He put his hand on her little close-fitting hat and tilted back her head till her full, rather oriental lips were under his. He loved her long, satisfying kisses, so unlike the uneasy ones of most English girls—he told himself that it was this Eastern quality in her love, inherited through the Jewish blood of her fathers, which had made the last few weeks so wonderful.

A minute later the parlourmaid brought in tea, and they had it together beside the singing hearth. There was no light in the room except the dancing glow on beams and walls, the reflections from polished silver and lustre-ware. Vera did not talk much, for she was tired, and after tea she said she would like to go up to her room and lie down before dinner. Peter offered to go with her and read her to sleep—he could not bear to be away from her very long—but Vera said she would rather be quiet, in which no doubt she was wise, for the gods had not given Peter the gift of reading aloud.

Well, perhaps it was all to the good that she did not want him, because he would have to go up to Conster some time this evening, and he would rather go now than after dinner, when he could be sitting on the hearthrug at Vera's feet keeping their first watch together by their own fire. So though he was feeling a bit fagged himself after the journey, he put on his overcoat again and went out into the early darkness which was thick with a new drizzle.

Starvecrow was lost in the night, except for a golden square which was Vera's room, and the distant sulky glow of a lantern among the barns. Only a gleaming of puddles and the water in the ruts showed him the farm drive—which had remained a farm-drive in spite of the Ashers' wish that it should become an avenue; for, as he pointed out to them, his traffic of wagons would do for nothing more genteel. As he reached the bottom, the distant murmur of a car, far away in the network of lanes between Starvecrow and Vinehall, made him unaccountably think of Stella. Queer ... it must be just a year since he had seen her last. How many things had happened since then, and how seldom he thought of her now—poor little girl!... And yet he had loved her—there was no good making out that he hadn't—and he had been grief-stricken when she had gone away—thought a dozen times of calling her back and letting Starvecrow and the rest go hang.... It merely showed that Mary was right, and love,

like everything else, could die. Would his love for Vera die?—
why not, since his love for Stella had died?—but his love for
Vera was so warm and alive—so had his love for Stella been
once. Oh, damn! he was getting into a melancholy mood—it
must be the effect of the journey. Thank God! here he was
at Conster and wouldn't have much more time for the blues,
though the thought of seeing his family again did not give
him any overwhelming pleasure.

§2

He found his father and mother and two sisters in the drawing room, and it seemed to him that their greeting had a
queer, uneasy quality about it, a kind of abstraction—as if
their thoughts were centred on something more engrossing
than his return. When he had gone his round of kisses and
handshakes, Lady Alard seemed suddenly to express the real
interest of the party by crying in a heartbroken voice—

"Peter! what *do* you think has happened?"

"What?" cried Peter sharply. He had a vision of a foreclos-
ing mortgagee.

"It's Mary!" wailed Lady Alard—"Julian is divorcing her."

"Mary!"

Peter was genuinely shocked—the Alards did not appear
in the divorce court; also his imagination was staggered at the
thought of Mary, the fastidious, the pure, the intense, being
caught in the coarse machinery of the state marriage laws.

"Yes—isn't it utterly dreadful? It appears he's had her
watched by detectives ever since she left him, and now
they've found something against her—at least they think they
have. It was that time she went abroad with Meg Sellons, and

Charles joined them at Bordighera—which I always said was unwise. But the worst of all, Peter, is that she says she won't defend herself—she says that she's done nothing wrong, but she won't defend herself—she'll let Julian put her away, and everyone will think she's—oh, Peter, this will finish me—it really will. When I got Mary's letter I had the worst attack I've had for years—we had to send for Dr. Mount in the middle of the night. I really thought—"

Sir John interrupted her—

"You'd better let me finish, Lucy. The subject is legal, not medical. Mary has behaved like a fool and run her head into Julian's trap. I don't know how much there is in it, but from what she says I doubt if he has much of a case. If she'll defend it, she'll probably be able to clear herself, and what's more I bet she could bring a counter-petition."

"That would be a nasty mess, wouldn't it, Sir?" said Peter.

"Not such a nasty mess as my daughter being held up in all the newspapers as an adulteress!"

"Oh, John!" cried Lady Alard—"what a dreadful thing to say before the girls!"

"Doris is old enough to hear the word now if she's never heard it before, and Jenny—she's emancipated, and a great deal older than you and me. I tell you I object to my daughter being placarded in the penny papers as an adulteress, and I'd much rather she proved Julian an adulterer."

"Is that possible, Sir?" asked Peter.

"Of course it is—the man's been on the loose for a year."

"If that's all your evidence—"

"Well, I haven't had him followed by detectives, but I can turn a few on now, and—"

"Really, Sir, I do agree with Mary that it would be better to leave the matter alone. An undefended case can be slipped through the papers with very little fuss, while if you have a defence, to say nothing of a cross-petition ... it isn't as if she particularly wanted to keep Julian as a husband—I expect she's glad to have the chance of getting rid of him so easily."

"I daresay she is. I daresay she wants to marry that old ass Charles Smith. But what about her reputation?—what about ours? I tell you I'm not going to stand still and have filth thrown at me by the press. I'm proud of my name if you aren't."

"It really seems to me that the matter rests with Mary—if she doesn't want to defend herself...."

"Mary must think of her family—it ought to come before her private feelings."

The words seemed an echo of a far-back argument—they reminded Peter dimly of his own straits last year. The family must come first.... That time it was money, now it was reputation. After all, why not? There was no good holding to the one and letting the other go. But he was sorry for Mary all the same.

"Well, I can't stay any longer now. I must be getting back to dinner. I'll bring Vera up tomorrow morning."

"Mary's coming down in the afternoon."

"Oh, is she?"

"Yes—I've wired for her. I insist on her listening to reason."

So Mary would have to face Peter's choice—family duty against personal inclination.... Well, after all he hadn't made such a bad thing of it.... He thought of Vera waiting for him at Starvecrow, and in spite of the fret of the last half-hour a smile of childlike satisfaction was on his face as he went home.

§3

Peter was out early the next morning, when the first pale sunshine was stealing up the valley of the Tillingham, flooding all the world in a gleam of watery gold. He had awoken to the music of his farm, to the crowing of his cocks, to the stamping of his cattle in their stalls, to the clattering of his workmen's feet on the cobbles of the yard. Starvecrow was his home, his place for waking up and falling asleep, for eating his food and warming himself at his fire, for finding his wife at the end of the day, for the birth of his children.... He had, as he stood that morning in the yard, a feeling both of proud ownership and proud adoption.

The whole farm, house and buildings, looked tidy and prosperous. It had lost that rather dilapidated, if homely, air it had worn before his marriage. Though the Ashers might have neither enough capital nor inclination to pay off the debts of their son-in-law's family, they had certainly been generous in the matter of their daughter's home. But for them the place could never have been what it was now—trimmings and clippings, furnishings and restorings had been their willingly paid price for Alard blood. The whole farm had been repaired, replanted and restocked. Indeed Starvecrow was now not so much a farm as a little manor, a rival to Conster up on the hill. Was this exactly what Peter had intended for it?—he did not stop to probe. No doubt his imagination had never held anything so solid and so trim, but that might have been only because his imagination had planned strictly for the possible, and all that had been possible up to his falling in love with Vera was just the shelter of that big kindly roof, the simplicity of those common farmhouse rooms, with the hope and labour of slow achievement and slow restoration.

Still, he was proud of the place, and looked round him with satisfaction as he walked down the bricked garden path, beside the well-raked herbaceous border. He went into the yard where his men were at work—he now employed two extra hands, and his staff consisted of a stockman, a shepherd, a ploughman, and two odd men, as well as the shepherd's wife, who looked after the chickens and calves.

Going into the cowhouse he found Jim Lambard milking the last of the long string of Sussex cows. He greeted his master with a grin and a "good marnun, sur"—it was good to hear the slurry Sussex speech again. Peter walked to the end of the shed where two straw-coloured Jerseys were tethered—one of them, Flora, was due to calve shortly, and after inspecting her, he went out to interview the stockman. John Elias had held office not only in Greening's time, but in the days before him when Starvecrow was worked by a tenant farmer—he was an oldish man who combined deep experience and real practical knowledge with certain old-fashioned obstinacies. Peter sometimes found him irritating to an intense degree, but clung to him, knowing that the old obstinacies are better than the new where farm-work is concerned, and that the man who insists on doing his work according to the rules of 1770 is really of more practical value than the man who does it according to the rules of the Agricultural Labourers Union. Elias had now been up a couple of nights with the Jersey, and his keen blue eye was a trifle dim from anxiety and want of sleep. Peter told him to get off to bed for a few hours, promising to have him sent for if anything should happen.

He then sent for the ploughman, and discussed with him the advisability of giving the Hammer field a second ploughing. There was also the wheat to be dressed in the threshing machine before it was delivered to the firm of corn-merchants who had bought last year's harvest. A final talk with his shepherd about the ewes and prospects for next month's lambing—and Peter turned back towards the house, sharpset for breakfast and comfortably proud of the day's beginning. He liked to think of the machinery of his farm, working efficiently under his direction, making Starvecrow rich.... Conster might still shake on its foundations but Starvecrow was settled and established—he had saved Starvecrow.

The breakfast-room faced east, and the sunshine poured through its long, low window, falling upon the white cloth of the breakfast table, the silver, the china and the flowers. The room was decorated in yellow, which increased the effect of lightness—Peter was thrilled and dazzled, and for a moment did not notice that breakfast had been laid only for one. When he did, it gave him a faint shock.

"Where's your mistress?" he asked the parlourmaid, who was bringing in the coffee—"isn't she coming down?"

"No, Sir. She's taking her breakfast upstairs."

Peter felt blank. Then suddenly he realised—of course she was tired! What a brute he was not to think of it—it was all very well for him to feel vigorous after such a journey, and go traipsing round the farm; but Vera—she was made of more delicate stuff.... He had a feeling as if he must apologise to her for having even thought she was coming down; and running upstairs he knocked at her door.

"Come in," said Vera's rather deep, sweet voice.

Her room was full of sunshine too, but the blind was down so that it did not fall on the bed. She lay in the shadow, reading her letters and smoking a cigarette. Peter had another shock of the incongruous.

"My darling, are you dreadfully tired?"

"No—I feel quite revived this morning," and she lifted her long white throat for him to kiss.

"Have you had your breakfast?"

"All I want. I'm not much of a breakfast eater, that's one reason why I prefer having it up here."

"But—but aren't you ever coming down?"

"Poor boy—do you feel lonely without me?"

"Yes, damnably," said Peter.

"But, my dear, I'd be poor company for you at this hour. I'm much better upstairs till ten or eleven—besides it makes the day so long if one's down for breakfast."

Peter looked at her silently; her argument dispirited him: "the day so long."... For him the day was never long enough. He suddenly saw her as infinitely older and tireder than himself.

"Run down and have yours, now," she said to him, "and then you can come up and sit with me for a bit before I dress."

§4

The next day Mary Pembroke came to Conster, and that same evening was confronted by her family. Sir John insisted on everyone being present, except Gervase—whom he still considered a mere boy—and the daughters-in-law. Vera was glad to be left out, for she had no wish to sit in judgment on a fellow woman, in whose guilt she believed and with whose lies she sympathised, but Rose was indignant, for she detected a slight in the omission.

"Besides," she said to her husband, "I'm the only one who considers the problem chiefly from a moral point of view—the rest think only of the family, whether it will be good or bad for their reputation if she fights the case."

"What about me?" asked her husband, perhaps justly aggrieved—"surely you can trust me not to forget the moral side of things."

"Well, I hope so, I'm sure. But you must speak out and not be afraid of your father."

"I'm not afraid of him."

"Indeed you are—you never can stand up to him. It's he who manages this parish, not you."

"How can you say that?"

"What else can I say when you still let him read the lessons after he created such a scandal by saying 'damn' when the pages stuck together."

"Nobody heard him."

"Indeed they did—all the three first rows, and the choir boys. It's so bad for them. If I'd been in your place he shouldn't have read another word."

"My dear, I assure you it wasn't such a scandal as you think—certainly not enough to justify a breach with my father."

"That's just it—you're afraid of him, and I want you to stand your ground this time. It's not right that we should be looked down upon the way we are, but we always will be if you won't stick up for yourself—and I really fail to see why you should countenance immorality just to please your father."

Perhaps it was owing to this conversation with his wife that during most of the conference George sat dumb. As a matter of fact, nobody talked much, except Sir John and Mary. Mary had a queer, desperate volubility about her—she who was so aloof had now become familiar, to defend her aloofness. Her whole nature shrank from the exposure of the divorce court.

"But what have you got to expose?" cried Sir John when she used this expression, "you tell me you've done nothing."

"I've loved Julian, and he's killed my love for him—I don't want that shown up before everybody."

"It won't be—it doesn't concern the case."

"Oh, yes, it does—that sort of thing always comes out— 'the parties were married in 1912 and lived happily together till 1919, when the respondent left the petitioner without any explanation'—it'll be all to Julian's interest to show that he made me an excellent husband and that I loved him devotedly till Something—which means Somebody—came between us."

"He'll do that if you don't defend the case."

"But it won't be dwelt on—pored over—it won't provide copy for the newspapers. Oh, can't anybody see that when a woman makes a mistake like mine she doesn't want it read about at the breakfast tables of thousands of—of—"

"One would understand you much better," said Doris, who for a few moments had been swallowing violently as a preliminary to speech—"one would understand you much

better if what you objected to was thousands of people reading that you'd been unfaithful to the husband you once loved
so much."

"But it wouldn't be true."

"They'd believe it all the same—naturally, if the decree
was given against you."

"I don't care about that—it's what's true that I mind people knowing."

"Don't be a fool," interrupted Sir John—"you're not going
to disgrace your family for an idea like that."

"I'll disgrace it worse if I give the thing all the extra pub-
licity of a defended suit."

"But, Mary dear," said Lady Alard—"think how dreadful
it will be for us as well as for you if the decree is given against
you. There's Jenny, now—it's sure to interfere with her prospects—What did you say, Jenny?"

"Nothing, Mother," said Jenny, who had laughed.

"But you don't seem to consider," persisted Mary, "that
even if I defend the case I may lose it—and then we'll all be
ever so much worse off than if I'd let it go quietly through."

"And Julian have his revenge without even the trouble of
fighting for it!" cried Sir John. "I tell you he's got nothing of a
case against you if you choose to defend it."

"I'm not so sure of that. Appearances are pretty bad."

"Egad, you're cool, Ma'am!—But I forgot—you don't care
tuppence what people think as long as they don't think what's
true. But, damn it all, there's your family to be considered as
well as yourself."

"Is it that you want to marry Charles Smith?" asked Peter.
"If she does, Sir, it's hardly fair to make her risk...."

"Listen to me!" George had spoken at last—the voice of morality and religion was lifted from the chesterfield. "You must realise that if the decree is given against her, she will not be free in the eyes of the Church to marry again. Whereas if she gets a decree against her husband, she would find certain of the more moderate-minded clergy willing to perform the ceremony for the innocent partner."

"I don't see that," said Peter rudely—"she'd be just as innocent if she lost the suit."

"She wouldn't be legally the innocent partner," said George, "and no clergyman in the land would perform the ceremony for her."

"Which means that the Church takes the argument from law and not from facts."

"No—no. Not at all. In fact, the Church as a whole condemns, indeed—er—forbids the re-marriage of divorced persons. But the Church of England is noted for toleration, and there are certain clergy who would willingly perform the ceremony for the innocent partner. There are others—men like Luce, for instance—who are horrified at the idea of such a thing. But I've always prided myself on—"

"Hold your tongue, George," broke in his father, "I won't have you and Peter arguing about such rubbish."

"I'm not arguing with him, Sir. I would scarcely argue with Peter on an ecclesiastical subject. In the eyes of the Church—"

"Damn the eyes of the Church! Mary is perfectly free to re-marry if she likes, innocent or guilty. If the Church won't marry her, she can go to the registrar's. You think nothing can be done without a clergyman, but I tell you any wretched little civil servant can do your job."

"You all talk as if I wanted to marry again—" Mary's voice shot up with a certain shrill despair in it. "I tell you it's the last thing in the world I'd ever do—whatever you make me do I would never do that. Once is enough."

"It would certainly look better if Mary didn't re-marry," said Doris, "then perhaps people would think she'd never cared for Commander Smith, and there was nothing in it."

"But why did you go about with him, dear?" asked Lady Alard—"if you weren't really fond of him?"

"I never said I wasn't fond of him. I am fond of him—that's one reason why I don't want to marry him. He's been a good friend to me—and I was alone ... and I thought I was free ... I saw other women going about with men, and nobody criticising. I didn't know Julian was having me watched. I didn't know I wasn't free—and that now, thanks to you, I'll never be free."

She began to cry—not quietly and tragically, as one would have expected of her—but loudly, noisily, brokenly. She was broken.

§5

The next morning Sir John drove up to London to consult his solicitors. The next day he was there again, taking Mary with him. After that came endless arguments, letters and consultations. The solicitors' advice was to persuade Julian Pembroke to withdraw his petition, but this proved impossible, for Julian, it now appeared, was anxious to marry again. He had fallen in love with a young girl of nineteen, whose parents were willing to accept him if Mary could be decorously got rid of.

This made Sir John all the more resolute that Mary should

not be decorously got rid of—if mud was slung there was always a chance of some of it sticking to Julian and spoiling
his appearance for the sweet young thing who had won the
doubtful prize of his affections. He would have sacrificed a
great deal to bring a counter-petition, but very slight investi-
gations proved that there was no ground for this. Julian knew
what he was doing, and had been discreet, whereas Mary had
put herself in the wrong all through. Sir John would have to
content himself with vindicating his daughter's name and
making it impossible for Julian to marry his new choice.

Mary's resistance had entirely broken down—the family had crushed her, and she was merely limp and listless in
their hands. Nothing seemed to matter—her chance of a
quiet retreat into freedom and obscurity was over, and now
seemed scarcely worth fighting for. What did it matter if her
life's humiliation was exposed and gaped at?—if she had to
stand up and answer dirty questions to prove her cleanness?...
She ought to have been stronger, she knew—but it was difficult to be strong when one stood alone, without weapon or
counsellor.

Jenny and Gervase were on her side, it is true, but they
were negligible allies, whether from the point of view of im-
pressing the family, or of any confidence their advice and arguments could inspire in herself. Vera Alard, though she did
not share the family point of view, had been alienated by her
sister-in-law's surrender—"I've no sympathy with a woman
who knows what she wants but hasn't the courage to stand
out for it," she said to Peter. In her heart she thought that
Mary was lying—that she had tried Charles Smith as a lover
and found him wanting, but would have gladly used him as a

means to freedom, if her family hadn't butted in and made a scandal of it.

As for Peter, he no longer felt inclined to take his sister's part. He was angry with her for her forgetfulness of her dignity. She had been careless of her honour, forgetting that it was not only hers but Alard's—she had risked the family's disgrace, before the world and before the man whose contempt of all the world's would be hardest to bear. Peter hated such carelessness and such risks—he would do nothing more for Mary, especially as she had said she did not want to marry Charles Smith. If she had wanted that he would have understood her better, but she had said she did not want it, and thus had lost her only claim to an undefended suit. For Peter now did not doubt any more than his family that Julian would fail to prove his case.

Outside the family, Charles Smith did his best to help her. He came down to see her and try to persuade her people to let the petition go through undefended. But he was too like herself to be much use. He was as powerless as she to stand against her family, which was entering the divorce court in much the same spirit as its forefathers had gone to the Crusades—fired by the glory of the name of Alard and hatred of the Turk.

"I'm disappointed in my first co-respondent," said Gervase to Jenny after he had left—"I'd expected something much more spirited—a blend of Abelard, Don Juan and Cesare Borgia, with a dash of Shelley. Instead of which I find a mild-mannered man with a pince-nez, who I know is simply dying to take me apart and start a conversation on eighteenth-century glass."

"That's because he isn't a real co-respondent. You've only to look at Charles Smith to be perfectly sure he never did anything wrong in his life."

"Well, let's hope the Judge and jury will look at him, then."

"I hope they won't. I'm sure Mary wants to lose."

"Not a defended case—she'd be simply too messed up after that."

"She'll be messed up anyhow, whether she wins or loses. There'll be columns and columns about her and everything she did—and didn't do—and might have done. Poor Mary.... I expect she'd rather lose, and then she can creep quietly away."

"Do you think she'll marry Smith?"

"No, I don't. He'd like to marry her, or he thinks he'd like to, but I'm pretty sure she won't have him."

"Then she'd better win her case—or the family will make her have him."

"George says she can't marry again unless she's the innocent party."

"I don't think what George says will make much difference. Anyhow, it's a silly idea. If the marriage is dissolved, both of 'em can marry again—if the marriage isn't dissolved, neither of 'em can, so I don't see where George's innocent party comes in. That's Stella's idea—part of her religion, you know—that marriage is a sacrament and can't be dissolved. I think it's much more logical."

"I think it's damned hard."

"Yes, so do I. But then I think religion ought to be damned hard."

"I'll remind you of that next time I see you lounging in front of the fire when you ought to be in church. You know you hurt George's feelings by not going."

"I'm not partial to George's sort of religion."

"I hope you're not partial to Stella's—that would be another blow for this poor family."

"Why?—it wouldn't make any difference to them. Not that you need ever be afraid of my getting religion ... but if I did I must say I hope it would be a good stiff sort, that would give me the devil of a time. George arranges a nice comfortable service for me at eleven, with a family pew for me to sleep in. He preaches a nice comfortable sermon that makes me feel good, and then we all go home together in the nice comfortable car and eat roast beef and talk about who was there and how much there was in the collection. That isn't my idea of the violent taking the Kingdom of Heaven by storm."

"Are you trying to make me think that you'd be pious if only you were allowed to wear sandals and a hair shirt?"

"Oh, no, Jenny dear. But at least I can admire that sort of religion from a distance."

"The distance being, I suppose, from here to Birmingham?"

"May I ask if you are what is vulgarly called getting at me?"

"Well, I'd like to know how long this correspondence between you and Stella has been going on."

"Almost ever since she left—but we've only just got on to religion."

"Be careful—that's all. I don't want you to hurt yourself."

"How?—with Stella or with Stella's ideas?"

"Both," said Jenny darkly.

§6

Charles Smith was not allowed to come down again. The solicitors declared it advisable that Mary should see nothing of
him while proceedings were pending. Indeed it was necessary
to guard her reputation like a shrine. She stayed at Conster
while the weeks dragged through the spring, and when in
May Sir John and Lady Alard went for their yearly visit to
Bath, it was decided that she should go to the Vicarage, so
that a polish of sanctity and ecclesiastical patronage might be
given to her stainlessness.

So she packed her belongings—helped by Jenny instead
of Gisèle, whose wages had been beyond her means ever
since her plunge for freedom—and they were taken to where
Leasan Parsonage stood hidden among May trees and lilac
bushes down Leasan lane.

Mary was not personally looking forward to the change,
though the atmosphere of Conster was eruptive, and though
one felt the family solidarity more strongly at the Manor
than at the Parsonage, and was also—in spite of luxury—
more conscious of the family's evil days. Her feeling for
Rose was almost fear—her bustle, her curiosity, her love of
rule, her touch of commonness provoked an antipathy which
was less dislike than alarm. She also shrank from the ugliness and discomforts of the Vicarage life—Rose was supposed to have a gift for training Raw Girls, and, as Gervase
once said, even when the girls ceased to be actually raw, they
were still remarkably underdone. Chatter, scoldings, creaking
footsteps, and the smell of bad cooking filled the house all
day—George, whom Mary was inclined to like in spite of

his stupidity, took the usual male refuge in flight, and spent most of his time shut up in his study, which shared the sanctity of Leasan church and could be invaded by no one but his wife.

There were also two rather colourless children, Lillian and Edna, whose governess—a more cultured type of Raw Girl—made a sixth at luncheon. It had always been a secret grief to Rose that she had never had a son; her only comfort was that no other Alard had done so up till now. But this comfort would probably be taken from her soon. Vera would be sure to have a son—Jewesses always did.... Rose thought vaguely about Abraham....

§7

The day started early at Leasan Parsonage—not that there was any particular reason why it should, but eight o clock breakfast was Rose's best protest against the sloppy ways of Conster, where you came down to breakfast when you liked, or had it upstairs. Mary was addicted to the latter vice, and on her first morning at Leasan came down heavy-eyed, with that especial sense of irritation and inadequacy which springs from a hurried toilet and a lukewarm bath.

"So you wear a tea-gown for breakfast," said Rose, who wore a sports coat and a tweed skirt.

"A breakfast gown."

"It's the same thing. In fact you might call it a dressing-gown with those sleeves. Edna, don't drink your tea with a spoon."

"It's too hot, Mother."

"Well, leave it till it gets cooler. Don't drink it with a

spoon—you'll be pouring it into your saucer next. George, what are your letters about today?"

"Income tax mostly—and there's Mr. Green writing again about a Choral Celebration."

"Well, you must be firm with him and tell him we can't possibly have one. I told you what it would be, engaging an organist who's used to such things—they won't give them up."

"I thought it might be possible to arrange it once a month, at an hour when it won't interfere with Matins."

"Nonsense, dear. The boys' voices could never manage it and the men would go on strike."

"They're becoming fairly general, you know, even in country churches."

"Well, I think it's a pity. I've always distrusted anything that tends to make religion emotional."

"I can't understand anyone's emotions—at least voluptuous emotions—being stirred by anything our choir could do."

"George!—'voluptuous'"—a violent shake of the head—"pas devant les enfants. Who's your cheque from?"

"Dr. Mount. He's very generously subscribing to the Maternity Fund. He says 'I feel I've got a duty to Leasan as well as Vinehall, as I have patients in both parishes.'"

"I call that very good of him, for I know he never makes more than five hundred a year out of the practice. By way, have you heard that Stella's back?"

"No—since when?"

"I saw her driving through Vinehall yesterday. Edna and Lillian, you may get down now for a great treat, and have a run in the garden before Miss Cutfield comes."

"May we go to meet Miss Cutfield?"

"If you don't go further than the end of the lane. That's right, darlings—say your grace—'for what we *have* received,' Edna, not 'about to'—now run away."

"Why are you sending away the children?" asked George.

"Because I want to talk about Stella Mount."

"But why is Stella unfit to discuss before the children?"

"Oh, George—you must know!—it was simply dreadful the way she ran after Peter."

"You don't think she's still running after him?"

"I think it's a bad sign she's come back."

"Her father wanted her, I expect. That chauffeur-secretary he had was no good. Besides, I expect she's got over her feeling for Peter now."

"I'm sure I hope she has, but you never know with a girl like Stella. She has too many ways of getting out of things."

"What do you mean, dear?"

"Oh, confession and all that. All she has to do is to go to a Priest and he'll let her off anything."

"Come, come, my dear, that is hardly a fair summary of what the Prayer Book calls 'the benefit of absolution.' My own position with regard to confession has always been that it is at least tolerable and occasionally helpful."

"Not the way a girl like Stella would confess," said Rose darkly—"Oh, I don't mean anything wrong—only the whole thing seems to me not quite healthy. I dislike the sort of religion that gets into everything, even people's meals. I expect Stella would rather die than eat meat on Friday."

"But surely, dear," said George who was rather dense—"that sort would not encourage her to run after a married man."

"Well, if you can't use your eyes! ... she's been perfectly open about it."

"But she hasn't been here at all since he married."

"I'm talking of before that—when she was always meeting him."

"But if he wasn't married you can hardly accuse her of running after a married man."

"He's married now. Don't be so stupid, dear."

§8

Peter was a little annoyed to find that Stella had come back. It would perhaps be difficult to say why—whether her return was most disturbing to his memory or to his pride. He would have angrily denied that to see her again was in any sense a resurrection—and he would just as angrily have denied that her attitude of detached friendliness was disagreeable to his vanity. Surely he had forgotten her ... surely he did not want to think that she could ever forget him....

He did not press these questions closely—his nature shrank from unpleasant probings, and after all Stella's presence did not make anything of that kind necessary. He saw very little of her. She came to tea at Starvecrow, seemed delighted with the improvements, was becomingly sweet to Vera—and after that all he had of her was an occasional glimpse at Conster or on the road. It could not be said, by any stretch of evidence, that she was running after a married man. But Rose Alard soon had a fresh cause for alarm. Stella was seeing a great deal too much of Gervase. She must somehow have got into touch with the younger brother during her absence from home, for now on her return there seemed to be a friendship already established. They were occasionally seen out walking together in the long summer evenings, and on Sundays he sometimes went with her to church at Vinehall—which was a double crime, since it disparaged George's ministrations at Leasan.

"I should hate to say she was mercenary," said Rose reflectively, "but I must say appearances are against her—turning to the younger brother as soon as she's lost the elder."

"I don't see where the mercenariness comes it," said Mary—"Gervase won't have a penny except what he earns, and there's Peter and his probable sons, as well as George, between him and the title."

"But he's an Alard—I expect Stella would like to marry into the family."

"I fail to see the temptation."

"Well, anyhow, I think it very bad taste of her to take him to church at Vinehall—it's always been difficult to get him to come here as it is, and George says he has no influence over him whatever."

Mary only sighed. She could not argue with Rose, yet she had a special sympathy for a woman who having had love torn out of her heart tried to fill the empty aching space as best she could. Of course it was selfish—though not so selfish in Stella as it had been in herself, and she hoped Stella would not have to suffer as she had suffered. After all, it would do Gervase good to be licked into shape by a woman like Stella—he probably enjoyed the hopelessness of his love—if indeed it was hopeless ... and she could understand the relief that his ardent, slightly erratic courtship must be after Peter's long series of stolid blunders.

But Stella was not quite in the position Mary fancied. She was not letting Gervase court her, indeed he would never have thought of doing so. She seemed definitely apart from any idea of lovemaking—she set up intangible barriers round herself, which even his imagination could not cross. Perhaps some day ... but even for "some day" his plans were not so much of love as of thinking of love.

Meanwhile she fulfilled a definite need of his, just as he fulfilled a need of hers. She gave him an outlet for the pent-up thoughts of his daily drives, and the society of a mind which delighted him with its warmth and quickness. Gervase too had a quick mind, and his and Stella's struck sparks off each other, creating a glow in which he sometimes forgot that his heart went unwarmed. Their correspondence had been a slower, less stimulating version of the same process. They had discussed endless subjects through the post, and now Stella had come home in the midst of the most interesting. It was the most interesting to him because it was obviously the most interesting to her. She had bravely taken her share in their other discussions, but he soon discovered that she was too feminine to care about politics, too concrete to grasp abstractions, and that in matters of art and literature her taste was uncertain and often philistine. But in the matter of religion she showed both a firmer standing and a wider grasp. Indeed he was to find that her religion was the deepest, the most vital and most interesting part of her—in it alone did the whole Stella come alive.

The topic had been started by the tragedy of Mary's marriage, and at first he had been repulsed by her attitude, which he thought strangely unlike her in its rigidity. But as time went on he began to contrast it favourably with George's compromises—here was a faith which at least was logical, and which was not afraid to demand the uttermost.... They continued the discussion after she had come home, and he was surprised to see what he had hitherto looked upon equally as a fad and a convention, a collection of moral and intellectual lumber, show itself almost shockingly as an adventure and a power. Not that Stella had felt the full force of it yet—her life had always run pretty smoothly through the simplicities of joy and sorrow, there had been no conflict, no devastation. But strangely enough he, an outsider, seemed able to see what she herself possibly did not realise—that she carried in her heart a force which might one day both make and break it.

It had been his own suggestion that he should go with her to church, though he did not know whether it was to satisfy a hope or dismiss a fear. He had lost the detached attitude with which he had at first approached the subject, much as he would have approached Wells's new novel or the Coalition Government. To his surprise he found himself at ease in the surroundings of Vinehall's Parish Mass. Its gaiety and homeliness seemed the natural expression of instinctive needs. Vinehall church was decorated in a style more suggestive of combined poverty and enterprise than of artistic taste; the singing—accompanied rather frivolously on a piano—was poor and sometimes painful; the sermon was halting and trite. These things were better done by brother George at Leasan. But the Mass seemed strangely independent of its outward expression, and to hold its own solemn heart of worship under circumstances which would have destroyed the devotions of Leasan. Here, thought Gervase, was a faith which did not depend on the beauty of externals for its appeal—a faith, moreover, which was not afraid to make itself hard to men, which threw up round itself massive barriers of hardship, and yet within these was warm and sweet and friendly—which was furthermore a complete adventure, a taking of infinite risks, a gateway on unknown dangers....

As he knelt beside Stella in a silence which was like a first kiss, so old in experience did it seem, in spite of the shock of novelty, he found that the half-forgotten romances of his childhood were beginning to take back their colours and shine in a new light. Those figures of the Mother and her Child, the suffering Son of Man, the warm-hearted, thick-headed, glorious company of the apostles, which for so long had lived for him only in the gilt frames of Renaissance pictures, now seemed to wake again to life and friendliness. Once more he felt the thrill of the Good Shepherd going out to see the lost sheep ... and all the bells of heaven began to ring.

§9

George Alard could not help being a little vexed at Gervase's new tendencies. He told himself that he ought to be glad the boy was going to church at all, for he had been negligent and erratic for a long time past—he ought not to feel injured because another man had won him to some sense of his duty. But he must say he was surprised that Luce had succeeded where he himself had failed—Luce was a dry, dull fellow, and hopelessly unenterprising; not a branch in his parish of the C.E.M.S. or the A.C.S. or the S.P.G., no work-parties or parish teas, and no excitement about the Enabling Act and the setting up of a Parochial Church Council which was now occupying most of George's time. Still, he reflected, it was probably not so much Luce as Stella Mount who had done it—she was a pretty girl and perhaps not too scrupulous, she had persuaded Gervase. Then there had always been that curious streak in his brother's character which differentiated him from the other Alards. George did not know how to describe it so well as by Ungentlemanliness. That part of Gervase which had revolted from a Gentleman's Education and had gone into an engineering shop instead of to Oxford was now revolting from a Gentleman's Religion and going to Mass instead of Dearly Beloved Brethren. There had always seemed to George something ungentlemanly about Catholicism, though he prided himself on being broad-minded, and would have introduced one or two changes on High Church lines into the services at Leasan if his father and his wife had let him.

"Apart from every other consideration, I'm surprised he doesn't realise how bad it looks for him to go Sunday to Vinehall when his brother is Vicar of Leasan."

"He goes with Stella," said Mary.

"I think that makes it worse," said Rose.

"Why?" asked Peter.

He had come in to see George about his election to the Parochial Church Council, which his brother was extremely anxious should take place, but for which Peter had no wish to qualify himself. George had hoped that the bait of a seat on the Council, with the likelihood of being elected as the Parish's representative at the Diocesan Conference, might induce Peter to avail himself once more of the church privileges which he had neglected for so long. It was uphill work, thought poor George, trying to run a parish when neither of one's brothers came to church, and one's father said 'damn' out loud when reading the lessons....

"Why?" asked Peter, a little resentful.

Rose looked uneasy—

"Well, everyone knows she used to run after you and now she's running after Gervase."

"She didn't run after me and she isn't running after Gervase," said Peter; then he added heavily—"I ran after her, and Gervase is running after her now."

"Oh!" Rose tossed her head—"I own I once thought ... but then when you married Vera ... well, anyhow I think she ought to discourage Gervase more than she does, and I insist that it's in extremely bad taste for her to take him to church at Vinehall."

"Perhaps he likes the service better," said Mary, who during this discussion had been trying to write a letter and now gave up the effort in despair.

"Oh, I daresay he does—he's young and excitable."

"There's nothing very exciting at Vinehall," said George— "I don't think Luce has even a surpliced choir these days."

"Well, there's incense and chasubles and all that—Gervase always did like things that are different."

"I must say," said Mary, who was perhaps a little irritated at having nowhere to write her letter (the Raw Girl being in devastating possession of her bedroom)—"I must say that if I had any religion myself, I'd like a religion which at least was religion and not soup."

"What do you mean?"

Both George and Rose sat up stiffly, and even Peter looked shocked.

"Well, your religion here seems chiefly to consist in giving people soup-tickets and coal-tickets, and having rummage sales. Stella Mount's religion at least means an attempt at worship, and at least.... Oh, well—" she broke down rather lamely—"anyhow it makes you want something you haven't got."

"We can most of us do that without religion," said Peter, getting up.

Rose looked meaningly after him as he went out of the room, then she looked still more meaningly at her husband—it was as if her eyes and eyebrows were trying to tell him her conviction that Peter was finding life unsatisfactory in spite of Vera and Starvecrow, indeed that he regretted Stella—had he not championed her almost grotesquely just now? ... and he had talked of wanting something he had not got....

George refused to meet her eyes and read their language. He too rose and went out, but he did not follow Peter. He felt hurt and affronted by what Mary had said—"soup"... that was what she had called the religion of her parish church, of her country, indeed, since George was convinced that Leasan represented the best in Anglicanism. Just because he didn't have vestments and incense and foreign devotions, but plain, hearty, British services—because he looked after people's bodies as well as their souls—he was to be laughed at by a woman like Mary, who—but he must not be uncharitable, he was quite convinced of Mary's innocence, and only wished that her prudence had equalled it.

He walked out through the French windows of his study, and across the well-kept Vicarage lawn. Before him, beyond the lilacs Leasan's squat towers stood against a misty blue sky. With its wide brown roof spreading low over its aisles almost

to the ground the church was curiously like a sitting hen. It
squatted like a hen over her brood, and gave a tender impression of watchfulness and warmth.... The door stood open,
showing a green light that filtered in through creeper and
stained glass. George went in, and the impression of motherly
warmth was changed to one of cool emptiness. Rows of shining pews stretched from the west door to the chancel with its
shining choir-stalls, and beyond in the sanctuary stood the
shining altar with two shining brass candle sticks upon it.

George went to his desk and knelt down. But there was
something curiously unprayerful in the atmosphere—he
would have felt more at ease praying in his study or at his
bedside. The emptiness of the church was something more
than an emptiness of people—it was an emptiness of prayer.
Now he came to think of it, he had never seen anyone at
prayer in the church except at the set services—a good collection of the neighbouring gentlefolk at Matins, a hearty as-
sembly of the villagers at Evensong, a few "good" people at
the early celebration, and one or two old ladies for the Litany
on Fridays—but never any prayer between, no farm lad ever
on his knees before his village shrine, or busy mother coming
in for a few minutes rest in the presence of God....

But that was what they did at Vinehall. He had looked
into the church several times and had never seen it empty—
there was always someone at prayer ... the single white lamp
... that was the Reserved Sacrament of course, theologically
indefensible, though no doubt devotionally inspiring ... devotion—was it that which made the difference between religion
and soup?

George felt a sudden qualm come over him as he knelt

in his stall—it was physical rather than mental, though the memory of Mary's impious word had once again stirred up his sleeping wrath. He lifted himself into a sitting position— that was better. For some weeks past he had been feeling ill— he ought to see a doctor ... but he daren't, in case the doctor ordered him to rest. It was all very well for Mary to gibe at his work and call it soup, but it was work that must be done. She probably had no idea how hard he worked—visiting, teaching, sitting on committees, organising guilds, working parties, boy scouts, Church of England Men's Society ... and two sermons on Sunday as well.... He was sure he did more than Luce, who had once told him that he looked upon his daily Mass as the chief work of his parish.... Luce wouldn't wear himself out in his prime as George Alard was doing.... Soup!

§10

Mary went back to Conster for the uneasy days of the Summer. Her heart sickened at the dragging law—her marriage took much longer to unmake that it had taken to make. She thought of how her marriage was made—Leasan church ... the smell of lilies ... the smell of old lace ... lace hanging over her eyes, a white veil over the wedding-guests, over her father as he gave her away, over her brother as he towered above her in surplice and stole, over her bridegroom, kneeling at her side, holding her hand as he parted her shaking fingers ... "with this ring I thee wed" ... "from this day forward, till death do us part.".... How her heart was beating—fluttering in her throat like a dove ... now she was holding one fringed end of George's stole, while Julian held the other—"that which God hath joined together let not man put asunder."

And now the unmaking—such a fuss—such a business this putting asunder! Telegrams, letters, interviews ... over and over again the story of her disillusion, of her running away, of her folly ... oh, it was all abominable, but it was her own fault—she should not have given in. Why could she never endure things quite to the end? When she had found out that Julian the husband was not the same as Julian the lover, but an altogether more difficult being, why had her love failed and died? And now that love was dead and she had run away from the corpse, why had she allowed her family to persuade her into this undignified battle over the grave? Why had she not gone quietly out of her husband's life into the desolate freedom of her own, while he turned to another woman and parted her fingers to wear the pledge of his eternal love.

If only she had been a little better or a little worse!... A little better, and she could have steadied her marriage when it rocked, a little worse and she could have stepped out of it all, cast her memories from her, and started the whole damn thing over again as she had seen so many women do. But she wasn't quite good enough for the one or bad enough for the other, so she must suffer as neither the good nor the bad have to suffer. She must pay the price for being fine, but not fine enough.

In Autumn the price was paid. For three days counsel argued on the possibility or impossibility of a woman leaving one man except for another—on the possibility or impossibility of a woman being chaste when in the constant society of a male friend—on the minimum time which must be allowed for misconduct to take place. Waiters, chambermaids, chauffeurs gave confused evidence—there was "laughter

in court"—the learned judge asked questions that brought
shame into the soft, secret places of Mary's heart—Julian
stood before her to tell her and all the world that she had
loved him once.... She found herself in the witness-box, receiving from her counsel the wounds of a friend.... Of course
Julian must be blackened to account for her leaving him—
was she able to paint him black enough? Probably not, since
the verdict was given in his favour.

Most of the next day's papers contained photographs of
Mrs. Pembroke leaving the divorce court after a decree nisi
had been obtained against her by her husband, Mr. Julian
Pembroke (inset).

§11

In spite of the non-committal attitude of his solicitors, Sir
John Alard had been sure that to defend the suit would be
to vindicate Mary and her family against the outrageous Julian. He would not believe that judgment could go against his
daughter except by default, and now that this incredible thing
had happened, and Mary had been publicly and argumen-
tatively stripped of her own and Alard's good name, while
Julian, with innocence and virtue proclaimed by law, was set
free to marry his new choice, he felt uncertain whether to
blame most his daughter's counsel or his daughter herself.

Counsel had failed to make what he might out of Julian's
cross-examination ... what a fruitful field was there! If only
Sir John could have cross-examined Julian himself! There
would have been an end of that mirage of the Deceived and
Deserted Husband which had so impressed the court.... But
Mary was to blame as well as counsel. She really had been

appallingly indiscreet ... her cross-examination—Lord! what
an affair! What a damn fool she had made of herself!—Hang
it all, he'd really have thought better of her if she'd gone the
whole hog ... the fellow wasn't much good in the witness-box
either ... but he'd behaved like a gentleman afterwards. He
had made Mary a formal proposal of marriage the morning
after the decree was given. The only thing to do now was for
her to marry him.

Lady Alard marked her daughter's disgrace by sending for
Dr. Mount in the middle of the night, and "nearly dying on
his hands" as she reproachfully told Mary when she returned
to Conster the next afternoon. Mary looked a great deal more
ill than her mother—dazed and blank she sat by Lady Alard's
sofa, listening to the tale of her sorrows and symptoms, only
a slow occasional trembling of her lip showing that her
heart was alive and in torment under the dead weight of her
body's stupefaction. All her mind and being was withdrawn
into herself, and during the afternoon was in retreat, seeking
strength for the last desperate stand that she must make.

After tea, Peter arrived, looking awkward and unhappy—
then George, looking scared and pompous. Mary knew that
a family conclave had been summoned, and her heart sank.
What a farce and a sham these parliaments were, seeing that
Alard was ruled by the absolute monarchy of Sir John. No
one would take her part, unless perhaps it was Gervase—
Uranus in the Alard system—but he would not be there today; she must stand alone. She gripped her hands together
under the little bag on her lap, and in her dry heart there was
a prayer at last—"Oh, God, I have never been able to be quite
true to myself—now don't let me be quite untrue."

As soon as the servants had cleared away the last of the tea things—there had been a pretence of offering tea to Peter and George, as if they had casually dropped in—Sir John cast aside all convention of accident, and opened the attack.

"Well," he said to his assembled family—"It's been a dreadful business—unexpectedly dreadful. Shows what the Divorce Court is under all this talk about justice. There's been only one saving clause to the whole business, and that's Smith's behaviour. He might have done better in the witness box, but he's stuck by Mary all through, and made her a formal offer of marriage directly the decree was given."

"That was the least he could do," said Peter.

"Of course; you needn't tell me that. But I've seen such shocking examples of bad faith during the last three days.... It's a comfort to find one man behaving decently. I'm convinced that the only thing Mary can do is to marry him as soon as the decree is made absolute."

George gave a choking sound, and his father's eye turned fiercely upon him.

"Well, Sir—what have *you* to say?"

"I—I—er—only that Mary can't marry again now—er—under these new circumstances ... only the innocent partner...."

"You dare, Sir! Damn it all—I'll believe in my own daughter's innocence in spite of all the courts in the country."

"I don't mean that she isn't innocent—er—in fact—but the decree has been given against her."

"What difference does that make?—if she was innocent before the decree she's innocent after it, no matter which way it goes. Damn you and your humbug, Sir. But it doesn't matter in the least—she can marry again, whatever you say;

the law allows it, so you can't stop it. She shall be married in Leasan church."

"She shall not, Sir."

A deep bluish flush was on George's cheek-bones as he rose to his feet. Sir John was for a moment taken aback by defiance from such an unexpected quarter, but he soon recovered himself.

"I tell you she shall. Leasan belongs to me."

"The living is in your gift, Sir, but at present I hold it, and as priest of this parish, I refuse to lend my church for the marriage of the guil—er—in fact, for—the marriage."

"Bunkum! 'Priest of this parish'—you'll be calling yourself Pope next. If you can't talk sense you can clear out."

George was already at the door, and the hand he laid upon it trembled violently.

"Don't go!"—it was Mary who cried after him—"there's no need for you to upset yourself about my marriage. I haven't the slightest thought of getting married."

But George had gone out.

§12

There was an uneasy shuffle of relief throughout the room. The situation, though still painful, had been cleared of an exasperating side-issue. But at the same time Mary was uncomfortably aware that she had changed the focus of her father's anger from her brother to herself.

"What do you mean?" he rapped out, when the sound of George's protesting retreat had died away.

"I mean that you and George have been arguing for nothing. As I told you some time ago, I haven't the slightest intention of marrying Charles."

"And why not, may I ask?"

"Because I've had enough of marriage."

"But Mary, think of us—think of your family," wailed Lady Alard—"what are we going to do if you don't marry?"

"I can't see what difference it will make."

"It will make all the difference in the world. If you marry Charles and go abroad for a bit, you'll find that after a time people will receive you—I don't say here, but in London. If you don't marry, you will always be looked upon with suspicion."

"Why?"

"Married women without husbands always are."

"Then in spite of all the judges and juries and courts and decrees, I'm still a married woman?"

"I don't see what else you're to call yourself, dear. You're certainly not a spinster, and you can't say you're a widow."

"Then if I marry again I shall have two husbands, and in six months Julian will have two wives."

Lady Alard began to weep.

"For God's sake! let's stop talking this nonsense," cried Sir John. "Mary's marriage has been dissolved, and her one chance of reinstating herself—and us—is by marrying this man who's been the cause of all the trouble. I say it's her duty—she's brought us all into disgrace, so I don't think it's asking too much of her to take the only possible way of getting us out, even at the sacrifice of her personal inclinations."

"Father—I never asked you to defend the case. I begged you not to—all this horror we have been through is due to your defence."

"If you'd behaved properly there would have been no case at all, and if you had behaved with only ordinary discretion the defence could have been proved. When I decided that we must, for the honour of the family, defend the case, I had no idea what an utter fool you had been. Your cross-examination was a revelation to me as well as to the court. You've simply played Old Harry with your reputation, and now the only decent thing for you to do is to marry this man and get out."

"I can get out without marrying this man."

"And where will you go?"

"I shall go abroad. I have enough money of my own to live on quietly, and I needn't be a disgrace to anyone. If I marry Charles I shall only bring unhappiness to both of us."

"Oh, Mary, do be reasonable!" cried Lady Alard—"do think of the girls"—with a wave that included both twenty-two and thirty-eight—"and do think how all this is your own fault. When you first left Julian, you should have come here and lived at home, then no one would ever have imagined anything. But you would go off and live by yourself, and think you could do just the same as if you weren't married—though I'm sure I'd be sorry to see Jenny going about with anyone as you went about with Charles Smith. When I was engaged to your father, we were hardly ever so much as left alone in a room together—"

"Your reminiscences are interesting, my dear," said Sir John, "but cast no light on the situation. The point is that Mary refuses to pay the price of her folly, even though by doing so she could buy out her family as well as herself."

"I fail to see how."

"Then you must be blind."

"It seems to me it would be much better if I went right away. I've made a hideous mess of my life, and brought trouble upon you all—I acknowledge that; but at least there's one thing I will not do—and that is walk with my eyes open into the trap I walked into ten years ago with my eyes shut."

"Then you need expect nothing more from your family."

"I won't."

"Father," said Peter—"if she isn't fond of the chap ..."

Mary interrupted him.

"Don't—it isn't quite that. I am fond of him. I'm not in love with him or anything romantic, but I'm fond of him, and for that very reason I won't take this way out. He's twenty years older than I am, and set in his bachelor ways and I firmly believe that only chivalry has made him stand by me as he has done. He doesn't in his heart want to marry a woman who's ruined and spoiled ... and I won't let him throw himself away. If I leave him alone, he can live things down—men always can; but if I marry him, he'll sink with me. And I've nothing to give him that will make up to him for what he will suffer. I won't let him pay such a price for ... for being ... kind to me."

Nobody spoke a word. Perhaps the introduction of Charles Smith's future as a motive for refusing to use him to patch up the situation struck the Alards as slightly indecent. And Mary suddenly knew that if the argument were resumed she would yield—that she was at the end of her resources and could stand out no longer. Her only chance of saving Charles's happiness and her own soul now lay in the humiliation of flight. There is only one salvation for the weak and that is to realise their weakness. She rose unsteadily to her feet. A dozen miles seemed to yawn between her and the door....

"Where are you going, Mary?" asked Sir John—"we haven't nearly finished talking yet."

Would anybody help her?—yes—here was Jenny unexpectedly opening the door for her and pushing her out. And in the hall was Gervase, his Ford lorry throbbing outside in the drive.

"Gervase!" cried Mary faintly—"if I pack in ten minutes, will you take me to the station?"

§13

It was a very different packing from that before Mary's departure eighteen months ago. There was no soft-treading Gisèle, and her clothes, though she had been at Leasan six months, were fewer than when she had come for a Christmas visit. They were still beautiful, however, and Mary still loved them—it hurt her to see Jenny tumbling and squeezing them into the trunk. But she must not be critical, it was as well perhaps that she had someone to pack for her who did not really care for clothes and did not waste time in smoothing and folding ... because she must get out of the house quickly, before the rest of the family had time to find out what she was about. It was undignified, she knew, but her many defeats had brought her a bitter carelessness.

The sisters did not talk much during the packing. But Mary knew that Jenny approved of what she was doing. Perhaps Jenny herself would like to be starting out on a flight from Alard. She wondered a little how Jenny's own affair was going—that unacknowledged yet obsessing affair. She realised rather sadly that she had lost her sister's confidence—or perhaps had never quite had it. Her own detachment, her own passion for aloofness and independence had grown up like a mist between them. And now when her aloofness was destroyed, when some million citizens of England were acquainted with her heart, when all the golden web she had spun round herself was torn, soiled and scattered, her sister was gone. She stood alone—no longer set apart, no longer veiled from her fellows by delicate self-spun webs—but just alone.

"Shall I ring for Pollock?" said Jenny.

"No, I'd much rather you didn't."

"Then how shall we manage about your trunk? It's too heavy for us to carry down ourselves."

"Can't Gervase carry it?"

"Yes—I expect he could."

She called her brother up from the hall, and he easily swung up the trunk on his shoulder. As he did so, and Mary saw his hands with their broken nails and the grime of the shop worked into the skin, she realised that they symbolised a freedom which was more actual than any she had made. Gervase was the only one of the family who was really free, though he worked ten hours a day for ten shillings a week. Doris was not free, for she had accepted the position of idle daughter, and was bound by all the ropes of a convention which had no substance in fact. Peter was not free because he had, Mary knew, married away from his real choice, and was now bound to justify his new choice to his heart—George was not free, he was least free of all, because individual members of the family had power over him as well as the collective fetish. Jenny was not free, because she must love according to opportunity. Slaves ... all the Alards were slaves ... to Alard—

to the convention of the old county family with its prosperity of income and acres, its house, its servants, its ancient name and reputation—a convention the foundations of which were rotten right through, which was bound to topple sooner or later, crushing all those who tried to shelter under it. So far only two had broken away, herself and Gervase—herself so feebly, so painfully, in such haste and humiliation, he so calmly and carelessly and sufficiently. He would be happy and prosperous in his freedom, but she ... she dared not think.

However, Jenny was thinking for her.

"What will you do, Mary?" she asked, as they crossed the hall—"where are you going?"

"I'm going back to London. I don't know yet what I'll do."

"Have you enough money? I can easily lend you something—I cashed a cheque yesterday."

"Oh, I'm quite all right, thanks."

"Do you think you'll go abroad?"

"I'll try to. Meg is going again next month. I expect I could go with her."

They were outside. Mary's box was on the back of the lorry, and Gervase already on the driver's seat. It was rather a lowly way of leaving the house of one's fathers. Mary had never been on the lorry before, and had some difficulty in climbing over the wheel.

Jenny steadied her, and for a moment kept her hand after she was seated.

"Of course you know I think you're doing the only possible thing."

"Yes ... thank you, Jenny; but I wish I'd done it earlier."

"How could you?"

"Refused to defend the case—spared myself and everybody all this muck."

"It's very difficult, standing up to the family. But you've done it now. I wish I could.... Goodbye, Mary dear, and I expect we'll meet in town before very long."

"Goodbye."

The Ford gargled, and they ran round the flower-bed in the middle of Conster's gravel sweep. Jenny waved farewell from the doorstep and went indoors. Gervase began to whistle; he seemed happy—"I wonder," thought Mary, "if it's true that he's in love."

§14

During the upheaval which followed Mary's departure, George Alard kept away from Conster. He wouldn't go any more, he said, where he wasn't wanted. What was the good of asking his advice if he was to be insulted—publicly insulted when he gave it? He brooded tenaciously over the scene between him and his father. Sir John had insulted him not only as a man but as a priest, and he had a right to be offended.

Rose supported him at first—she was glad to find that there were occasions on which he would stand up to his father. George had been abominably treated, she told Doris—really one was nearly driven to say that Sir John had no sense of decency.

"He speaks to him exactly as if he were a child."

"He speaks to us all like that."

"Then it's high time somebody stood up to him, and I'm very glad George did so."

"My dear Rose—if you think George stood up...."

After a time Rose grew a little weary of her husband's attitude. Also, though she was always willing to take up arms against the family at Conster, she had too practical an idea of her own and her children's interests to remain in a state of war. George had made his protest—let him now be content.

But George was nursing his injury with inconceivable perseverance. Hitherto she had often had to reproach him for his subservience to his father, for the meekness with which he accepted his direction and swallowed his affronts.

"If you can put up with his swearing in church, you can put up with what he said to you about Mary."

"He has insulted me as a priest."

"He probably doesn't realise you are one."

"That's just it."

She seemed to have given him fresh cause for brooding. He sulked and grieved, and lost interest in his parish organisations—his Sunday School and Mothers Union, his Sewing Club and Coal Club, his Parochial Church Council—now established in all its glory, though without Peter's name upon the roll, his branches of the S.P.G., the C.E.M.S., all those activities which used to fill his days, which had thrilled him with such pride when he enumerated them in his advertisements for a locum in the *Guardian*.

He developed disquieting eccentricities, such as going into the church to pray. Rose would not have minded this if he had not fretted and upset himself because he never found anyone else praying there.

"Why should they?" she asked, a little exasperated—"They can say their prayers just as well at home."

"I've never been into Vinehall church and found it empty."

"Oh, you're still worrying about Gervase going to Vinehall?"

"I'm not talking about Gervase. I'm talking about people in general. Vinehall church is used for prayer—mine is always empty except on Sundays."

"Indeed it's not—I've often seen people in it, looking at the old glass, and the carving in the South Aisle."

"But they don't pray."

"Of course not. We English don't do that sort of thing in public. They may at Vinehall; but you know what I think of Vinehall—it's un-English."

"I expect it's what the whole of England was like before the Reformation."

"George!" cried Rose—"you must be *ill*."

Only a physical cause could account for such mental disintegration. She decided to send for Dr. Mount, who confirmed her diagnosis rather disconcertingly. George's heart was diseased—had been diseased for some time. His case was the exact contrast of Lady Alard's—those qualms and stabs and suffocations which for so long both he and his wife had insisted were indigestion, were in reality symptoms of the dread angina.

He must be very careful not to overstrain himself in any way. No, Dr. Mount did not think a parish like Leasan too heavy a burden—but of course a complete rest and holiday would do him good.

This, however, George refused to take—his new obstinacy persisted, and though the treatment prescribed by Dr. Mount did much to improve his general condition, mental as well as physical, he evidently still brooded over his grievances. There were moments when he tried to emphasise his sacerdotal dignity by a new solemnity of manner which the family at Conster found humorous, and the family at Leasan found irritating. At other times he was extraordinarily severe, threatening such discipline as the deprivation of blankets and petticoats to old women who would not come to church—the most irreproachable Innocent Partner could not have cajoled the marriage service out of him then. He also started reading his office in church every day, though Rose pointed out to him that it was sheer waste of time, since nobody came to hear it.

§15

Social engagements of various kinds had always filled a good deal of George Alard's life—he and Rose received invitations to most of the tea-parties, tennis-parties and garden-parties of the neighbourhood. He had always considered it part of his duty as a clergyman to attend these functions, just as he had considered it his duty to sit on every committee formed within ten miles and to introduce a branch of every episcopally blessed Society into his own parish. Now with the decline of his interest in clubs and committees came a decline of his enthusiasm for tennis and tea. Rose deplored it all equally—

"If you won't go to people's parties you can't expect them to come to your church."

"I can and I do."

"But they won't."

"Then let them step away. The Church's services aren't a social return for hospitality received."

"George, I wish you wouldn't twist everything I say into some ridiculous meaning which I never intended—and I *do* think you might come with me to the Parishes this afternoon. You know they're a sort of connection—at least everyone hopes Jim won't marry Jenny."

"I don't feel well enough," said George, taking a coward's refuge—"not even to visit such close relations," he added with one of those stray gleams of humour which were lost on Rose.

"Well, this is the second time I've been out by myself this week, and I must say.... However, if you don't feel well enough.... But I think you're making a great mistake—apart from my feelings...."

She went out, and George was left to the solitude and peace of his study. It was a comfortable room, looking out across the green, cedared lawn to the little church like a sitting hen. The walls were lined with books, the armchairs were engulfing wells of ease—there was a big writing-table by the window, and a rich, softly-coloured carpet on the floor. Rose's work-bag on a side-table gave one rather agreeable feminine touch to the otherwise masculine scene. The room was typical of hundreds in the more prosperous parsonages of England, and George had up till quite recently felt an extraordinarily calm and soothing glow in its contemplation. It was ridiculous to think that a few words from his father—his father who was always speaking sharp, disparaging words—could have smashed all his self-satisfaction, all his pride of himself as Vicar of Leasan, all his comfortable possession of Leasan Vicarage and Leasan Church.... But now he seemed to remember that the dawn of that dissatisfaction had been in Leasan Church itself, before his father had spoken—while he was kneeling there alone among all those empty, shining pews.... He would go out for a walk. If he stopped at home he would only brood—it would be worse than going to the Parishes. He would go over and see Dr. Mount—it would save the doctor coming to the Vicarage, perhaps—there must be a visit about due and they could have a chat and some tea. He liked Dr. Mount—a pleasant, happy, kind-hearted man.

The day was good for walking. The last of Autumn lay in ruddy veils over the woods of Leasan and Brede Eye. The smell of hops and apples was not all gone from the lanes. George walked through his parish with a professional eye on the cottages he passed. Most of the doors were shut in the afternoon stillness, but here and there a child swinging on a gate would smile at him shyly as he waved a Vicarial hand, or a woman would say "Good afternoon, Sir." The cottages nearly all looked dilapidated and in want of paint and repair.

George had done his duty and encouraged thrift among his parishioners, and the interiors of the cottages were many of them furnished with some degree of comfort, but the exterior structures were in bad condition owing to the poverty of the Manor. He cleared his throat distressfully once or twice—had one the right to own property when one could not afford to keep it in repair?... His philanthropic soul, bred in the corporal works of mercy, was in conflict with his racial instinct, bred in the tradition of the Squires.

When he came to Vinehall, he found to his disappointment that Dr. Mount was out, and not expected to be home till late that evening. George felt disheartened, for he had walked three miles in very poor condition. He would have enjoyed a cup of tea.... However, there was nothing to be done for it, unless indeed he went and called on Luce. But the idea did not appeal to him—he and the Rector of Vinehall were little more than acquaintances, and Luce was a shy, dull fellow who made conversation difficult. He had better start off home at once—he would be home in time for a late tea.

Then he remembered that the carrier's cart would probably soon be passing through Vinehall and Leasan on its way from Robertsbridge station to Rye. If he went into the village he might be able to pick it up at the Eight Bells. Unfortunately he had walked the extra half-mile to the inn before he remembered that the cart went only on Tuesdays, Thursdays and Saturdays, and today was Wednesday. He would have to walk home, more tired than ever. However, as he passed through the village, he thought of the church, partly because he was tired and wanted to rest, partly because Vinehall church always had a perverse fascination for him—he never could pass it without wanting to look in … perhaps he had a secret, shameful hope that he would find it empty.

He crossed the farmyard, wondering why Luce did not at all costs provide a more decent approach, a wonder which was increased when, on entering the church, he found he had admitted not only himself but a large turkey, which in the chase that followed managed somehow to achieve more dignity than his pursuer. After three laps round the font it finally disappeared through the open door, and George collapsed on a chair, breathing hard, and not in the least devout.

The church had none of the swept, shiny look of Leasan, nor had it Leasan's perfume of scrubbing and brass-polish; instead it smelt of stale incense, lamp-oil and old stones— partly a good smell and partly an exceedingly bad one. It was seated with rather dilapidated chairs, and at the east end was a huge white altar like a Christmas cake. There were two more altars at the end of the two side aisles and one of them was furnished with what looked suspiciously like two pairs of kitchen candle sticks. But what upset George most of all were the images, of which, counting crucifixes, there must have been about a dozen. His objections were not religious but aesthetic—it revolted his artistic taste to see the Christ pointing to His Sacred Heart, which He carried externally under His chin, to see St. Anthony of Padua looking like a girl in a monk's dress, to see the Blessed Virgin with her rosary painted on her blue skirt—and his sense of reverence and decency to see the grubby daisy-chain with which some village child had adorned her. Luce must have bought his church furniture wholesale at a third-rate image shop....

George wished he could have stopped here, but he was bound to look further, towards the white star which hung in the east. Yes ... it was just as usual ... a young man in working clothes was kneeling there ... and an immensely stout old woman in an apron was sitting not far off. Certainly the spectacle need not have inspired great devotional envy, but George knew that in his own parish the young man would probably have been lounging against the wall opposite the Four Oaks, while the old woman would have been having a nap before her kitchen fire. Certainly neither would have been found inside the church.

There was a murmur of voices at the back of the south aisle, and looking round George saw one or two children squirming in the pews, while behind a rather frivolous blue curtain showed the top of a biretta. Luce was hearing confessions—the confessions of children.... George stiffened—he felt scandalised at the idea of anyone under twelve having any religious needs beyond instruction. This squandering of the sacraments on the young ... as if they were capable of understanding them....

He turned to go out, feeling that after all the scales had dropped on the debit side of Vinehall's godliness, when he heard behind him a heavy tread and the flutter of a cassock. Luce had come out of his confessional.

"Why—Mr. Alard."

George was a little shocked to hear him speak out loud, and not in the solemn whisper he considered appropriate for church. The Rector seemed surprised to see him—did he want to speak to him about anything?

"Oh, no—I only looked in as I was passing."

"Seen our new picture?" asked Luce.

"Which one?" The church must have contained at least a dozen pictures besides the Stations of the Cross.

"In the Sacrament Chapel."

They went down to the east end, where Luce genuflected, and George, wavering between politeness and the Bishop of Exeter's definition of the Real Presence, made a sort of curtsey. There was a very dark oil painting behind the Altar—doubtful as to subject, but the only thing in the church, George told himself, which had any pretence to artistic value.

"Mrs. Hurst gave us that," said Luce—"it used to hang in her dining-room, but considering the subject she thought it better for it to be here."

He had dropped his voice to a whisper—George thought it must be out of respect to the Tabernacle, but the next minute was enlightened.

"She's asleep," he said, pointing to the stout old woman.

"Oh," said George.

"Poor old soul," said Luce—"I hope the chair won't give way—they sometimes do."

He genuflected again, and this time the decision went in favour of the Bishop of Exeter, and George bowed as to an empty throne. On their way out his stick caught in the daisy chain which the Mother of God was wearing, and pulled it off.

§16

He and Luce walked out of the church together and through the farmyard without speaking a word. The silence oppressed George and he made a remark about the weather.

"Oh, yes, I expect it will," said Luce vaguely.

He was a tall, white-faced, red-headed young man, who spoke with a slight stutter, and altogether, in his seedy cassock which the unkind sun showed less black than green, seemed to George an uninspiring figure, whose power it was difficult to account for. How was it that Luce could make his church a house of prayer and George could not? How was it that people thought and talked of Luce as a priest, consulted him in the affairs of their souls and resorted to him for the sacraments—whereas they thought of George only as a parson, paid him subscriptions and asked him to tea?

He was still wondering when they came to the cottage where the Rector lived—instead of in the twenty-five-roomed Rectory which the Parish provided, with an endowment of a hundred and fifty pounds a year. They paused awkwardly at the door, and the awkwardness was increased rather than diminished by Luce inviting him to come in. George's first impulse was to decline—he felt he would rather not have any more of the other's constraining company—but the next minute he realised that he now had the chance of a rest and tea without the preliminary endurance of a long and dusty walk. So he followed him in at the door, which opened disconcertingly into the kitchen, and through the kitchen into the little study-living-room beyond it.

It was not at all like George's study at Leasan—the floor had many more books on it than the wall, the little leaded window looked out into a kitchen garden, and the two arm chairs both appeared so doubtful as possible supports for George's substantial figure that he preferred, in spite of his fatigue, to sit down on the kitchen chair that stood by the writing-table. He realised for the first time what he had always known—that Luce was desperately poor, having nothing but what he could get out of the living. Probably the whole did not amount to two hundred pounds ... and with post-war prices.... George decided to double his subscription to the Diocesan Fund.

Meantime he accepted a cigarette which was only just not a Woodbine, and tried to look as if he saw nothing extraordinary in the poverty-stricken room. He thought it would be only charitable to put the other at his ease.

"Convenient little place you've got here," he remarked— "better for a single man than that barrack of a Rectory."

"Oh, I could never have lived in the Rectory. I wonder you manage to live in yours."

George muttered something indistinct about private means.

"It's difficult enough to live here," continued Luce—"I couldn't do it if it wasn't for what people give me."

"Are your parishioners generous?"

"I think they are, considering they're mostly poor people. The Pannells across the road often send me over some of their Sunday dinner in a covered dish."

George was speechless.

"And I once found a hamper in the road outside the gate. But after I'd thanked God and eaten half a fowl and drunk a bottle of claret, I found it had dropped off the carrier's cart and there was no end of a fuss."

"Er—er— hum."

There was a knock at the outer door, and before Luce could say "Come in," the door of the study opened and a small boy stuck his head in.

"Please, Father, could you lend us your ink?—Mother wants to write a letter."

"Oh, certainly, Tom—take it—there it is; but don't forget to bring it back."

The small boy said nothing, but snatched his booty and went out.

"Are your people—er—responsive?" asked George.

"Responsive to what?"

"Well—er—to you."

"Oh, not at all."

"Then how do you get them to come to church?"

"I don't—Our Lord does."

George coughed.

"They come to church because they know they'll always find Him there—in spite of me."

George could not keep back the remark that Reservation was theologically indefensible.

"Is it?" Luce did not seem much interested. "But I don't keep the Blessed Sacrament in my church for purposes of theology, but for practical use. Suppose you were to die tonight—where would you get your last Communion from if not from my tabernacle?"

George winced.

"This is the only church in the rural deanery where the Blessed Sacrament is reserved and the holy oils are kept. The number of people who die without the sacraments must be appalling."

George had never been appalled by it.

"But why do you reserve publicly?" he asked—"That's not primitive or catholic—to reserve for purposes of worship."

"I don't reserve for purposes of worship—I reserve for Communion. But I can't prevent people from worshipping Our Lord. Nobody could—not all the Deans of all the cathedrals in England. Oh, I know you think my church dreadful—everybody does. Those statues ... well, I own they're hideous. But so are all the best parlours in Vinehall. And I want the people to feel that the church is their Best Parlour—which they'll never do if I decorate it in Anglican good taste, supposing always I could afford to do so. I want them to feel at home."

"Do you find all this helps to make them regular communicants?"

"Not as I'd like, of course; but we're only beginning. Most of them come once a month—though a few come every week. I've only one daily communicant—a boy who works on Ellenwhorne Farm and comes here every evening to cook my supper and have it with me."

George was beginning to feel uncomfortable in this strange atmosphere—also he was most horribly wanting his tea. Possibly, as Luce had supper instead of dinner, he took tea later than usual.

"Of course," continued the Rector, "some people in this place don't like our ways, and don't come to church here at all. Some of my parishioners go to you, just as some of yours come to me."

"You mean my brother Gervase?"

"I wasn't thinking of him particularly, but he certainly does come."

"The Mounts brought him."

"In the first instance, I believe. I hope you don't feel hurt at his coming here—but he told me he hadn't been to church for over a year, so I thought ..."

Not a sign of triumph, not a sign of shame—and not a sign of tea. It suddenly struck George as a hitherto undreamed-of possibility that Luce did not take tea. His whole life seemed so different from anything George had known that it was quite conceivable that he did not. Anyhow the Vicar of Leasan must be going—the long shadows of some poplars lay over the garden and were darkening the little room into an early twilight. He rose to depart.

"Well, I must be off, I suppose. Glad to have had a chat. Come and preach for me one day," he added rashly.

"With pleasure—but I warn you, I'm simply hopeless as a preacher."

"Oh, never mind, never mind," said George—"all the better—I mean my people will enjoy the change—at least I mean—"

He grabbed desperately at his hat, and followed his host through the kitchen to the cottage door.

"Here's Noakes coming up the street to cook supper," said Luce—"I didn't know it was so late."

George stared rather hard at the Daily Communicant—having never to his knowledge seen such a thing. He was surprised and a little disappointed to find only a heavy, fair-haired young lout, whose face was the face of the district—like a freckled moon.

"I'm a bit early tonight, Father; but Maaster sent me over to Dixter wud their roots, and he said it wun't worth me coming back and I'd better go straight on here. I thought maybe I could paint up the shed while the stuff's boiling."

"That's a good idea—thanks, Noaky."

"Father, there's a couple of thrushes nesting again by the Mocksteeple. It's the first time I've seen them nest in the fall."

"It's the warm weather we've been having."

"Surelye, but I'm sorry for them when it turns cold.... Father, have you heard?—the Rangers beat the Hastings United by four goals to one...."

§17

When George had walked out of the village he felt better—he no longer breathed that choking atmosphere of a different world, in which lived daily communicants, devout children, and clergymen who hadn't always enough to eat. It was not, of course, the first time that he had seen poverty among the clergy, but it was the first time he had not seen it decently covered up. Luce seemed totally unashamed of his ... had not made the slightest effort to conceal it ... his cottage was, except for the books, just the cottage of a working man; indeed it was not so comfortable as the homes of many working men.

George began to wonder exactly how much difference it would have made if he had been poor instead of well-to-do—if he had been too poor to live in his comfortable vicarage, too poor to decorate his church in "Anglican good taste" ... not that he wouldn't rather have left it bare than decorate it like Vinehall ... what nonsense Luce had talked to justify himself! The church wasn't the village's Best Parlour ... or was it?

He felt quite tired when he reached Leasan, and Rose scolded him—"You'd much better have come with me to the Parishes." ... However, it was good to sit at his dinner table and eat good food off good china, and drink his water out of eighteenth-century glass that he had picked up in Ashford.... Luce was not a total abstainer, judging by that story of the claret.... It is true that the creaking tread of the Raw Girl and the way she breathed down his neck when she handed the vegetables made him think less disparagingly of the domestic offices of the Daily Communicant; but somehow the Raw Girl fitted into the scheme of things—it was only fitting that local aspirants for "service" should be trained at the Vicarage—whereas farm-boys who came in to cook your supper and then sat down and ate it with you ... the idea was only a little less disturbing than the idea of farm-boys coming daily to the altar.... He wondered if Rose would say it was un-English.

"Oh, by the way, George"—Rose really was saying—"a message came down from Conster while you were out, asking you to go up there after dinner tonight."

George's illness had brought about a kind of artificial peace between the Manor and the Vicarage.

"What is it now? Have you been invited too?"

"No—I think Sir John wants to speak to you about something."

"Whatever can it be?—Mary's in Switzerland. It can't be anything to do with her again."

"No—I believe it's something to do with Gervase. I saw Doris this evening and she tells me Sir John has found out that Gervase goes to confession."

"Does he?—I didn't know he'd got as far as that."

Yes—he goes to Mr. Luce. Mrs. Wade saw him waiting his turn last Saturday when she was in Vinehall church taking rubbings of the Oxenbridge brass. I suppose she must have mentioned it when she went to tea at Conster yesterday."

"And my father wants me to interfere?"

"Of course—you're a clergyman."

"Well, I'm not going to."

"George, don't talk such nonsense. Why, you've been complaining about your father's disrespect for your priesthood, and now when he's showing you that he does respect it—"

"He's showing it no respect if he thinks I'd interfere in a case like this."

"But surely you've a right—Gervase is your brother and he doesn't ever come to your church."

"I think it would be unwise for me to be my brother's confessor."

"It would be ridiculous. Whoever thought of such a thing?"

"Then why shouldn't he go to Luce?—and as for my

church, he hasn't been to any church for a year, so if Luce can get him to go to his ... or rather if Our Lord can get him to go to Luce's church ..."

"I do hope it won't rain tomorrow, as I'd thought of going into Hastings by the 'bus."

Rose had abrupt ways of changing the conversation when she thought it was becoming indelicate.

§18

George went up to Conster after all. Rose finally persuaded him, and pushed him into his overcoat. She was anxious that he should not give fresh offence at the Manor; also she was in her own way jealous for his priestly honour and eager that he should vindicate it by exercising its functions when they were wanted instead of when they were not.

There was no family council assembled over Gervase as there had been over Mary. Only his father and mother were in the drawing-room when George arrived. Gervase was a minor in the Alard household, and religion a minor matter in the Alard world—no questions of money or marriage, those two arch-concerns of human life, were involved. It was merely a case of stopping a silly boy making a fool of himself and his family by going ways which were not the ways of squires. Not that Sir John did not think himself quite capable of stopping Gervase without any help from George, but neither had he doubted his capacity to deal with Mary without summoning a family council. It was merely the Alard tradition that the head should act through the members, that his despotism should be as it were mediated, showing thus his double power both over the rebel and the forces he employed for his subjection.

"Here you are, George—I was beginning to wonder if Rose had forgotten to give you my message. I want you to talk to that ass Gervase. It appears that he's gone and taken to religion, on the top of a dirty trade and my eldest son's ex-fiancée."

"And you want me to talk him out of it?" George was occasionally sarcastic when tired.

"Not out of religion, of course. Could hardly mean that. But there's religion and religion. There's yours and there's that fellow Luce's."

"Yes," said George, "there's mine and there's Luce's."

"Well, yours is all right—go to church on Sundays—very right and proper in your own parish—set a good example and all that. But when it comes to letting religion interfere with your private life, then I say it's time it was stopped. I've nothing against Luce personally—"

"Oh, I think he's a perfectly dreadful man," broke in Lady Alard—"he came to tea once, and talked about God—in the drawing-room!"

"My dear, I think this is a subject which would be all the better without your interference."

"Well, if a mother hasn't a right to interfere in the question of her child's religion...."

"You did your bit when you taught him to say his prayers—I daresay that was what started all the mischief."

"John, if you're going to talk to me like this I shall leave the room."

"I believe I've already suggested such a course once or twice this evening."

Lady Alard rose with dignity and trailed to the door.

"I'm sure I hope you'll be able to manage him," she said

bitterly to George as she went out, "but as far as I'm concerned I'd much rather you argued him out of his infatuation for Stella Mount."

"There is always someone in my family in love with Stella Mount," said Sir John, "and it's better that it should be Gervase than Peter or George, who are closer to the title, and, of course, let me hasten to add, married men. But this is the first case of religious mania we've ever had in the house—therefore I'd rather George concentrated on that. Will you ask Mr. Gervase to come here?"—to the servant who answered his ring.

"Mr. Gervase is in the garage, Sir."

"Send him along."

Gervase had been cleaning the Ford lorry, having been given to understand that his self-will and eccentricity with regard to Ashford were to devolve no extra duties on the chauffeur. His appearance, therefore, when he entered the drawing-room, was deplorable. He wore a dirty suit of overalls, his hands were black with oil and grime, and his hair was hanging into his eyes.

"How dare you come in like that, Sir?" shouted Sir John.

"I'm sorry, Sir—I thought you wanted me in a hurry."

"So I do—but I didn't know you were looking like a sweep. Why can't you behave like other people after dinner?"

"I had to clean the car, Sir. But I'll go and wash."

"No, stay where you are—George wants to speak to you."

George did not look as if he did.

"It's about this new folly of yours," continued Sir John. "George was quite horrified when I told him you'd been to confession."

"Oh, come, not 'horrified,'" said George uneasily—"it was only the circumstances.... Thought you might have stuck to your parish church."

"And *you*'d have heard his confession!" sneered Sir John.

"Well, Sir, the Prayer Book is pretty outspoken in its commission to the priest to absolve—"

"But you've never heard a confession in your life."

This was true, and for the first time George was stung by it. He suddenly felt his anger rising against Luce, who had enjoyed to the full those sacerdotal privileges which George now saw he had missed. His anger gave him enough heat to take up the argument.

"I'm not concerned to find out how Luce could bring himself to influence you when you have a brother in orders, but I'm surprised you shouldn't have seen the disloyalty of your conduct. Here you are forsaking your parish church, which I may say is also your family church, and traipsing across the country to a place where they have services exciting enough to suit you."

"I'm sorry, George. I know that if I'd behaved properly I'd have asked your advice about all this. But you see I was the heathen in his blindness, and if it hadn't been for Father Luce I'd be that still."

"You're telling me I've neglected you?"

"Not at all—no one could have gone for me harder than you did. But, frankly, if I'd seen nothing more of religion than what I saw at your church I don't think I'd ever have bothered about it much."

"Not spectacular enough for you, eh?"

"I knew you'd say something like that."

"Well, isn't it true?"

"No."

"Then may I ask in what way the religion of Vinehall is so superior to the religion of Leasan?"

"Just because it isn't the religion of Vinehall—it's the religion of the whole world. It's a religion for everybody, not just for Englishmen. When I was at school I thought religion was simply a kind of gentlemanly aid to a decent life. After a time you find out that sort of life can be lived just as easily without religion—that good form and good manners and good nature will pull the thing through without any help from prayers and sermons. But when I saw Catholic Christianity I saw that it pointed to a life which simply couldn't be lived without its help—that it wasn't just an aid to good behaviour but something which demanded your whole life, not only in the teeth of what one calls evil, but in the teeth of that very decency and good form and good nature which are the religion of most Englishmen."

"In other words and more briefly," said Sir John, "you fell in love with a pretty girl."

Gervase's face darkened with a painful flush, and George felt sorry for him.

"I don't deny," he said rather haltingly, "that if it hadn't been for Stella I should never have gone to Vinehall church. But I assure you the thing isn't resting on that now. I've nothing to gain from Stella by pleasing her. We're not on that footing at all. She never tried to persuade me, either. It's simply that after I'd seen only a little of the Catholic faith I realised that it was what I'd always unconsciously believed ... in my heart.... It was my childhood's faith—all the things I'd 'loved long since and lost awhile.'"

"But don't you see," said George, suddenly finding his feet in the argument, "that you've just put your finger on the weak spot of the whole thing? This 'Catholic faith' as you call it was unconsciously your faith as a child—well, now you ought to go on and leave all that behind you. 'When I became a man I put away childish things.'"

"And 'whosoever will not receive the kingdom of heaven as a little child shall in no wise enter therein.' It's no good quoting texts at me, George—we might go on for ever like that. What I mean is that I've found what I've always been looking for, and it's made Our Lord real to me, as He's never been since I was a child—and now the whole of life seems real in a way it didn't before—I don't know how to explain, but it does. And it wasn't only the romantic side of things which attracted me—it was the hard side too. In fact the hardness impressed me almost before I saw all the beauty and joy and romance. It was when we were having all that argument about Mary's divorce…. I saw then that the Catholic Church wasn't afraid of a Hard Saying. I thought, 'Here's a religion which wouldn't be afraid to ask anything of me—whether it was to shut myself up for life in a monastery or simply to make a fool of myself.'"

"Well, on the whole, I'm glad you contented yourself with the latter," said Sir John.

George said—"I think it's a pity Gervase didn't go to Oxford."

"Whether he's been to Oxford or not, he's at least supposed to be a gentleman. He may try to delude himself by driving off every morning in a motor lorry, but he does in fact belong to an old and honourable house, and as head of that house I object to his abandoning his family's religion."

"I never had my family's religion, Sir—I turned to Catholicism from no religion at all. I daresay it's more respectable to have no religion than the Catholic religion, but I don't mind about being respectable—in fact, I'd rather not."

"You're absorbing your new principles pretty fast—already you seem to have forgotten all family ties and obligations."

"I can't see that my family has any right to settle my religion for me—at least I'm Protestant enough to believe I must find my own salvation, and not expect my family to pass it on to me. I think this family wants to do too much."

"What d'you mean, Sir?"

"It wants to settle all the private affairs of its members. There's Peter—you wouldn't let him marry Stella. There's Mary, you wouldn't let her walk out by the clean gate—"

"Hold your tongue! Who are you to discuss Peter's affairs with me? And as for Mary—considering your disgraceful share in the business...."

"All right, Sir. I'm only trying to point out that the family is much more autocratic than the Church."

"I thought you said that what first attracted you to the Church was the demands it made on you. George!"

"Yes, Sir."

"Am I conducting this argument or are you?"

"You seem better able to do it than I, Sir."

"Well, what did I send you to Oxford for, and to a theological college for, and put you into this living for, if you can't argue a schoolboy out of the Catholic faith?"

"I've pointed out to Gervase, Sir, that the so-called Catholic movement is not the soundest intellectually, and that I don't see why he should walk three miles to Vinehall on

Sundays when he has everything necessary to salvation at his parish church. I can't go any further than that."

"How d'you mean?"

"I can't reason him out of his faith—why should I? On the contrary, I'm very glad he's found it. I don't agree with all he believes—I think some of it is extravagant—but I see at least he's got a religion which will make him happy and keep him straight, and really there's no cause for me to interfere with it."

George was purple.

"You're a fool!" cried Sir John—"you're a much bigger fool than Gervase, because at least he goes the whole hog, while you as usual are sitting on the fence. It's just the same now as when I asked you to speak to Mary. If you'd go all the way I'd respect you, or if you'd go none of the way I'd respect you, but you go half way.... Gervase can go all the way to the Pope or to the devil, whichever he pleases—I don't care now—he can't be as big a fool as you."

He turned and walked out of the room, banging the door furiously behind him. The brothers were left alone together. Gervase heaved a sigh of relief.

"Come along with me to the garage," he said to George, "and help me take the Ford's carburetor down."

"No, thanks," said George dully—"I'm going home."

§19

He had failed again. As he walked through the thick yellow light of the Hunter's Moon to Leasan, he saw himself as a curiously feeble and ineffective thing. It was not only that he had failed to persuade his brother by convincing arguments, or that he had failed once more to inspire his father with any sort of respect for his office, but he had somehow failed in regard to his own soul, and all his other failures were merely branches of that most bitter root.

He had been unable to convince Gervase because he was not convinced himself—he had been unable to inspire his father because he was not inspired himself. All his life he had stood for moderation, toleration, broad-mindedness ... and here he was, so moderate that no one would believe him, so tolerant that no one would respect him, so broad-minded that the water of life lay as it were stagnant in a wide and shallow pond instead of rushing powerfully between the rocky, narrow banks of a single heart....

He found Rose waiting for him in the hall.

"How late you are! I've shut up. They must have kept you an awful time."

"I've been rather slow coming home."

"Tired?"

"I am a bit."

"How did you get on? I expect Gervase was cheeky."

"Only a little."

"Have you talked him round?"

"I can't say that I have. And I don't know that I want to."

"George!"

Rose had put out the hall lamp, and her voice sounded hoarse and ghostly in the darkness.

"Well, the boy's got some sort of religion at last after being a heathen for years."

"I'm not sure that he wouldn't be better as a heathen than believing the silly, extravagant things he does. I don't suppose for a minute it's gone really deep."

"Why not?"

"The sort of thing couldn't. What he wants is a sober, sensible, practical religion—"

"Soup?"

"George!"

"Well, that's what Mary called it. And when I see that boy has found adventure, discipline and joy in faith, am I to take it away and offer him soup?"

"George, I'm really shocked to hear you talk like that. Please turn down the landing light—I can't reach it."

"Religion is romance," said George's voice in the thick darkness of the house—"and I've been twelve years trying to turn it into soup...."

§20

Rose made up her mind that her husband must be ill, therefore she forebore further scolding or argument, and hurried him into bed with a cup of malted milk.

"You've done too much," she said severely—"you said you didn't feel well enough to come with me to the Parishes, and then you went tramping off to Vinehall. What can you expect when you're so silly? Now drink this and go to sleep."

George went to sleep. But in the middle of the night he awoke. All the separate things of life, all the differences of time and space, seemed to have run together in one sharp moment. He was not in the bed, he was not in the room ... the room seemed to be in him, for he saw every detail of its trim mediocrity ... and there lay George Alard on the bed beside a sleeping Rose ... but he was George Alard right enough, for George Alard's pain was his, that queer constricting pain which was part of the functions of his body, of every breath he drew and every beat of his heart ... he was lying in bed ... gasping, suffering, dying ... this was what it meant to die.... Rose! Rose!

Rose bent over her husband; her big plaits swung in his face.

"What's the matter, George?—Are you ill?"

"Are you ill?" she repeated.

Then she groped for a match, and as soon as she saw his face, jumped out of bed.

No amount of bell-ringing would wake the Raw Girls, so Rose leaped upstairs to their attic, and beat on the door.

"Annie! Mabel! Get up and dress quickly, and go to Conster Manor and telephone for Dr. Mount. Your master's ill."

Sundry stampings announced the beginning of Annie's and Mabel's toilet, and Rose ran downstairs to her husband. She lit the lamp and propped him up in bed so that he could breathe more easily, thrusting her own pillows under his neck.

"Poor old man!—Are you better?" Her voice had a new tender quality—she drew her hand caressingly under his chin—"Poor old man!—I've sent for Dr. Mount."

"Send for Luce."

It was the first time he had spoken, and the words jerked out of him drily, without expression.

"All right, all right—but we want the doctor first. There, the girls are ready—hurry up, both of you, as fast as you can, and ask the butler, or whoever lets you in, to 'phone. It's Vinehall 21—but they're sure to know."

She went back into the room and sat down again beside George, taking his hand. He looked dreadfully ill, his face was blue and he struggled for breath. Rose was not the sort of woman who could sit still for long—in a moment or two she sprang to her feet, and went to the medicine cupboard.

"I believe some brandy would do you good—it's allowed in case of illness, you know."

George did not seem to care whether it was allowed or not. Rose gave him a few drops, and he seemed better. She smoothed his pillows and wiped the sweat off his face.

She had hardly sat down again when the hall door opened and there was the sound of footsteps on the stairs. It must be the girls coming back—Rose suddenly knew that she was desperately glad even of their company. She went to the door, and looked out on the landing. The light that streamed over her shoulder from the bedroom showed her the scared, tousled faces of Gervase and Jenny.

"What's up, Rose?—Is he very bad?"

"I'm afraid so. Have you 'phoned Dr. Mount?"

"Yes—he's coming along at once. We thought perhaps we could do something?"

"I don't know what there is to do. I've given him some brandy. Come in."

They followed her into the room and stood at the foot of the bed. Jenny, who had learned First Aid during the war, suggested propping him higher with a chair behind the pillows. She and Gervase looked dishevelled and half asleep in their pyjamas and great-coats. Rose suddenly realised that she was not wearing a dressing-gown—she tore it off the foot of the bed and wrapped it round her. For the first time in her life she felt scared, cold and helpless. She bent over George and laid her hand on his, which were clutched together on his breast.

His eyes were wide open, staring over her shoulder at Gervase.

"Luce ..." he said with difficulty—"Luce ..."

"All right," said Gervase—"I'll fetch him."

"Wouldn't you rather have Canon Potter, dear?—He could come in his car."

"No—Luce ... the only church ... Sacrament ..."

"Don't you worry—I'll get him. I'll go in the Ford."

Gervase was out of the room, leaving Jenny in uneasy attendance. A few minutes later Doris arrived. She had wanted to come with the others, but had felt unable to leave her room without a toilet. She alone of the party was dressed—even to her boots.

"How is he, Rose?"

"He's better now, but I wish Dr. Mount would come."

"Do you think he'll die?" asked Doris in a penetrating whisper—"ought I to have woken up Father and Mother?"

"No—of course not. Don't talk nonsense."

"I met Gervase on his way to fetch Mr. Luce."

"That's only because George wanted to see him—very natural to want to see a brother clergyman when you're ill. But it's only a slight attack—he's much better already."

She made expressive faces at Doris while she spoke.

"There's Dr. Mount!" cried Jenny.

A car sounded in the Vicarage drive and a few moments later the doctor was in the room. His examination of George was brief. He took out some capsules.

"What are you going to do?" asked Rose.

"Give him a whiff of amyl nitrate."

"It's not serious?... He's not going to ..."

"Ought we to fetch Father and Mother?" choked Doris.

"I don't suppose Lady Alard would be able to come at this hour—but I think you might fetch Sir John."

Rose suddenly began to cry. Then the sight of her own tears frightened her, and she was as suddenly still.

"I'll go," said Jenny.

"No—you'd better let me go," said Doris—"I've got my boots on."

"Where's Gervase?" asked Dr. Mount.

"He's gone to fetch Mr. Luce from Vinehall—George asked for him."

"How did he go? Has he been gone long?"

"He went in his car—he ought to be back quite soon. Oh, doctor, do you think it's urgent ... I mean ... he seems easier now."

Dr. Mount did not speak—he bent over George, who lay motionless and exhausted, but seemingly at peace.

"Is he conscious?" asked Rose.

"Perfectly, I should say. But don't let him speak."

With a queer abandonment, unlike herself, Rose climbed on the bed, curling herself up beside George and holding his hand.

The minutes ticked by. Jenny, feeling awkward and self-conscious, sat in the basket arm-chair by the fireplace. Dr. Mount moved quietly about the room as in a dream—Rose watched him set two lighted candles on the little table by the bed. There was absolute silence, broken only by the ticking of the clock. Rose began to feel herself again—the attack was over—George would be all right—it was a pity that Gervase had gone for Mr. Luce. She began to feel herself ridiculous, curled up with George in the bed ... she had better get out before Sir John came and sneered at her very useful flannel dressing-gown ... then suddenly, as she looked down on it, George's face changed—once more the look of anguish convulsed it, and he started up in bed, clutching his side and fighting for his breath.

It seemed an age, though it was really only a few minutes, that the fight lasted. Rose had no time to be afraid or even pitiful, for Dr. Mount apparently could do nothing without her—as she rather proudly remembered afterwards, he wouldn't let Jenny help at all, but turned to Rose for everything. She had just begun to think how horrible the room smelt with drugs and brandy, when there was a sound of wheels below in the drive.

"That's Gervase," said Jenny.

"Or perhaps it's Sir John...."

But it was Gervase—the next minute he came into the room.

"I've brought him," he said—"is everything ready?"

"Yes, quite ready," said Dr. Mount.

Then Rose saw standing behind Gervase outside the door a tall stooping figure in a black cloak, under which its arms were folded over something that it carried on its breast.

The Lord had come suddenly to Leasan Parsonage.

Immediately panic seized her, a panic which became strangely fused with anger. She sprang forward and would have shut the door.

"Don't come in—you're frightening him—he mustn't be disturbed.... Oh, he'd be better, if you'd only let him alone...."

She felt someone take her arm and gently pull her aside—

the next moment she was unaccountably on her knees, and crying as if her heart would break. She saw that the intruder no longer stood framed in the doorway—he was beside the bed, bending over George, his shadow thrown monstrous on the ceiling by the candle-light.... What was he saying?...

"Lord, I am not worthy that Thou shouldest come under my roof...."

PART III

FOURHOUSES

FOURHOUSES

§1

GEORGE ALARD'S death affected his brother Peter out of all proportion to his life. While George was alive, Peter had looked upon him rather impatiently as a nuisance and a humbug—a nuisance because of his attempts to thrust parochial honours on his unwilling brother, a humbug because religion was so altogether remote from Peter's imagination that he could not credit the sincerity of any man (he was not so sure about women) who believed in it. But now that George was dead he realised that, in spite of his drawbacks, he had been a link in the Alard chain, and that link now was broken. If Peter now died childless, his heir would be Gervase—Gervase with his contempt of the Alard traditions and ungentlemanly attitude towards life. Gervase was capable of selling the whole place. It would be nothing to him if Sir Gervase Alard lived in a villa at Hastings or a flat at West Kensington, or a small holding at his own park gates, whatever was the fancy of the moment—no, he had forgotten it was to be a garage— "Sir Gervase Alard. Cars for hire. Taxies. Station Work."

These considerations made him unexpectedly tender towards his sister-in-law Rose when she moved out of Leasan Parsonage into a small house she had taken in the village. Rose could not bear the thought of being cut off from Alard, of being shut out of its general councils, of being deprived of its comfortable hospitality half as daughter, half as guest. Also she saw the advantages of the great house for her children, the little girls. Her comparative poverty—for George had not left her much—made it all the more necessary that she should prop herself against Conster. Living there under its wing, she would have a far better position than if she set up her independence in some new place where she would be only a clergyman's widow left rather badly off.

Peter admired Rose for these tactics. She would cling to Alard, even in the certainty of being perpetually meddled with and snubbed. He lent her his car to take her and her more intimate belongings to the new house, promised her the loan of it whenever she wanted, and gave her a general invitation to Starvecrow, rather to Vera's disquiet. He had hated Rose while his brother was alive—he had looked upon her as a busybody and an upstart—but now he loved her for her loyalty, self-interested though it was, and was sorry that she had for ever lost her chance of becoming Lady Alard.

He made one or two efforts to impress Gervase with a sense of his responsibility as heir-apparent, but was signally unsuccessful.

"My dear old chap," said his irreverent brother—"you'll probably have six children, all boys, so it's cruel to raise my hopes, which are bound to be dashed before long."

Peter looked gloomy. Gervase had hit him on a tender,

anxious spot. He had now been married more than a year, and there was no sign of his hopes being fulfilled. He told himself he was an impatient fool—Jewish women were proverbially mothers of strong sons. But the very urgency of his longing made him mistrust its fulfilment—Vera was civilised out of race—she ran too much to brains. She had, to his smothered consternation, produced a small volume of poems and essays, which she had had typed and sent expectantly to a publisher. Peter was not used to women doing this sort of thing, and it alarmed him. If they did it, he could not conceive how they could also do the more ordinary and useful things that were expected of them.

His father laughed at him.

"Peter—you're a yokel. Your conception of women is on a level with Elias's and Lambard's."

"No, it isn't, Sir—that's just what's the matter. I can't feel cocksure about things most men feel cocksure about. That's why I wish you'd realise that there's every chance of Gervase coming into the property—"

"My dear Peter, you are the heir."

"Yes, Sir. But if I don't leave a son to come after me...."

"Well, I refuse to bother about what may happen forty years after I'm dead. If you live to my age—and there's no reason you shouldn't, as you're a healthy man—it'll be time to think about an heir. Gervase may be dead before that."

"He's almost young enough to be my son."

"But what in God's name do you want me to do with him? Am I to start already preparing him for his duties as Sir Gervase Alard?"

"You might keep a tighter hand on him, Sir."

"Damn it all! Are you going to teach me how to bring up my own son?"

"No, Sir. But what I feel is that you're not bringing him up as you brought up George and me and poor Hugh—you're letting him go his own way. You don't bother about him because you don't think he's a chance of coming into the property. And two of the three of us have got out of his way since he was sixteen.... He's precious near it now. And yet you let him have his head over that engineering business, and now you've given way about his religion."

"The engineering business was settled long ago, and has saved us a lot of money—more than paid for that fool Mary's fling. What we've spent on the roundabouts we've saved on the swings all right. As for the religion—he'll grow out of that all the quicker for my leaving him alone. I got poor George to talk to him, but that didn't do any good, so I've decided to let him sicken himself, which he's bound to do sooner or later the way he goes at it."

"The fact is, Sir—you've never looked upon Gervase as the heir, and you can't do so now, though he virtually *is* the heir."

"Indeed he isn't. The heir is master Peter John Alard, whose christening mug I'm going to buy next Christmas"— and Sir John made one or two other remarks in his coarse Victorian fashion.

Peter knew he was a fool to be thinking about his heir. His father, though an old man, was still hale—his gout only served to show what a fighter he was; and he himself was a man in the prime of life, healthy and sound. Was it that the war had undermined his sense of security?—He caught uneasy glimpses of another reason, hidden deeper ... a vague

sense that it would be awful to have sacrificed so much for
Alard and Starvecrow, and find his sacrifice in vain—to have
given up Stella Mount (who would certainly not have given
him a book instead of a baby) only that his brother Gervase
might some day degrade Alard, sell Starvecrow and (worst of
all) marry Stella.

§2

For in his heart Peter too expected Gervase to marry Stella.
He knew there was a most unsuitable difference in their ages,
but it weighed little against his expectation. He expected
Gervase to marry Stella for the same reason that he expected
to die without leaving an heir—because he feared it. Besides,
his family talked continually of the possibility, and here again
showed that obtuseness in the matter of Gervase that he deplored. They had no objection to his marrying Stella Mount,
because he was the younger son, and it wasn't imperative for
him to marry money, as it had been for Peter. Another reason
for Peter's expectation was perhaps that he could not understand a man being very much in Stella's society and not wanting to marry her. She was pretty, gentle, capable, comfortable,
and oh! so sweet to love—she would make an excellent wife,
even to a man many years younger than herself; she would be
a mother to him as well as to his children.

This did not mean that Peter was dissatisfied with Vera.
His passion for her had not cooled at the end of a year. She
was still lovely and desirable. But he now realised definitely
that she did not speak his language or think his thoughts—
the book of poems was a proof of it, if he had required other
proof than her attitude towards Starvecrow. Vera was all right

about the family—she respected Alard—but she was remarkably out of tune with the farm. She could not understand the year-in-year-out delight it was to him. She had even suggested that they should take a house in London for the winter—and miss the ploughing of the clays, the spring sowings, and the early lambing! "The country's so dreary in winter," she had said.

This had frightened Peter—he found it difficult to adjust himself to such an outlook ... it was like the first morning when he had found she meant always to have breakfast in bed.... Stella would never have suggested that he should miss the principal feasts of the farmer's year.... But Stella had not Vera's beauty or power or brilliance—nor had she (to speak crudely) Vera's money, and if he had married her Starvecrow would probably now have been in the auction market.

Besides, though loyal to Starvecrow, Stella had always been flippant and profane on the subject of the family, and in this respect Vera was all that Peter could wish. She was evidently proud of her connection with Alard—she kept as close under its wing as Rose, and for more disinterested reasons. She had her race's natural admiration for an ancient family and a noble estate, she felt honoured by her alliance and her privileges—she would make a splendid Lady Alard of Conster Manor, though a little unsatisfactory as Mrs. Peter Alard of Starvecrow Farm.

As part of her lien with Alard, Vera had become close friends with Jenny. It was she who told Peter that Jenny had broken off her engagement to Jim Parish.

"I didn't know she was engaged to him."

"Oh, Peter, they've been engaged more than three years."

"Well, I never knew anything about it."

"You must have—you all did, though you chose to ignore it."

"I always thought it was just an understanding."

"That's the same thing."

"Indeed it isn't!"—At that rate he had been engaged to Stella and had behaved like a swine.

"Well, whatever it was, she's through with it now."

"What did she turn him down for?"

"Oh, simply that there was no chance of their marrying, and they were getting thoroughly tired of each other."

"A nice look-out if they'd married."

"That would have been different. They might not have got tired of each other then. It's these long engagements, that drag on and on without hope of an ending. I must say I'm sorry for poor Jenny. She's been kept hanging about for three years, and she's had frightfully little sympathy from anyone—except perhaps Mary. They were all too much afraid that if they encouraged her she'd dash off and get married on a thousand a year or some such pittance."

"I've always understood Parish paid three hundred a year towards the interest on the Cock Marling mortgages—that would leave him with only seven hundred," said Peter gravely.

"Impossible, of course. They'd have been paupers. But do you know that till I came down here I'd no idea how fashionable mortgages are among the best county families?"

§3

Peter did not meet Jenny till some days later. She had been to see Vera, and came out of the house just as Peter was talking to young Godfrey, the farmer of Fourhouses. This farm did not belong to the Alards—it stood on the southern fringe of their land in Icklesham parish. At one time Sir William Alard had wanted to buy it, but the owners held tight, and his grandchildren lived to be thankful for the extra hundred acres weight that had been spared them. Now, the situation was reversed, and the Godfreys were wanting to buy the thirty acres of Alard land immediately adjoining Fourhouses.

Sir John was willing to sell, and the only difficulty was the usual one of the mortgage. Godfrey, however, still wished to buy, for he believed that the land would double its value if adequate money was spent on it, and this he was prepared to do, for his farm had prospered under the government guarantees. For generations the Godfreys had been a hard-working and thrifty set, and the war—though it had taken Ben Godfrey himself out to Mesopotamia—had made Fourhouses flourish as it had never done since the repeal of the Corn Laws.

The problem became entirely one of price, and Peter had done his best to persuade his father not to stand out too stiffly over this. The family badly needed hard cash—the expenses of Mary's suit had been heavy, and as their money was tied up in land it was always difficult to put their hand on a large sum. Here was a chance which might never happen again— for no one was likely to want the Snailham land under its present disabilities, except Godfrey, whose farm it encroached on. If they did not sell it now, it might become necessary (and this was Peter's great fear) to sell the free lands of Starvecrow. Therefore if the Snailham land brought in the ready money they wanted, they must try to forget that it was going for little more than half what Sir William had given for it seventy years ago.

"Well, I'll talk it over with Sir John," he said to Godfrey, who was on horseback in the drive. It was then he saw Jenny coming towards them out of the house.

"Wait a minute," he said to her—"I want to speak to you."

He was uncertain whether or not he ought to introduce the young farmer to his sister. Godfrey did not call himself a gentleman farmer—indeed he was inclined to despise the title—but he came of good old yeoman stock, and his name went back nearly as far as Alard into the records of Winchelsea.

"Jenny, this is Mr. Godfrey of Fourhouses—my sister, Miss Jenny Alard."

Godfrey took off his soft hat. He had the typical face of the Sussex and Kent borders, broad, short-nosed, blue-eyed; but there was added to it a certain brownness and sharpness, which might have come from a dash of gipsy blood. A Godfrey had married a girl of the Boswells in far-back smuggling days.

He and Peter discussed the Snailham snapes a little longer—then he rode off, and Peter turned to Jenny.

"I didn't know you'd come over," he said, "and I wanted to talk to you a bit—it's an age since I've seen you."

He was feeling a little guilty about his attitude towards her and Jim Parish—he had, like all the rest of the family, tried to ignore the business, and he now realised how bitter it must have been to Jenny to stand alone.

"Vera told me that you'd broken off your engagement," he added as they walked down the drive.

"So it was an engagement, was it?" said Jenny rather pertly.

"Well, you yourself know best what it was."

"I should have called it an engagement, but as neither his family nor mine would acknowledge it, perhaps it wasn't."

"There was no chance of your getting married for years, so it seemed better not to make it public. I can't tell you I'm sorry you've broken it off."

"I should hardly say it's broken off—rather that it's rotted away."

Her voice sounded unusually hard, and Peter felt a little ashamed of himself.

"I'm frightfully sorry, Jenny"—taking her arm—"I'm afraid we've all been rather unsympathetic, but—"

"Gervase hasn't. It was he who advised me to end things."

"The deuce it was!"

"Yes—he saw it as I did—simply ridiculous."

"So it was, my dear—since you couldn't get married till the Lord knows when."

"That wasn't what made it ridiculous. The ridiculous part was that we could have got married perfectly well if only I hadn't been Jenny Alard of Conster Manor and he Jim Parish of Cock Marling Place."

"What do you mean?"

"Well, he's got over seven hundred a year. Most young couples would look upon that as riches, but it's poverty to us—partly because he has to pay away half of it in interest on mortgages, and partly because we've got such an absurd standard of living that we couldn't exist on anything less than two or three thousand."

"Well, I hope you'd never be such a fool as to marry on seven hundred."

"That's just it—I'm refusing to marry on seven hundred. But I'll tell you, Peter—I'd do it like a shot for a man who didn't look upon it as a form of suicide. If ever I meet a man who thinks it enough for him, I promise you it'll be enough for me."

"That's all very well, Jenny. But Parish must think of Cock Marling."

"He is thinking of it. It's Cock Marling that's separated us just as Conster separated you and Stella."

Peter was annoyed.

"You've no right to say that. What makes you think I wanted to marry Stella? It's not fair to Vera to suggest such a thing."

"I'm sorry, Peter. I oughtn't to have said it. But I did once think ... But anyhow, I'm glad you didn't."

"So am I."

"And I'm glad I'm not going to marry Jim."

"Then you needn't be angry with Cock Marling."

"Yes, I am—because I know I could have been happy with Jim if there'd been no Cock Marling. It's all very well for you to talk, Peter—but I think ... Oh, these big country houses make me sick. It's all the same—everywhere I go I see the same thing—we're all cut to a pattern. There's always the beautifully kept grounds and the huge mortgaged estate that's tumbling to pieces for want of money to spend on it. Then, when you go in, there are hothouse flowers everywhere, and beautiful glass and silver—and bad cooking. And we're waited on badly because we're too old-fashioned and dignified to employ women, so we have the cheapest butler we can get, helped by a footman taken from the plough. Upstairs the bedrooms want painting and papering, but we always have two cars—though we can't afford motor traction for our land. We're falling to pieces, but we hide the cracks with pots of flowers. Why can't we sell our places and live in comfort? We Alards would be quite well-to-do if we lived in a moderate sized house with two or three women servants and either a small car or none at all. We could afford to be happy then."

"Jenny, you're talking nonsense. You're like most women and can't see the wood for the trees. If we gave up the cars tomorrow and sacked Appleby and Pollock and Wills, and sold the silver and the pictures, it wouldn't do us the slightest good in the world. We'd still have the estate, we'd still have to pay in taxes more than the land brings in to us. You can't sell land nowadays, even if it isn't mortgaged. Besides—damn it all!—why should we sell it? It's been ours for centuries, we've been here for centuries, and I for one am proud of it."

"Well, I'm not. I'm ashamed. I tell you, Peter, our day is over, and we'd better retire, while we can retire gracefully— before we're sold up."

"Nonsense. If we hang on, the value of the land will rise, we'll be able to pay off the mortgages—and perhaps some day this brutal government will see the wickedness of its tax- ation and—"

"Why should it? It wants the money—and we've no right to be here. We've outlived our day. Instead of developing the land—we're ruining it, letting it go to pieces. We can't afford to keep our tenants' farms in order. It's time we ceased to own half the country, and the land went back to the people it used to belong to."

"I see you've been talking to Gervase."

"Well, he and I think alike on this subject."

"I'm quite sure you do."

"And we've made up our minds not to let the family spoil our lives. It's taken Jim from me—but that was his fault. It's not going to smash me a second time. If I want to marry a poor man, I shall do so—even if he's really poor—not only just what we call poor."

"Well, you and Gervase are a precious couple, that's all I've got to say."

The next moment he softened towards her, because he remembered that she was unhappy and spoke out of the bitterness of her heart. But though he was sorry for her, he had a secret admiration for Jim Parish, who had refused to desert the Squires.

§4

He was intensely worried that his sister and brother could take up such an attitude towards the family. They were young socialists, anarchists, bolsheviks, and he heartily disapproved of them. He brooded over Jenny's words more than was strictly reasonable. She wasn't going to let the family spoil her life, she said—she wasn't going to sacrifice herself to the family—she wasn't going to let the family come between her and the man she loved as he had let it come between him and Stella. She'd no right to say that—it wasn't true. He couldn't really have loved Stella or he wouldn't have sacrificed her to Alard and Starvecrow. Yes, he would, though yes, he had. He had loved her—he wouldn't say he hadn't, he wouldn't deny the past. He had loved her, but he had deliberately let her go because to have kept her would have meant disloyalty to his family. So what Jenny had said was true.

This realisation did not soothe, though he never doubted the rightness of what he had done. He wondered how much he had hurt Stella by putting her aside ... poor little Stella—she had loved him truly, and she had loved Starvecrow. He had robbed her of both.... He remembered the last scene between them, their goodbye—in the office at Starvecrow, in the days of its pitch-pine and bamboo, before he had put in the Queen Anne bureau and the oak chests. He wondered what she would think of it now. She would have fitted into Starvecrow better than Vera ... bah! he'd always realised that, but it was just as well to remind himself that if he had married her, there would have been no Starvecrow for her to fit into. He hadn't sacrificed her merely to Alard but also to Starvecrow—and she had understood that part of the sacrifice. He remembered her saying, "I understand your selfish reason much better than your unselfish one."

Well, there was no good brooding over her now. If he had loved her once, he now loved her no longer ... and if she had loved him once, she now loved him no longer. She was consoling herself with Gervase. She might be Lady Alard yet, and save Starvecrow out of the wreck that her husband would make of the estate. Peter felt sick.

The next day he met her at tea at Conster Manor, whither he had been asked with Vera to meet George's successor, the new Vicar of Leasan. She was sitting on the opposite side of the room beside the Vicar's wife—a faded little woman, in scrappy finery, very different from her predecessor who was eating her up from her place by Lady Alard. Peter had met Stella fairly often in public, but had not studied her closely till today. Today for some reason he wanted to know a great deal about her—whether she was still attractive, whether she was happy, whether she was in love with Gervase, though this last was rather difficult to discover, as Gervase was not there.

On the first two points he soon satisfied himself. She was certainly attractive—she did not look any older than when he had fallen in love with her during the last year of the war. Her round, warmly coloured face and her bright eyes held the double secret of youth and happiness—yes, he saw that she was happy. She carried her happiness about with her. After all, now he came to think of it, she did not lead a particularly happy life—dispensing for her father and driving his car, it was dull to say the least. He could not help respecting her for her happiness, just as he respected her for her bright neat clothes contrasting so favourably with the floppy fussiness of bits and ends that adorned the Vicar's wife.

He could not get near her and he could not hear what she was saying. The floor was held by Mr. Williams, the new Vicar. The Parsonage couple were indeed the direct contrast of their predecessors—it was the husband who dominated, the wife who struggled. Mr. Williams had been a chaplain to the forces, and considered Christianity the finest sport going. A breezy, hefty shepherd, he would feed his flock on football and billiards, as George had fed them on blankets and Parochial Church Councils. It was inconceivable that anyone in Leasan should miss the way to heaven.

"I believe in being a man among men," he blew over Sir John, who was beginning to hate him, though he had chosen him out of twenty-one applicants—"That's what you learnt in France—no fuss, no frills, just playing the game."

"You'd better have a few words with my youngest son," said Sir John, resolving to give him a hard nut to crack—"He's turned what used to be called a Puseyite in my young days, but is now called a Catholic, I believe."

"A Zanzibarbarian—what? Oh, he'll grow out of that. Boys often get it when they're young."

"And stay young all their lives if they keep it," said Stella— "I'm glad Gervase will be always young."

The Vicar gave her a look of breezy disapproval. Peter was vexed too—not because Stella had butted into the conversation and thrown her opinion across the room, but because she had gone out of her way to interfere on behalf of Gervase. It was really rather obvious ... one couldn't help noticing ... and in bad taste, too, considering Peter was there.

"Here he is," said Sir John, as the Ford back-fired a volley in the drive—"you can start on him now."

But Gervase was hungry and wanted his tea. He sat down beside his mother and Rose, so that he could have a plate squarely set on the table instead of balancing precarious slices of cake in his saucer. Peter watched him in a manner which he hoped was guarded. There was no sign of any special intelligence between him and Stella—Gervase had included her in his general salutation, which he had specialised only in the case of the Vicar and his wife. At first this reassured Peter, but after a while he realised that it was not altogether a reassuring sign—Gervase should have greeted Stella more as a stranger, shaken hands with her as he had shaken hands with the strangers, instead of including her in the family wave and grin. They must be on very good terms—familiar terms....

Stella rose to go.

"Have you got the car?" asked Gervase.

"No—Father's gone over to Dallington in her."

"Let me drive you back—I've got Henry Ford outside."

"But have you finished your tea? You've only eaten half the cake."

"I'll eat the other half when I come back—it won't take me more than a few minutes to run you home."

"Thanks very much, then," said Stella.

She had never been one to refuse a kindness, or say "No, thanks," when she meant "Yes, please." None the less Peter was angry. He was angry with her for accepting Gervase's offer and driving off in his disreputable lorry, and he was angry with her for that very same happiness which he had admired her for earlier in the afternoon. It was extremely creditable of her to be happy when she had nothing to make her so, when her happiness sprang only from the soil of her contented heart; but if she was happy because of Gervase ...

"He's an elegant fellow, that young son of mine," said Sir John, as the lorry drove off amidst retchings and smoke— "No doubt the day will come when I shall see him drink out of his saucer."

§5

The woman Peter loved now left Conster more elegantly than the woman he had loved once. The Sunbeam floated over the lane between Conster and Starvecrow, and pulled up noiselessly outside the house almost directly it had started. Peter was beginning to feel a little tired of the Sunbeam—he had hankerings after a lively little two-seater. An eight-cylindered landaulette driven by a man in livery was all very well for Vera to pay calls in, or if they wanted to go up to town. But he wanted something to take him round to farms on business, and occasionally ship a bag of meal or a load of spiles. He couldn't afford both, and if they had the two-seater Vera could still go out in it to pay her calls—or up to London, for that matter. But she refused to part with the Sunbeam—it

was her father and mother's wedding present, and they would
be terribly hurt if she gave it up. Two-seaters were always uncomfortable. And why did Peter want to go rattling round
to farms?—Couldn't he send one of his men?—Vera never
would take him seriously as a farmer.

This evening, thanks to the Sunbeam, they reached home
too early to dress for dinner. Peter asked Vera to come for a
stroll with him in the orchard, but she preferred the garden
at the back of the house. The garden at Starvecrow used to be
a plot of ragged grass, surrounding a bed of geraniums from
the middle of which unexpectedly rose a pear-tree. Today it
was two green slips of lawn divided by a paved pathway shad-
ed by a pergola. The April dusk was still warm, still pricked
with the notes of birds, but one or two windows in the house
were lighted, orange squares of warmth and welcome beyond
the tracery of the pergola.

"It's lovely, isn't it?" murmured Peter, taking Vera's arm
under her cloak—"Oh, my dear, you surely wouldn't be in
London now."

"No," said Vera—"not when it's fine."

"What did you think of Williams?"

"Oh, he seemed all right—I didn't talk to him much. But
his wife's a bore."

"I felt sorry for poor Rose, having to welcome her."

"You needn't worry—she didn't do much of that."

"She had to sit there and be polite, anyhow."

"I didn't notice it. But I tell you what really interested
me—and that was watching Stella Mount and Gervase."

"Oh!"

"They were most amusing."

"I never noticed anything."

"No, my dear old man, of course you didn't, because you never do. But it's perfectly plain that it's a case between them. I've thought so for a long time."

"He may be in love with her, but I'm sure she isn't in love with him."

"Well, she seemed to me the more obviously in love of the two. She had all the happy, confident manner of a woman in love."

"She couldn't be in love with him—he's a mere boy."

"Very attractive to women, especially to one past her early youth. Stella must be getting on for thirty now, and I expect she doesn't want to be stranded."

For some reason Peter could not bear to hear her talked of in this way.

"I know she's not in love with him," he said doggedly.

"How can you know?"

"By the way she looks and behaves and all that—I know how Stella looks when she's in love."

"Of course you do. But since she couldn't get you perhaps she'd like to have Gervase."

Peter felt angry.

"I wish you wouldn't talk like that. Stella isn't that sort at all—and she didn't love me any more than I loved her."

"Really!"

"You all talk—I've heard Doris and Rose at it as well as you—you all talk as if Stella had been running after me and I wouldn't have her. But that isn't the truth—I loved her, and I'd have had her like a shot if it had been possible, but it wasn't."

He felt a stiffening of Vera's arm under his, though she did not take it away. He realised that he had said too much. But he couldn't help it. There in the garden of Starvecrow, which Stella had loved as well as he, he could not deny their common memories ... pretend that he had not loved her ... he had a ridiculous feeling that it would have been disloyal to Starvecrow as well as to Stella.

"You needn't get so angry," Vera was saying—"I had always been given to understand that the affair wasn't serious—a wartime flirtation which peace showed up as impossible. There were a great many like that."

"Well, this wasn't one of them. I loved Stella as much as she loved me."

"Then why didn't you marry her?"

"I couldn't possibly have done so—and anyhow," shame-facedly, "I'm glad I didn't."

"Then I still say you didn't really love her. If you had, you'd have married her even though the family disapproved and she hadn't a penny. She'd have done it for you—so if you wouldn't do it for her, it shows that you didn't love her as much as she loved you."

"I did"—almost shouted Peter.

Vera took her arm away.

"Really, Peter, you're in a very strange mood tonight. I think I'll go indoors."

"I'm only trying to make you understand that though I don't love Stella now, I loved her once."

"On the contrary—you're making me understand that though you didn't love her once, you love her now."

"How can you say that!"

"Because you're giving yourself away all round. You're jealous of your brother, and you're angry with me because I don't speak of Stella in a way you quite approve of. Don't worry, my dear boy. We've been married over a year, and I can hardly expect your fancy never to stray. But I'd rather you weren't quite such a boor over it."

She walked quickly into the house.

Peter felt as if he had been struck. He told himself that Vera was unjust and hard and cynical. How dare she say he was jealous of Gervase? How dare she say he had never really loved Stella?—that was her own infernal jealousy, he supposed. How dare she say he loved Stella now?—that again was her infernal jealousy. He took one or two miserable turns up and down the path, then went in to dress for dinner.

A wood fire was burning sweetly in his dressing-room, and his clothes had been laid out by the parlourmaid, who was as good a valet as only a good parlourmaid can be. Under these combined influences Peter learned how material comforts can occasionally soothe a spiritual smart, dressing there in warmth and ease, he began to slip out of those distressing feelings which had raged under the pergola. After all, Vera had made him supremely happy for a year. It was ungrateful to be angry with her now, just because she had taken it into her head to be a little jealous. That was really a compliment to him. Besides, now he came to think of it, he had not spoken or behaved as he ought. What a fool he had been to kick up such a dust just because Vera had doubted the reality of his dead love for Stella. No wonder she had drawn conclusions … and instead of trying to soothe and reassure her, he had only got angry.

He made up his mind to apologise at once, and paused at her door on his way downstairs. But he heard the voice of the maid inside, and decided to wait till they were alone in the drawing-room before dinner. She was nearly always down a few minutes before eight.

However, tonight, perversely, she did not appear. The clock struck eight, and to Peter's surprise, Weller, the parlour-maid, came into the room.

"Dinner is served, Sir."

"But your mistress isn't down yet."

"She has ordered her dinner to be sent up to her room, Sir."

§6

Peter was not to be let off so easily as in the simplicity of his heart he had imagined. He had transgressed the laws of matrimony as Vera understood them, by refusing to say that he had never really loved Stella. He ought properly to have said that he had never really loved anyone until he met his wife, but that, Peter told himself, was nonsense in a man of his age. He told it to himself all the more vehemently because he had an uneasy feeling that a year ago he would have said what Vera wanted, that he himself would have believed she was the only woman he had really loved.

The next morning he went into her room as usual while she was having her breakfast, and they said the usual things to each other as if nothing had happened. But Peter felt awkward and ill at ease—he wanted, childishly, to "make it up," but did not know how to get through the invisible wall she had built round herself. Also he knew that she would accept nothing less than a recantation of all that he had said yesterday—he would have to tell her that he had never loved Stella, that all that part of his life had been dreaming and self-deception. And he would not say it. With a queer obstinacy, whose roots he would not examine, he refused to deny his past, even to make the present happier and the future more secure.

"What are you doing today?" asked Vera coolly, as she stirred her coffee.

"I'm going over to an auction at Canterbury—they're selling off some old government stuff."

As a matter of fact, he had not meant to go, but now he felt that he must do something to get himself out of the house for the day.

"Then you won't be in for lunch?"

"No—not much before dinner, I expect."

"Shall you go in the car?"

"Only as far as Ashford—I'll take the train from there."

It was all deadly. Going out of her room, going out of the house, he was conscious of a deep sense of depression and futility. Vera was displeased with him because he would not be disloyal to the past.... After all, he supposed it was pretty natural and most women were like that ... but Vera was different in the way she showed her displeasure—if only she'd say things!—become angry and coaxing like other women—like Stella when he had displeased her. He remembered her once when she had been angry—how differently she had behaved—with such frankness, such warmth, such wheedling.... Vera had just turned to ice, and expressed herself in negations and reserves. He hated that—it was all wrong, somehow.

He fretted and brooded the whole way to Ashford. It was

not till he was nearly there that he remembered he had an appointment with Godfrey at Starvecrow that afternoon. Vera was making him not only a bad husband but a bad farmer.

§7

Godfrey did not forget his appointment. He arrived punctually at three o clock, and not finding Peter at home, waited with the patience of his kind. A further symptom of Peter's demoralisation was his forgetting to tell anyone at Starvecrow when he would be back, so Godfrey, who was really anxious to have his matter settled and could scarcely believe that anything so important to himself should seem trivial in the stress of another's life, felt sure that Mr. Alard would soon come in, and having hitched his reins and assured himself that Madge would stand for ever, went into the office and waited.

Here Jenny Alard found him at about half-past three, just wondering whether it would be good manners for him to smoke. She had come up to see Vera, but finding she had gone out in the car, looked in at the office door in hopes of finding Peter. Godfrey was sitting rather stiffly in the gate-backed chair, turning his box of gaspers over and over in his large brown hands. Jenny came into the room and greeted him at once. She and her family always took pains to be cordial to their social inferiors. If the man in the office had been an acquaintance of her own rank, she would probably have bowed to him, made some excuse and gone out to look for her brother—but such behaviour would never do for anyone who might imagine it contained a slight.

"Good afternoon. Are you waiting for my brother? Do you know when he'll be in?"

He rose to greet her, and as they shook hands she realised what a shadow his inferiority was. He stood before her
six feet high, erect, sun-burned—his thick hair and bright
eyes proclaiming his health, his good clothes proclaiming his
prosperity, a certain alert and simple air of confidence speaking of a life free from conflict and burden.

"Mr. Alard made an appointment for three. But they tell
me he's gone to Canterbury."

"It's a shame to keep you waiting. You're busy, I expect."

"Not so terrible—and it's the first time he's done it. I
reckon something's gone wrong with the car."

"He hasn't got the car—Mrs. Alard is out in it. Perhaps
he's missed his train."

"If he's done that he won't be here for some time, and I
can't afford to wait much longer. I've a man coming to Fourhouses about some pigs after tea."

"I expect there's a time-table somewhere—let's look."

She rummaged among the papers at the top of the desk
—auction catalogues, advertisements for cattle foods and farm
implements—and at last drew out a local time-table. Their
heads bent over it together, and she became conscious of a
scent as of straw and clean stables coming from his clothes.
She groped among the pages not knowing her way, and then
noticed that his hands were restless as if his greater custom
were impatient of her ignorance.

"No—it's page sixty-four—I remember ... two pages back
... no, not there, you've missed it."

His hands hovered as if they longed to turn over the
leaves, but evidently he forbade them—and she guessed that
he shrank from the chance of touching hers. She looked at his

hands—they were well-shaped, except for the fingers which work had spoiled, they were brown, strong, lean—she liked them exceedingly. They were clean, but not as Peter's or Jim's or her father's hands were clean; they suggested effort rather than custom that he washed when he was dirty in order to be clean rather than when he was clean in order to prevent his ever being dirty.... What a queer way her thoughts were running, and all because of his hands— Well, she would like to touch them ... it was funny how he held back even from such a natural contact as this—typical of his class, in which there was always consciousness between the sexes ... no careless, casual contacts, no hail-fellow and hearty comradeship, but always man and woman, some phase of courtship ... romance....

"I can't find it."

She thrust the book into his hands, and their fingers touched. He begged her pardon—then found the page. She did not notice what he said—her pulses were hammering. She was excited not so much by him as by herself. Why had her whole being lit up so suddenly?—What had set it alight? Was it just this simple deferential consciousness of sex between them, so much more natural than the comradeship which was the good- form of her class? Sex-consciousness was after all more natural than sex-unconsciousness, the bridling of the flirt more natural than the indifference of the "woman who has no nonsense about her." She felt a deep blush spreading over her face—she became entirely conscious before him, uneasy under his alert, dignified gaze.

He was picking up his hat—he was saying something about the two-forty-five being in long ago and his having no time to wait till the four-forty.

"I'll call in tomorrow—I'll leave word with Elias that I'll call in at twelve tomorrow."

"I'm so sorry you've come all this way for nothing," she faltered.

"Oh, it's no matter. I'm not busy today. Mr. Alard must have missed his train."

She found herself going out of the room before him. His smart gig stood outside the door—the mare whinnied at the sight of him. Jenny thought how good it must be to drive horse-flesh instead of machinery.

"You haven't taken to a motor-car yet, I see."

"I don't think I ever shall. It 'ud feel unfriendly."

"Yes, I expect it would after this"—and she patted the mare's sleek neck.

"A horse knows you, you see—and where you go wrong often he'll go right—but a car, a machine, that's got no sense nor kindness in it, and when you do the wrong thing there's nothing that'll save you."

Jenny nodded. He warmed to his subject.

"Besides, you get fond of an animal in a way you can't of a machine. This Madge, here. I've raised her from a filly, and when I take her out of the shafts she'll follow me round the yard for a bit of sugar—and you heard her call to me just now when I came out? That's her way. You may pay three thousand pounds for a Rolls Royce car but it won't never say good-evening."

He laughed at his own joke, showing his big splendid teeth, and giving Jenny an impression of sweetness and happiness that melted into her other impressions like honey.

"Did she recognise you when you came back from the war?—You were in Mesopotamia weren't you?"

"Yes—three years. I can't say as she properly recognised me, but now I've been back a twelve-month I think she fits me into things that happened to her before I left, if you know what I mean."

"Yes, I understand."

He had been talking to her with his foot on the step, ready to get into his gig. Then suddenly he seemed to remember that she did not live at Starvecrow, that she too had a journey before her and no trap to take her home.

"Can I give you a lift, Miss Alard?—I'm passing Conster."

"Yes—thank you very much," said Jenny.

§8

That evening, sitting at dinner with her family, she felt vaguely ashamed of herself—she had let herself go too far. As she watched her mother's diamond rings flashing over her plate, as she listened to her father cynically demolishing the Washington conference, as she contemplated Doris eating asparagus in the gross and clumsy manner achieved only by the well-bred, the afternoon's adventure took discreditable colours in her mind. What had made her feel like that towards Godfrey? Surely it was the same emotion which draws a man towards a pretty housemaid. The young farmer was good-looking and well-built—he had attracted her physically—and her body had mocked at the barriers set up by her mind, by education, birth, breeding and tradition.

She wondered guiltily what Jim would think of her if he knew. He would probably see a fresh reason for congratulating himself on the rupture of those loose yet hampering ties which had bound them for so long. She had never felt like that towards Jim, though she had accepted the physical element in their relation—thought, indeed, sometimes, that it was unduly preponderating, holding them together when ideas and ambitions would have drawn them apart. Was it possible after all that Godfrey's attraction had not been merely physical—that there had been an allure in his simple, unaccustomed outlook on life as well as in his splendid frame?

Gervase came in late to dinner, and being tired did not talk much. After the meal was over, and Jenny was playing bridge with her parents and Doris, he sat in the window, turning over the pages of a book and looking out between the curtains at the pale Spring stars. When Lady Alard's losses made her decide she was too tired to play anymore and the game was broken up, Jenny went over and sat beside him. It had struck her that perhaps his life at the works, his association with working men, might enable him to shed some light on her problem. Not that she meant to confide in him, but there seemed to be in Gervase now a growing sanity of judgment; she had a new, odd respect for the experiences of the little brother's mind.

"Gervase," she said—"I suppose you could never make friends with anyone at the shop?"

"No—I'm afraid I couldn't. At least not with anyone there now. But we get on all right together."

"I suppose it's the difference in education."

"Partly—but chiefly the difference in our way of looking at things."

"Surely that's due to education."

"Yes, if by education you mean breeding—the whole life. It's not that we want different things, but we want them in a different way."

"Do all men want the same things?"

He smiled.

"Yes—we all want money, women, and God."

Jenny felt a little shocked.

"Some want one most, and some want another most," continued Gervase—"and we're most different in our ways of wanting money and most alike in our ways of wanting God."

"How do you want money in different ways?"

"It's not only the fact that what's wealth to them is often poverty to us—it's chiefly that they get their pleasure out of the necessities of life and we out of the luxuries. It's never given you any actual pleasure, I suppose, to think that you've got a good house to live in and plenty to eat—but to those chaps it's a real happiness and I'm not talking of those who've ever had to go without."

Jenny was silent a moment. She hesitated over her next question.

"And what's the difference in your ideas about women?"

He shrugged his shoulders.

"Their talk about women makes me sick—I feel in that matter we've got the pull over them. When men of our own set get on the subject, it's different altogether, even at its worst. But I sometimes think that this is because their ideal of women is really so high that they don't look upon a certain class of them as women at all."

"You think their ideal of women in general is high?"

"Yes, that's why their women are either good or bad. They won't stand the intervening stages the way we do. They expect a great deal of the women they make their wives."

"I suppose that a friendship between a woman of our class

and a man of theirs would be much more difficult than a friendship between two men of different classes."

"It would be quite impossible. They don't understand friendship between men and women for one thing. I'm not sure that they haven't got too much sense."

Jenny rose and moved away. She found the conversation vaguely disturbing. Though, after all, she cried impatiently to herself, why should she? They hadn't been discussing Godfrey—only the men where Gervase worked, who belonged altogether to a different class. But Godfrey, yeoman farmer of Fourhouses, solid, comfortable, respectable, able to buy land from impoverished Alard ... why should she think of him as in a class beneath her? Her parents would think so certainly, but that was because their ideas had grown old and stiff with Alard's age ... mentally Alard was suffering from arterial sclerosis ... oh, for some new blood!

§9

Peter was vexed with himself for having forgotten Godfrey's appointment—not that he thought his forgetfulness would jeopardise the business between Conster and Fourhouses, but such a lapse pointed degradingly to causes beneath it. He had been careless and forgetful as a farmer because he was unhappy as a husband. His private life was hurting him and its convulsions had put his business life out of order.

On his return from Canterbury there was a reconciliation between him and Vera. His long day of futile loneliness had broken his spirit—he could endure their estrangement no longer, and in order to make peace was willing to stoop to treacheries which in the morning he had held beneath his

honour. He had made Stella a burnt offering to peace. No—
he said to Vera—he had never really loved her—she had just
been "one of the others" before he met his wife.... He took
her glowing memory and put it in the prison house where he
had shut up the loves of a month and a week and a day ... he
saw her in that frail company, looking at him from between
the bars, telling him that she did not belong there. But he
spoke to her roughly in his heart—"Yes you do—you're one
of the thieves who stole a bit of the love I was keeping for
Vera—just that."

Vera, after the first frigidities, graciously accepted his con-
trition. As he was willing to acknowledge that he had never
really loved Stella, she was willing to drop the other half of the
argument and allow that he was not belatedly in love with her
now. Once more there was love and harmony at Starvecrow—
warmth in the low rooms, where the firelight leaped on creamy
walls and the rustle of Vera's silk seemed to live like an echo, a
voluptuous ghost. The cold, thin Spring seemed shut outside
the house—the interior of Starvecrow, its ceilings, doors, walls
and furniture meant more to Peter now than its barns and
stacks and cobbled yard, even than its free woods and fields.

The cold, thin Spring warmed and thickened in the woods.
The floods receded from the Tillingham marshes, and the river ran through a golden street of buttercups to the sea. The
winter sowings put a bloom of vivid green into the wheat
fields, the blossom of apple, cherry, pear and plum drifted
from the boughs of the orchard to the grass, leaving the first
green hardness of the fruits among the leaves; and as the outer
world grew warm and living, once more the heart of the house
grew cold. Peter and Vera were not estranged, but the warm

dusk of their rapture had given place to the usual daylight, in
which Peter saw the ugly things his peace contained.

He was not blinded by the wonder that had happened,
by the knowledge that probably, almost certainly, Vera was
to have a child—that there would be an heir to Conster and
Alard, and lovely Starvecrow would not go to strangers. He
felt intensely relieved that his fears would not be realised, that
he was not inevitably building for Gervase to throw down—
but there was less glamour about the event than he had antic-
ipated, it could not set his heart at rest, nor make Vera shine
with all the old light of the honeymoon.

He had always thought and heard that expecting a child
brings husband and wife even closer together than the first
days of love—he was vexed that the charm did not work.
Was it because of his feeling that if the child were a girl it
might just as well not be born? That was certainly the wrong
thing to feel, for much as he longed for an heir, he should not
forget that a girl would be his child, the child of the woman he loved. Then one day he had a dreadful realisation—the
conviction that if he were waiting for Stella's child it would
all have been different, that he would have thought of the
child as much as now he thought of the heir. Of course he
would still have wanted an heir, but he would not have had
the feeling that if it did not give him a boy his wife's childbearing was in vain.... In vain—in vain.... He would not have
known that word which now he found in his mind so often
"Marriage in vain if there is no child ... childbearing in vain
if there is no heir." He saw his marriage as a mere tool of
Alard's use, a prop to that sinking edifice of the Squires.... He
felt as miserable as in the first days of the cold, thin Spring.

§10

He now no longer denied that in one sense he had made a mistake in marrying Vera. He still found her brilliant and beautiful, a charming if sometimes a too sophisticated companion. But she was not the wife of his heart and imagination. Her personality stood queerly detached from the rest of his life—apart from his ideas of home and family. He felt coldly angry with her for the ways in which she refused or failed to fulfil his yearnings, and he could never, he felt, quite forgive her for having demanded Stella as a sacrifice. His denial of his love for Stella, which he had made in the interests of peace, now pierced his memory like a thorn—partly he reproached himself, and partly he reproached Vera. And there was a reproach for Stella too.

But he still told himself that he was glad he had married Vera. After all, he had got what he wanted. All he no longer had was the illusion that had fed him for a year after marriage, the illusion that in taking Vera he had done the best thing for himself as a man as well as an Alard. He could no longer tell himself that Vera was a better wife and a sweeter woman than he would have found Stella—that even without family considerations he had still made the happiest choice. That dream had played its part, and now might well die, and yet leave him with the thought that he had chosen well.

He need not look upon his marriage as mercenary because it was practical rather than romantic, nor himself as a fool because he had been heated and dizzied into taking a step he could never have taken in cold blood. He had always planned to marry money for the sake of Alard and Starvecrow, and he could never have done so without the illusion of love. Nature had merely helped him carry out what he had unnaturally planned.... And Starvecrow was safe, established and under his careful stewardship the huge, staggering Conster estate would one day recover steadiness. The interest on the mortgages was always punctually paid, and he had hopes of being able in a year or two to pay off some of the mortgages themselves. By the time he became Sir Peter Alard he might be in a fair way of clearing the property.... So why regret the romance he had never chosen?

He told himself he would regret nothing if he was sure that Stella would not marry Gervase—that having very properly shut romance out of his own house, he should not have to see it come next door. In his clearer moments he realised that this attitude was unreasonable, or that, if reasonable, it pointed to an unhealthy state of affairs, but he could never quite bully or persuade himself out of it. He had to confess that it would be intolerable to have to welcome as a sister the woman he had denied himself as a wife. Anything, even total estrangement, would be better than that—better than having to watch her making his brother's home the free and happy place she might have made his own, throwing her sweetness and her courage into the risks of his brother's life, bearing his brother's children, made after all the mother of Alards ... perhaps the mother of Alard's heir. This last thought tormented him most. He saw a preposterous genealogical table:

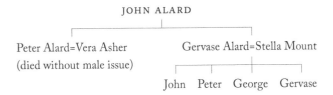

JOHN ALARD

Peter Alard=Vera Asher
(died without male issue)

Gervase Alard=Stella Mount

John   Peter   George   Gervase

From the family's decaying trunk he saw a new healthy branch springing through the grafting in of Stella's life— healthy but alien, for the children Stella gave Gervase would not be Alards in the true sense of the children she might have given Peter. They would be soaked in their father's disloyal ideas. His bad sense, his bad form. John, Peter, George and Gervase would probably smash up what was left of the tradition and the estate.... Peter saw them selling Starvecrow, selling Conster, opening shops and works, marrying indiscriminately.... He hated these insurgent nephews his mind had begotten.

Now and then he told himself that his fears were ill-founded. If Stella was going to marry Gervase surely something definite would be known about it by this time. She was not so young that she could afford to wait indefinitely. But against this he knew that Gervase was scarcely twenty-one, and that neither of them had a penny. A long, public engagement would be difficult for many reasons. There might be some secret understanding. His brother still spent most of his Sundays at Vinehall ... better not deceive himself with the idea that he went merely for devotional reasons, to gratify this newly-formed taste which to Peter smacked as unseemly as an appetite. No, he went to see Stella, sit with her, talk with her ... kiss her, hold her on his knee, feel the softness of her hair between his fingers ... oh damn! if only he knew definitely one way or the other, he could choke down his imagination.... His imagination was making a hopeless fool of him with its strokings and its kisses—with its John, Peter, George and Gervase....

His uneasiness finally drove him to take what a little earlier would have seemed an impossible way out of his difficulties. One day, at the end of the brooding of a lonely walk, he met Stella unexpectedly in Icklesham street, and after the inevitable platitudes of greeting followed the first wild plunges of his mind.

"I say, Stella—forgive my asking you—but am I to congratulate you and Gervase?"

The colour rushed over her face, and he had an uneasy moment, wondering whether he had guessed right or merely been impertinent.

"No—you'll never have to do that," she answered firmly the next minute.

"I—I beg your pardon."

He was flushing too, partly with relief, partly with apprehension at the rejoiced, violent beating of his heart.

"Oh, it doesn't matter a bit. Other members of your family have been half-asking—hinting ... so I'd rather you asked outright. Of course, seeing that I'm seven years older than Gervase, one would have thought ... but I suppose people must have something to talk about."

He assented weakly—and it suddenly struck him that she was wondering why he had asked her instead of Gervase.

"As a matter of fact," she continued, "I don't see so much of him as people think. He comes over to us on Sundays, but that's partly for Father Luce. He serves the Parish Mass, and they both have lunch with us afterwards—and in the afternoon he helps with the children."

Peter felt inexpressibly relieved that there was no truth in his picture of Gervase and Stella in the afternoon—no kisses, no strokings of her hair, which was like fine silk between your fingers ... like a child's hair.... Fresh and bright and living as ever, it curled up under the brim of her hat ... he wondered if she saw how he was staring at it—yes, she must, for she put up her hand rather nervously and pushed a curl under the straw.

"Please contradict anything you hear said about him and me," she said.

"Yes, I promise I will. It was Vera put it into my head. She said she was quite sure Gervase was in love with you."

"Well, please contradict it—it will be annoying for Gervase as well as for me."

A sudden fear seized Peter—a new fear—much more unreasonable and selfish than the old one. It expressed itself with the same suddenness as it came, and before he could check himself he had said—

"Stella ... there isn't ... there isn't anyone else?"

He knew that moment that he had given himself away, and he could not find comfort in any thought of her not having noticed. For a few seconds she stared at him silently with her bright perplexed eyes. Then she said—

"No, there isn't.... But, Peter, why shouldn't there be?"

He murmured something silly and surly—he was annoyed with her for not tactfully turning the conversation and covering his blunder.

"I'm nearly twenty-eight," she continued—"and if I can manage to fall in love, I shall marry."

"Oh, don't wait for that," he said, still angry—"you can marry perfectly well without it. I have, and it's been most successful."

He knew that he had hurt her in the soft places of her heart; and with his knowledge a fire kindled, setting strange hot cruelties ablaze.

"Besides, it's easy enough to fall in love, you know—I've done it lots of times, and so have you, I expect—easy enough to fall in love and just as easy to fall out."

She answered him sweetly.

"Oh, I can do both—I've done both—but it's not been easy, not a bit."

"Well, I'll wish you luck."

He took off his hat and passed on. For a quarter of a mile he hated her. He hated her because he had wounded her, and because she would not be proud enough to hide the wound—because from outside his life she still troubled it—because he had lied to her—because he had treated her badly—because he had once loved her and because he had denied it—because he loved her still and could not deny it any more.

§11

He was so busy hating and loving her that he did not notice the large car that passed him at the cross roads till he heard it slithering to a stop. Then he looked up and saw it was his mother's. Jenny stuck her head out of the window.

"Hullo, Peter! Like a lift home?"

"No thanks, I'm not going home. I've got to call at Fourhouses."

"Haven't you finished that dreadful business yet?" asked Lady Alard in a tragic voice. The selling of thirty acres to the farm which had originally owned them struck her as the deepest humiliation the family had had yet to swallow.

"Yes—the agreement's been signed, but there's a few minor matters cropped up over the transfer."

"Why don't you make him come and see you? Why should

you walk six miles across country to interview a man like Godfrey?"

"Because I wanted a walk," said Peter shortly.

"You've got terribly restless lately. This is the second time I've met you tramping about like a—like a—"

"I call it very sensible of him," said Jenny—"we're a lazy lot—rolling about in cars. I've half a mind to get down and walk with him."

"But he's going to Fourhouses, dear."

"Never mind—I'd like to see Fourhouses."

"Your shoes are too thin for walking."

"Not on a day like this."

Peter opened the door—he was anxious for Jenny's company, she would take his thoughts off recent complications. He helped her out, and signed to Appleby to drive on.

"We've been paying calls in Winchelsea," said Jenny with a grimace—"Oh, Peter, this is a dog's life."

Peter would not have liked himself to spend an afternoon paying calls, but he regarded it as part of a woman's duty, and rather disapproved of Jenny's rebellion. He liked her, and admired her for her young well-bred loveliness, but lately he had begun to think she was getting too like Gervase....

"Somebody must pay calls," he said a little gruffly.

"Why?" asked Jenny.

"Don't be silly, my dear. You know it's a social necessity."

"Well, it oughtn't to be—just knowing a lot of dull people because they live in the same neighbourhood and are of the same social standing as ourselves—keeping up our intercourse by means of perfunctory visits which we hate paying as much as they hate receiving ... carefully dodging the tea-hour, so that there'll be no chance of any real hospitality...."

"So that's how you choose to describe it—"

"That's how it is."

Peter said nothing. He told himself emphatically that Stella probably had exactly the same ideas. Now Vera, for all her intellect and modernity, never shirked her social obligations. Oh, he had done right, after all.

Jenny was enjoying the walk, in spite of her thin shoes and the gruffness of her companion—in spite of some feelings of trepidation at her own recklessness. She was going to see Godfrey again after an interval of nearly two months ... she was going to see him through her own deliberate choice and contrivance. Directly Peter had mentioned Fourhouses she had made up her mind to go with him. If Godfrey's attraction had not been merely good health and good looks, but his character, his circumstances, she would know more of her own feelings when she saw him in his proper setting, against the background of Fourhouses. His background at present was her own revolt against the conditions of her life—for two months she had seen him standing like a symbolic figure of emancipation among the conventions, restrictions and sacrifices which her position demanded. Life had been very hard for her during those months, or perhaps not so hard as heavy. She had missed the habit of her relation to Jim Parish and felt the humiliation of its breaking off—the humiliation of meeting him casually as he dangled after an heiress....
"He'll do like Peter—he'll make himself fall in love with a girl with money and live happy ever afterwards." She had felt the galling pettiness of the social round, the hollowness of the disguises which her family had adopted, the falseness of the standards which they had set up. "We must at all costs have as many acres of land as we can keep together—we must

have our car and our menservants—our position as a 'county family.' We call ourselves the New Poor, though we have
all these. But we're not lying, because in order to keep them
we've given up all the really good things of life—comfort and
tranquillity and freedom and love. So we're Poor indeed."

She was frankly curious to see the home of the man
whose values were not upside down, who had not sacrificed
essentials to appearances, who found his pleasure in common things, who, poorer than the poverty of Alard, yet called
himself rich. Godfrey had captured her imagination, first no
doubt through his virile attraction, but maintaining his hold
through the contrast of her brief glimpse of him with the life
that was daily disappointing her. She asked Peter one or two
questions about Fourhouses. It ran to about four hundred
acres, mostly pasture. Godfrey grew wheat, as well as con-
servatively maintaining his hop-gardens, but the strength of
the farm was in live-stock. His father had died twelve years
ago, leaving the place in surprisingly good condition for those
days of rampant free trade—he had a mother and two sisters
living with him, Peter believed. Yes, he had always liked Godfrey, a sober, steady, practical fellow, who had done well for
himself and his farm.

§12

Fourhouses showed plainly the origin of its name. The original dwelling-house was a sturdy, square structure to which
some far-back yeoman had added a gabled wing. An inher-
itor had added another wing, and a third had incorporated
one of the barns—the result was many sprawling inequalities
of roof and wall. No one seemed to have thought about the

building as a whole, intent only on his own improvements, so that the very materials as well as the style of its construction were diverse—brick, tile, stone, timber—Tudor austerity, Elizabethan ornament, Georgian convention.

There was no one about in the yard, so Peter walked up to the front door and rang the bell. It was answered by a pretty, shy young woman whose pleasant gown was covered by an apron.

"Good afternoon, Miss Godfrey. Is your brother in?"

"Yes, Mr. Alard. If you'll step into the parlour I'll tell him you're here."

Jenny glanced at Peter, asking silently for an introduction. But her brother seemed abstracted, and forgot the courtesy he had practised at Starvecrow.

The young woman ushered them into a little stuffy room beside the door. There was a table in the middle of it covered by a thick velvet cloth, in the midst of which some musky plant was enthroned in a painted pot. There were more plants in the window, their leaves obscuring the daylight, which came through them like green water oozing through reeds. Jenny felt a pang of disappointment. This little room which was evidently considered the household's best showed her with a sharp check the essential difference between Alard and Godfrey. Here was a worse difference than between rough and smooth, coarse and delicate, vulgar and refined—it was all the difference between good taste and bad taste. Ben Godfrey's best clothes would be like this parlour—he would look far more remote from her in them than he looked in his broad cloth and gaiters.

Fortunately he was not wearing his best clothes when he

came in a few minutes later. He came stooping under the low door, all the haymaking's brown on his face since their last meeting.

"Well, this is good of you, Mr. Alard, coming all this way. Why didn't you send me a line to call around at Starvecrow? Good evening, Miss Alard—have you walked all the way from Conster too?"

"Oh no, I drove as far as Icklesham. The car's making me lazy."

"Well, you've had a good walk anyway. Won't you come in and have a cup of tea? We're just sitting down to it."

It was six o clock and neither Peter nor Jenny had remembered that there were human beings who took tea at this hour.

"Thank you so much," said Jenny—"I'll be glad." She had had her tea at Conster before leaving to pay the calls, but she said to herself "If I go in now and see them all having six o clock tea together, it'll finish it." Since she had seen the parlour she had thought it would be a good job if she finished it.

Godfrey led the way down a flagged passage into the oldest part of the house. The room where his family were having tea had evidently once been a kitchen, but was now no longer used as such, though the fireplace and cupboards remained. The floor was covered with brick, and the walls bulged in and out of huge beams, evidently ship's timber and riddled with the salt that had once caked them. Similar beams lay across the ceiling and curved into the wall, showing their origin in a ship's ribs—some Tudor seafarer had settled down ashore and built his ship into his house. Long casement windows let in the fullness of the evening sun, raking over the fields from

Snowden in the west—its light spilled on the cloth, on the blue and white cups, on the loaf and the black teapot, on the pleasant faces and broad backs of the women sitting round.

"This is my mother—Miss Alard; and my sister Jane, and my sister Lily...." He performed his introductions shyly.

The women stood up and shook hands—Jane Godfrey found a chair for Jenny, and Mrs. Godfrey poured her out a cup of very strong tea. There was a moment's constraint and some remarks about the weather but soon an easier atmosphere prevailed. This was partly due to Peter, who was always at his best with those who were not socially his equals. Jenny had often noticed how charming and friendly he was with his father's tenants and the village people, whereas with his own class he was often gruff and inarticulate. She knew that this was not due to any democratic tastes, but simply to the special effort which his code and tradition demanded of him on such occasions. She had never realised so plainly the advantages of birth and breeding, as when at such times she saw her unsociable brother exert himself, not to patronage but to perfect ease.

She herself found very little to say—she was too busy observing her surroundings. The "best parlour" atmosphere had entirely vanished—the contrast which the kitchen at Fourhouses presented with the drawing-room at Conster was all in the former's favour. She found a comfort, dignity and ease which were absent from the Alard ceremonial of afternoon tea, in spite of Wills and the Sevres china. Whether it was the free spill of the sunshine on table and floor, the solid, simple look of the furniture, the wonder of the old ship's beams, or the sweet unhurried manners of the company, she could

not say, but the whole effect was safe and soothing—there
was an air of quiet enjoyment, of emphasis on the fact that
a good meal eaten in good company was a source of pleasure
and congratulation to all concerned.

She ate a substantial tea of bread and butter and lettuce,
listening while Peter and Ben Godfrey talked post-war politics, now and then responding to a shy word from one of the
Godfrey women. She was reluctant to praise what she saw
around her, to comment on the charm and dignity of the
house, for fear she should seem to patronise—but a remark
ventured on its age found Mrs. Godfrey eager to talk of her
home and able to tell much of its history. After tea she offered to show Jenny the upstairs rooms.

"This is a fine old house, I've been told. The other day a
gentleman came over from Rye on purpose to see it."

They walked up and down a number of small twisting
passages, broken with steps and wanting light. Rooms led in-
conveniently out of one another—windows were high under
the ceiling or plumb with the floor. There was a great deal of
what was really good and lovely—old timber-work, old cupboards, a fine dresser, a gate-legged table and a couple of tall
boys and a great deal that recalled the best parlour, the iron
bedsteads, marble-topped washstands, flower-painted mir-
rors and garlanded wall-paper of the new rural tradition. All,
however, was good of its kind, comfortable and in sound repair. Mrs. Godfrey was proud of it all equally.

"But I suppose, Miss Alard, you don't find it much of a
house compared to your own."

"I think it's lovely," said Jenny—"much more exciting than
Conster."

Mrs. Godfrey was not sure whether a house had any right to be exciting, so she made no reply. They went downstairs again, and fearing the best parlour, Jenny suggested that they should go out into the yard and find the men.

"They must have finished their business by now."

"They'll be in Ben's office—leastways in what he calls his office," said Mrs. Godfrey with a small tolerant laugh.

She led the way into one of the barns where a corner was boarded off into a little room. Here stood a second-hand roll-topped desk and a really good yew-backed chair. The walls were covered with scale-maps of the district and advertisements for cattle food, very much after the style of the office at Starvecrow. Jenny looked round for some individual mark of Ben, but saw none, unless the straightness and order of it all were an index to his character.

"He'll be showing Mr. Alard the stock—he's proud of his stock," said Mrs. Godfrey, and sure enough the next minute they heard voices in the yard, and saw Godfrey and Peter coming out of the cow-shed.

"Here you are," cried Peter to his sister—"I want you to look at Mr. Godfrey's Sussex cattle. He's got the finest I've seen in the district."

Jenny could not speak for a moment. She had seen a look in Godfrey's eyes when they fell on her that deprived her of speech. Her heart was violently turned to the man from his surroundings in which she had sought a refuge for her self-respect—Fourhouses, its beauties and its uglinesses, became dim, and she saw only what she had seen at first and been ashamed of—the man whom she could—whom she must—love.

§13

Having tea at Fourhouses had not "finished it"; and she was glad, in spite of the best parlour. The Godfreys' life might be woefully lacking in ornament, but she had seen enough to know that it was sound in fundamentals. Here was the house built on a rock, lacking style perhaps, but standing firm against the storms—while Alard was the house built on the sand, the sand of a crumbled and obsolete tradition, still lovely as it faced the lightning with its towers, but with its whole structure shaken by the world's unrest.

She did not take in many impressions of her last few minutes at the farm. The outhouses and stables, tools and stock, were only a part of this bewildered turning of herself. They scarcely seemed outside her, but merged into the chaotic thought processes which her mind was slowly shaking into order. A quarter of an hour later she found herself walking with Peter along the road that winds at the back of Icklesham mill....

"Uncommon good sort of people, those Godfreys," her brother was saying.

"Yes, I liked them very much."

"I think there's no class in England to equal the old-fashioned yeoman farmer. I'd be sorry to see him die out."

"Do you think he will die out?"

"Well—land is always getting more and more of a problem. There aren't many who can keep things up as well as Godfrey. He's had the sense to go for livestock—it's the only thing that pays nowadays. Of course the farmers are better off than we are—they aren't hit the same way by taxation. But rates are high, and labour's dear and damn bad. I really don't know what's going to become of the land, but I think the yeoman will last longer than the Squire. Government supports him, and won't do a thing for us."

Jenny said nothing. She felt unequal to a discussion in her present mood.

"I envy Godfrey in a lot of ways," continued Peter—"He's been able to do for his place things that would save ours if only we could afford them. He's broken fifteen acres of marsh by the Brede River and gets nine bushels to the acre. Then you saw his cattle.... Something to be proud of there. If we could only go in for cattle-breeding on a large scale we might get the farms to pay."

"I like the way they live," said Jenny—"they seem so quiet and solid—so—so without a struggle."

"Oh, Godfrey must be pretty well off, I suppose. I don't know how he's made his money—I expect his father did it for him. But he paid us cash down for the land, and doesn't seem to feel it."

"I don't suppose they're better off than we are. It's simply that they aren't in the mess we're in—and they haven't got to keep up appearances. They're free, so they're contented."

Peter evidently suspected a fling at Alard in this speech, for he answered gravely.

"All the same, it's up to us to stand by our own class. I daresay the Godfreys are happier and more comfortable than we are, but we can't ever be like them. We can't shelve our responsibilities. We've got a tradition as old as theirs, and we have to stick to it, even if at present it seems to be going under. Personally I'm proud of it."

Again Jenny felt herself unable to argue, to tell Peter, as Gervase would have done, that what he called responsibilities were only encumbrances, that what he called tradition was only a false standard. Instead she was acutely conscious of her disloyalty to her people's cause, of how near she stood to betraying it.

She had not quite realised this before, she had not grasped the full implications of the inward movements of her heart. She had seen herself first, in bitter shame, as a young woman whose sexual consciousness had been stirred by a young man of a lower class; then she had seen herself as enticed not merely by his health and comeliness but by his happy independence, his freedom from the shackles that bound her—till at last he had become a symbol of the life outside the Alard tradition, of the open country beyond the Alard estate, a contrast to all that was petty, arbitrary and artificial in her surroundings. And now, this evening, at Fourhouses, she had met the man again, and met him without shame. She knew now that she was attracted to him not merely in spite of his class but because of it—because he belonged to the honourable class of the land's freemen. He appealed to her as a man, speaking to her with his eyes the language that is common to all men, and he appealed to her as a freeman, because she knew that if she went to him she would be free—free of all the numberless restrictions and distresses that bound her youth.

The problem before her now was not whether she should be ashamed or not ashamed of his attraction, but whether she should yield to it or turn away. She faced these new thoughts during the rest of her walk with Peter, between the dry, abstracted phrases of her conversation—during dinner and the long dreary evening of cards and desultory talk—and at last, in greater peace, when she had gone to bed and lay watching the grey moonlight that moved among the trees of the plantation.

What was she to do? What had she done? Had she fallen in love with Godfrey? Was she going to tear her life out of its groove and merge it with his, just on the strength of those three meetings? She did not know—she was not sure. She could not be in love yet, but she felt sure that she was going to be. At least so she should have said if he had been a man of her own class. Then why should she act any differently because he was not? Her defiance grew. Godfrey's class was a good class—his family was old, substantial and respected. It was silly and snobbish to talk as if he belonged to some menial order—though, hang it all, any order was better than the order of impoverished country families to which she belonged.

Resentfully Jenny surveyed her tribe. She saw the great families of the Kent and Sussex borders struggling to show the world the same front that they had shown before they were shaken. She saw them failing in that struggle one by one—here a great house was closed, and for sale, with no buyers because of its unwieldy vastness and long disrepair—here another was shorn of its estate—stripped off it in building plots and small holdings—yet another had lost its freedom in mortgages, and kept its acres only at the price of being bound to their ruin. There was no need for Gervase to tell that the Squires, having outlived their day, were going under—her broken romance with Jim Parish had shown her that. She had realised then that it was not likely that she would ever marry into her own class. The young men who were her friends and associates in the life of the county must marry wealth. Peter had gone outside the county and married money—she too one day would have to go outside and marry money— or marry where money did not matter. The days were gone when Manor mated with Manor and Grange with Grange— mighty alliances like the marriages of Kings. Nowadays, just as Kings could no longer mate with the blood royal but sought consorts among their subjects, so the Squires must seek their wives outside the strict circle of the "county"— and not even in the professional classes, which were nearly as hard-hit as themselves, but in the classes of aspiring trade, nouveaux-riches, war-profiteers....

Jenny grimaced—yet, after all, what else was there to do? Remain a spinster like Doris, or induce some hot-blooded heir of impoverished acres to forget them in a moment of romance, from which he would wake one day to reproach her.... No, she would have to be like the rest and marry outside the tribe. But since she must go out, why shouldn't she go out in the direction she chose? Why was it very right and proper to marry into trade as long as it is wealthy, and somehow all wrong if it is not? Why was Peter without reproach for marrying Vera Asher, whose grandfather had kept a clothes-mart in the city, while she would never be forgiven if she married Ben Godfrey, whose grandfather, with his father and fathers before him, had been a yeoman farmer of ancient land?

The answer of course was plain, and she must not be cynical in giving it. If she acknowledged that the excuse was money she must also acknowledge that it was money for the family's sake—money to keep the family alive, to save its estates from dispersal and its roof from strangers. These men and women married into a class beneath them to save their families. But if they did so to save their families, why shouldn't she do so to save herself? Why was there always this talk of the group, the tribe, the clan, while the individual was sacrificed and pushed under? Both she and Jim Parish had been sacrificed to his family.... Doris had been sacrificed to hers ... and there was Mary, sacrificed to the family's good name, escaping, it is true, at the last, but not till after her wings had been broken ... there was Peter, marrying a rich woman and becoming dull and stuffy and precise in consequence. Only Gervase so far had not been sacrificed—probably he would never be, for he had already chosen his escape. And she—she now had her chance ... but she did not know if she would take it.

Lying there in the white break of the dawn, her mind strung with sleeplessness, she faced the danger. If she did not escape Alard would have her—she would have to offer herself to it either as Doris had offered herself or as Peter had offered himself.... Why should she? Why should she sacrifice her youth to prop its age—an age which must inevitably end in death. "Things can't go on much longer—it's only a question of putting off the end." If the house was bound to fall, why should she be buried in the ruins?... She had a momentary pang—for she knew that Peter had great schemes for Alard, great dreams for it—that he hoped to save it and give it back, even in the midst of the world's shaking, some of its former greatness. But she could not help that. For Peter the family might be the biggest thing in life—for her it was not, and she would be betraying the best of herself if she did not put it second to other things. What she wanted most in the world was love—love, peace, settlement, the beauty of content ... these no one but Ben Godfrey could give her.

The sky was faintly pink behind the firs. A single bird's note dropped into the still air. She heard a movement in the room next to hers—she and Gervase still slept at the top of the house in the two little rooms they had had as girl and boy. Her brother was getting up—first, she knew, to serve the altar at Vinehall, then to drive away over the Kentish hills to his work among bolts and screws and nuts and rods and grease ... there is more than one way out of the City of Destruction.

§14

After that she must have slept, for when she next opened her eyes she had made up her mind. Jenny was not naturally ir-resolute but she was diffident, and this problem of escape was the biggest she had ever had to tackle. However, sleep had straightened out the twisted workings of her thought—the way was clear at last.

She sprang out of bed, alive with a glowing sense of de-termination. She knew that she had a great deal to plan and to do. This love affair, apart from its significance, was entirely different from any other she had had. Her intuition told her that she would have to make the openings, carry on all the initial stages of the wooing. She would have to show Godfrey that she cared, or his modesty would make him hang back. In common language she would have to "make the running." Rather to her surprise, she found that she enjoyed the pros-pect. She remembered once being a little shocked by Stella

Mount, who had confided that she liked making love herself just as much as being made love to.... Well, Jenny was not exactly going to make love, but she was going to do something just as forward, just as far from the code of well-bred people—she was going to show a man in a class beneath her that she cared for him, that she wanted his admiration, his courtship....

She hurried over her bath and dressing, urged by the conviction that she must act, take irretraceable steps, before she had time to think again. She had already thought enough—more thought would only muddle her, wrap her in clouds. Action would make things clearer than any amount of reflection. She would go over to Fourhouses—a litter of collie-pups she had confusedly admired the day before would give her an excuse for a visit, an excuse which would yet be frail enough to show that it alone had not brought her there.

She was the first at breakfast that morning, and hoped that no one else would come down while she was in the room. Her father was generally the earliest, but today she did not hear his footstep till she was leaving the table. There were two doors out of the breakfast room, and Jenny vanished guiltily through one as Sir John came in at the other. She was ashamed of herself for such Palais Royal tactics, but felt she would stoop to them rather than risk having her resolution scotched by the sight of her father.

She had decided to go on foot to Fourhouses—not only would it mean a more unobtrusive departure from Conster, but it would show Godfrey her determination. The purchase of a puppy she had scarcely noticed the day before was a flimsy excuse for walking five miles across country the first thing next morning. He would be bound to see at least part of its significance—and she had known and appraised enough men to realise that his was the warm, ready type which does not have to see the whole road clear before it advances.

The early day was warm; a thick haze clotted the air, which was full of the scents of grass and dust, of the meadowsweet and the drying hay. The little lanes were already stuffy with sunshine, and before Jenny had come to Brede she realised that the light tweed suit she had put on was too heavy, and her summer-felt hat was making a band of moisture round her head, so that her hair lay draggled on her brows. She took off her coat and slung it over her arm ... phew! how airless this part of the country was, with its old, old lanes, trodden by a hundred generations of hobnails to the depth of fosses ... when she was across the marsh with its trickery of dykes she would leave the road and take to the fields. The way had not seemed so long yesterday in the cool of the evening.... What would Peter say if he could see her now?—Poor old Peter! It would be dreadful for him if she carried out her scheme. He felt about things more strongly than anyone.... She was sorry for Peter.

Then she wondered what Godfrey would think when he saw her, arriving hot and tired and breathless, with her trumped up excuse for seeing him again. Would he despise her?—Perhaps, after all, he did not particularly care about her—she was a fool to be so sure that he did. He probably had that slow, admiring way with all women. Besides, it's ridiculous to go by the look in a man's eyes ... silly ... schoolgirlish ... novel-read-ing-old-maidish ... she was losing her balance in her hatred of things. She would probably find out that he was in love with

some girl of his own class.... Her heart beat painfully at such
an idea and her ridiculous mind denied it, but she knew that
her mind was only obeying her heart.

... Or he might fail to see anything significant in her
coming. He probably had one of those slow-moving country
brains on which everything is lost but the direct hit. He most
likely was a dull dog ... and she had thought he could make
her happy—Jenny Alard, with her quick mind, high breeding
and specialised education. Her longing to escape had driven
her into fancying herself in love. All she wanted was to get
away from home—and this door stood open. Beyond it she
might find even worse restrictions and futilities than those
from which she fled.

She was losing heart, and almost lost purpose as well. She
stopped in the lane at the foot of Snailham hill, and looked
back towards the north. Conster was hidden behind the ridge
of Udimore but she was still on Alard ground—there was
Crouch's Farm beside the Brede River—and Little Float and
Cockmartin, both Alard farms—and all that green width of
marsh was Alard's, with its dotted sheep. She had a preposterous feeling that if she walked off the estate on to Godfrey's
land it would be too late to turn back ... if she was going back
she must go back now.

She stood in the pebbly marle, looking over the marsh
to the trees where Udimore church showed a hummock of
roof. She tried to examine herself, to find out in a few giddy seconds why she was going to Fourhouses. Was it simply
because she was tired of convention—of county shams—of
having to go without things she wanted in order to have
things she didn't want?—or was she in love with Ben God-

frey, and going to him in spite of the efforts of her class instinct to keep her back? She suddenly knew that the latter
was the only good reason. If it was true that she had fallen in
love with Godfrey the second time she had seen him—that
afternoon, weeks back, at Starvecrow—and if all this hatred
of Alard ways, this ramp against convention, was no genuine
revolt against either but just the effort of her mind to justify her heart—then she had better go forward. But if, on the
other hand, she really hated her life and was willing to take
any way of escape—particularly if her unrest was due to the
collapse of her affair with Jim Parish—if she was going to
Fourhouses only to escape from Conster—then she had better turn back.

She stood for a moment hesitating, her heels deep in the
silt of the lane, her eyes strained towards Udimore. Then a
footstep made her start and turn round. She had the confused
impression of a man and a gun, of a recognition and a greeting, all blurred together in the mists of her surprise. She had
not expected to meet him so far from his farm, right off his
own land ... she felt a quake of disappointment, too; for the
boundaries of the two estates had now a mysterious significance, and she was sorry that she had met him before she had
left Alard ground, before she had escaped.

"Good morning, Miss Alard. You've come a long way so
early."

"Yes; I was coming to Fourhouses—it struck me that you
might be willing to sell one of those collie pups you showed
me yesterday."

This was not how she had meant to speak. She knew her
voice was clipped and cold. Hang it! she might have man-

aged to break through the wall on this special occasion. First words are the most significant, and she had meant hers to have a more than ordinary warmth, instead of which they had a more than ordinary stiffness. But it was no good trying— she would never be able so to get rid of the traditions of her class and of her sex as to show this young man that she loved him ... if indeed she really did love him.

He was speaking now—she forced herself to listen to what he said.

"I'd never sell you one of those—they're not worth paying for. It's only I'm that soft-hearted I couldn't think of drowning them. I got rid of the last litter quite easily, just giving them away. So I'll be grateful if you'll accept one."

"Thank you—but I really couldn't allow—I mean ..."

"Won't you come up to the place and look at them? You'll see for yourself they're not much. I could let you have a really good retriever-pup later, but these collies—it's just my sister's Lizzie that one of our old men gave her years ago, and she's no particular breed, and the sire's their dog at Wickham."

"Thanks ever so much—but you're out with your gun, so I won't trouble you to turn back."

She wondered if he would make any explanation, offer some apology for carrying his gun over Alard fields. But he merely urged her again to come up to Fourhouses, and slack after her conflict, she gave way and turned with him.

"Are you bothered much with rabbits?" she asked as they walked up the hill. "We're simply over-run with them at Conster."

"They're pretty bad, especially now the corn's up. I generally take out my gun when I go round the place."

"But is this your land?—I thought I was still on ours."

"This is the land I have just bought from your father, Miss Alard. It was yours three months ago, but it belongs to Fourhouses now."

§15

Jenny had known before that love could make her superstitious—only under its influence had she occasionally respected the mascots, charms, black cats and other gods of the age, or yielded to the stronger, stranger influences of buried urgencies to touch and try.... But she was surprised at the sudden relief which she felt at Godfrey's words. She tried to reason herself out of the conviction that she had definitely crossed the frontier and could now never go back. She could not help feeling like one of those escaped prisoners of war she had sometimes read of during the last five years, who passed unaware the black and orange boundary posts of Holland, and, after hiding for hours from what they took for German sentries, found themselves at last confronted by the friendly Dutch guards. In vain she told herself that it made no difference whether she met Godfrey on land belonging to Conster or to Fourhouses—she was in the grip of something stronger than reason; she could not argue or scold herself out of her follies.

The answer to all her questionings was now pretty plain. She was coming to Fourhouses for the man, not for escape. No need of her own could have made a fool of her like this. She was not fancying herself in love with Ben Godfrey—she really loved him, attracted physically at first, no doubt, but as she advanced finding ever more and more solid reason for attachment. She wanted him, and why in the world shouldn't she have him?—if he had been rich, not even the lowest rank would have made him ineligible in her people's eyes. But because he was only "comfortable," only had enough to live on in peace and happiness and dignity, her family would be horrified at such an alliance—"a common farmer," she could hear them calling him, and her cheeks reddened angrily as she walked up the hill.

"Are you tired?" asked Godfrey—"let me carry your coat—it's a terrible hot day."

She let him relieve her, pleased at the accidental touch of his hand under the stuff. She wondered if he would say "I beg your pardon" as he had said the first time. But he was silent, indeed the whole of the way to Fourhouses he said very little, and she wondered if he was pondering her in his mind, perhaps asking himself why she had come, trying to argue away his surprise, telling himself it was just a lady's way to be impulsive and tramp five miles to buy a mongrel pup she had scarcely noticed the day before. Now and then his glance crept towards her, sweeping sideways from deepset blue eyes, under the fringe of dark lashes. She liked his eyes, because they were not the brown bovine eyes of the mixed race who had supplanted the original South Saxons, but the eyes of the Old People, who had been there before the Norman stirred French syllables into the home-brew of Sussex names. They were the eyes of her own people, though she herself had them not, and they would be the eyes of her children ... she felt the colour mounting again, but this time it was not the flush of indignation, and when next she felt his gaze upon her, her own was impelled to meet it. For the first time on that walk to Fourhouses their eyes met, and she saw that his face was as red as hers with the stain of a happy confusion.

When they came to the farm, he invited her in, saying that he would bring her the puppies. For a moment she saw him hesitate at the parlour door, but to her relief he passed on, leading the way to the kitchen.

"Mother, here's Miss Alard come again to see Lizzie's pups"—he ushered her in rather proudly, she thought, standing back against the door which he flung wide open.

· "You're welcome" said Mrs. Godfrey—"please sit down."

She was ironing at the table, but stopped to pull forward a chair to the window, which was open. There was no fire in this, the big outer room, but from a smaller one within came the sound of cracking wood and occasional bursts of singing.

"I'm afraid I've come at an awkward time," said Jenny.

"Oh, no—we're never too busy here—and Ben 'ull be proud to show you the little dogs, for all he makes out to look down on them, they being no sort of class and him a bit of a fancier as you might say. You've had a hot walk, Miss Alard— can I get you a drink of milk? It's been standing in the cool some while and 'ull refresh you."

Jenny was grateful and glad. Mrs. Godfrey fetched her the milk in a glass from the dairy, then went back to her ironing. She was a stout, middle-aged woman, bearing her years in a way that showed they had not been made heavy by too much work or too much childbearing. She could still show her good white teeth, and her hair had more gloss than grey in it. She talked comfortably about the weather and the hay-making till her son came back with the two most presentable of Lizzie's family.

"If you'll be kind enough to take one of these little chaps, Miss Alard...."

They spent twenty minutes or so over the puppies, and in the end Jenny made her choice and accepted his gift.

"He won't be ready to leave his mother for a week or two yet."

"I'll come back and fetch him."

"Won't you come before then?"

They were alone in the great kitchen—Mrs. Godfrey had gone into the inner room to heat her iron, and they stood between the table and the window, Jenny still holding the puppy in her arms. The moment stamped itself upon her memory like a seal. She would always remember that faint sweet scent of freshly ironed linen, that crack of a hidden fire, that slow ticking of a clock and Ben Godfrey's face before her, so brown, strong and alive, so lovable in its broad comeliness. The last of her reserve dropped from her—he ceased to be a problem, a choice, a stranger; he became just a fond, friendly man, and her heart went out to him as to a lover, forgetting all besides.

"Yes, of course I'll come"—she said gently—"whenever you want me."

§16

The rest of that day did not seem quite real—perhaps because she would not let herself think of what she had done in the morning, what she had committed herself to. And when the day was over and she lay flat on her back in her bed, with the bedclothes up to her chin, the morning still seemed like something she had watched or dreamed rather than something she had lived.

She did not actually live till the next day at breakfast, when she turned over the letters beside her plate. Among them lay one in handwriting she did not know, small and laborious. She looked at the postmark and saw it was from Icklesham, and immediately found herself tingling and blushing. Her first impulse was to put it away and read it in solitude later on, but a contrary impulse made her open it at once—partly because she could not bear the suspense, and partly because she could not bear the shame of her own foolishness. Why should she be so sure it was from Fourhouses? Ben Godfrey was not the only person she knew in Icklesham ... though the only person she knew who was likely to write in that careful, half-educated hand.... Yes, it was from Fourhouses.

My dear Miss Alard,

I hope this letter finds you in the best of health, and I hope you will not think I am taking a liberty to ask if you could meet me by the Tillingham Bridge on the road from Brede Eye to Horns Cross next Thursday afternoon at three p.m. I have something very particular to say to you. Ever since you were kind enough to call this morning and said you would come back any time I wanted I have been thinking that perhaps you would like my freindship. Dear Miss Alard, I hope you do not think I am taking a liberty, and if you do not want my freindship perhaps you will kindly let me know. But ever since you came over with Mr. Peter Alard I thought perhaps you would like my freindship. I must not say any more. But I would like to talk to you on Thursday at three p.m. if you will meet me on the Tillingham Bridge by Dinglesden Farm. I think that is better than me coming to your house—["yes, I think so too," said Jenny]—and I should

be very much obliged if you would come. My dear Miss
Alard I hope you do not think I am taking a liberty on so
short an acquaintance, but I feel I should like to be your fre-
ind. If you would rather not have my freindship perhaps you
will kindly let me know. Having no more to say, I will now
draw to a close.

Yours sincerely,

BENJAMIN GODFREY

Jenny was half surprised to find herself choking with
laughter.

"Here I am, down to brass tacks," she thought to herself—
"I must put this letter with the best parlour and the Sunday
clothes" ... then suddenly, deep in her heart—"Oh, the darling! the darling!"

"Your letters seem to be amusing," said Doris from the
other end of the table.

"Yes, they are."

"I wish mine were. I never seem to get anything but bills.
I'm glad you're more lucky—though I expect it makes a difference not hearing from Jim."

"Oh, we never corresponded much—we met too often."

"It was always the other way round with me ... the piles of
letters I used to get.... I expect you remember."

Jenny could remember nothing but a fat letter which appeared every other day for about three weeks, from an Indian
civil servant who was presumptuous enough to think himself
fit to mate with Alard.

"Well, I've had my good times," continued Doris, "so
I oughtn't to grumble. Things seem to have been different
when I was your age. Either it was because there were more

men about, or"—she smiled reminiscently. "Anyhow, there weren't any gaps between. I put an end to it all a little while ago—I had to—one finds these things too wearing ... and I didn't want to go on like Ninon de l'Enclos—I don't think it's dignified."

"Perhaps not," said Jenny absently. She was wondering what Doris would say to her letter if she could see it.

After breakfast she took it up to the old schoolroom and read it again. This time it did not make her laugh. Rather, she felt inclined to cry. She thought of Ben Godfrey sitting at the kitchen table with a sheet of note-paper and a penny bottle of ink before him—she saw him wiping his forehead and biting his penholder—she saw him writing out the note over and over again because of the blots and smudges that would come. Yes, she must remember the debit side—that he was not always the splendid young man she saw walking over his fields or driving his trap. There were occasions on which he would appear common, loutish, ignorant.... But, and this was the change—she saw that she loved him all the better for these occasions—these betraying circumstances of letter writing, best parlour and best clothes, which seemed to strip him of his splendour and show him to her as something humble, pathetic and dear.

"Dear Mr. Godfrey," she said to herself—"I shall be very humbly grateful for your freindship ... and I can't imagine it spelt any other way."

She found it very difficult to answer the letter, as she was uncertain of the etiquette which ruled these occasions. Evidently one said little, but said it very often. In the end all she did was to write saying she would meet him on the Tillingham bridge, as he suggested. She thought it was rather rash of him to appoint a tryst on her father's land, but they could easily go off the road on to the marsh, where they were not likely to be seen.

She posted the letter herself in the box at the end of the drive, then gave herself up to another twenty-four hours' in reality of waiting.

§17

The next day was heavy with the threat of thunder. The ragged sky hung low over the trees, and clouds of dust blew down the lanes, through the aisles of the fennel. Jenny was exactly punctual at her tryst. She did not know whether or not he would expect to be kept waiting, but she had resolved to weigh this new adventure by no false standards of coquetry, and walked boldly on to Dinglesden bridge just as the thin chimes of Conster's stable-clock came across the fields.

He was nowhere in sight, but in a couple of minutes he appeared, riding this time on a big-boned brown horse, who swung him along at a slow, lurching pace. Evidently he had not expected to find her there before him.

Directly he caught sight of her he jerked the reins and finished the last hundred yards at a canter, pulling up beside her on the crest of the bridge.

"Good-day, Miss Alard. I hope I haven't kept you waiting."

She was pale with shyness. Hitherto she had never, under any circumstances, felt ill at ease with a man, but now she was incomprehensibly too shy to speak. He had dismounted, and was leading his horse towards the gate opening on the marsh by Dinglesden Farm. She found herself walking beside him.

"Bit thundery," he remarked—"maybe we'll have a storm."

"Do you think so?"

"I'm not sure—it may blow over. I hope it does, for I've still a couple of fields uncut."

"The hay's been good this year."

"Not so bad—but a bit stalky."

They were through the gate now, walking side by side over the grass-grown, heavy rutted track that leads past the barns of Dinglesden down the Tillingham marsh, between the river and the hop-gardens. Jenny was glad they were off the road—soon they would be out of sight of it. The hop-gardens that covered the slope and threw a steamy, drowsy scent into the heaviness of the day, would hide them completely from any-one who went by. She began to feel very much alone with Godfrey ... and still neither of them spoke. They had not spo-ken since they had left the road.

Only a few hundred yards brought them to the turn of the valley, where the Tillingham swings southward towards Rye. Behind them the farm and the bridge were shut out by the sloping hop-gardens, before them the marsh wound, a green street, between the sorrel-rusted meadows, with the Mock-steeple standing gaunt and solitary on the hill below Barline.

"It's very good of you to have come," said Ben.

"I—I wanted to come."

He checked his horse, and they stood still.

"You—you don't think it cheek—I mean, that I'm taking a liberty—in wanting to know you?"

"No...."

"When you came that evening to the farm, I—I wanted to say all sorts of things, and I didn't like ... for I didn't know...."

"I should like to be your friend."

Her voice came firmly at last.

"I should like to be your friend," she repeated.

She knew what the word "friend" meant in his ears. "My friend" was what a girl of his class would say when she meant "my lover."

"Well, then...."

He took her hand and blushed.

"Let's sit down for a bit," he said.

A stripped and fallen tree lay on the grass, and they sat down on it when he had hitched his horse to the fence of the hop-garden. Long hours seemed to roll by as they sat there side by side ... the sun came out for a moment or two, sending the shadow of the hop-bines racing over the ground. There was a pulse of thunder behind the meadows in the north. Then suddenly, for some unfathomable reason, Jenny began to cry.

At first he seemed paralysed with astonishment, while she leaned forward over her knees, sobbing uncontrollably. But the next moment his arms came round her, drawing her gently up against him, her cheek against his homespun coat that smelt of stables.

"My dear ... my little thing ... don't cry! What is it?—Are you unhappy? What have I done?"

She could not speak—she could only lift her face to his, trying to smile, trying to tell him with her streaming eyes that she was not unhappy, only silly, only tired. He seemed to understand, for he drew her closer, and she could feel his whole body trembling as he put his mouth shyly against hers.

One or two drops of rain splashed into the ruts, and a

moan of wind suddenly came through the hop-bines. He lifted his head, still trembling. He looked at her sidelong, as if
for a moment he expected her to be angry with him, to chide
his presumption. He would have taken away his arm, but she
held it about her.

"You'll get wet," he said reluctantly—"we should ought to
move."

"I don't care—I don't want to move. Let me stay like this."

"Then you aren't angry with me for—"

"Why should I be?"

"Well, we aren't long acquainted...."

§18

During the next two months Jenny grew sweetly familiar
with that strip of marsh between the hop-gardens and the
River Tillingham. The Mocksteeple, standing out on the hill
above the river's southward bend, had become one of many
joyful signs. Once more the drab, ridiculous thing looked
down on Alard loves, though now it was not a cynical Alard
Squire making sport of the country girls, but an Alard girl
tasting true love for the first time with a yeoman. Her earlier
love-affairs, even that latest one with Jim Parish, became thin,
frail things in comparison.

Godfrey was contemptuous of Jim.

"He couldn't have loved you, or he'd never have let you go.
He'd have let his place go first."

"Would you let Fourhouses go for me, Ben?"

"Reckon I would."

"Thank God you haven't got to choose."

"I'm sorry I haven't got to choose, for I'd like to show you."

"Well, I'm glad, for whichever way you chose it 'ud be hard for you."

"No—not hard."

"You don't know, because you're safe; you haven't even got to think of it. But I'm sorry for some of our men—yes, for Jim Parish, and even for Peter. You see, it's not merely choosing for themselves. They have their families to consider. You can't dish all your relations just because you want to get married."

Love was making her soft in judgment.

"No relation that had any heart would stand in the way of a young chap's marrying a good girl. My mother 'ud sooner turn out and live in a cottage than see me go without a wife."

"But would you turn your mother out, Ben?"

"We'd all go out together—for my wife."

His love-making was a delightful blend of diffidence and ardour. At first it had been difficult to show him that she was touchable, approachable to caresses. Yet once she had shown him the way, he had required no more leading. He had a warm, gentle nature, expressing itself naturally in fondness. His love for her seemed to consist in equal parts of passion and affection. It lacked the self-regarding element to which she was accustomed, and though it held all the eager qualities of fire, there was about it a simplicity and a shyness which were new to her. After a time she discovered that he had a mind like a young girl's, and an experience very nearly as white. He had spent his life in the society of animals and good women, and the animals had taught him to regard them not as symbols of license but as symbols of order, and the women had taught him that they were something more than animals. He had the fundamental cleanness of a man who takes nature naturally.

There had been another surprise for her, too, and this had lain in his attitude towards her position and her family. She discovered that his deference for her was entirely for her as a woman, and he had no particular respect for her as an Alard. His courtship would have been as diffident if she had been the daughter of the farmer of Glasseye or the farmer of Ellenwhorne. He was grateful to her for loving him, and infinitely careful of her love, as a privilege which might be withdrawn, but he saw no condescension in her loving him, no recklessness in her seeking him. Indeed, the only time she found a stiffness in him was when she told him that their love would have to be secret as far as her family was concerned. He had come to see her openly and innocently at Conster, and though luckily her people had been out, and she had been able to convey to the servants that he had only called on business, she had had to warn him that he must not come again.

"But why not?—I'm not ashamed of loving you."

"It isn't that, Ben."

"Nor ashamed of myself, neither."

"Oh, darling, can't you understand that it's because of my parents—what they'll think and say—and do, if they get the chance?"

"You mean they won't hold with us marrying?"

"No—they won't hold with it at all."

"I expect they'd like you to marry a lord."

"It isn't so much a lord that they want as someone with money."

"Well, I've got plenty of that, my lovely."

"Not what they'd call plenty—they want a really rich man, who'll be able to put us on our feet again."

"Reckon he'd be hard to find. You'd need fifty thousand to do that, I reckon."

Jenny nodded.

"Thank God," he said, "my land's free."

"You're lucky."

"It's only because I haven't bitten off more than I can chew, nor my father before me. That piece I bought from your father is the first that Fourhouses has bought for sixty years. We're not grand landlords, us. Maybe" ... he hesitated a moment ... "your father and mother 'ud think you were marrying beneath you to marry me. I reckon we're not gentry, and I was sent to the National School. But my folk have had Fourhouses two hundred years, and we've kept ourselves honest, for all that my grandfather married a gipsy. There was a lady I met on leave in Egypt asked me to marry her," he added naively, "and Lord! she was beautiful and had lovely gowns, and was a great man's widow. But I couldn't feel rightly towards her, so I declined the favour she would do me, but was honoured all the same. What are you laughing at, duck?"

"Not at you."

She realised that the war was probably in part responsible for his failure to see the barriers between them—its freedoms coupled with his own inherited consciousness of a good inheritance and an honest history. She was not sorry for this—it showed that he was aware of no maladjustments in their comradeship, in their tastes, views, thoughts, ideas, which now they exchanged freely. It made their courtship much more natural. All she feared was his resentment at her family's attitude.

But she found him unexpectedly mild on this point. His self-respect was solid and steady enough not to be shaken by what would have upset a man standing less securely. He was proud of his yeoman birth, his prosperous farm and free inheritance, and could laugh at the contempt of struggling, foundering Conster. Moreover, he loved Jenny, and, since she loved him, could forgive those who did not think him good enough for her. He agreed that their engagement should be kept from her people, though it was known to his, till she could find a proper time for disclosing it. Meanwhile they met either at Fourhouses, where the kindly, dignified welcome of his mother and sisters saved their love from any sordid touch of the clandestine, or else, nearer Jenny's home, at Brede Eye or the Mocksteeple.

As time went on she felt the necessity of taking at least one member of her family into her confidence—partly to make contrivance more easy, and partly as a help in the ultimate crisis which must come before long. Ben was slow in his methods, and did not belong to a class who made marriages in haste, but she knew that the last months of the year would probably be crucial. She would then have somehow to declare herself, and she saw the need for an ally.

Of course there was only Gervase. She knew that he alone was in the least likely to take her part; and in spite of her growing approach to Peter, she realised that it would be folly to turn to him now. He had married a girl whose grandfather Ben Godfrey's grandfather would have despised, nevertheless he would be horror-stricken at the marriage she proposed to make—he would talk as if she was marrying beneath her, as if she was making herself cheap and degrading her name. She could not bear it.... No, Peter would have to stay outside. Gervase was altogether different—he had accomplished his own revolt, and would encourage hers. Besides, he had always been her special brother, and though lately his new interests and long absences had a trifle estranged them, she knew she had only to turn to him to find their old alliance standing.

It was with this special decision that she came from the Mocksteeple one evening in September. She had told Ben that she meant to confide in Gervase, and he had agreed, though she knew that he too was sorry it could not be Peter. She felt the approach of relief—it would be a relief to have someone with whom she could discuss her difficulties, on whose occasional co-operation she could depend, and whose goodwill would support her during the catastrophic days of disclosure. Gervase seemed greater to her in all these capacities than he seemed to Ben. She knew that Ben thought him a mere boy, whose knowledge of their circumstances might, far from giving them support, actually lead to their confusion. But Jenny still had her queer new respect for Gervase. No doubt he was a hothead, a rather uncritical revolutionary; but his ideas seemed lately to have grown more stable; they seemed less ready-made, more the fruit of his own thinking. His contempt of his people's gods had no longer such a patent origin in youthful bumptiousness, but seemed rather due to the fact of his having built his own holy places. She wondered what had taught him wisdom—which of the new elements that had lately come into his life. Was it work, religion, love, or merely his growing older?

§19

She did not find an opportunity for speaking to him alone till after dinner. He went out, saying that he had some work to do at the garage, and as Rose Alard had dined at Conster and now made the fourth at bridge, Jenny was soon able to slip away after him.

She found him guiding an electric light bulb to and fro among the inward parts of the Ford. Gervase always did his own cleaning and repairs, which meant a lot of hard work, as the run to Ashford must be made every day, no matter how dirty the roads and the weather, and the lorry, which had long lost its youth when he first took it over, was now far advanced in unvenerable old age.

"Hullo, Jenny," he cried when he saw her—"so you've escaped from the dissipations of the drawing-room."

"Yes, Rose is playing tonight, thank heaven! and I've come out to talk to you."

"That's good. I'm sorry to be in this uncivilised place, but I can't help it. Henry Ford has appendicitis, and I must operate at once. He's got one wheel in the grave, I'm afraid, but with a little care and coddling I can make him last till I'm through with Ashford."

"When will that be?"

"Next January."

"And what will you do then?"

"Get some sort of a job, I suppose."

She thought he looked fagged and jaded, though it might have been the light, and the ugliness of his dirty blue slops buttoned up to his collarless chin. After all, now she came to think of it, he must have a pretty hard life—up every morning at six or earlier, driving fifteen miles to and fro in all weathers, working hard all day, and then coming home late, generally to finish the day with cleaning and repairs.

"Gervase," she said abruptly—"are you happy?"

"Yes, Jen—quite happy. Are you?"

"Oh, Gervase...."

He looked up at the change in her voice.

"I've something to tell you," she said hurriedly—"I'm going to be married."

"What! To Jim Parish?"

"Oh, no, not to him. That's all over. Gervase, I want you to stand by me; that's why I'm telling you this. I'm making a great venture. I'm marrying Ben Godfrey."

"Ben Godfrey...."

He repeated the name vaguely. Evidently it conveyed nothing to him. He was so much away that he heard little of the talk of the estate.

"Yes. The farmer of Fourhouses. Don't you know him? I've known him three months, and we love each other. Father and Mother and Peter and everyone will be wild when they know. That's why I want to have you on my side."

"Jenny, dear...." He carefully deposited Henry Ford's appendix on the shelf, wiped his oily fingers on a piece of rag, and came and sat beside her on the packing case where she had perched herself—"Jenny, dear, this is too exciting for words. Do tell me more about it."

Jenny told him as much as she could—how meeting Ben Godfrey had set her mind on a new adventure and a new revolt—how she had resolved not to let her chance slip by, but had let him know she cared—how eager and sweet his response had been, and how happy life was now, with meeting and love-making. Her manner, her looks, her hesitations told him as much as her words.

"You will stand by me, won't you, Gervase?"

"Of course I will, Jen. But do you mind if I ask you one or two questions?"

"Ask whatever you like. As you're going to help me, you've a right to know."

"Well, are you quite sure this is going to last?"

"My dear! I never thought you'd ask that."

"I daresay it sounds a silly and impertinent question. But I must ask it. Do you think he's pulled your heart away from your judgment? And do you think it's possible that you may have been driven towards him by reaction, the reaction from all that long, meandering, backboneless affair with Jim Parish, and all the silly, trivial things that did for it at last? Don't be angry with me. I must put that side of the question to you, or I'd never forgive myself."

"Do you think I've never put it to myself? Oh, Gervase, it was exactly what I thought at the beginning. I told myself it was only reaction—only because I was bored. But when I met him at Fourhouses I couldn't help seeing it was more than that, and now I know it's real—I know, I *know*."

"Have you tastes and ideas in common?"

"Yes, plenty. He has very much the same sort of abstract ideas as I have—thinks the same about the war and all that. And he's read, too—he loves Kipling, and Robert Service's poems, though he reads boys' books as well. He really has a better literary taste than I have—you know what Vera thinks of my reading. And he's travelled much more than I have, seen more of the world. He's been in Mesopotamia, and Egypt, and Greece, and France. And yet he's so simple and unassuming. He's much more of a 'gentleman' in his speech and manners than lots of men I know."

"Have you ever seen him in his Sunday clothes?"

"Yes, I have, and survived. He wears a ready-made brown suit with a white stripe in it. And that's the worst there is about him."

"What are his people like?"

"They're darlings. His mother is solid and comfortable and motherly, and the girls are about my own age, but with much better manners. When Ben and I are married, the others will live in a part of the house which is really quite separate from the rest—has a separate door and kitchen—the newest of the four houses. Oh, I tell you, Gervase, I've faced everything—tastes, ideas, family, Sunday clothes—and there's nothing that isn't worth having, or at least worth putting up with for the sake of the rest, for the sake of real comfort, real peace, real freedom, real love...."

Her eyes began to fill, and he felt her warm, sobbing breath on his cheek.

"Jenny, I want to kiss you. But I should have to make too many preparations first—take off my slops, wash my hands with soda, and clean my teeth, because I've been smoking woodbines all day. So I think I'd better put it off till Sunday. But I do congratulate you, dear—not only on being in love but on being so brave. I think you're brave, Jenny; it's so much more difficult for a woman to break away than for a man. But you'd never have found happiness in the family groove, and sometimes I was afraid that ... never mind, I'm not afraid now."

"And you'll stand by me, Gervase?"

"Of course I will. But you've got to show me the young man. I won't stand by an abstraction. I want to see if I like him as flesh and blood."

"I'll take you over to Fourhouses on Saturday afternoon. And I'm quite sure you'll like him."

"I've made up my mind to, so he'll be a pretty hopeless washout if I don't. I wonder that I haven't ever met him, but I expect it's being away so much."

Jenny was about to enlarge further on her young man's qualities, when she remembered that there is nothing more tiresome to an unprosperous lover than the rhapsodies of someone whose love is successful and satisfied. Gervase had loved Stella Mount for two years—everybody said so—but nothing seemed to have come of it. It must distress him to hear of her happiness which had come so quickly. She wondered if his worn, fagged look were perhaps less due to hardship than to some distress of his love. She was so happy that she could not bear to think of anyone being miserable, especially Gervase, whom, next to Ben, she loved better than all the world. She checked her outpourings, and took his grimy, oil-stained hand in hers, laying it gently in her satin lap.

"Kid—do tell me. How are things between you and Stella?"

"There aren't any 'things' between me and Stella."

"Oh, Gervase, don't tell me you're not in love with her."

"I won't tell you anything so silly. Of course I'm in love with her, but it's not a love that will ever give her to me. It can't."

"Why?"

"Because she doesn't care for me in that way. I don't suppose she thinks of me as anything but a boy."

"Doesn't she know you love her?"

"She may—I daresay she does. But I'm sure she doesn't love me."

"Have you ever asked her?"

"No."

"Well, then ... Gervase!"

"One can find out that sort of thing without asking."

"Indeed one can't—not with a girl like Stella. If you didn't speak, she'd probably try very hard not to influence you in any way, because she realises that there *are* difficulties, and would be afraid of leading you further than you felt inclined."

"I haven't seen so very much of her lately. We never meet except on Sundays. I can't help thinking that she's trying to keep me at a distance."

"Perhaps she's surprised at your not speaking. How long have you been friends?"

"About three years, I suppose."

"And all that time people have been bracketing you together, and you've said nothing. I expect she's wondering why on earth you don't make love to her."

"I shouldn't dare."

"Not to Stella?—She seems to me a girl one could make love to very easily."

"I agree—once she'd said 'yes.' But she's a girl one couldn't take risks with—she'd be too easily lost. I've a feeling that if I made a move in that direction without being sure of her, she'd simply go away—fade out. And I'm terrified of losing the little I've got of her."

"But you may lose her through not being bold enough. It sickens a girl frightfully when a man hangs round and doesn't speak. The reason that she seems to avoid you now may be that she's offended."

"Jenny, you don't know Stella. She's so candid, so transparent, that if she had any such feelings about me, I'd be sure to see it. No, I think she stands away simply because she's found out that people are talking, and wants to keep me at a distance."

"But you can't be sure. You may be quite mistaken. If I was a man I'd never let things go by default like that. She won't 'fade out' if you do the thing properly. Women are always pleased to be asked in marriage—at least if they're human, and Stella's human if she's nothing else."

"And so am I. That's why I can't bear the thought of her saying 'no.'"

"I'll be surprised if she says 'no.' But anyhow I'd rather lose a good thing through its being refused me than through not having the spirit to ask for it."

"Yes, I think you're right there."

He fell into a kind of abstraction, stroking his chin with one hand, while the other still lay in her lap. Then he rose suddenly and went over to the shelf where he had put his tools.

"Well, I can't leave Henry Ford with his inside out while I talk about my own silly affairs. You may be right, Jen—I dunno. But I'm frightfully, ever so, glad about you—you dear."

"Thank you, Gervase. It's such a relief to have you on my side."

"When are you going to spring it on the family?"

"Oh, not just yet—not till Christmas, perhaps. We want to have everything settled first."

"I think you're wise."

"Remember, you're coming with me to Fourhouses on Saturday."

"Rather! That's part of the bargain. I must see the young man."

"And I'm sure you'll like him."

"I can very nearly promise to like him."

She went up to him and put her hands on his shoulders.

"Good night, old boy. I must be going in now—I suppose you're here till bed time?"

"And beyond—good night, Jenny."

"Gervase, you're getting thin—I can feel your bones."

"I'd be ashamed if you couldn't. And do run along—I've just had a vision of Wills carrying in the barley water tray. Clairvoyantly I can see him tripping over Mother's footstool, clairaudiently I can hear Father saying 'Damn you, Wills. Can't you look where you're going?'... Leave the busy surgeon now, there's a dear."

He stepped back from under her hands, and thoughtfully held up Henry Ford's appendix to the light.

§20

Jenny had made more impression than she knew on Gervase's ideas of Stella. Hitherto he had always tacitly accepted a tolerated position—she had allowed him to go for walks with her, to come and see her on Sundays, to write to her, to talk to her endlessly on the dull topic of himself; she had always been friendly, interested, patient, but he had felt that if she loved him she would not have been quite all these—not quite so kind or friendly or patient. And lately she had withdrawn herself—she had found herself too busy to go for walks, and in her father's house there was always the doctor or the priest. He respected and thought he understood her detachment.

People were "talking," as long ago they had "talked" about her and Peter, and she wanted this new, unfounded gossip to die.

Now it struck him that there was a chance that Jenny might be right, and that Stella fled before the gossip not because she wanted to disprove it, but because she wished it better founded, was perhaps a little vexed with him that it was not. Of course, if all these three years she had been wanting him to speak.... For the first time he saw a certain selfishness in his conduct—he was ashamed to realise that he had been content with his position as hopeless lover, so content that he had never given a thought to wondering if it pleased her. There had been a subtle self-indulgence in his silent devotion.... "Lord! I believe it's as bad as if I'd pestered her."

But he really could not believe that if Stella loved him he would not know it. One of her chief qualities was candour, and she was impulsive enough to make him think that she would readily give expression to any attraction that she felt. If Jenny, who was so much more cold and diffident, could have been quickened by love into taking the first step towards Ben Godfrey, how much more swiftly and decisively would ardent Stella move when her heart drove her. Of course she might see the drawbacks and dangers of marrying a man so much younger than herself—she might have held back for his sake ... perhaps that was why she was holding back now.... But he did not really think so—love was the last emotion that a nature like Stella's could hide, however resolute her will.

There seemed no way of solving his doubts but to do as Jenny suggested and to ask her. He shrank from putting his fate to the test.... But that was only part of this same selfishness he had discovered. By speaking, he could harm nobody but himself. He might indeed turn himself out of Paradise, that garden of hopeless loving service which was home to him now. But he could not hurt or offend Stella—she could not accuse him of precipitancy after three years—and if it was true that she cared, as might be just possible, then he would have put an end to a ridiculous and intolerable state of things.

In this indecision he went with Jenny to Fourhouses on Saturday. He did not talk to her about his own affairs—for hers were too engrossing for both of them. She was desperately anxious that he should like Ben Godfrey, not only because it would put their alliance on firm and intimate ground, but because she wanted her brother's friendship to apologise and atone to her lover for the slights of the rest of her family. As she grew in love for Ben and in experience of his worth she came fiercely and almost unreasonably to resent what she knew would be the attitude of her people towards him. She came more and more to see him from his own point of view—a man as good as Alard, and more honourably planted in the earth. She marvelled at herself now because she had once thought that she was stooping—she laughed at her scheme for holding out the sceptre.

But though she was anxious, she was not surprised that the two men should like each other. Ben Godfrey had all the qualities that Gervase admired, and young Alard was by this time quite without class consciousness, having lost even the negative kind which comes from conscientious socialism. He had had very little of congenial male society during the last two and a half years, as his work at Ashford had kept him chiefly among men with whom he had little in common. The farmer of Fourhouses belonged altogether to a different breed from the self-assertive young mechanics at Gillingham and Golightly's ... there was no need to warn Jenny here of fatal differences in the pursuit of wealth, women and God.

Gervase was very favourably impressed by all he saw, and came home a little envious of his sister. She had found a happiness which particularly appealed to him, for it was of both common and adventurous growth. She would be happy in the common homely things of life, and yet they would not be hers in quite the common way—she would hold them as an adventurer and a discoverer, for to win them she would have dared and perhaps suffered much.

That was how Gervase wanted happiness—with double roots in security and daring. He wondered if only the kingdom of heaven was happy in that way, and if he could not find homeliness and adventure together on earth. He did not want one without the other, he did not want peace with dullness, nor excitement with unrest. He had learned that the soul could know adventure with profoundest quiet— might not the body know it too? Walking home in the sunset from Fourhouses, Gervase longed for the resurrection of the body—for his body to know what his soul knew; and his heart told him that only Stella could give him this, and that if she would not, he must go without it.

§21

On Sunday mornings Gervase always went to see his mother before breakfast. It was to make up, he said, for seeing so little of her during the rest of the week. Lady Alard was subtly pleased and flattered by these visits. No one else ever paid them. He would sit on the bed and talk to her—not as the rest of the family talked, in a manner carefully adapted to her imbecility, but as one intelligent being to another, about politics and books and other things she could not understand. This pleased her all the more because he was careful to suggest her part of the conversation as well as carrying on his own; he never let her expose her ignorance. And though she secretly knew he was aware of it, and that he knew that she knew, the interview never failed to raise her in her own esteem, as a mother in whom her son confided.

This particular Sunday he stayed rather longer than usual, giving her the right attitude towards Queen Victoria, as to which she had always been a little uncertain. He had just been reading Lytton Strachey's *Life*, and they laughed together over the tartan upholstery of Balmoral, and shook their heads and wondered over John Brown. From John Brown the conversation somehow wandered to Gervase's work at Ashford, and finally ended in a discussion of the days not so very far ahead when he should have finished at the workshop and be his own master.

"What shall I do with myself then, Mother? Shall I open a garage in Leasan, so that you can sack Appleby and sell the car, and hire off me? Or would you like just to sack Appleby and let me drive the car? You'd find me most steady and reliable as a shuvver, and it would be such fun having tea with the maids when you went calling."

"I wish you'd taken up a more dignified profession. There really doesn't seem to be anything for you to do now that isn't rather low."

"I'm afraid I like doing low things, Mother. But I really don't know what I'm going to do when I leave Gillingham's. It's funny—but my life seems to stop at Christmas. I can't look any further. When I first went into the works I was always making plans for what I'd do when I came out of them. But now I can't think of anything. Well, anyhow, I've got more than three months yet—there'll be time to think of something before then. Did you know that I start my holiday next week?—Ten whole, giddy days—think of that!"

"Shall you be going away?"

"No, I don't think so. A man I was with at Winchester asked me to come and stop with his people. But he lives in Scotland, and I can't afford the journey. Besides it wouldn't be worth it just for a week."

"I thought you said you'd got ten days."

"Yes—but I'm going to spend four of them at Thunders Abbey near Brighton. Father Luce thought it would be a good idea if I went to a retreat."

"Oh, Gervase!—is it a monastery?"

"The very same. It's the chief house of the Order of Sacred Pity."

"But, my dear—are you—oh, you're not going to become a monk?"

"No fear—I'm just going into retreat for four days, for the good of my soul."

"Well, I don't know what a retreat is, but I feel it would do you much more good if you went to Scotland. You're looking quite white and seedy. Are you sure your heart's all right? You know we've got angina in the family. I've had it for years and years, and poor George died of it. I'm so afraid you've got it too."

"I haven't—honour bright. I'm looking white because I

want a holiday—and I'm going to have one—for both body and soul.... And now I really must go down to breakfast or I shan't be able to get more than my share of the kidneys."

Sunday breakfast was an important contrast with the breakfasts of the week. On week-days he either scrambled through a meal half-cooked by the kitchen-maid, or shared the dry short-commons of Father Luce's cottage. On Sundays he ate his way exultingly through porridge, bacon, kidneys, toast and honey, with generally three cups of coffee and a slice of melon. As a rule the family were all down together on Sunday, having no separate engagements, but an hour of united loafing before Appleby brought round the car to take to church such of them as felt inclined for it.

Gervase had to start earlier—directly breakfast was over. His Parish Mass was at half-past ten, in consideration for Vinehall's Sunday dinners, since there the rich and the poor were not separated into morning and evening congregations. Also he was Master of the Ceremonies, and had to be in the sacristy well before the service began, to make the usual preparations, and exhort and threaten the clumsy little servers, who came tumbling in at the last moment with their heads full of Saturday's football. Gervase was not a ritualist, and his aim was to achieve as casual an effect as possible, to create an atmosphere of homeliness and simplicity round the altar. But so far he had got no nearer his ideal than a hard-breathing concentration—the two torch-bearers gripped their torches as if they were to defend their lives with them, and the panting of the thurifer mingled with the racket of his cheap brass censer.

It was not till the sermon began that he had time to look

for Stella. When he had taken his seat in the Sanctuary with his arms folded, and had seen that the three little boys were also sitting with their arms folded instead of in more abandoned attitudes, he was free to search for her face through the incense-cloud that floated in the nave. He found her very soon, for a ray of golden, dusty sunshine fell upon her as she sat with her arm through Dr. Mount's. The sunshine had dredged all the warm brown and red tints out of her hair and face, giving her a queer white and golden look that made her unreal. As he looked at her, she smiled, and he found that her smile had come in response to a smile of his which had unknowingly stolen over his face as he watched her. Her smile was rather sad, and he wondered if the sadness too was a response.

Mr. Luce was delivering one of Newman's Parochial Sermons in his own halting words, and though Gervase always made it a point of discipline to listen to sermons, however much they bored him, he found that this morning attention was almost impossible. Stella seemed to fix his thoughts so that he could not drag them from her. He knew that his attitude towards her was changing—it was becoming more disturbed, more desperate. His heart must have been ready for this change, for he did not think that Jenny's words would have had power to work it of themselves. He wondered where it was leading him ... he wondered if it had anything to do with this feeling as of a ditch dug across his life at the end of the year.... But probably his leaving the works after Christmas would account for that. Well, anyhow, he would have to put an end to the present state of affairs—they were the result of mere selfishness and cowardice on his part. Perhaps he ought to go away—leave Stella altogether, since she did not love him and his heart was unquiet because of her ... he would have his chance to go away in January—right away.... But he could not—he could never bear to live away from her. And he had no certain knowledge that she did not love him—perhaps she did—perhaps Jenny was right after all.... "In the Name of the Father and of the Son and of the Holy Ghost. Amen."

§22

After Mass, Gervase and the Vicar walked together to Hollingrove.

"I've heard from Thunders Abbey," said Gervase to Luce, "and there's a vacancy for the eighteenth. So I shall go."

"I wonder how you'll like it."

"So do I. But I'm glad I'm going. They're full up really, but Father Lawrence said I could sleep at the farm."

"Then you'll have to get up early. It's fifteen minutes' walk from the Abbey, and Mass is at half-past six and of obligation."

"Never mind—I'm used to hardships, though I know you think I wallow in unseemly luxuries. But I'm getting keen on this, Father. Whether I like it or not, I know it will be exciting."

"Exciting! That's a nice thing to expect of a retreat."

"Well, religion generally is exciting, isn't it, so the more I get the more exciting it's likely to be."

"Um—too exciting perhaps."

"What do you mean, Father?"

But Luce would not tell him, and in another minute they

were at Dr. Mount's cottage, where they always had mid-day dinner on Sundays. It was cooked by Stella herself, helped by the little maid, so she did not appear till it was ready. She had changed her frock and bore no traces of her labours beyond a face heated by the fire. Her cheeks were flushed and her eyes bright—she looked absurdly young. How old was she, Gervase wondered? Twenty-eight or twenty-nine? But she did not look a bit over twenty. She did not look as old as he did. It must be her vitality which kept her young like this—her vitality ... and the way she did her hair. He smiled.

"What are you smiling at, Gervase?"

"At you, Stella."

"And why at me?"

"Because you look so absurdly young. And I've been very knowing, and have decided that it's the way you do your hair."

"Really, Gervase, you're not at all gallant. Surely I look young because I am young. If you think different you oughtn't to say so."

"This is a poor beginning for your career as a ladies' man," said Dr. Mount.

"Just as well he should start it on me," said Stella—"then he'll know the technique better by the time it really matters."

Her words stabbed Gervase—they showed him how he stood with her. She did not take him seriously—or if she did, she was trying to show him that it was all no use, that he must give up thinking of her. The result was that he thought of her with concentrated anxiety for the rest of the meal, his thoughts making him strangely silent.

He was not wanted at Catechism that afternoon, so he could spend it with her, and for the first time he found the privilege unwelcome. He remembered other Sunday afternoons when he had lain blissfully slack in one of the armchairs, while Stella curled herself up in the other with a book or some sewing. They had not talked consecutively, but just exchanged a few words now and then when the processes of their minds demanded it—it had all been heavenly and comfortable and serene.... He found himself longing almost angrily to be back in his old attitude of contented hopelessness. But he knew that he could never go back, though he did not exactly know why. What had happened that he could no longer find his peace in her unrewarded service? Had he suddenly grown up and become dependent on realities—no longer to be comforted with dreams or to taste the sweet sadness of youth?

He had half a mind to go for a walk this afternoon and leave her—he knew that she would not try to make him stay. But, in spite of all, he hankered after her company; also there was now growing up in him a new desire to come to grips with her, to know exactly where he stood—whether, though she did not want his love she still wanted his friendship, or whether she would like him to go away. So when Father Luce went off to his Catechism, and the doctor to see a couple of patients at Horns Cross, Gervase stayed behind in the sitting room where they had had their coffee, and asked Stella, according to custom, if she would mind his pipe.

"You know, Gervase, you're always allowed to smoke your pipe if I'm allowed to mend my stockings. Neither is exactly correct behaviour in a drawing-room, but if you dispense me from the rules of feminine good-breeding, I'll dispense you from the rules of masculine etiquette."

"Thank you."

He took out his pipe, and she fetched her work-basket from the back of the sofa. Nothing could have looked more domestic than the two of them sitting each side of the fire, he smoking, she darning, both silent. But the unreality of it vexed him this afternoon. He could not play the childish game he had sometimes played, of pretending they were married, and being content. "When I became a man I put away childish things...." He wanted to have the power to go over to her as she sat absorbed in her work, turn up her face and kiss her—or else pick her off the chair and set her on his knee....

"Stella," he said gruffly.

"Well?"

"I want to speak to you."

"What is it?"

"Well ... our friendship isn't the same as it used to be."

He would be furious if she contradicted him—or if she said, "Oh, really? I haven't noticed anything." But she said at once—

"I know it isn't."

"And what do you put that down to?"

She hedged for the first time.

"I don't know."

"You're trying to keep me at a distance."

She did not speak, but he saw the colour burning on the face that she bent hurriedly over her work.

He edged his chair closer, and repeated—

"Yes, you are, Stella—trying to keep me off."

"I—I'm sorry."

"You needn't be sorry; but I wish you'd tell me why you're

doing it. It isn't that you've only just discovered that I love you—you've always known that."

"I'm wasting your time, Gervase. I shouldn't keep you dangling after me."

"You mean that I've hung about too long?"

"Oh, no...." She was obviously distressed.

"Stella, I've loved you for years, and you know it—you've always known it. But I've never asked anything of you or expected anything. All I've wanted has been to see you and talk to you and do anything for you that I could. It hasn't done me any harm. I'm only just old enough to marry, and I have no means.... And up till a little while ago I was content. Then you changed, and seemed to be trying to put me off—it hurt me, Stella, because I couldn't think why...."

"Oh, I can't bear to hurt you." To his surprise he saw that her tears were falling. She covered her face.

"Stella, my little Stella."

By leaning forward he could put his hand on her knee. It was the first caress that he had ever given her, and the unbearable sweetness of it made him shiver. He let his hand lie for a few moments on her warm knee, and after a time she put her own over it.

"Gervase, I'm so sorry—I'm afraid I've treated you badly. I let you love me—you were so young at first, and I saw it made you happy, and I thought it would pass over. Then people began to talk, as they always do, and I took no notice—it seemed impossible, me being so much older than you—until I found that ... I mean, one day I met Peter, and he really thought we were engaged...."

It was not her words so much as the burst of bitter weeping that followed them which showed Gervase the real state of her heart. She still loved Peter.

"It's nothing to regret, dear," he said hurriedly—"you were perfectly right. And now I understand...."

"But it's wrong, Gervase, it's wrong...." By some instinct she seemed to have discovered that he guessed her secret ... "it's wrong; but oh, I can't help it! I wish I could. It seems dreadful not to be able to help it after all these years."

She had gripped his hand in both hers—her body was stiff and trembling.

"Stella, darling, don't be so upset. There's nothing wrong in loving—how could there be? Surely you know that."

"Yes I do. It's not the loving that's wrong, but letting my whole life be hung up by it. Letting it absorb me so that I don't notice other men, so that I can't bear the thought of marrying anyone else—so that I treat you badly."

"You haven't treated me badly, my dear. Get that out of your head at once."

"I have—because I've spoilt our friendship. I couldn't go on with it when I knew...."

"It's high time our friendship was spoilt, Stella. It was turning into a silly form of self-indulgence on my side, and it ought to be put an end to. Hang it all! why should I get you talked about?—apart from other considerations. You've done me good by withdrawing yourself, because you've killed my calf-love. For the last few weeks I've loved you as a man ought—I've known a man's love, though it's been in vain."

"Oh, Gervase...."

"Don't think any more about me, dear; you've done me nothing but good."

She had hidden her face in the arm of the chair, and he suddenly saw that he must leave her. Since she did not love him, his own love was not enough to make him less of an intruder. There were dozens of questions he wanted to ask her—answers he longed to know. But he must not. He rose and touched her shoulder.

"I'm going, my dear. It's nearly time for Adoration. I shan't come back next Sunday—and later, next year, I'll be going away ... don't fret ... it'll all be quite easy."

It wasn't easy now. She held out one hand without lifting her head, and for a moment they held each other's hands in a fierce clasp of farewell. He felt her hot, moist palm burning against his, then dropped it quickly and went out.

So that was the end. He had finished it. But Stella herself had taught him that one did not so easily finish love. He supposed that he would go on loving her as she had gone on loving Peter.

It was a quarter to four as he went into church. Quietly and methodically he lit the candles for Devotions, and watched the slight congregation assemble in the drowsy warmth of the September afternoon. He could not feel acutely—he could not even turn in his sorrow to the Sacred Victim on the Altar, whose adoration brought the children's service to a close.

O Sacred Victim, opening wide
The gate of heaven to men below....

The well-known words rose out of the shadows of the aisles behind him. They bruised his heart with their familiar sweetness.

"Our foes press round on every side,
Thine aid supply, thy strength bestow."

The candles that jigged in the small draughts of the sanctuary blurred into a cloud of rising incense, and then more thickly into a cloud of unshed tears. He fought them back, ashamed. He was beginning to feel again, and he would rather not feel—like this. It was intolerable, this appeal to his bruised emotion—it was like compelling him to use a wounded limb. He felt as if he could not bear any more of the wan, lilting music, the faint, sweet voices of the faithful, the perfumed cloud that rose like smoke before the altar and then hung among the gilding and shadows of the chancel roof. And now the virile tenor of the Priest seemed to bring a definitely sexual element into the tender dream.... What was this he was saying about love?...

"O God, who has prepared for them that love thee, such good things as pass man's understanding, pour into our hearts such love towards thee, that we, loving thee above all things ..."

§23

The clear pale sunlight of late October glittered on the River Tillingham, and seemed to be all light. No warmth was in the evening ray, and Jenny's woollen scarf was muffled to her throat as she came to the Mocksteeple. From far off she had seen the tall figure waiting beside the kiln. She wondered if he would hear her footsteps in the grass, or whether till she had called his name he would stand looking away towards where the light was thickening at the river's mouth.

Her feet made a sucking noise in the ground which was

spongy with autumn rains. He turned towards her and immediately held out his arms.

"My lovely...."

She was enfolded.

His warmth and strength made her think of the earth, and there was a faint scent of earth about him as she hid her face on his breast. There was also that smell of the clean straw of stables which she had noticed when she first met him. She rubbed her cheek childishly and fondly against the roughness of his coat then lifted her mouth for his slow, hard kisses....

"My lovely—oh, my lovely."

"How long can you stay?" he asked her a few minutes later, when they had huddled down together under the wall of the Mocksteeple, from which came a faint radiation of warmth, as the tar gave out the heat it had absorbed during the day.

"Not very long, I'm afraid, Benjie. There are people coming to dinner tonight, and I'll have to be back in good time. But we must fix about Monday. I've already told them I'm going up to town for a day's shopping, and I've written to a friend to choose me a couple of frocks at Debenham's and send them down—to make the lie hold water. I'm afraid I'm getting quite a resourceful liar."

"But you are going shopping, dear."

"Yes, but I can't tell them it's furniture, stupid. Oh, Ben, won't it be wildly exciting choosing things for Fourhouses! But we mustn't be extravagant, and you've got some lovely bits already."

"I want you to have the whole house to please you—nothing in it that you don't like."

"I like everything except the parlour, and those iron bedsteads they have upstairs. We'll want some chests too, to use instead of the washstands. Then Fourhouses will be perfect inside and out."

"You have real taste—that's what you have," he said admiringly.

"It's so dear of you to give me what I want."

"It's my wedding-present to you, sweetheart; and Mother and the girls are giving you sheets and table linen, so reckon we'll be well set up in our housekeeping."

She drowsed against him, her head on his shoulder, her arm across his knees. He put his mouth to her ear.

"My sweet," he murmured—"my little sweet—when is it going to be?"

"I've told you, Ben. At the beginning of January."

"That's your faithful word?"

"My faithful word."

"I'm glad—for oh, my dearest, it seems I've waited long enough."

"It won't seem so very long now—and, Ben, I've made up my mind about one thing. I'm not going to tell the family till it's all over."

"You're not!"

"No—because if I told them before it happened they'd try to stop it; and though they couldn't stop it, it would be a nuisance having them try."

"Does your brother agree with this?"

"It was he that suggested it."

"Well, I've a great respect for that brother of yours. But, sweetheart, it seems so dreadful, us marrying on the quiet, when I'm so proud of you and 'ud like to hold you before all the world."

"You shall hold me before all the world—after our marriage. But there's no good having a row with the parents, especially as they're old. It'll be bad enough for them anyhow, but I think they'll take it easier if they know it's too late to do anything."

He acquiesced, as he usually did, for he respected her judgment, and his natural dignity taught him to ignore this contempt of Alard for Godfrey. The rest of their short time together must not be spoiled by discussion. Once more he drew her close, and his kisses moved slowly from her forehead to her eyes, from her eyes to her cheeks, then at last to her mouth. His love-making gave her the thrill of a new experience, for she knew what a discovery and a wonder it was to him. It was not stale with repetition, distressed with comparison, as it was to so many men—as it was to herself. She felt a stab of remorse, a regret that she too was not making this adventure for the first time. She was younger than he, and yet beside him she felt shabby, soiled.... She strained him to her heart in an agony of tender possession. Oh, she would make his adventure worthwhile—he should not be disappointed in experience. They would explore the inmost heart of love together.

§24

Jenny was glad that the numbers in the drawing-room made it unnecessary for her to sit down to cards. She and Rose Alard had both cut out, and as Rose liked to sit and watch the play, Jenny felt she had an excuse to mutter something about "having one or two things to see to," and escape from the room. She wanted to be alone if only for half an hour, just to savour again in memory the comfort of her lover's arms, his tender breathing, the warmth of his kisses and the darkness of his embrace. She shut her eyes and heard him say "My lovely ... oh, my lovely!"

A full moon was spilling her light over the garden, and instinctively Jenny turned out of doors. She had put on her fur coat, and the still, moon-dazzled night was many degrees from frost. In the garden she would be sure of solitude, and at the same time would not be without the response of nature, so necessary to her mood. "One deep calleth another," and her heart in its new depth of rapture called to the moon and trees and grass, and received from them an answer which those self-absorbed human beings, crowded over cards, could never give.

She walked to and fro on the wide path beside the tennis lawn then turned into the darkness of the shrubbery, threading her way through moon-spattered arbutus and laurel till she came to a little garden-house which had been built in the reign of Queen Anne. It had the characteristics of its age— solid brick walls, high deepset windows, and a white pediment which now gleamed like silver in the light of the moon. It had been built by the nonjuring Gervase Alard, and here he had studied after his deprivation of the Vicarage of Leasan, and written queer crabbed books on a revised liturgy and on reunion with the Eastern Church. No one ever worked in it now, and it contained nothing but a bench and a few dilapidated garden chairs—it would hold only just enough warmth for her to sit down and rest.

To her surprise she found it was not empty; a movement startled her as she crossed the threshold, and the next moment she discovered Gervase, leaning back in one of the chairs. He was just a blot of shadow in the deeper darkness, except where his face, hands and shirt front caught the moonshine in ghostly patches of white.

"Hullo, Gervase—I'd no notion you'd come here."

He had left the drawing-room before coffee was brought in.

"I've been strolling about and got rather cold."

"Same here. Is there a whole chair beside you?"

At first she had been sorry to find him and had meant to go away, but now she realised that he was the only person whose company would not be loss.

"If not, there's one under me, and you shall have that.... Ah, here's something luxurious with rockers. Probably you and I are mad, my dear, to be sitting here. But I felt I simply must run away from the party."

"So did I."

She sat down beside him. In spite of the ghastly moonlight that poured over his face, he looked well—far less haggard than he had seemed in the kinder light a month ago. It struck her that he had looked better ever since his holiday, and his parting from Stella Mount, which he had told her of a few days after it happened. He had had a bad time, she knew, but he seemed to have come through it, and to have found a new kind of settlement. As she looked at him more closely in the revealing light, she saw that his mouth was perhaps a little too set, and that there were lines between nose and chin which she had not noticed before. He looked happy, but he also looked older.

"And how goes it, my dear?" he asked.

"Well, Gervase—extremely well."

She was too shy of intimate things to enquire how it went with him.

"I saw Ben this afternoon," she continued, "and I told him what you and I thought about not telling the parents till afterwards."

"And did he agree?"

"Yes, he agreed. I really think he's been wonderful about it all when you consider how he must feel...."

"He's got some sense of proportion—he's not going to let his love be spoilt by family pride. Jenny, if I've learnt anything in these first years of my grown-up life, it is that love must come before everything else."

She was surprised at this from him.

"You would put it before religion?"

"Religion is the fulfilment of love."

She repelled the awkward feelings which invariably oppressed her at the mention of such things. She wanted to know more of this young brother of hers, of the conflicts in which he triumphed mysteriously.

"Gervase, I wish I understood you better. I can't make out how it is that you, who are so modern and even revolutionary in everything else, should be so reactionary in your religion. Why do you follow tradition there, when you despise it in other things."

"Because it's a tradition which stands fast when all the others are tumbling down. It's not tradition that I'm out against, but all the feeble shams and conventions that can't stand when they're shaken."

"But does religion stand? I thought it was coming down like everything else."

"Some kinds are. Because they're built on passing ideas instead of on unchanging instincts. But Catholic Christianity stands fast because it belongs to an order of things which doesn't change. It's made of the same stuff as our hearts. It's the supernatural satisfaction of all our natural instincts. It doesn't deal with abstractions, but with everyday life. The sacraments are all common things—food, drink, marriage, birth and death. Its highest act of worship is a meal—its most sacred figures are a dying man, and a mother nursing her child. It's traditional in the sense that nature and life are traditional...."

It was many months since she had heard him talk like this. It reminded her of the old days when they were both at school, and he had brought her all his ideas on men and things, all his latest enthusiasms and discoveries.

"Jenny," he continued, "I believe that we've come to the end of false traditions—to the removing of those things which are shaken, that those things which cannot be shaken may remain. "

"Is there anything besides religion which can't be shaken?"

"Yes—my dear, the earth. The land will still be there though the Squires go, just as the faith will still be there though the Parsons go. The Parson and the Squire will go, and their places will be taken by the Yeoman and the Priest who were there before them."

"Go back to the Middle Ages?"

"Lord, no! Too much has happened since then. We've got industry and machinery and science—we can't go back to sack and maypoles. What I mean is that, instead of the country being divided among a few big landlords who don't and can't farm their own land, it will be divided into a lot of small farms of manageable size. Instead of each country parish being in the charge of a small country gentleman who has to keep up state on an income of two hundred a year, and is cut off from his parishioners by his social position and the iron gates of his parsonage, there'll be a humble servant living among them as one of themselves, set above them only by his vocation. It'll be a democracy which will have the best of aristocracy kept alive in it. The Parson and the Squire don't belong to any true aristocracy—they're Hanoverian relics—and they're going, and I'm glad."

"Yes, I think they're going all right, but I can't feel so glad as you, because I'm not so sure as to who will take their place. The yeoman isn't the only alternative to the squire—there's also the small-holder and the garden-city prospector. As for the parson—I don't know much about church affairs, but I should think he's just as likely to lose the spiritual side of himself as the material, and we'll have men that aren't much better than relieving officers or heads of recreation clubs."

"Don't try and burst my dream, Jenny. It's a very good sort of dream, and I like to think it will come true. And I know it will come true in a sense, though possibly in a sense which will be nonsense to most people. That's a way some of the best dreams have."

He was silent and thoughtful for a moment. Perhaps he was thinking of another Gervase Alard, who had long ago sat where he sat, and dreamed a dream which had not come true.

"But don't let's have any more of me and my dreams," he said after a while. "Talk to me about Ben. We started talking about him, you know, and then drifted off into Utopia. I should think that was a good sign."

"I'm meeting him in London on Monday to do some shopping."

"What are you going to buy?"

"Furniture. I want to pick up one or two really nice old pieces for Fourhouses. They're to be his wedding-present to me. First of all we'll go to Duke Street, and then to Puttick and Simpson's in the afternoon."

"Are you going to refurnish the house?"

"No, only get rid of one or two abominations. I had thought of doing up the Best Parlour, but now I've decided to let that stand. If I'm to be a farmer's wife I must get used to the Family Bible and aspidestras and wool mats."

"I think you're wise. It's just as well not to try to alter more of his life than you can help."

"I don't want to alter his life. I'm quite persuaded that his life is better than mine. And as for him not having our taste, or rather a different kind of bad taste from what we've got—it doesn't matter. I've made up my mind I must take Ben as he comes and as a whole, and not try to ignore or alter bits of him. I'm going to do the thing properly—make his friends my friends, pour out tea for the old ladies of Icklesham, ask the farmers who call round on business to stay to dinner or supper, go to see them at their farms and make friends with their wives. I know I can do it if only I do it thoroughly and don't make any reservations. Of course I'll go on being friends with our set if they'll let me, but if they won't, it's they who'll have to go and not the others. Gervase, I'm sick of Jenny Alard, and I'm thankful that she's going to die early next year, and a new creature called Jenny Godfrey take her place."

"My dear, you're going to be very happy."

"I know I am. I'm going to be the only happy Alard."

"The only one?"

"Yes—look at the others. There's Doris, a dreary middle-aged spinster, trodden on by both the parents, and always regretting the lovers she turned down because they weren't good enough for the family. There's Mary, living alone in private hotels and spending all her money on clothes; there's Peter, who's married a rich girl who's too clever for him, and who—worst of all—thinks he's happy and has become conventional. No—I can't help it—I pity them all."

"And what about me, Jenny? You've left me out. Do you pity me?"

She had ignored him deliberately—perhaps because she did not quite know where to place him.

"O Gervase, I hope you'll be happy—I'm sure you will, because you're different from the rest."

"Yes, I'm sure too. I'm going to be happy—as happy as you. I don't quite know how"—and he gave her a wry smile—"but I know that I shall be."

PART IV

STARVECROW

STARVECROW

§1

"FATHER," said Stella Mount—"I'm afraid I must go away again."

"Go away, child? Why?"

"I—I can't fall out of love with Peter."

"But I thought you'd fallen out of love with him long ago."

"Yes—I thought so too. But I can't have done it really, or if I did I must have fallen in again. I'm frightfully sorry about it ... leaving you a second time, just because I'm not strong-minded enough to.... But it's no use.... I can't help ..."

"Don't worry, dear. If you're unhappy you shall certainly go away. But tell me what's happened. How long have you been feeling like this?"

"Ever since I knew Peter still cared."

"Peter!—he hasn't said anything to you, has he?"

"Oh, no—not a word. But I could see—I could see he was jealous of Gervase."

"How could he possibly be jealous of Gervase?"

335

"He was. I met him one day in Icklesham street, and he congratulated me ... he said someone had told him Gervase and I were engaged...."

"The idea!—a boy six years younger than yourself!"

"Yes, I know. I never took him seriously—that was my mistake. Peter was ever so worked up about it, and when I told him it wasn't true he seemed tremendously relieved. And every time I've met him since his manner's been different. I can't describe it, but he's been sort of shy and hungry—or else restless and a bit irritable; and for a long time I could see he was still jealous—and it worried me; I felt I couldn't bear doing anything Peter didn't like, and I was wild at people talking, and upsetting him, so I pushed off poor Gervase and became cold and unfriendly."

"Is that why he's given up coming here on Sundays?"

"No—not exactly. We had rather a scene when he last came, just before his holiday, and he said he wouldn't come back. You see he cares, Father—he cares dreadfully. I'm ever so sick with myself for not having realised it. I was so wrapped up in Peter.... I thought it was only a rave, like what the Fawcett boy had—but now I'm sure he really cares, and it must be terrible for him. That's why I want to go away, for I'll never be able to care for anyone else while I feel for Peter as I do."

"But, my dear, it's just as well you shouldn't fall in love with Gervase. He's a nice boy, but he's much too young."

"Yes, I know—it isn't that. It's being sure that however much he was the right age I couldn't have cared—not because of anything lacking in him—but because of what's lacking in me ... because of all that I've given to Peter, and that Peter can't take.... Oh, Father, I've made some discoveries since

Gervase went. I believe I refused Tom Barlow because of Peter. The reason I'm single now is because for years I've been in love with a man I can't have. And that's wrong—I know it's wrong. It sounds 'romantic' and 'faithful' and all that—but it isn't really—it's wrong. Not because Peter's a married man, but because I'm an unmarried woman. He's keeping me unmarried, and I ought to get married—I don't like Spinsters—and I know I was meant to be married."

"So do I; and I'm sure that one day you will be."

"But I can't fall in love with anyone while I love Peter ... that's why I must go away. I ought to go somewhere really far, out of the country perhaps. I feel dreadful leaving you, daddy, but I know I must go. It's even more necessary than it was the first time. And there's no good saying I could help Peter if I stayed—I don't help him—I can see that I only make him unhappy; I'm not cold enough to be able to help him. A calm strong dignified woman might be able to help him, but I'm not that sort. I want his love, his kisses, his arms round me.... I want to give.... O Father, Father...."

She sobbed breathlessly, her face hidden in the back of her chair. Dr. Mount stood beside her in silence; then he touched her gently and said—

"Don't cry like that my dear—don't—I can't bear it. You shall go away—we'll both go away. I've been in this place twenty years, and it's time I moved on."

"But you don't want to go, and you mustn't. You're happy here, and I'd never forgive myself if you left because of me."

"I'd like to see a bit more of the world before I retire. This isn't the first time I've thought of a move, and if you want to go away, that settles it. I might get a colonial practice...."

Stella thought of some far away country with flat roofs and dust and a devouring sun, she thought of hundreds of miles of forest and desert and ocean lying between her and Peter, and her tears were suddenly dried up as with the hot breath of that far land. Dry sobs tore her throat, as she clutched the back of the chair. She pushed her father away—

"Go, dear—don't stay—when I'm like this."

He understood her well enough to go.

For a few seconds she sobbed on, then checked herself, and perfunctorily wiped her eyes. The four o'clock sun of early November was pouring into the room, showing all its dear faded homeliness, giving life to the memories that filled it. Long ago Peter had sat in that chair—she had sat on the arm ... she seemed to feel his warm hand on her cheek as he held her head down to his shoulder. O Peter, Peter—why had he left her when he loved her so?... Oh, yes, she knew he had treated her badly, and had only himself to blame. But that didn't make her love him less. She felt now that she had been in love with him the whole time—all along—all through and since their parting. All the time that she thought she was indifferent, and was happy in her busy life—driving the car, seeing her friends, talking and writing to Gervase, cooking and sewing and going to church, wearing pretty frocks at the winter dances and summer garden-parties—all that time her love for Peter was still alive, growing and feeding itself with her life. It had not died and been buried as she had thought but had entered a second time into its mother's womb to be born. She had carried it secretly, as a mother carries her child in her womb, nourishing it with her life, and now it was born—born again—with all the strength of the twice-born.

§2

It would be difficult to say how the rumour got abroad in
Vinehall and Leasan that the Mounts were going away. It
may have been servants' gossip, or the talk of some doctor
come down to view the practice. But, whatever the source, the
story was in both villages at the end of the month, and in the
first week of December Rose Alard brought it to Starvecrow.

She had come to have tea with Vera, and Peter was there
too. Vera was within three months of the heir, and displayed
her condition with all the opulence of her race. Not even her
purple velvet tea-gown could hide lines reminiscent of Sar-
ah's and Hannah's exulting motherhood. Her very features
seemed to have a more definitely Jewish cast—she was now
no longer just a dark beauty, but a Hebrew beauty, heir of Re-
becca and Rachel and Miriam and Jael. As Jenny had once
said, one expected her to burst into a song about horses and
chariots. She had for the time lost those intellectual and artistic interests which distinguished her from the other Alards.
She no longer seemed to care about her book, for which she
had so far been unable to find a publisher, but let it lie forgotten in a drawer, while she worked at baby clothes. Nevertheless she was inclined to be irritable and snap at Peter,
and Peter himself seemed sullen and without patience. Rose
watched him narrowly—"He's afraid it's going to be a girl."

Aloud she said—

"Have you heard that the Mounts are leaving Vinehall?"

Her news caused all the commotion she could have
wished.

"The Mounts leaving!"—"When?"—"Why?"—"Both of
them?"

"Yes, both. I heard it at the Hursts; they seemed quite positive about it, and you know they're patients."

"But where are they going?" asked Vera.

"That I don't know—yet. The Hursts said something about a colonial appointment."

"I'm surprised, I must say. Dr. Mount's getting old, and you'd think he'd want to stay on here till he retired—not start afresh in a new place at his age."

"If you ask me, it's Miss Stella's doing. She's lived here nearly all her life and hasn't got a husband, so she thinks she'll go and try somewhere else before it's too late."

"Then they'd certainly better go to the Colonies—there are no men left in England. But I'm sorry for Dr. Mount."

"I suppose you know it's all over between her and Gervase?"

"Oh, is it—at last?"

"Yes—he hasn't been there since his holiday in September. He has his dinner on Sundays either at the Church Farm or alone with Mr. Luce."

"Rose, how do you find out all these things?"

"The Wades told me this. They say she's been looking awful."

"Peter!" cried Vera irritably, as a small occasional table went to the ground.

"No harm done," he mumbled, picking it up.

"But you're so clumsy. You're always knocking things over...." She checked herself suddenly, pleating angry folds in her gown.

Peter got up and went out.

"I'm glad he's gone," said Rose—"It's much easier to talk without a man in the room. I really do feel sorry for Stella— losing her last chance of becoming Lady Alard."

"You think it's Gervase who's cooled off, not she who's turned him down?"

"Oh, she'd never do that. She's much too keen on getting married."

"Well, so I thought once. But I'm not so sure now. I used to think she was in love with Gervase, but now I believe she only kept him on as a blind."

"To cover what?"

"Peter."

"You mean...."

"That they've been in love with each other the whole time."

"Vera!"

Excitement at the disclosure was mingled in Rose's voice with disappointment that she had not been the one to make it.

"Yes," continued her sister-in-law in a struggling voice— "they've always been in love—ever since he married me—ever since he gave her up. They've never been out of it—I know it now."

"But I always thought it was all on her side."

"Oh, no, it wasn't. Peter was infatuated with her, for some strange reason—she doesn't seem to me at all the sort of girl a man of his type would take to. Being simple himself, you'd think he'd like something more sophisticated."

"But Stella is sophisticated—she's artful. Look how she got Gervase to change his religion, and break his poor brother's heart. I often think that it was Gervase's religion which killed poor George, and Stella was responsible for that. She may have pretended to be in love with him just to get him over. You see she can be forgiven anything she does by just going to confession."

"Well, she needs forgiveness now if she never did before. So it's just as well she knows where to get it."

"But, Vera, do you really think there's anything—I mean anything wicked between them?"

"I don't know what you call wicked, Rose, if keeping a man's affections away from his wife who's soon going to have her first child ... if that isn't enough for you.... No, I don't suppose he's actually slept with her"—Vera liked shocking Rose—"She hasn't got the passion or the spunk to go so far. But it's bad enough to know Peter's heart isn't mine just when I need him most—to know he only married me just to put the estate on its legs, and now is bitterly regretting it"—and Vera began to cry.

"But how do you know he's regretting it? He doesn't go about with Stella, I can tell you that. I'd be sure to have heard if he did."

"No, I daresay he doesn't go about with her. I shouldn't mind if he did, if only his manner was the same to me. But it isn't—every time we're together I can see he doesn't love me any more. He may have for a bit—he did, I know—but Stella got him back, and now every time he looks at me I can see he's regretting he ever married me. And if the baby's a girl ... my only justification now is that I may be the mother of an heir ... if the baby's a girl, I hope I'll die. Oh, I tell you, Stella may be Lady Alard yet."

She threw herself back among the cushions and sobbed unrestrainedly. Rose felt a thrill. She had always looked upon Vera as a superior being, remote from the commonplaces of existence in Leasan; and here she was behaving like any other jealous woman.

"Oh, I wish I'd never married," sobbed Vera—"at least not this sort of marriage. My life's dull—my husband's dull—my only interests are bearing his children and watching his affair with another woman. I'm sick of the County families—they've got no brains, they've got no guts—I'd much better have married among my own people. They at least are alive."

Rose was shocked. However, she valiantly suppressed her feelings, and patted the big olive shoulder which had shrugged abandonedly out of the purple wrappings.

"Don't worry, dear," she soothed—"you're upset. I'm sure Peter's all right. It's often rather trying for men in times like these...." she heaved on the edge of an indelicate remark ... "so they notice other women more. But I'm quite sure there's nothing really wrong between him and Stella; because if there was," she added triumphantly, "Stella wouldn't be going away."

"Oh, wouldn't she!"

"No, of course not. I expect she's going only because she knows now definitely that she'll never get Peter back."

"Nonsense."

"It isn't nonsense, dear. Don't be so cross."

"I'm sorry, Rose, but I'm ... anyhow Dr. Mount can't go before I'm through, and that's three months ahead. I've half a mind not to have him now. I feel sick of the whole family."

"That would be very silly of you, Vera. Dr. Mount's the best doctor round here for miles, and it would only be spiting yourself not to have him. After all he's not responsible for Stella's behaviour."

"No, I suppose not. Oh, I daresay I'm an ass, going on like this."

She sat up, looking more like the author of "Modern Rhymes." Rose, who had always been a little afraid of her, now had the privileged thrill of those who behold the great in their cheaper moments.

"You'll be all right, dear," she said meaningly, "in three months' time."

"All right, or utterly done in. O God, why can't someone find out a way of deciding the sex of children? I'd give all I possess and a bit over to be sure this is going to be a boy. Not that I want a boy myself—I like girls much better—but I don't want to see Peter go off his head or off with Stella Mount."

"I don't believe she's got a single chance against you once you're yourself again. Even now I could bet anything that it's all on her side."

"She's got no chance against me as a woman, but as an Ancient Habit she can probably do a lot with a man like Peter. But I'm not going to worry about her any more—I've given way and made an utter fool of myself, and it's done me good, as it always does. Rose, you promise not to say a word of this to anyone."

"Of course I won't. But I might try to get at the facts...."

"For God's sake don't. You'll only make a mess."

As she revived she was recovering some old contempt for her sister-in-law.

§3

The post arrived just as Stella was setting out with the car one day early the next month to meet her father in Ashford. He had been in Canterbury for a couple of days, attending a dinner and some meetings of the Medico-Chirurgical Society, and this afternoon she was to meet him at Ashford Station and drive him home. She was in plenty of time, so when she saw Gervase's writing on the envelope handed to her, she went back into the house and opened it.

It was now three months since she had spoken to Gervase or heard anything directly from him. He still came over to Vinehall on Sundays and to certain early masses in the week, but he never called at Dr. Mount's cottage, nor had she seen him out of church, nor heard his voice except in dialogue with the Priest—"I will go unto the Altar of God" ... "Even unto the God of my joy and gladness"....

She wondered what he could have to say to her now. Perhaps he had recovered, and was coming back. She would be pleased, for she missed his company—also it would be good to have his letters when she was out in Canada.... But Stella knew what happened to people who "recovered" and "came back," and reflected sadly that it would be her duty to discourage Gervase if he thought himself cured.

But the letter did not contain what she expected.

Conster Manor,
Leasan,
Sussex.

Jan. 2, 1922

My dear Stella,

I'm writing to tell you something rather funny which has happened to me. I don't mean that I've fallen out of love with you—I never shall and don't want to. But I'm going to do something with my love which I never expected.

You know that in September, I went into retreat for four days at Thunders Abbey. I was sure I'd hate it—and so I did in a way—but when I'd got there I saw at once that it was going to be more important than I'd thought. At first I thought it was just a dodge of Father Luce's for making me uncomfortable—you know he looks upon me as a luxury-loving young aristocrat, in need of constant mortification. I don't know what it was exactly that made me change—it was partly, I think, the silence, and partly, I know, the Divine Office. At the end of my visit I knew that Office as the great work of prayer, and Thunders Abbey as just part of that heart of prayer which keeps the world alive. And, dear, I knew that my place was in that heart. I can't describe to you exactly what I felt—and I wouldn't if I could. But you're a Catholic, so you won't think I'm talking nonsense when I say that I feel I belong there, or, in plainer language, that I have a vocation. You don't believe that vocations come only to priggish maidens and pious youth, but much more often to ordinary healthy, outdoor people like you and me. Of course I know that even you will think (as Father Luce and the Father Superior have thought) that my vocation may possibly be another name for disappointment in love. I've thought it myself, but I don't believe it. Anyhow it's at last been settled that I'm going to be allowed to try. As soon as I've finished at Gillingham's I shall go. You know the community, of course. It's an order for work among the poor, and has houses in London, Birmingham and Leeds. At Thunders Abbey there's a big farm for drunkards, epileptics, idiots, and other pleasant company. I'd be useful there, as they've just started motor traction, but I don't know where they'll send me. Of course I may come out again; but I don't think so. One knows a sure thing, Stella, and I never felt so sure about anything as about this and it's all the more convincing, because I went in without a thought of it. I expect you will be tremendously surprised, but I know you won't write trying to dissuade me, and telling me all the good I could do outside by letting out taxis for hire and things like that. You dear! I feel I owe everything to you—including this new thing which is so joyful and so terrifying. For I'm frightened a bit—I'm not just going in because I like it—I don't know if I do. And yet I'm happy.

Don't say a word to anyone, except your father. I must wait till the time is ripe to break the news to my family, and then, I assure you, the excitement will be intense. But I felt I must write and tell you as soon as I knew definitely they'd let me come and try, because you are at the bottom of it all—I don't mean as a disappointment in love, but as the friend who first showed me the beauty of this faith which makes such demands on us. Stella, I'm glad you brought me to the faith before I'd had time to waste much of myself. It's lovely to think that I can give Him all my grown-up life. I can never pay you back for what you've done, but I can come nearest to it by taking my love for you into this new life. My love for you isn't going to die, but it's going to become a part of prayer.

May I come and see you next Sunday? I thought I would write and tell you about things first, for now you know you won't feel there are any embarrassments or regrets between us. Dear Stella, I think of you such a lot, and I'm afraid you must still be unhappy. But I know that this thing I am going to do will help you as much as me. Perhaps, too, some day I shall be a Priest—though I haven't thought about that yet— and then I shall be able to help you more. Oh my dear, it isn't every man who's given the power to do so much for the

woman he loves. I bless you, my dear, and send you in antic-
ipation one of those free kisses we shall all give one another
in Paradise.

GERVASE

P.S. There is a rumour that you are going away, but as I
can't trace its succession back further than Rose, I pronounce
it of doubtful validity.

  P.P.S. Dear, please burn this—it's more than a love-letter.

  P.P.P.S. I hope I haven't written like a prig.

Stella let the letter fall into her lap. She was surprised.
Somehow she had never thought of Gervase as a religious;
she had never thought of him except as a keen young engineer—attractive, self-willed, eccentric, devout. His spiritual
development had been so like hers—and she, as she knew
well, had no vocation to the religious life—that she was surprised now to find such an essential difference. But her surprise was glad, for though she brushed aside his words of
personal gratitude, she felt the thrill of her share in the adventure, and a conviction that it would be for her help as well
as for his happiness. Moreover, this new development took
away the twinges of self-reproach which she could not help
feeling when she thought of her sacrifice of his content to
Peter's jealousy.

But her chief emotion was a kind of sorrowful envy. She
envied Gervase not so much the peace of the cloister—not so
much the definiteness of his choice—as his freedom. He was
free—he had made the ultimate surrender and was free. She
knew that he had now passed beyond her, though she had
had a whole youth of spiritual experience and practice and

he barely a couple of years. He was beyond her, not because of his vocation, but because of his freedom. His soul had escaped like a bird from the snare, but hers was still struggling and bound.

She would never feel for Peter as Gervase felt for her. Her utmost hope was, not to carry her love for him into a new, purged state, but to forget him—if she aimed at less she was deceiving herself, forgetting the manner of woman she was. She had not Gervase's transmuting ecstasy—nor could she picture herself giving Peter "free kisses" in a Paradise where flesh and blood had no inheritance. Her loves would always be earthly—she would meet her friends in Paradise, but not her lovers.

§4

Well, there was no time for reflection, either happy or sorrowful—she must start off for Ashford, or her father would be kept waiting. Once again, after many times, she experienced the relief of practical action. Her disposition was eminently practical, and the practical things of love and life and religion—kisses and meals and sacraments—were to her the realities of those states. A lover who did not kiss and caress you, a life which was based on plain living and high thinking, a religion without good outward forms for its inward graces, were all things which Stella's soul would never grasp.

So she went out to the little "tenant's fixture" garage, filled the Singer's tank and cranked her up, and drove off comforted a little in her encounter with life's surprises. The day was damp and mild. There was a moist sweetness in the air, and the scent of ploughed and rain-soaked earth. Already the spring-sowings had begun, and the slow teams moved solemnly to and fro over the January fields. Surely, thought Stella, ploughing was the most unhurried toil on earth. The plough came to the furrow's end, and halted there, while men and horses seemed equally deep-sunk in meditation. Whole minutes later the whip would crack, and the team turn slowly for the backward furrow. She wouldn't like to do a slow thing like that—and yet her heart would ache terribly when it was all gone, and she would see the great steam ploughs tearing over the mile-long fields of the West ... she would then think sorrowfully of those small, old Sussex fields—the oldest in the world—with their slow ploughing; she would crave all the more for the inheritance which Peter might have given her among them....

She was beginning to feel bad again—and it was a relief to find that the car dragged a little on the steering, pulling towards the hedge, even though she knew that it meant a punctured tyre. The Singer always punctured her tyres like a lady—she never indulged in vulgar bursts, with a bang like a shot-gun and a skid across the road. Stella berthed her beside the ditch, and began to jack her up.

Well, it was a nuisance, seeing that her father would be kept waiting. But she ought to be able to do the thing in ten minutes ... she wished she was wearing her old suit, though. She would make a horrible mess of herself, changing wheels on a dirty day.... The car was jacked up, and Stella was laying out her tools on the running board when she heard a horse's hoofs in the lane.

It seemed at first merely a malignant coincidence that the rider should be Peter; yet, after all, the coincidence was not so great when she reflected that she was now on the lane between Conster and Starvecrow. She had heard that Peter had lately taken to riding a white horse—it was all part of the picture he was anxious to paint of himself as Squire. He would emphasise his Squirehood, since to it he had sacrificed himself as freeman and lover.

She had never seen him looking so much the Squire of tradition as he looked today. He wore a broadcloth coat, corduroy breeches, brown boots and leggings and a bowler hat. Of late he had rather increased in girth, and looked full his forty years. Unaccountably this fact stirred up Stella's heart into a raging pity—Peter middle-aged and getting stout, Peter pathetically over-acting his part of country gentleman—it stirred all the love and pity of her heart more deeply than any figure of romance and youth. She hoped he would not stop, but considering her position she knew she was hoping too much.

He hitched the white horse to the nearest gate and dismounted. They had not been alone together since the summer, though they had met fairly often in company, and now she was conscious of a profound embarrassment and restraint in them both.

"Have you punctured?" he asked heavily.

"No, but the tyre has," said Stella.

The reply was not like herself, it was part of the new attitude of defence—a poor defence, since she despised herself for being on guard, and was therefore weaker.

"You must let me help you change the wheel."

"I can do it myself, quite easily. Don't bother, Peter—you know I'm used to these things."

"Yes, but it's dirty work for a woman. You'll spoil your clothes."

She could not insist on refusing. She went to the other side of the car, where her spare wheel was fastened, and bent desperately over the straps. She wondered how the next few minutes would pass—in heaviness and pertness as they had begun, or in technical talk of tyres and nuts and jacks, or in the limp politeness of the knight errant and distressed lady.

The next moment Peter made a variation she had not expected.

"Stella, is it true that you're going away?"

"I—I don't know. It isn't settled.... Who told you?"

"Rose told me—but it can't be true."

"Why not?"

"Your father surely would never go away at his time of life—and Rose spoke of the Colonies. He'd never go right away and start afresh like that."

"Father's heard of a very good billet near Montreal. We haven't settled anything yet, but we both feel we'd like a change."

"Why?"

"Well, why shouldn't we? We've been here more than twenty years, and as for Father being old, he's not too old to want to see a bit more of the world."

Peter said nothing. He was taking off the wheel. When he had laid it against the bank he turned once more to Stella.

"It's queer how I always manage to hear gossip about you. But it seems that this time I'm right, while last time I was wrong."

"Everyone gets talked about in a little place like this."

She tried to speak lightly, but she was distressed by the way he looked at her. Those pale blue eyes ... Alard eyes, Saxon eyes ... the eyes of the Old People looking at her out of the Old Country, and saying "Don't go away...."

The next minute his lips repeated what his eyes had said: "Don't go away."

She trembled, and stepped back from him on the road.

"I must go."

"Indeed you mustn't—I can't bear it any longer if you do."

"That's why I must go."

"No—no—"

He came towards her, and she stepped back further still.

"Don't go, Stella. I can't live here without you."

"But, Peter, you must. What good am I doing you here?"

"You're here. I know that you're only a few miles away. I can think of you as near me. If you went right away...."

"It would be much better for both of us."

"No, it wouldn't. Stella, it will break me if you go. My only comfort during the last six hellish months has been that at least you're not so very far from me in space, that I can see you, meet you, talk to you now and then...."

"But, Peter, that's what I can't bear. That's why I'm going away."

Her voice was small and thin with agitation. This was worse, a hundred times worse, than anything she had dreaded five minutes ago. She prayed incoherently for strength and sense.

"If that's what you feel, you've got to stay," Peter was saying. "Stella, you've shown me—Stella, you still care.... Oh, I'll own up, I'll own that I've been a fool, and a blackguard to you. But if you still care, I can be almost happy. We've still something left. Only you'll have to stay."

"You mustn't talk like this."

"Why not—if you still care? Oh, Stella, say it's true—say you still care ... a little."

She could not deny her love, even though she was more afraid of his terrible happiness than she had been before of his despair. To deny it would be a profaning of something holier than truth. All she could say was—

"If I love you, it's all the more necessary for me to go away."

"It's not. If you love me, I can be to you at least what you are to me. But if you go away, you'll be as wretched as I shall be without you."

"No ... if I go away, we can forget."

"Forget!—What?—each other?"

"Yes."

The word was almost inaudible. She prayed with all her strength that Peter would not come to her across the road and take her in his arms. His words she could fight, but not his arms....

"Stella—you're not telling me that you're going away to forget me?"

"I must, Peter. And you'll forget me, too. Then we'll be able to live instead of just—loving."

"But my love for you is my life—all the life I've got."

"No—you've got Vera, and soon you'll have your child. When I've gone you can go back to them."

"I can't—you don't know what you're talking about. If you think I can ever feel again for Vera what I felt when I was fool enough—"

"Oh, don't...."

"But I will. Why should you delude yourself, and think I'm just being unfaithful to my wife? It's to you I've been unfaithful. I was unfaithful to you with Vera—and now I've repented and come back."

They faced each other, two yards apart in the little muddy lane. Behind Peter the three-wheeled car stood forlornly surrounded by tools, while his horse munched the long soaking tufts under the hedge. Behind Stella the hedge rose abruptly in a soaring crown. Looking up suddenly, she saw the delicate twigs shining against a sheet of pale blue sky in a faint sunlight. For some reason they linked themselves with her mind's effort and her heart's desire. Here was beauty which did not burn.... She suddenly found herself calm.

"Peter, dear, there's no good talking like that. Let's be sensible. Rightly or wrongly you've married someone else, and you've got to stand by it and so have I. If I stay on here we will only just be miserable—always hankering after each other, and striving for little bits of each other which can't satisfy. Neither of us will be able to settle down and live an ordinary life, and after all that's what we're here for—not for adventures and big passions, but just to live ordinary lives and be happy in an ordinary way."

"Oh, damn you!" cried Peter.

It was like the old times when he used to rail against her "sense," against the way she always insisted that their love should be no star or cloud, but a tree, well rooted in the earth.

It made it more difficult for her to go on, but she persevered.

"You've tried the other thing, Peter—you've tried sacrificing ordinary things like love and marriage to things like

family pride and the love of a place. You've found it hasn't
worked, so don't do the whole thing over again by sacrificing
your home and family to a love which can never be satisfied."

"But it can be," said Peter—"at least it could if you were
human."

Stella, a little to his annoyance, didn't pretend not to know
what he meant.

"No, it couldn't be—not satisfied. We could only satisfy a
part of it—the desire part—the part which wants home and
children would always have to go unsatisfied, and that's as
strong as the rest, though it makes less fuss."

"And how much satisfaction shall we get through never
seeing each other again?"

"We shall get it—elsewhere. You will at least be free to go
back to Vera—and you did love her once, you can't deny it—
you did love her once. And I—"

"—Will be free to marry another man."

"I don't say that, Peter—though also I don't say that I
won't. But I shall be free to live the life of a normal human
being again, which I, can't now. I shan't be bringing unrest
and misery wherever I go—to myself and to you. Oh, Peter, I
know we can save ourselves if we stop now, stop in time. We
were both quite happy last time I was away—I was a fool ever
to come back. I must go away now before it's too late."

"You're utterly wrong. When you first went away I could
be happy with Vera—I couldn't now. All that's over and done
with for ever, I tell you. I can never go back to her, whether
you go or stay. It's nothing to do with your coming back—it's
her fault—and mine. We aren't suited, and nothing can ever
bring us together again now we've found it out."

"Not even the child?..."

"No—not even that. Besides, how do I know.... Stella, all the things I've sacrificed you to have failed me, except Starvecrow."

"You've still got Starvecrow."

"Yes, but I.... Oh, Stella, don't leave me alone, not even with Starvecrow. The place wants you, and when you're gone I'm afraid.... Vera doesn't belong there; it's your place. Oh, Stella, don't say you can live without me, any more than I can live without you."

She longed to give him the answer of her heart—that she could never, never live without him, go without the dear privilege of seeing him, of speaking to him, of sacrificing to him all other thoughts and loves. But she forced herself to give him the answer of her head, for she knew that it would still be true when her heart had ceased to choke her with its beating.

"Peter, I don't *feel* as if I could live without you, but I *know* I can—and I know you can live without me, if I go away. What you've said only shows me more clearly that I must go. I could never stop here now you know I love you."

"And why not?—it's your damned religion, I suppose—teaching you that it's wrong to love—that all that sort of thing's disgusting, unspiritual—you've got your head stuffed with all the muck a lot of celibate priests put into it, who think everything's degrading."

She felt the tears come into her eyes.

"Don't, my dear. Do you really believe—you who've known me—that I think love is degrading?—or that my religion teaches me to think so? Why, it's because all that is so lovely,

so heavenly and so good, that it mustn't be spoilt—by secrecy
and lies, by being torn and divided. Oh, Peter, you know I love
love...."

"So much that you can apparently shower it on anyone as
long as you get the first victim out of the way."

They both turned suddenly, as the jar of wheels sounded
up the hill. It would be agony to have the discussion broken
off here, but Stella knew that she mustn't refuse any opportunity of ending it. No longer afraid of Peter's arms, she crossed
swiftly to the dismantled car.

"Please don't wait. I can manage perfectly now. Please go,
Peter—please go."

"I'll go only if you promise to see me again before you
leave."

"Of course I will—I'll see you again; but you must go now."

The wagon of Barline, heavy with crimson roots, was
lurching and skidding down the hill towards them. Peter
went to his standing horse, and rode him off into the field.
Stella turned to the car, and, crouched in its shelter, allowed
herself the luxury of tears.

§5

She dried her eyes, came up from behind the car, and lost
herself in the sheer labour of putting on the wheel. She was
late, she must hurry; she strove, she sweated, and at last was
once more in her seat, the damaged wheel strapped in its
place, all the litter of tools in the dickie. She switched on the
engine, pressed the self-starter pedal, slid the gear lever into
place, and the little car ran forward. Then she realised what a
relief it was to find herself in motion—some weight seemed

to lift from her mind, and her numb thoughts began to move, to run to and fro. She was alive again.

But it hurt to be alive. Perhaps one was happier dead. For the thoughts that ran to and fro were in conflict, they formed themselves into two charging armies, meeting with horrible impact, terror and wounds. Her mind was a battlefield, divided against itself, and as usual the movement of the car seemed to make her thoughts more independent, more free of her control. They moved to the throb and mutter of the engine, as to some barbaric battle-music, some monotonous drum. She herself seemed to grow more and more detached from them. She was no longer herself—she was two selves—the self that loved Peter and the self that loved God. She was Stella Mount at prayer in Vinehall church—Stella Mount curled up on Peter's knees ... long ago, at Starvecrow—Stella Mount receiving her soul again in absolution.... Stella Mount loving, loving, with a heart full of fiery sweetness.... Well, aren't they a part of the same thing—love of man and love of God? Yes, they are—but today there is schism in the body.

During the last few months love had given her nothing but pain, for she had seemed to be swallowed up in it, away from the true richness of life. She had lost that calm, cheerful glow in which all things, even the dullest and most indifferent, had seemed interesting and worthwhile. Love had extinguished it. The difference she saw between religion and love was that religion shone through all things with a warm, soft light, making them all friendly and sweet, whereas love was like a fierce beam concentrated on one spot, leaving the rest of life in darkness, shining only on one object, and that so blindingly that it could not be borne.

She felt a sudden spasm of revolt against the choice forced upon her. Why should she have to choose between heaven and earth, which she knew in her heart were two parts of one completeness? Why should God want her to give up for His sake the loveliest thing that He had made?... Why should He want her to *burn*?

Now had come the time, she supposed, when she would have to pay for the faith which till then had been all joy, which in its warmth and definiteness had taught her almost too well how to love. It had made her more receptive, more warm, more eager, and had deprived her of those weapons of self-interest and pride and resentment which might have armed her now. Perhaps it was because they knew religion makes such good lovers that masters of the spiritual life have urged that the temptations of love are the only ones from which it is allowable to run away. It was her duty to run away from Peter now, because the only weapons with which she could fight him were more unworthy than surrender. With a grimmer, vaguer belief she might have escaped more easily—she might have seen evil in love, she might have distrusted happiness and shunned the flesh. But then she would not have been Stella Mount—she owed her very personality to her faith—she owed it all the intense joy she had had in human things. Should she stumble at the price?

If only the price were not Peter—Peter whom she loved, whom the love of God had taught her to love more than her heart could ever have compassed alone. Why must he be sacrificed? After all, she was offering him up to her own satisfaction—to her anxiety to keep hold of heavenly things. Why should he be butchered to give her soul a holiday? She almost hated herself—hated herself for her odious sense, for her cold-blooded practicalness. She proposed to go away not only so as to be out of temptation—let her be honest—but so that she could forget him and live the life of a normal happy woman ... which of course meant some other man.... No wonder he was disgusted with her—poor, honest, simple, unsatisfied Peter. She was proposing to desert him, sure of interior comforts he had never known, and secretly sure that the detestable adaptability of her nature would not allow her to mourn him long once he was far away. Oh, Peter—Peter!... "I will give you back the years that the locust hath eaten—I have it in my power. I can do it—I can give you back the locust's years. I can do it still...."

She could do it still. She could tell her father that she did not want to go away after all—and he would be glad ... poor Father! He was only going for her sake. He would be glad to stay on among the places and the people that he loved. And she ... she could be a good, trusty friend to Peter, someone he could turn to in his loneliness, who would understand and help him with his plans for Alard and Starvecrow.... What nonsense she was talking. Silly hypocrite! Both sides of her, the Stella who loved Peter and the Stella who loved God, saw the futility of such an idea. She could never be any man's friend—least of all Peter's. If she stayed, it would be to love Peter, to be all that it was still possible for her to be to him, all that Vera was and the more that she was not.

But could she? Had she the power to love Peter with a love unspoilt by regret? Would she be able to bear the thought of her treachery to the Lord whose happy child she had been so long?—to His Mother and hers—to all His friends and hers, the saints—to all the great company of two worlds whom she would betray? For her the struggle contained no moral issue. It was simply a conflict between love and love. And all the while she knew in the depth of her heart that love cannot really be divided, and that her love of God held and sustained her love of Peter, as the cloud holds the rain-drop, and the shore the grain of sand.

The first houses of Ashford slid past, and she saw the many roofs of the railway-works. Traffic dislocated the strivings of her mind, and in time her thoughts once more became numb. They lay like the dead on the battle-field, the dead who would rise again.

§6

Gervase came to see Stella, according to promise, the following Sunday. He found her looking tired and heavy-headed, and able only mechanically to sustain her interest in his plans. Also he still found her unapproachable—she was not cold or contrary, but reserved, feeding on herself.

He guessed the source of her trouble, but shrank from probing it—keeping the conversation to his own affairs with an egotism he would normally have been ashamed of. What he noticed most was the extinction of joy in her—she had always seemed to him so fundamentally happy, and it was her profound and so natural happiness which had first attracted him towards her religion. But now the lamp was out. He was not afraid for her—it did not strike him that she could possibly fail or drop under her burden; but his heart ached for her, alone in the Dark Night—that very Dark Night he himself had come through alone.... Now he stood, also alone, in a strange dawn which had somehow changed the world, as the fields are changed in the whiteness of a new day.

It was not till he got up to go that he dared try to come closer. They had been talking about the difficulties of the life he had chosen.

"I'm afraid Christianity's a hard faith, my dear," he said as he took her hand—"the closer you get to the Gospel the harder it is. You've no idea what a shock the Gospels gave me when I read them again last year, not having looked at them since I was a kid. I was expecting something rather meek-and-mild, with a gentle, womanly Saviour, and all sorts of kind and good-natured sentiments. Instead of which I find that the Kingdom of Heaven is for the violent, while the Lion of Judah roars in the Temple courts.... He built His Church upon a Rock, and sometimes we hit that Rock mighty hard."

"But I do hope you'll be happy, Gervase."

"I'm sure of that, though whether it will be in a way that will be easily recognised as happiness I'm not so sure."

"When are you going?"

"It's not quite settled yet. I leave off at Gillingham's on the twenty-fifth, and I expect I'll go to Thunders early in February. I'll come and see you again before then. Goodbye, my dear."

He kissed her hand before letting it go.

§7

He had said nothing to her about his sister Jenny, though her marriage was so close as to seem almost more critical than his own departure. He felt the unfairness of sharing with Stella so difficult a secret, also he realised that the smaller the circle to which it was confined the smaller the catastrophe when it was either accidentally discovered or deliberately revealed.

About a week before the day actually fixed for the wedding, the former seemed more likely. Jenny met Gervase on his return from Ashford with a pale, disconcerted face.

"Father guesses something's up," she said briefly.

"What?—How?—Has anyone told him?"

"No—he doesn't really know anything, thank heaven—at least anything vital. But he's heard I was at tea at Fourhouses twice last week. One of the Dengates called for some eggs, I remember, and she must have told Rose when Rose was messing about in the village. He's being heavily sarcastic, and asking me if I wouldn't like Mrs. Appleby asked in to tea, so that I won't have to walk so far to gratify my democratic tastes."

"But Peter's had tea with them, too—you told me it was he who introduced you."

"Yes, but that only makes it worse. Peter's been at me as well—says he'd never have taken me there if he'd thought I hadn't a better sense of my position. He was very solemn about it, poor old Peter."

"But of course they don't suspect any reason."

"No, but I'm afraid they will. I'm not likely to have gone there without some motive—twice, too—and, you see, I've been so secret about it, never mentioned it at home, as I should have done if I'd had tea at Glasseye or Monkings or anywhere like that. They must think I've some reason for keeping quiet.... I hope they won't question me, for I'm a bad liar."

"You'll be married in ten days—I don't suppose they'll get really suspicious before that."

However, a certain amount of reflection made him uneasy, and after dinner he drove over to Fourhouses, to discuss the matter with Ben Godfrey himself.

When he came back, he went straight up to Jenny's room—she had gone to bed early, so as to give her family less time for asking questions.

"Well, my dear," he said when she let him in, "I've talked it over with Ben, and we both think that you'll have to get married at once."

"At once!—But can we?"

"Yes—the law allows you to get married the day after to-morrow. It'll cost thirty pounds, but Fourhouses can rise to that, and it's much better to get the thing over before it's found out. Not that anyone could stop you, but it would be a maddening business if they tried, and anyhow I think the parents will take it easier if it's too late to do anything."

"I think you're quite right, absolutely right. But—"

"But what?"

"Oh, nothing—only it seems such a jump, now I'm standing right on the edge."

"You're not afraid, Jenny?"

"No—only in the way that everyone's afraid of a big thing. But you're absolutely right. Now there's a chance of us being found out, we must act at once. I don't want to have to tell any lies about Ben. I suppose he'll go up to town tomorrow."

"Yes, and you and I will follow him the day after. I must see about a day off. I'm not quite clear as to what one does exactly to get a special license, but he'll go to the Court of Faculties and they'll show him how. He's going to wire me at Gillingham's—lucky I'm still there."

"I don't envy you, Gervase, having to break the news to Father and Mother."

"No, I don't think it'll be much fun. But really it will be better than if you wrote—I can let them down more gently, and they won't feel quite so outraged. As for the row—there'll be one about my own little plan in a short time, so I may as well get used to them."

Jenny said nothing. She had known of Gervase's "little plan" only for the last week, and she had for it all the dread and dislike which the active Englishwoman instinctively feels for the contemplative and supernatural—reinforced now by the happy lover's desire to see all the world in love. The thought of her brother, with all his eager experimental joy in life, all his profound yet untried capacity for love, taking vows of poverty and celibacy, filled her with grief and indignation—she felt that he was being driven by the backwash of his disappointment over Stella Mount, and blamed "those Priests," who she felt had unduly influenced him at a critical time. However, after her first passionate protest, she had made no effort to oppose him, feeling that she owed him at least silence for all that he had done to help her in her own adventure, and trusting to time and recovery to show him his folly. She was a little reassured by the knowledge that he could not take his final vows for many years to come.

He was aware of this one constraint between them, and coming over to her as she lay in bed, he gave her a kiss. For some unfathomable reason it stung her, and turning over on her side she burst into tears.

"Jenny, Jenny darling—don't cry. Oh, why.... Jenny, if you've any doubts, tell me before it's too late, and I'll help you out—I promise. Anything rather than...."

"Oh, don't, Gervase. It isn't that. Can't you understand? It's—oh, I suppose all women feel like this—not big enough ... afraid...."

§8

The wedding had always been planned to take place in London, so it was merely the time that was being altered. Both Gervase and Jenny had seen, and Ben Godfrey had been brought reluctantly to see, that to be married at home would double the risks; so a room had been taken and a bag of Godfrey's clothes deposited in a Paddington parish, where the Vicar was liberal in his interpretation of the laws of residence, and an ordinary licence procured. The change of plans necessitated a special licence, and Jenny had to wait till Gervase came home the next evening to know if all was in order. However, after the shock of its inception, the new scheme worked smoothly. Jenny came down early the next morning and breakfasted with Gervase, then drove off in Henry Ford, leaving a message with Wills that she had gone to London for the day, and her brother was driving her as far as Ashford.

Everything was so quiet and matter-of-fact as to seem to her almost normal—she could not quite realise that she had left her old life behind her at Conster, even more completely than most brides leaving their father's house; that ahead of her was not only all the difference between single and married, but all the difference between Alard and Godfrey, Conster and Fourhouses. She was not only leaving her home, but her class, her customs, her acquaintance. It was not till she was standing beside Godfrey in a strange, dark church, before a strange clergyman, that she realised the full strangeness of it all. For a moment her head swam with terror—she found

herself full of a desperate longing to wake up in her bed at
Conster and find it was a dream—she thought of the catastrophe of Mary's marriage, and she knew that she was taking far bigger risks than Mary.... And through all this turmoil
she could hear herself saying quite calmly—"I, Janet Christine, take thee, Benjamin, to be my wedded husband." Some
mechanical part of her was going on with the business, while
her emotions cowered and swooned. Now she was signing
her name in the register—Janet Christine Godfrey—now
she was shaking hands with the clergyman and answering his
inane remarks with inanities of her own. It was too late to
draw back—she had plunged—Jenny Alard was dead.

They had lunch at a restaurant in Praed Street, and afterwards Gervase went with them to Paddington Station and
saw them off to Cornwall. They were not going to be away
long, partly on account of Godfrey's spring sowings, and
partly because Jenny felt that she could not leave her brother
any length of time to stand the racket. She would still have
liked to suppress his share in the business, but Gervase was
firm—"It's treating them better," he said, "and, besides, it will
help them a lot to have a scapegoat on the premises."

Jenny felt almost sentimental in parting from the little
brother, who had helped her so much in the path she had
chosen, and who had taken for himself so rough and ridiculous a road. She kissed him in the carriage doorway, made
him promise to write to her, and then did her best to put him
out of her head for the first happy hours of the honeymoon.

Circumstances made this fairly easy. By the time they
were at Mullion, watching the low lamps of the stars hanging
over the violet mists that veiled Poldhu, even Gervase seemed

very far away, and the household and life of Conster Manor almost as if they had never been. Nothing was real but herself and Ben, alone together in the midst of life, each most completely the other's desire and possession. When she looked into his eyes, full of their new joy and trouble, the husband's eyes which held also the tenderness of the father and the simplicity of the child, there was no longer any past or future, but only the present—"I love."

The next day, however, recalled her rather abruptly to thoughts of her scapegoat. She received a telegram—

"Father kicked me out address Church Cottage Vinehall don't worry Gervase."

Jenny was conscience-stricken, though she knew that Gervase would not be much hurt by his exile. But she was anxious to hear what had happened, and waited restlessly for a letter. None came, but the next morning another telegram.

"Father had stroke please come home Gervase."

So Jenny Godfrey packed up her things and came home after two days' honeymoon. Happiness is supposed to make time short, but those two days had seemed like twenty years.

§9

Gervase reproached himself for having done his part of the business badly, though he never felt quite sure how exactly he had blundered. He had reached Conster two hours before dinner, and trusted that this phenomenon might prepare his father for some surprise. But, disappointingly, Sir John did not notice his return—he had grown lately to think less and less about his youngest son, who was seldom at home and whom he looked upon as an outsider. Gervase had deliber-

ately alienated himself from Alard, and Sir John could never, in spite of Peter's efforts, be brought properly to consider him as an heir. His goings out and his comings in were
of little consequence to the head of the house. So when at
six o clock Gervase came into the study, his father was quite
unimpressed.

"May I speak to you for a minute, Sir?"

"Well, well—what is it?"

Sir John dipped *Country Life* the fraction of an inch to
imply a temporary hearing.

"It's about Jenny, Sir."

"Well, what about her?"

"She's—I've been with her in town today. I've just come
back. She asked me to tell you about her and young Godfrey."

"What's that? Speak up, Sir, can't you? I can't hear when
you mumble. Come and stand where I can see you."

Gervase came and stood on the hearth-rug. He was beginning to feel nervous. Uncomfortable memories of childhood rushed up confusedly from the back of his mind, and
gave him sore feelings of helplessness and inferiority.

"It's about Jenny and young Godfrey, Sir."

"Godfrey! Who's Godfrey?"

"Benjamin Godfrey of Fourhouses—the man who bought
your Snailham land."

"Well, what about him?"

"It's about him and Jenny, Sir."

"Well, *what* about 'em? What the devil's he got to do with
Jenny?"

"Don't you remember she went to tea at Fourhouses last
week?"

"She hasn't been there again, has she?"

Gervase considered that the subject had been sufficiently led up to—anyhow he could stand no more of the preliminaries.

"Well, yes, Sir—at least she's having tea with him now—at least not tea ... I mean, they were married this morning."

Sir John dropped *Country Life*.

"Married this morning," he repeated in a lame, normal voice.

"Yes, Sir, at St. Ethelburga's, Paddington. They've been in love with each other for some time, but as they didn't expect you'd quite see things as they did, they thought they'd better wait to tell you till after the ceremony."

"And where—where are they now?"

"At Mullion, Sir—in Cornwall."

Sir John said nothing. His face turned grey, and he trembled. Gervase was distressed.

"Don't take it so dreadfully to heart, Father. I'm sure it's really for the best. He's a decent chap, and very well-to-do—he'll be able to give her everything she's been accustomed to"—remembering an old tag.

"Get out!" said Sir John suddenly.

"I'm frightfully sorry if you think we've treated you badly, Sir. But really we tried to do it in the way we thought would hurt you least."

"Get out!" repeated his father—"get out of here. This is your doing, with your socialism, with your contempt for your own family, with your.... Get out of the room, or I'll...."

His shaking hand groped round for a missile, and Gervase moved hastily to the door, too late, however, to escape a bound volume of *Punch*, which preceded him into the hall.

Wills was standing outside the dining-room door with

a tray, and Gervase found it very difficult to look dignified. Such an attitude was even more difficult to keep up during the alarms that followed. He retreated to his bedroom, taking *Punch* with him, partly as a solace, partly in a feeble hope of persuading Wills that to have a book thrown at your head is a normal way of borrowing it. He had not been alone a quarter of an hour before he was summoned by Speller, his mother's maid.

There followed an interview which began in reproaches, passed on to an enquiry into Jenny's luggage—had she bought brushes and sponges in London, since she had taken nothing away?—and ended cloudily in hysterics and lavender water. Gervase went back to his room, which ten minutes later was entered by the sobbing Doris, who informed him he had "killed Mother," who apparently required a post-mortem interview. Once again he went down to the boudoir with its rose-coloured lights and heavy scents of restoratives, and to the jerky accompaniment of Doris's weeping told his story over again. He had to tell it a fourth time to Peter, who had been summoned from Starvecrow, and found that it was hardening into set phrases, and sounded rather like the patter of a guide recounting some historic elopement from a great house.

"They've been in love for some time, but as they didn't expect you'd quite see things as they did—"

"My God!" said Peter.

He was perhaps the most scandalised of all the Alards, and had about him a solemn air of wounding which was more distressing to Gervase than his father's wrath.

"I introduced him to her," he said heavily—"I introduced

him. I never thought ... how *could* I think ... that she held herself so cheap—all of us so cheap."

"You really needn't treat the matter as if Jenny had married the rag-and-bone man—"began Gervase.

"I know Godfrey's position quite well."

"He farms his own land, and comes of good old stock. He's well off, and will be able to give her everything she's been accustomed to—"

"He won't. She's been accustomed to the society of gentlepeople, and he'll never be able to give her that. She's gone to live on a farm, where she'll have her meals in the kitchen with the farm-men. I tell you I know the Godfreys, and they're nothing more than a respectable, good sort of farming people who've done well out of the war. At least, I won't call them even that now," he added fiercely—"I won't call a man respectable who worms himself into intimacy with my sister on the strength of my having introduced him."

"However, it's some comfort to think they've gone to the Poldhu hotel at Mullion," said Lady Alard; "the Blakelocks were there once, you know, Doris, and the Reggie Mulcasters. She won't notice the difference quite so terribly since he's taken her there."

"Yes, she will," said Peter—"she'll notice the difference between the kind of man she's been used to meeting here and a working farmer, who wasn't even an officer during the war. If she doesn't—I'll think worse of her even than I do now. And as for you—" turning suddenly on Gervase—"I don't trust myself to tell you what I think of you. I expect you're pleased that we've suffered this disgrace—that a lady of our house has married into the peasantry. You think it's democratic and all that. You're glad—don't say you're not."

"Yes, I am glad, because Jenny's happy. You, none of you, seem to think of that. You don't seem to think that 'the kind of man she's been meeting here' hasn't been the slightest use to her—that all he's done has been to trouble her and trifle with her and then go off and marry money—that now at last she's met a man who's treated her honourably—"

"Honourably! He's treated her like the adventurer he is. Oh, it's a fine thing of him to marry into our family, even if she hasn't got a penny—his ancestors were our serfs—they ran at our people's stirrups, and our men had the *droit du seigneur* of their women—"

"And pulled out the teeth of your wife's forefathers," said Gervase, losing his temper. "If you're going back five hundred years, I don't think your own marriage will bear the test."

He knew that if he stayed he would quarrel with them all, and he did not want to do that, for he was really sorry for them, wounded in their most sensitive feelings of family pride. He walked out of the room, and made for the attic stairs, seeking the rest and dignity of solitude. But it was not to be. The door of his father's dressing-room opened as he passed, and Sir John came out on the landing, already dressed for dinner.

"You understand that after what has happened I cannot keep you here."

He was quite calm now, and rather terrifying.

"I—oh, no—I mean yes, of course," stammered Gervase.

"You have work at Ashford, so you can go and lodge near it. Or you can go to your Ritualist friends at Vinehall. I refuse to have you here after your treachery. You are a traitor, Sir— to your own family."

"When—when would you like me to go?"

"You can stay till tomorrow morning."

"Thanks—I'll leave tonight."

So the day's catastrophe ended in Gervase driving off through the darkness in Henry Ford, his suit-case and a few parcels of books behind him. He had decided to go to Luce— the Priest would take him in till he was able to go to Thunders Abbey.

"Well, anyhow, I'm spared that other row," he thought to himself; "or, rather, I've got through two rows in one. Father won't mind what I do with myself after this."

He felt rather forlorn as the lorry's lights swept up the Vinehall road. During the last few months he had been stripped of so many things—his devotion to Stella, his comradeship with Jenny—he knew that he could never be to her what he had been before she married—and now his family and his home. And all he had to look forward to was a further, more complete stripping, even of the clothes he wore, so that in all the world he would own nothing.

§10

Any lack of cordiality in Luce's welcome was made up by his quite matter-of-fact acceptance of this sudden descent upon him at a late hour of a young man and all his worldly goods, including a Ford lorry. The latter was given the inn stable as a refuge, while Gervase was told he could have the spare bedroom as long as he liked if he would clear out the apples. This done and some porridge eaten, he went to bed, utterly worn out, and feeling less like Gervase Alard than he had ever felt in his life.

The next day he went off to work as usual, sending a telegram to Jenny on his way. When he came back he found a message had arrived from Conster—he must go home at once; his father had had a stroke.

"I've a ghastly feeling it was brought on by this row," he said to Luce, as he filled up the lorry's tank for the new journey.

"It must have been," was all the reassurance he got.

Gervase felt wretched enough. The message, which had been left by Dr. Mount, gave no details, and as the cottage was empty when he called, there had been no verbal additions or explanations. He thought of calling at the doctor's on his way to Leasan—he had meant to go there anyhow this evening and tell them about Jenny's marriage—but he decided it was best to lose no time, and drove straight to Conster.

Here he received his first respite. The stroke was not a severe one, and Dr. Mount was practically certain Sir John would get over it. However, he seemed to think the other members of the family ought to be sent for, and Doris had telegraphed to Mary but not to Jenny, as she didn't think Jenny deserved it after what she had done. She did not think Gervase deserved it, either, but evidently Dr. Mount had taken it upon himself to decide, and left a message without consulting her.

He was not allowed to go near his father that night, and spent the hours intermittently sleeping and waking in his little cold bedroom, now empty of everything that was really his. The next morning he went out and sent a telegram to Jenny. But by the time she arrived her presence was useless. Sir John had recovered consciousness and would see none of his erring children. Mary, Gervase and Jenny waited together in the drawing-room in hopes that the edict would be revoked. But, as Doris came down to tell them at intervals, it was no use whatever. He refused to let them come near him—indeed, the mere mention of their names seemed to irritate him dangerously. Towards evening Dr. Mount advised them to go away.

"I'm afraid there's no hope, at present anyhow—and it's best not to worry him. There's often a very great irritability in these cases. He may become calmer as his condition improves."

So Jenny, scared and tired, was taken away by her husband to the shelter of Fourhouses, and Gervase prepared to go back to Vinehall. They were both rather guiltily conscious that they did not pity those who had been denied the presence so much as those who were bound to it—Doris, who as unofficial nurse and substitute scapegoat, was already beginning to show signs of wear and tear—and Peter, worn with a growing sense of responsibility and the uncertain future brought a step nearer ... no doubt the younger ones had made an easy escape.

Only Mary looked a bit wistful.

"It's so long since I've seen him," she said as she stood on the steps, waiting for the car which was to take her back to Hastings.

"Cheer up, my dear—he'll change his mind when he gets better," said Gervase.

Mary shook her head. She had altered strikingly since he had seen her last. She seemed all clothes—faultless, beautiful clothes, which seemed mysteriously a part of herself so that it was difficult to imagine her without them. Her real self had

shrunk, faded, become something like a whisper or a ghost—
she was less Mary Pembroke than a suit of lovely grey velvet
and fur which had somehow come alive and taken the simu-
lacrum of a woman to show off its beauty.

"Where are you going?" he asked her, moved with a sudden anxious pity.

"Back to Hastings. I've found a very comfortable small
hotel, and I think I'll stay there till I know more how things
are going with Father. I expect I shall run over and see Jenny
now and then."

"I'm glad you're going to do that," he cried warmly—"it'll
mean a lot to her to have one of the family with her—especially when I'm gone."

"You?—where are you going?"

He found himself quite unable to tell her of what he was
looking forward to.

"Oh, my work at Ashford comes to an end in a week, and
I'll have to pack off somewhere else."

He kissed her before she went away, and found an unexpected warmth in her lips. After all, the real Mary had always
lived very far beneath the surface, and as years went by and
the surface had become more and more ravaged she had retreated deeper and deeper down. But he was glad to think
that at the bottom, and perhaps by queer, perverse means, she
had somehow managed to keep herself alive.

§11

Jenny's sudden return had the disadvantage of bringing her
back into the midst of her family while the scandal of her
marriage was still hot. As her father refused to see her, Ben

had suggested taking her away again, but Jenny did not like to leave while Sir John was still in any danger, and by the time all danger was past, her husband's affairs had once more fast bound him to the farm—besides, the various members of her family had adjusted themselves to her defection, and settled down either into hostility or championship, according to their own status in the tribe.

It was characteristic of the house of Alard that even its revolted members camped round it in its evil hour, held to it by human feeling after all other links were broken. No one would leave the neighbourhood while Sir John continued ill and shaken. Mary stayed at Hastings, and Gervase stayed at Vinehall, even after his apprenticeship to Gillingham's had finally come to an end, and the men had given him a farewell oyster supper at the White Lion, with a presentation wristwatch to add to the little stock of possessions he would have to give up in a few weeks.

However, by the beginning of February, Sir John had so far recovered as to make any waiting unnecessary. He still refused to see his disloyal son and rebellious daughters. His illness seemed to have hardened his obstinacy, and to have brought about certain irritable conditions which sometimes approached violence and made it impossible to attempt any persuasion.

He came downstairs and took up his indoor life as usual, though out of doors he no longer rode about on his grey horse. The entire overseership of the estate devolved on Peter, with the additional burden that his responsibility was without authority—his father insisted on retaining the headship and on revising or overthrowing his decisions. Nothing could be done without reference to him, and his illness seemed to have

made him queerly perverse. He insisted that an offer from
a firm of timber-merchants for the whole of Little Sowden
Wood should be refused, though Peter explained to him that
at present the wood actually cost more in its upkeep than was
realised by the underwood sales in the local market.

"Why should I have one of the finest woods on my estate
smashed up by a firm of war-profiteers? Confound you, Sir!
Many's the fox that hounds have put up in Sowden, and the
place was thick when Conster started building."

"But we're in desperate need of ready money, Father. We
can't afford to start repairs at Glasseye, and this is the third
year we've put off. There's Monkings, too,—the place is falling to pieces, and Luck says he'll quit if he has to wait any
longer."

"Quit?—Let him. He needn't threaten me. Tenants aren't
so scarce."

"Good tenants are. We aren't likely to get a man who
farms the land as well as Luck. He got the Penny field to carry seven bushel to the acre last year. He's clockwork with the
rent, too—you know the trouble we have over rent."

"But I won't have Sowden cut down to keep him. Timber!
I thought we were done with that shame when the war ended, and we'd lost Eleven Pounder and Little Horn."

"But I can't see anything more shameful in selling timber than in selling land, and you sold that Snailham piece last
year to—"

Peter tried to retrieve his blunder, but his mind was not
for quick manoeuvres and all he could do was to flush and
turn guiltily silent. His father's anger blazed at once.

"Yes—we sold land last year, and a good business we

made of it, didn't we! The bounder thought he'd bought my daughter into the bargain. He thought he'd got the pull of us because we were glad to sell. I tell you, I'll sell no more of my land, if it puts such ideas into the heads of the rascals that buy it, if it makes all the beastly tenants and small-holders within thirty miles think they can come and slap me on the back and make love to my daughters and treat me as one of themselves. I'll not sell another foot as long as I live. When I die, Sir, you may not get a penny, but you'll get the biggest estate in East Sussex."

Peter groaned.

§12

Gervase did not think it advisable to go near his family when the time came for him to leave Vinehall for Thunders Abbey. He would have liked to see his mother, but knew too well that the interview would end only in eau de Cologne and burnt feathers. Since he was exiled, it was best to accept his exile as a working principle and not go near the house. He knew that later on he would be given opportunities to see his parents, and by then time might have made them respectively less hostile and less hysterical.

So he wrote his mother a very affectionate letter, trying to explain what he was going to do, but not putting any great faith in her understanding him. He told her that he would be able to come and see her later, and sent his love to Doris and Peter and his father. He also wrote a line to Mary. His personal farewells were for Stella and Jenny only.

To Stella he said goodbye the day before he left. He found her making preparations for her own departure. She and her father were leaving for Canada as soon as Mrs. Peter Alard was through her confinement, which she expected in a couple of weeks. The practice had been sold, and the escape into a new life and a new country was no longer a possible resort of desperation but a fixed doom for her unwilling heart.

All she had been able to do during the last weeks had been to let her father act without interference. Her entire conflict had been set in withholding herself from last-moment entreaties to stay, from attempts at persuading him to withdraw from negotiations over the practice, from suggestions that their departure should be put off to the end of the summer. So negative had been her battle that she had never felt the thrill of combat—instead she felt utterly crushed and weary. She felt both dead and afraid ... the only moments in which she seemed to live were the moments in which she encountered Peter, passing him occasionally on the road or meeting him in a neighbour's house. They were terrible moments of fiery concentrated life—she was glad afterwards to fall back into her stupor. She and he had had no more private conversations—she was able to pursue her negative battle to the extent of avoiding these—but his mere presence seemed to make alive a Stella Mount who was dying, whose death she sometimes thought of as a blessing and sometimes as a curse.

When she saw Gervase, so quiet and sweet-tempered and happy, she wondered if she would possibly be like that when her love for Peter was dead, as his for her was dead. But then his love for her was not dead—that was the whole point; like Enoch, it was translated—it was not, because God had taken it. As she looked into his peaceful eyes, her own filled with tears. She wondered if he had won his battle so quickly because it had been a slighter one than hers, or because he was better armed. Probably because of both. He was younger than she, his passions still slept in his austere, hard-working youth—and would probably awake only to find themselves reborn in his religious life—also, she realised that he might be naturally spiritual, whereas she had never been more than spiritually natural—a distinction. He was a man born to love God as she had been born to love men, and she knew that, in spite of all he said, he would have found his beloved sooner or later without any help of hers.

"Goodbye, dear Gervase," she said, and pressed his hand.

"Goodbye, Stella"—surprisingly he kissed her, like another girl. She had not thought he would dare kiss her at all, and this warm, light, natural kiss—the kiss of a gentle friend—showed her a self-conquest more complete than any she had imagined—certainly than any she would ever know. She might be strong enough to deny her kisses to Peter, but she would never be able to give him the kiss of a friend.

§13

The next day Gervase drove off to Thunders Abbey, and went by way of Icklesham. It was a windless afternoon; the first scent of primroses hid in the hollows of the lanes, and the light of the sun, raking over the fields, was primrose-coloured on the grass. The browsing sheep and cattle cast long shadows, and the shadows of the leafless trees were clear, a delicate tracery at their roots.

As he drove up and down the steep, wheel-scarred lanes he watched familiar farms and spinneys go by as if it were for the last time. He knew that he would see them all many times after this, but somehow it would not be the same. Gervase Alard would be dead, as Jenny Alard was dead, and he felt as Jenny had felt the night before her wedding—glad and yet afraid. He remembered her words—"Can't you understand?—It's because I don't feel big enough ... afraid." He, too, felt afraid of his new life, and for the same reason—because he knew he was not big enough. Yet, in spite of her fear, Jenny had gone on, and now she was happy. And he was going on, and perhaps he would be happy, too.

He found her baking little cakes for tea. She tapped on the kitchen window when the lorry rattled into the yard, and he came in and took her in his arms, in spite of her protest that she was all over flour.

"Hullo, Gervase! this is splendid—I haven't seen you for ages."

She was wearing a blue gingham overall, and with her face flushed at the fire, and her background of brick, scrubbed wood and painted canisters, she looked more like a farmer's wife than he could ever have imagined possible. She had grown plump, too, since her marriage, and her eyes had changed—they looked bright, yet half asleep, like a cat's eyes.

"I've come to say goodbye, Jen. I'm off to Thunders."

"When?—Tomorrow?"

"No—this very evening. I'll go straight on from here."

"Gervase!"

She looked sad—she understood him less than ever now.

"Father Lawrence wrote two days ago and said they were able to take me—and I've nothing to wait for. Father won't see me. I've written to Mother—I thought it better than farewells in the flesh."

"And Stella?"

"I've said goodbye to her."

"Gervase, I know—I feel sure you're only doing this because of her."

"Well, I can't show you now that you're wrong, but I hope time will."

"I hope it won't show you that *you*'re wrong—when it's too late. My dear—" She went up to him and put her hands on his shoulders—"My dear, you're so young."

"Don't, Jen."

"But it's true. Why can't you wait till you've seen more of life—till you've lived, in fact?"

"Because I don't want to give God just the fag-end of myself, the leavings of what you call life. I want to give Him the best I've got—all my best years."

"If Stella had accepted you, you would have married her, and we shouldn't have heard anything about all this."

"That's true. But she refused me, and it was her refusal which showed me the life I was meant for. The fact that I loved Stella, and she would not have me, showed me that God does not want me to marry."

He seemed to Jenny transparent and rather silly, like a child.

"But you're only twenty-one," she persisted gently, as she would with a child. "You'd have been sure to fall in love again and marry someone else."

"And there's no good telling you I'm sure I shouldn't. However, my dear, I'm not going to prison on a life sentence—I can come out tomorrow if I don't like it; and probably for a year or so the whole community will be trying to turn me out—they're as much afraid of a mistake as you are."

"I don't trust them. They only too seldom get hold of men in your position."

"My dear, don't let's talk any more about me. It's making us quarrel, and probably this is the last time I shall see you for months. Tell me how you've been getting on. Has the County called yet?"

"Not so as you'd notice. As a matter of fact, the Fullers left cards the other day. Agney's far enough off for it not to matter very much, and I think Mrs. Fuller has a reputation for being broad-minded which she's had to live up to. But I'm getting to like Ben's friends—I told you I should. There's the Boormans of Frays Land and the Hatches of Old Place, and a very nice, well-educated bailiff at Roughter, who collects prints and old furniture. I see a lot of them—they've been here and I've been to their houses; and as Mrs. Godfrey and the girls keep to their own part of the house, I've got my hands full from morning to night, and don't have much time to think about anything I may have lost."

"It seems to suit you, anyhow. You look fine."

"I feel splendid. Of course, I couldn't do it if it wasn't for Ben. I don't pretend I've found everything in the life agreeable, after what I've been used to. But Ben makes everything worth doing and worth bearing."

"And that's how it is with me. Can't you understand now, Jen?—I've got something, too, which makes it all worth doing and worth bearing—though I don't pretend, any more than you do, that I expect to find everything in my life agreeable."

"I'll try to understand, Gervase; but I don't suppose I'll succeed—and you really can't expect it of me."

"All right, I won't, just yet." He picked his cap and gloves off the table—"I really must be going now."

"Won't you stay and have some tea? I've got over the failure stage in cakes—I really think these will be quite eatable."

"No, thanks very much, I mustn't stay. It'll take Henry quite two hours to get to Brighton."

She did not seem to hear him—she was listening. He could hear nothing, but a moment later a footstep sounded in the yard.

"There he is," said Jenny.

She went out into the passage and closed the door behind her.

He was left alone in the big kitchen. The fire and the kettle hummed together to the ticking of the clock, and there was a soft, sweet smell of baking cakes. The last of the sunshine was spilling through the window on to the scrubbed, deal table, and over all the scene hung an impalpable atmosphere of comfort, warmth and peace. Outside in the passage he could hear the murmuring of a man's and a woman's voices.... His eyes suddenly filled with tears.

They were gone when Jenny came back into the room with Ben, who had evidently been told the reason for his brother-in-law's visit, for he shook hands in clumsy silence.

"How do you do?" said Gervase—"and goodbye."

Ben still said nothing. He neither approved nor understood young Alard's ways. Religion was for him the ten commandments, Parson's tithes, and harvest thanksgivings—anything further smacked of Chapel and the piety of smallholders. But he was too fond of Gervase to say openly what was in his heart, and as he was not used to saying anything else, he was driven into an awkward but well-meaning silence.

"I'm glad you're taking Henry with you," said Jenny, attempting lightness—"It would have been dreadful if you'd had to leave him behind."

"Yes—'The Arab's Farewell to His Steed' wouldn't have been in it. But I'm taking him as my dowry. They'll find some use for him at Thunders—he's got at least one cylinder working. If they hadn't wanted him I'd have given him to Ben—just to encourage him to start machinery on the farm."

"I'd sooner keep my horses, thank you," said Ben, relieved at having something to say at last. "Give me a horse-ploughed field, even if it does take twice the labour."

"But you'll be getting a tractor soon, won't you? That's another idea altogether, and you'll never find horses to beat that."

Thus talking of machinery the three of them went to the door, and said goodbye under cover of argument.

"You'll see me again before long," cried Gervase, as he drove off.

"Will you be able to write to us?"

"Of course I will—look out for a letter in a day or two."

With hideous grindings, explosions and plaints, the lorry went off down the drive. As it disappeared between the hedgerows, Jenny felt her heart contract in a pang of helpless pity.

"Oh, Ben.... He's so young—and he's never had anything."

She would have cried, but her husband's arm slipped round her, drawing her back into the darkening house.

§14

Jenny had been candid with Gervase in her account of herself. She was happy—supremely so—but there was much that would have been difficult were it not for the love which "made everything worth doing and worth bearing." She had nothing to complain of in Ben himself. He was after marriage the same as he had been before it—gentle, homely, simple and upright, with a streak of instinctive refinement which compensated for any lack of stress on the physical cleanliness which was the god of her former tribe. It is true that he expected more of her than Jim Parish, for instance, would have done. The sight of Jenny rising at half-past six to light the kitchen fire, cooking the breakfast, and doing all the housework with the help of one small girl, did not strike him as the act of wifely devotion and Spartan virtue that it seemed to her and would have seemed to Jim. It was what the women of his experience did invariably, and with a certain naive thickheadedness he had not expected Jenny, taken from a home of eight o clock risings, to be different. But in all other ways he was considerate—ways in which the men of her class would most probably not have considered her; and she soon became used to the physical labour of her days. Indeed, after the first surprise at his attitude, she realised that anything else would have brought an atmosphere of unreality into the life which she loved because it was so genuine. Farmers' wives—even prosperous farmers' wives—did not lie in bed till eight, or sit idle while the servants worked; and Jenny was now a farmer's wife—Mrs. Ben Godfrey of Fourhouses—with her place to keep clean, her husband and her husband's men to feed, her dairy and her poultry to attend to.

But though she loved Ben, and loved working for him, there were other things that were hard, and she was too clear-headed not to acknowledge the difficulties she had chosen. She often longed to be alone with her husband, instead of having to share him with his mother and sisters. According to yeoman custom, his wife had been brought into his home, which was also his family's home, and she must take what she found there. Jenny realised that she might have been worse off—she was genuinely fond of Mrs. Godfrey and Lily and Jane, and their separate quarters gave her a privacy and a freedom she would not have had on many farms—but she would have been less sensitive to the gulf between her new life and the old if she had been alone with Ben. His women, with their constant absorption in house-work—making it not so much a duty to be done and then forgotten as a religion pervading the whole life—with their arbitrary standards of decorum, and their total lack of interest in any mental processes—often begot in her revolt and weariness, especially when her husband was much away. She had not known till then how much she depended on stray discussions of books and politics, on the interchange of abstract and general ideas. Ben himself could give her these stimulations, for the war had enlarged his education, and his love for her made him eager to meet her on the ground she chose. But his work often took him into the fields soon after dawn, and he would not be privately hers again till night, for the meals at Fourhouses were communal and democratic; not only Mrs. Godfrey and her daughters, but the stockman, the cow-man, the carter and the ploughboys sat down to table with the master.

Moreover, after a month or two, she began to feel her

estrangement from her people. She did not miss her old acquaintances among the county families, but she felt the silence of her home more than she would ever have imagined
possible. No one from Conster—her father or mother or Doris—had come near her or sent her a word. There had been
the same silence up at Starvecrow which surprised her more,
for she and Vera had always been friends—though of course
Vera had her own special preoccupations now. Rose had
called, but evidently with a view to replenishing her stores
of gossip for Leasan tea-parties, and Jenny had done all she
could to discourage another visit. Mary generally came over
from Hastings once a week, but hers were only the visits of a
fellow-exile.

In her heart, the estrangement which Jenny felt the most
was between herself and Peter. She had not expected such
treatment from him. She had expected anger and disappointment, certainly, a stormy interview, perhaps, but not this blank.
Sometimes she told herself he was anxious about Vera, and
that his own troubles had combined with her misbehaviour to
keep him away. She forced herself to patience, hoping uncer-
tainly that the fortunate birth of an heir would bring old Peter
to a better frame of mind.

Meanwhile, she was reviving her friendship with Mary, or
rather was building up a new one, for in old times she had felt
a little afraid of her elegant, aloof sister. She was not afraid
of Mary now—indeed, from the vantage of her own happy
establishment she almost pitied this woman who had left so
much behind her in dark places.

Mary liked Ben—but her temperament had set her at a
great distance from his homely concreteness. Though she

stood by her sister in her adventure, she evidently could not think "what Jenny saw in him," and she was openly full of plans for his improvement and education.

"Why don't you lift him up to your level instead of stooping to his? You could easily do it. He's deeply in love with you, and, in my opinion, very much above his own way of life. Fourhouses is a good estate and he's got plenty of money to improve it—with a little trouble he could make it into a country house and himself into a small squire."

"Thanks," said Jenny—"That's what I've just escaped— from country houses and squires—and I don't want to start the whole thing over again. Why should Ben try to make himself a squire, when the squires are dying out all over the country, and their estates are being broken up and sold back to the people they used to belong to?"

"Jenny, you talk like a radical!—'God gave the land to the people' and all that."

"My husband's a vice-president of the Conservative Club. It isn't for any political reasons that I don't want to fight my way back into the county. It's simply that I'm sick of two things—struggle and pretence. Situated as I am, I've got neither—if I tried to keep what I gave up—when I married Ben, I'd have both."

"It's all very well for you to talk like this now—when everything's new. Even I know what the first months of marriage can be like…. But later on, when things have sobered down, you'll feel different—you'll want to see some of your old friends again, and wish you hadn't shut them out."

"If you mean the Parishes and the Hursts and the Wades and all that lot, nothing I could ever do would make them my friends again. You see, they're friends of Father's, and, considering his attitude towards my marriage—which would be the same whatever I did to raise myself—they can never be friends of mine. It isn't as if I'd moved thirty miles off and had a new sort of county to visit me. I'm in the middle of the old crowd, and they can never be friendly with me without offending my people. No, I must be content with Ben's friends—if I tried to improve him we'd lose those, too, and then I'd have nobody."

"I daresay you're right, my dear—you sound practical, anyway. And I've no right to teach anyone how to arrange their lives.... It's queer, isn't it, Jen? I took, generally speaking, no risks when I married. I married a man I loved, a man of my own class, whom my people approved of—and look at me now. You, on the other hand, have taken every imaginable risk—a runaway match, a different class, and the family curse."

"You'll have to look at me twelve years hence to compare me with you."

"I think you're going to be all right, though—even if you don't take my advice."

"I'm sure I shall be all right. You see, I'm doing everything with my eyes open. You didn't have your eyes open, Mary."

"I know I didn't. Very few women do. Most brides are like new-born kittens with their eyes shut."

"Are you happy now?"

It was the first time she had dared ask the question. Mary hesitated—

"Yes, I suppose I am happy. I have enough to live on, I have my friends—I travel about, and see places and people."

"Have you ever regretted that you didn't marry Charles?"

"Regretted! Good Lord, no! The very opposite. I didn't love him in that way, and we'd both have been wretched. Poor old dear! I'm glad I'd strength enough to spare him that, though I spared him nothing else...."

"Do you ever see him now?"

"Sometimes. He's married, you know—a very young thing, who doesn't like me too much. I didn't expect him to marry, but I believe he's happy. I hear that Julian is happy, too—he has two little boys and a baby girl. So I haven't really done either of my men much harm."

"No—it's you who've suffered the harm. Why haven't you married again, Mary? I've always expected you to."

Her sister shook her head.

"I can't—there's something in me lacking for that. I can't explain, and it sounds an extraordinary thing to say, but I feel as if I'd left it with Julian. I don't mean that I still love him or any nonsense like that—I hadn't loved him for a year before I left him ... but somehow one doesn't get rid of a husband as easily as the divorce-courts and the newspapers seem to suppose."

"If you'd married again you'd have forgotten Julian."

"No, I shouldn't, and I should have made another man un-happy—because of what's lacking in me. I know there are lots of women who can go from the church to the divorce-court and from the divorce-court to the registrar's, and leave noth-ing behind them in any of these places. But I'm not like that—I left my love with Julian and my pride with Charles. Sometimes I feel that if only I'd had the strength to stick to Julian a little longer, we'd have weathered things through—I'd have got back what I'd lost, and all this wouldn't have happened. But it's a waste of time to think of that now.... Don't worry about me, Jen. I'm happy in my own way—though it may not be yours, or many women's, for that matter. I've just managed to be strong enough not to spoil Charles's life—not to drag him down—so I've got one good memory.... And I'm free—that means more to me than perhaps you can realise—and I enjoy life as a spectator. I've suffered enough as an actor on the stage, and now I'm just beginning to feel comfortable in the stalls."

"Don't," said Jenny.

She could not bear any more—this was worse than Gervase. To have spent all the treasure of life on dust and wind was even worse than to give up that treasure unspent. She found the tears running out of her eyes as she put her arms round Mary—softness of furs and sweetness of violets, and in the midst of them a sister who was half doll and half ghost.

§15

Towards the end of March, Peter's daughter was born. He bore the disappointment better than anyone had expected. But lately it had not seemed to him to matter very much whether the child were a boy or a girl. His horizons were closing in upon him—they had even shut out his own inheritance, with the new powers and freedoms it would bring, and he could not look so far ahead as the prospects of his heir. Even Gervase's defection had not stirred him long. In his first shock of outrage and disgust he had motored over to Thunders Abbey and tried to persuade his brother to come back with him, but finding him obdurate, his emotions had col-

lapsed into a contempt which was queerly mixed with envy.
If Gervase preferred these debased states of life—first in a
garage and then in a monastery—to the decencies of his position as an Alard, then let him have what he wanted. It was
something to know what one wanted and take it unafraid.
Gervase might be a traitor, but he was not a fool.

So Peter heard unmoved Dr. Mount's announcement that
a little girl had been born, and only a trifle less unmoved received the woolly bundle of his little daughter into his arms.
He did not, as some men, awake to a new sense of fatherhood
at the touch of his firstborn. His failure as a husband seemed
to affect him as a father. He did not ask himself what he
would have felt if the child had been a boy. The only question
in his heart was what he would have felt if it had been Stella's
child ... but that was a useless question.

Vera was secretly glad to have a girl. She had always
wanted a daughter, and lately, as her mind had detached itself more and more from her husband's wishes, the want
had become anxious. A boy she always pictured as a second
Peter—heavy, obstinate, his heart set on things she did not
care about—but a girl would be a companion, and her own.
There would be, she felt, some chance of her growing up like
her mother and sharing her mother's adventures in intellect
and beauty; also, in that new florescence of her race which
had accompanied her pregnancy, she felt that her daughter would be truly a daughter of Abraham, whereas her son
would be born into a public-school tradition and the heirship
of a big estate—a child of the Goyim. So she stretched out
her arms gladly when the baby girl was put into them, and as
she looked down into the mysterious, ancient little face of the

newborn, her heart leapt with joy and pride to see the tokens of her blood already discernible, not so much in its later Hebraic characteristics as in some general oriental quality, older than Abraham.

"There's nothing of the Goy about her, is there?" she said to her mother, who had come to be with her in her confinement.

"No, indeed, there's not. She takes after us. It's curious how they nearly always do in a mixed marriage."

But, in the midst of her own gratification, Vera was glad to find that her husband was not bitterly disappointed. Poor old Peter! He had been estranged from her, she knew, and had wanted to marry the Mount woman, but she could forgive him in the triumph of her recovery. She had the child, and was rapidly getting well. When she was herself again she would win him back. She knew how ... it never failed.

In her presence Peter made his disappointment seem even less than it really was. The sight of her lying there in loveliness both opulent and exhausted—knowing vaguely what she had suffered and accepted—stirred in him a strange, admiring pity which forbade an unthankful word. He bore no resentment against her now. It was not her fault that she stood between him and Stella. Probably he had treated her badly— she might have suffered nearly as much as he.... And he was glad she had her reward.

But even when looking tenderly down on her, speaking tenderly to her, he could not picture himself going on with their marriage again. When his family and acquaintance tried to cheer him up for the disappointment of having a girl, they always said, "But it's only the first, Peter...." "The first never really matters...." and all the time he was feeling that there could not be another. It was a preposterous feeling, he knew, for, after Gervase's defection, it was imperative that he should have an heir; and men are not like women in these things. He had never had Stella—he could never have Stella. Why should he feel this aversion from doing his duty as a husband and an Alard? He did not know—but he felt it, almost to shrinking. He felt that his marriage was at an end—broken and yet binding—for Stella could not take him after divorce any more than she could take him without it. And everyone said "It's only the first" ... "It's just as well for the girl to come first—to be the oldest."...

A few days after the baby's birth Vera had a letter from Jenny, congratulating her and sending her love to Peter. She did not ask her brother to come over and see her, but Peter guessed what was behind her message. In the loneliness of those first days when the house seemed full of women and affairs from which he was shut out, he had a longing to go over to Fourhouses, and see Jenny and be friends again. But he was held back, partly by a feeling of awkwardness, a sense of the explanations and reproaches his visit would involve, partly by a remaining stiffness against her treachery, and most of all by a dull stirring sense of envy—the same as, though more accountable than, the envy he had felt for Gervase. Here again was someone who knew what she wanted and had got it, whom the family had not bound fast and swallowed up—and the worst of it all was that, unlike Gervase, she had got what Peter wanted, too. In vain he told himself that she could never be happy with Godfrey, could never adapt herself to the life she had chosen, that her plunge would be no more justified than his withdrawal. He dared not go near Fourhouses all the same.

§16

The hopes on which the baby's birth seemed to have fallen heaviest were Sir John's. The old man had had none of Peter's uncertainty or anxiety before the event—he had felt sure the child would be a boy. The news that it was a girl had been a terrible shock, and though it had not, as was feared at first, brought on another seizure, it was soon seen to have increased the nervous unsteadiness of his constitution. He alone, of all the Alards, did not join in the cry of "This is the first." First or last, it was probably the only grandchild he would live to see, and he expressed his disappointment with the candid selfishness of old age.

"Here have I been waiting for a boy—counting on a boy— and it's a girl after all. What good's a girl to us? We've got plenty of girls—or those who were once girls"—and he glared at Doris—"all they do is either to disgrace us in the divorce-courts, marry the sweep, or turn into bad-tempered old maids. We've got enough girls. It's a boy we want—with that Gervase gone off to be a monk. I've been badly served by my children."

"But, Father, it wasn't Peter's fault," urged Doris unskilfully.

"Wasn't it, Ma'am? You *do* know a lot—more than an unmarried woman ought to know about such things. I believe you even know that the baby wasn't found under a gooseberry bush."

"Oh, Father, don't talk in such a dreadful way—He's really getting quite awful," she said as she let Peter out—"I sometimes think there's something wrong with his brain."

"There probably is," said Peter.

Indeed, of late Sir John had grown alarmingly eccentric.

His love of rule had passed beyond the administration of his estate, and showed itself in a dozen ways of petty dominion. He seemed resolved to avenge his authority over the three rebellious children on the two who had remained obedient. Not only did he put up a forest of forbidding notices over his estate, to keep out the general public, which had hitherto had free entrance to most of his fields and woods, but he forbade his own children to use certain paths. He would not let Peter come by the field way from Starvecrow, but insisted on his going round by the road. He would stop Doris on the threshold of an afternoon's calling, and compel her to sit and read to him, by choice books which he calculated to offend her old-maidish susceptibilities. He found Doris better game than Peter, for whereas the son remained silent under his kicks, Doris never failed to give him all the fun he wanted in the way of protests, arguments, laments and tears. But from both he obtained obedience, through their dread of exciting him and bringing on another stroke.

His warfare was less open with his wife. He attacked her indirectly through the servants, who were always giving notice owing to his intimidation. Even Wills had once distantly informed his mistress that since Sir John did not seem to appreciate his services he might soon have to consider the advisability of transferring them elsewhere. Appleby had actually given notice, after a mysterious motor drive, from which Sir John had returned on foot—but had been persuaded by Peter to reconsider it and stay on. The female staff was in a state of perpetual motion. No cook would stand her master's comments on her performances, no housemaid endure his constant bullying and bell-ringing. He had perversely moved into a top-floor bedroom, so as to be out of reach of his wife and Speller, who disliked stairs. Here he would make tea at five o clock every morning with water from his hot-water bottle boiled up on a spirit lamp. This procedure filled Lady Alard with a peculiar horror when she discovered it; indeed, from her remarks it would appear that all her husband's other misdoings were negligible in comparison.

§17

A few days before Easter, Peter came suddenly to Fourhouses. He came early in the afternoon, and gave no explanation either of his coming or of his staying away. Jenny was upstairs, helping her mother-in-law turn out the conjugal bedroom, when she heard the sound of hoofs in the yard. She ran to the window, thinking it was Ben come home unexpectedly from an errand to Wickham Farm, but had no time to be disappointed in the rush of her surprise at seeing Peter.

"There's Peter—my brother—come at last!" she cried to Mrs. Godfrey, and, tearing off her dusting cap, she ran down stairs, still in her gingham overall. She wanted to open the door to him herself.

He could not have expected her to do this, for he was staring uninterestedly at his boots. Her gingham skirts evidently suggested a servant to him, for he lifted his eyes slowly, then seemed surprised to see her standing all bright and blowzed before him.

"Jenny!"

"Hullo, Peter! So you've come to see me at last."

He mumbled something about having been passing through Icklesham.

"Won't you come in?—the man'll take your horse. Hi! Homard—take Mr. Alard's horse round to the stable."

"I can't stop long," said Peter awkwardly.

"But you must, after all this time—come in."

She had meant to ask him why he had kept away so long and why he had come now; but when she found herself alone with him in the kitchen, she suddenly changed her mind, and decided to let things be. He probably had no reasonable explanation to offer, and unless she meant to keep the breach unhealed, she had better treat this visit as if there was nothing to explain about it.

"How's Vera?" she asked.

"She's getting on splendidly, thanks."

"And the baby?"

"That's getting on too."

"Do tell me about it—is it like her or like you?"

"It's like her—a regular little Yid."

"Never mind—she will probably grow up very beautiful."

Peter mumbled inaudibly.

Jenny looked at him critically. He seemed heavier and stupider than usual. He gave her the impression of a man worn out.

"You don't look well.... Are you worried? I do hope you aren't dreadfully disappointed the baby's a girl."

"It doesn't really matter."

"Of course not. The first one never does. You're sure to have others ... boys."

Peter did not answer, and Jenny felt a little annoyed with him. If this was the way he behaved at home she was sorry for Vera. It was curious how nervy these stolid men often were....

"How are Father and Mother?" she asked, to change the subject—"I suppose you go up to Conster every day."

"Twice most days. They're not up to much—at least Father isn't. He's had some pretty good shocks lately, you know. He was dreadfully upset at the baby's being a girl—and that fool Gervase's business was a terrible blow for him."

"It was a blow for me too. I did my best to put him off it, but it was no use. My only comfort is that apparently it'll be some time before he's really let in for it. He may come to his senses before then."

"I don't think so. He's as obstinate as the devil."

"What—have *you* tried arguing with him?"

"Yes—when I heard what he'd done, I drove over to Thunders Abbey or whatever it's called, and did my level best to bring him back with me. But it was all no good—you might as well try to argue with a dead owl."

"Good Lord!—you went over to Thunders, and tried to bring him back! Poor old Peter! But do tell me how he is, and what he's doing. What sort of place is it?"

"Oh a great big barrack, spoiling the country for miles round. But they've got some fine land and absolutely all the latest ideas in farming—motor traction and chemical fertilisation and all that."

"And was Gervase working on the farm?"

"No, Brother Joseph—that's what the fool's called now—Brother Joseph, when I saw him, was scrubbing out the kitchen passage on his hands and knees like a scullery maid. A dignified occupation for an Alard!"

"Poor old Gervase, how he'd hate that! But he'll be all the more likely to come to his senses and give it up, especially when he's got over his disappointment about Stella. I feel it's really that which was at the bottom of it all."

Peter did not speak for a moment. He leaned back in his wooden armchair, staring at the fire, which was leaping ruddily into the chimney's cavern.

"Do you mind if I light my pipe?" he asked after a bit.

"Of course not—do. I'm glad you're going to stay."

He took matches and his tobacco pouch out of his pocket, and she noticed suddenly that his hands were shaking. For the first time a dreadful suspicion seized her. His heaviness— his nerviness—his queer, lost manner ... was it possible, she wondered, that Peter *drank*?

"Have you heard when the Mounts are leaving?" she asked him, stifling her thoughts.

"No, I haven't."

"Stella was here three days ago, and she said that they've at last settled about the practice. She seemed to think they might be free to go at the end of May."

"Oh."

"I expect Vera's glad they didn't go off in a hurry, and leave her with a new man for the baby. Dr. Mount's the best maternity doctor for miles round."

"Yes, I've heard that."

He was falling back into silence, and no remark of hers on any topic seemed able to rouse him out of it, though she tried once or twice to re-animate him on the subject of Gervase. He lounged opposite her in his armchair, puffing at his pipe, and staring at the fire, now and then painfully dragging out a "yes" or a "no." She was beginning to feel bored with him and to think about her work upstairs. Was this all he

had to say to her after three months estrangement?—an estrangement which he had never troubled to explain. She had
been weak with him—let him off too easily—she ought to
have "had things out with him" about her marriage. She had
a right to know his reasons for forgiving her just as she had a
right to know his reasons for shunning her.... He had treated
her inexplicably.

She was working herself up to wrath like this when Peter
suddenly spoke of his own accord.

"This place is like what Starvecrow used to be."

"Used to be?—when?"

"Before Vera and I came to it—when the Greenings had
it. Do you remember the kitchen fireplace?—it was just like
this."

"Starvecrow is far grander than Fourhouses now. I'm just
a plain farmer's wife, Peter—I'm never going to pretend to be
anything else."

"And Starvecrow was just a plain farm; but we've changed
it into a country house."

"Mary's been wanting me to do the same for Fourhouses,
but I've told her I'd be very sorry to. I like it best as it is."

"So do I."

"Then are you sorry you've altered Starvecrow?"

"Yes."

"But it's a lovely place, Peter. You've made a perfect little
country house out of it. I'm sure you wouldn't be pleased to
have it the ramshackle old thing it used to be."

"Yes, I should."

"Well, Vera wouldn't, anyhow. You and she are in a totally different position from us. I'm not keeping Fourhouses as

it is because I don't think it's capable of improvement, but because I don't want to put myself outside my class and ape the county. You're just the opposite—you've got appearances to keep up; it would never do if you lived in the funny hole Starvecrow used to be in the Greenings time."

"I loved it then—it was just like this—the kitchen fire ... and the fire in the office—it used to hum just like this—as if there was a kettle on it. The place I've got now isn't Starvecrow."

"What is it, then?"

"I don't know—but it isn't Starvecrow. I've spoilt Starvecrow. I've changed it, I've spoilt it—Vera's people have spoilt it with their damned money. It isn't Starvecrow. Do you remember how the orchard used to come right up to the side wall? They've cut it down and changed it into a garden. The orchard's beyond the garden—then it doesn't look so much like a farm. A country house doesn't have an orchard just outside the drawing-room windows...."

He had left his chair, and was pacing up and down the room. His manner seemed stranger than ever, and Jenny felt a little frightened.

"I'm glad you don't want me to change Fourhouses," she said soothingly—"I must tell Mary what you've said."

"But I do want you to change it," he cried—"I can't bear to see it as it is—what Starvecrow used to be."

"Don't be silly, Peter. Starvecrow is much better now than it ever used to be."

He turned on her almost angrily—

"Goodbye."

She felt glad he was going, and still more glad to hear her husband's voice calling her from the yard.

"There's Ben. Must you really be going, Peter?"

"Yes—I must."

He walked out of the room, and she followed him—both meeting Ben on the doorstep. Young Godfrey was surprised to see his elder brother-in-law—he had made up his mind that Peter would never come to Fourhouses. He was still more surprised at his abstracted greeting.

"Hullo, Godfrey. Glad to see you —hat's a fine mare. Jenny, will you tell them to bring my horse round?"

"Yes.... Carter! Mr. Alard's horse.... Peter can't stay any longer, Ben. I told him you'd be sorry."

"I'm sure I'm very sorry, Sir"—he blushed at his slip into deference, but was quite unable to say "Peter"—"Is Mrs. Alard doing well?" he asked clumsily.

"Very well, thank you."

"I hope you'll come and see us again soon," said Jenny— "I'd like to show you the house."

"Yes, I'll come," he returned absently, and went to meet his horse, which was being led to him across the yard.

§18

The sun was still high as Peter rode back through the cross-country lanes to Starvecrow. The days were lingering now, and the fields were thickening for May. In the hay-fields the young crops were already marking their difference from the pastures with a rust of sorrel and a gilding of buttercups, and the hedges were losing their traceried outline in smothers of vetch and convolvulus.

Peter mechanically noted the progress of the winter sowings on Scragoak, Stonelink, and other farms he passed. These were all dependencies of Alard, and their welfare was bound up with Conster. Pleasant, homely places, their sprawling picturesqueness made up for any want of repair to all but the eye of his father's agent. Peter saw the needs of most of them—rebuilding, rethatching, redraining—and his mind, mechanically and from force of habit, deplored the impossibility of taking action. The position seemed quite hopeless, for he could do nothing now, and things would be even worse at his father's death, when the weight of death-duties and the pressure of mortgage holders would probably choke out the little life there was left in the Alard estates. But even this ultimate foreboding was only mechanical—his real emotions, his most vital pains, were all centred in himself.

He had spoken truly when he told Jenny that he could not bear the sight of Fourhouses. He could not even bear the thought of it. When he thought of that quiet, ancient house, with its bricked floors and wide, sunny spaces, with its humming kitchen fire and salt-riddled beam-work—above all when he thought of it as the home of loving hearts and the peace which follows daring—he felt unendurably the contrast of what he had made of Starvecrow. It was what Starvecrow used to be—it was what Starvecrow might have been ... for even if he had renounced the place he loved for the woman he loved, Starvecrow would have still gone on being the same, either as the home of another agent, or—if his father had really fulfilled his threat of selling it—the home of some honest farmer like Ben Godfrey, a man who would not only live in it but possess it, and give it back the yeoman dignity it had lost.

Starvycrow—Starvycrow.

What was it now? What had he made it? It was a small

country house, perfectly furnished and appointed, with a set of model buildings attached. It was the home of a burnt-out love, of the husks of marriage, of a husband and wife whose hearts were foes and whose souls were strangers, of lost illusions, of dead hopes, and wasted sacrifices. That was what it was now. That was what he had made it.

He remembered words which long ago he had spoken to Stella.... "Places never change—they are always the same. Human beings may change, but places never do." Those words were untrue—places can change, do change—Starvecrow had changed, he had changed it. While Stella, the woman, had not changed. She was still the same—the dear, the lovely ... and the unchanged, unchanging Stella might have been his instead of this changed Starvecrow. He had sacrificed the substance of life to a dream, a shadow, which without the substance must go up in smoke. He had sold his birth-right for a morsel of bread—or rather he had given away his bread for the sake of an inheritance in the clouds, which he could never hold.

His old hopes and his old fears had died together. Neither the fact that his newborn child was a girl, nor the final defection of Gervase the heir-apparent could make him hold his breath for Alard. These things had not killed his dreams, as once he had thought, but had merely shown that they were dead. The thought of his father's death, which could not now be far off, and his own succession to the property, with all the freedom and power it would bring, no longer stirred his flagging ambition. When he became Sir Peter he could probably save the House of Alard in spite of death duties and mortgagees. Without restrictions, master of his own economies, he

could put new life into the failing estate—or at least he could
nurse and shelter it through its difficult times till the days
came when the government *must* do something to set the
Squires on their legs again.... But the thought had no power
to move him—indeed Alard hardly seemed worth saving. It
was a monster to which he had sacrificed his uttermost human need. Gervase had been a wise man, after all. And Jenny
...Jenny had done what Peter might have done. He and Stella might now have been together in some wide farmhouse,
happy, alive and free. This child might have been her child....
Oh, how could he have been so blind? He had not known
how much he really loved her—he had thought she was just
like other women he had loved, and that he could forget her.
She would go away, and she would manage at last to forget
him; but he who stayed behind would never be able to forget her. He would live on and on, live on her memory—the
memory of her touch and voice, her narrow shining eyes, her
laughter and her kisses—live on and on until even memory
grew feeble, and his heart starved, and died.

Riding over the farms between Leasan and Vinehall
it suddenly struck him how easily he might turn aside and
go to see Stella. She had promised that she would see him
again before she went away. Should he go now and ask her
to redeem that promise? Should he go and plead with her as
he had never pleaded before? She could still save him—she
could still be to him what she might have been. In one mad
moment he saw himself and Stella seeking love's refuge at the
other end of the country, in some far, kindly farm in West-
moreland or Cornwall. Vera would divorce him—she would
be only too glad to get her freedom—and by the time he be-

came Sir Peter Alard he would have lived the scandal down. Stella still loved him—she was awake, alive, and passionate—she had none of the scruples and conventions, reserves and frigidities which keep most women moral—she had only her religion to stand between them, and Peter did not think much of that. A collection of dreams, traditions and prohibitions could not stand before his pleading—before the pleading of her own heart. He had not really pleaded with her yet....

For a moment he reined in his horse, hesitating at the mouth of the little lane which twists through the hollows of Goatham and Doucegrove towards Vinehall. But the next minute he went on again, driven by a question. What had he to offer Stella in exchange for all that he proposed to take from her?—What had he to give her in exchange for her father, her home, her good name, her peace of mind? The answer was quite plain—he had nothing but himself. And was he worth the sacrifice? Again a plain answer—No. He was worn, tired, disillusioned, shop-soiled, no fit mate for the vivid woman whom some hidden source of romance seemed to keep eternally young. Even suppose he could, by storming and entreaty, bend her to his desire, he would merely be bringing her to where he stood today. A few years hence she might stand as he stood now—looking back on all she had lost.... He would not risk bringing her to that. Three years ago he had sacrificed her to his desires—he had made her suffer.... It would be a poor atonement to sacrifice her again—to another set of desires. The least he could do for her was to let her follow her own way of escape—to let her go ... though still he did not know how he was to live without her.

§19

When he reached home he went upstairs to see Vera. Her mother and Rose were with her, and they were having tea.

"Hullo!" said his wife—"Where have you been all day?"

"I lunched over at Becket's House—Fuller asked me to stay. And in the afternoon I went to see Jenny."

He had not meant to tell them, but now he suddenly found he had done so. Vera lifted her eyebrows.

"Oh. So you've forgiven her at last. I think you might have told me before you went there. I want to thank her for writing to me, and you could have saved me the fag of a letter. She'll think it odd my not sending any message."

"I'm sorry, but I never thought of going till I found myself over there."

"And how is Jenny?" asked Rose.

"She seemed very well."

"And happy?"

"Yes—and happy."

"Is she still living like the wife of a working-man, with only one maid?"

"No, not like the wife of a working-man, who doesn't keep even one maid, but like the wife of a well-to-do farmer, which she is."

"You needn't bite my head off, Peter," said Rose.

"Your tea's in the drawing-room," said Vera—"I asked Weller to put it there ready for you when you came in. Nurse thinks it would be too much of a crowd if you had it up here. Besides, I know you'd rather be alone."

Peter rose from his seat at the bedside.

"All right—I'll go downstairs."

"I didn't mean now, you old silly," said Vera, pulling at his coat. "Hang it all, I haven't seen you the whole day."

Peter looked down at her hopelessly—at her large, swimming brown eyes, at her face which seemed mysteriously to have coarsened without losing any of its beauty, at the raven-black braids of her hair that showed under her lace nightcap, and last of all at her mouth—full, crimson, satisfied, devouring.... He became suddenly afraid—of her, with this additional need of him, this additional hold on him, which her motherhood had brought—and of himself, because he knew now that he hated her, quite crudely and physically hated her.

"I'm afraid I can't stay—I've got rather a headache ... and I'm going out directly to pot rabbits."

"That's an odd cure for a headache," said Vera. She looked hurt and angry, and he felt a brute to have upset her at such a time. But he could not help it—he had to go, and moved towards the door.

"Aren't you going to take any notice of your little daughter?" purred Mrs. Asher—"Baby dear, I don't think your daddy's very proud of you. He hasn't been near you since breakfast."

Speechlessly Peter went to the cradle and gazed down on the little wizened face. His heart felt hard; not one pang of fatherhood went through it. "You little sheeny—you little Yid"—he said to the baby in his heart.

"Isn't she a darling?" his mother-in-law breathed into his neck—"isn't she a love? Do you know, Vera thinks now that Miriam would do better than Rachel—it goes better with Alard."

Peter did not think that either went particularly well with

Alard, but he said nothing. Wasn't there a Jewish name which meant "The glory is departed from my house"?

He kissed the baby and went out, thankful to have escaped kissing the mother.

Some truth-loving providence had insisted on afflicting him with the headache he had claimed as an excuse for not sitting with Vera. His head ached abominably as he went into the drawing-room where his tea was laid. The firelight ruddied the white walls, the silver and the furniture, where comfort and cretonne were skilfully blended with oak and antiquity. His thoughts flew back to the evening when he and Vera had first come into this new room on their return from their honeymoon. He had thought it beautiful then—though even then he had realised it was not the right room for Starvecrow. It used to be one of the kitchens, and in the old days when he had first known it, had had a bricked floor and a big range, like the kitchen at Fourhouses. Tonight he hated it—it was part of the processes which had changed Starvecrow out of recognition. He rang the bell impatiently. He would have his tea carried into the office. That was the room which had altered least.

Even here there were changes, but they were of his own choice and making—he had planned them long before his marriage. The furniture of Greening's day—the pitchpine desk and cane-seated chairs—had been impossible; he had always meant to get a good Queen Anne bureau like this one, and some gate-backed chairs like these. There was nothing unfarmlike in this plainly furnished office, with its walls adorned with scale-maps and plans of fields and woods, and notices of auctions and agricultural shows.

Nevertheless today he found himself wishing he had it as it used to be. He would like to see it as it used to be—as Stella used to see it, when she came in fresh and glowing on a winter's afternoon, to sit beside the fire ... he could almost feel her cold cheek under his lips....

Then for one moment he saw it as it used to be. For an instant of strangeness and terror he saw the old scratched desk, with Greening's files and account-books upon it, saw Greening's book-shelves, with their obsolete agricultural treatises— saw the horse-hair armchair and the two other chairs with the cane seats, and the picture-advertisement of Thorley's cake on the wall.... He stood stock still, trembling—and then suddenly the room was itself again, and it didn't even seem as if it had altered.... But he felt dreadfully queer. He hurried to the door and went out through the passage into the little grass space at the back. God! he must be ill. What a fright he'd had! Suppose the hallucination had continued a moment longer, should he have seen Stella come into the room, unbuttoning her fur collar, her face all fresh with the wind?...

He went round to the front of the house, and fetched his hat and overcoat and gun. He'd go out after the rabbits, as he'd said. There were too many of them, and he'd promised Elias ... anyhow he couldn't stand the house. He whistled for Breezy, and the spaniel ran out to him, bounding and whimpering with delight. The sky was turning faintly green at the rims. The dusk was near.

He passed quickly through the yard. From the open doorway of the cowhouse came cheerful sounds of milking, and he could see his cows standing in shafts of mote-filled sunlight. The cowhouse had been enlarged and modernised—

Starvecrow could almost now be called a model farm. But he knew that the place wanted to be what it was in the old days before his wife's money had been spent on it. It was not only he who was dissatisfied with the changes—Starvecrow itself did not like them. He knew that tonight as he walked through the barns.... Starvecrow had never been meant for a well-appointed country house, or a model farm. It ought to have been, like Fourhouses, the home of happy lovers. It was meant to be a home.... It was not a home now—just a place where an unhappy man and woman lived, desiring, flee-ing, mistrusting, failing each other. He could have made it a home—brought Stella to it somehow, some day, at last. Per-haps—seeing his father's condition, that day would not have been far off now.... But like everything else, Starvecrow had been sacrificed to Alard. He had sacrificed it—he had be-trayed the faithful place. He saw now that he had betrayed not only himself, not only Stella, but also Starvecrow.

Starvycrow—Starvycrow.

Peter walked quickly, almost running, from the reproach of Starvycrow.

§20

At about seven o clock that evening a message came up from Conster, and as Peter was still out, it was brought to Vera. It was marked "immediate," so she opened it.

"Who brought this, Weller?"

"The gardener's boy, Ma'am."

"Tell him Mr. Alard is out at present, but I'll send him over as soon as he comes home—Sir John's had another stroke," she told her mother.

"Oh, my dear! How dreadful—I wish you hadn't opened the letter. Shocks are so bad for you."

"It wasn't a shock at all, thanks. I've been expecting it for weeks. Besides, one really can't want the poor old man to live much longer. He was getting a perfect nuisance to himself and everybody, and if he'd lived on might have done some real damage to the estate. Now Peter may just be able to save it, in spite of the death-duties."

"But, my dear, he isn't dead yet!" cried Mrs. Asher, a little shocked. She belonged to a generation to which the death of anybody however old, ill, unloved or unlovely, could never be anything but a calamity.

"He's not likely to survive a second stroke," said Vera calmly. "I'm sorry for the poor old thing, but really it's time he went. And I want Peter to come into the estate before he's quite worn out and embittered. It's high time he was his own master—it'll pull him together again—he's been all to pieces lately."

"And it'll quite settle the Stella Mount business," she added secretly to herself.

The next hour passed, and Weller came up to ask if she should bring in the dinner.

"What *can* have happened to Peter!" exclaimed Vera.

"I daresay he met the messenger on his way back, and went straight to Conster."

"Then it was very inconsiderate of him not to send me word. Yes, Weller, bring the dinner up here. You'll have it with me, won't you, Mother, as Peter isn't in?"

They were eating their fruit when Weller came in with another "Urgent." It was from Doris, and ran—

"Hasn't Peter come back yet? Do send him over at once whenever he does. Father is dying. Dr. Mount does not expect him to last the night. We have wired to Jenny and Mary and even Gervase. Do send Peter along. He ought to be here."

"How exactly like Doris to write as if we were deliberately keeping Peter away! *I* don't know where he is. Doris might realise that I'm the last person who'd know."

Her hands were trembling, and she whimpered a little as she crushed up the note and flung it across the room into the fireplace.

"Don't be upset, Vera darling. Nothing could possibly have happened to him—we should have heard. He's probably accepted a sudden invitation to dinner, the same as he did to lunch."

"I know nothing's happened to him—I'm not afraid of that. I know where he is...."

"Then if you know...."

"He's with Stella Mount," and Vera hid her face in the pillow, sobbing hysterically.

Mrs. Asher tried to soothe her, tried to make her turn over and talk coherently, but with that emotional abandonment which lay so close to her mental sophistication, she remained with her face obstinately buried, and sobbed on. Her mother had heard about Stella Mount, chiefly from Rose, but had never given the idea much credit. She did not credit it now. But to pacify Vera she sent over a carefully worded message to Dr. Mount's cottage, asking that if Mr. Peter Alard was there he should be told at once that he was wanted over at Conster.

The boy came back with the reply that Mr. Alard was not

at Vinehall, and had not been there that day. Everyone but the maid was out—Dr. Mount at Conster Manor and Miss Mount in church.

"That proves nothing," said Vera—"he needn't have met her at the house."

"But if she's in church—"

"How do we know she's in church? She only left word with the maid that she's gone there—" and Vera's sobs broke out again until the nurse begged her to calm herself for the sake of the child. Which she promptly did, for she was a good mother.

§21

At Conster all the family was by now assembled, with the exception of Peter and Gervase. Ben Godfrey had brought Jenny over from Fourhouses, and Mary had motored from Hastings; Rose was there too, with a daughter's privileges. They were all sitting in the dining-room over a late and chilly meal. They had been upstairs to the sick-room, where the prodigals had entered unforbidden, for Sir John knew neither sheep nor goat. His vexed mind had withdrawn itself to the inmost keep of the assaulted citadel, in preparation for its final surrender of the fortress it had held with such difficulty of late.

"There is no good saying that I expect him to recover this time," Dr. Mount had said. "I will not say it is impossible—doctors are shy of using that word—but I don't expect it, and, in view of his former condition which would be tremendously aggravated by this attack, I don't think anyone can hope it."

"Will it be long?" asked Doris, in a harsh, exhausted voice.

"I don't think it will be longer than forty-eight hours."

Doris burst into tears. Her grief was, the family thought, excessive. All her life, and especially for the last three months, her father had victimised her, browbeaten her, frustrated her, humiliated her—she had been the scapegoat of the revolted sons and daughters—and yet at his death she had tears and a grief which none of the more fortunate could share.

"I found him—it was I who found him"—she sobbed out her story for the dozenth time. "I came into the study with his hot milk—Wills has refused to bring it ever since poor Father threw it in his face—and I saw him sitting there, and he looked funny, somehow. I knew something was wrong— he was all twisted up and breathing dreadfully.... And I said 'Father, is anything the matter?—aren't you feeling well?' And he just managed to gasp 'Get out.' Those were the last words he uttered."

Sir John had not been put to bed in his attic-bedroom, the scene of his ignoble tea-making, but in his old room downstairs, leading out of Lady Alard's. She and the nurse were with him now while the others were at supper. She had a conviction that her husband knew her, as he made inartic- ulate sounds of wrath when she came near. But as he did the same for the nurse, the rest of the family were not convinced.

"When *is* Peter coming?" groaned Doris—"I really call it heartless of him to keep away."

"But he doesn't know what's happened," soothed Jenny— "he'll come directly he's heard."

"I can't understand what he's doing out at this hour. It's too late for any business, or for shooting—where can he have gone?"

"You'll be getting an answer to your second message soon," said Ben Godfrey.

"I daresay Peter thought he'd have his dinner first," continued Doris—"I expect he thought it didn't matter and he could come round afterwards."

"I don't think that's in the least likely," said Mary.

"Then why doesn't he come?—he can't be out at this hour."

"He must be out or he would have come."

"It's not so very late," said Jenny, "only just after nine."

"He may have gone out to dinner somewhere," said Rose.

"Yes, that's quite possible," said Jenny—"he may have gone somewhere on business and been asked to stay—or he may have met someone when he was out."

"I've a strong feeling that it mightn't be a bad plan to 'phone to Stella Mount."

"But Dr. Mount 'phoned there an hour ago, saying he'd be here all night. She'd have told him then if Peter was there."

"I think it quite probable that she would not have told him."

"What exactly do you mean by that, Rose?"

"Mean?—oh, nothing."

"Then there's no use talking of such a thing. I'm quite sure that if Peter had been at the Mounts', Stella would have sent him over directly she heard about Father."

At that moment Wills came into the room with a note for Doris.

"That must be from Starvecrow," she said, taking it. "Yes, it's from Mrs. Asher—'Peter hasn't been in yet, and we are beginning to feel anxious. He told us he was going out to shoot rabbits and one of the farm men saw him start out with his gun and Breezy. Of course he may have met someone and gone home with them to dinner. As you have a 'phone, perhaps you could ring up one or two places.'"

"We could ring up the Parishes," said Jenny—"he may have gone there. Or the Hursts—aren't they on the 'phone? I don't think the Fullers are."

"It's an extraordinary thing to me," said Rose, "that he should stop out like this without at least sending a message to his wife. He might know how anxious she'd be."

"Peter isn't the most thoughtful or practical being on earth. But there's no good making conjectures. I'm going to 'phone every place I can think of."

Jenny spoke irritably. Rose never failed to annoy her, and she was growing increasingly anxious about Peter. She had told the others of his visit that afternoon, but she had not told them of his queer, gruff, silent manner. Not that she had seen, or saw now, anything sinister in it, but she could not rid herself of the thought that Peter had been "queer," and that to queer people queer things may happen.

The telephone yielded no results. Neither the Parishes nor the Hursts were harbouring Peter, nor could she hear of him at the Furnace or Becket's House, or at the Vinehall solicitor's, or the garage at Iden, the final resorts of her desperation. Of course he had friends who were not on the telephone, but it was now after ten o'clock, and it was difficult to believe that if he had accepted a casual invitation to dine he would not have come home or sent word.

"Lord! How ghastly it is," she cried, as she hung up the receiver for the last time—"Father dying and Peter disappeared. What *are* we to do, Ben?"

"I think we ought to go and have a look for him," said her husband.

"How?—and who'd go?"

"I'll get a chap or two from here, and the men at Starvecrow. If he was only out after conies he wouldn't have gone far—down to the Bridge, most likely. We ought to search the fallows."

"Yes, do go," said Doris—"it's the only thing to be done now. I know something dreadful has happened to him. And perhaps tomorrow he'll be Sir Peter Alard...."

She had forgotten that Godfrey was the presumptuous boor who had disgraced her name. She saw in him only the man of the family—the only man of the family now.

"I'll ring for Wills, and he'll see about lanterns—and perhaps Pollock would go with you. And Beatup and Gregory know the district well—I'll have them sent for from the farm."

"Reckon I'd better go up to Starvecrow, John Elias would come with me, and Lambard and Fagge."

"If you're going to Starvecrow," said Jenny, "I'll go too, and see if I can do anything for poor Vera. I expect she's dreadfully worried and frightened."

"Don't go!" cried Doris—"suppose Father died...."

"I can't see what good I should be doing here. Vera needs me more than you do."

"She's got her mother. And it would be dreadful if Father died while you were out of the house."

"Not more dreadful than if I was in it. He doesn't know me, and wouldn't see me if he did."

"I think you're very heartless" and Doris began to cry—"Father might recover consciousness just before the end and want to forgive you."

"I don't think either is the least likely. Come along, Ben."

Her husband fetched her coat from the hall, and they set out together. Doris sat on in her chair at the head of the table, sobbing weakly.

"I think this is a terrible thing to have happened. Father and Peter going together.... It makes me almost believe there isn't a God."

"But we've no reason to think Peter's dead," said Mary—"a dozen other things may have happened. He may have broken his leg out in the fields and be unable to get home, in which case the men will soon find him. I don't see why you need take for granted that he's killed."

"I think it far more likely that he's gone off with Stella Mount," said Rose, relieved of Jenny's repressing presence.

"Why ever should you think that?" said Mary. "I wasn't aware that he was in love with her—now."

"He's been in love with her for the last year. Poor Vera's had a dreadful time. I'm sure she thinks Peter's gone with Stella."

"Really, Rose, you surprise me—and anyhow, Stella answered her father's 'phone call a short time ago, so she must be at home."

"She might just have been going to leave when he rang up."

"Well, the 'phone's in the next room if you like to give her a call—and know what to say to her. Personally I should find the enquiry rather delicate."

"It won't do any good my ringing up," sulked Rose—"if they're gone we can't stop them. If they've not gone then Doris is right, and Peter's probably killed or something. I don't know which would be the worst. It's dreadful to think of him chucking everything over when if he'd only waited another hour he'd have heard about Father's illness. He'd never have gone if he'd known he was to be Sir Peter so soon."

"Well, I'd rather he'd gone than was killed," said Doris— "the other could be stopped and hushed up—but if he's dead ... there's nobody left."

"What about Gervase?" asked Mary.

"He's no good."

"Surely he'd come out of his convent or whatever it is, if he knew he had succeeded to the property."

"I don't know. Gervase never cared twopence about the property. I don't think he'd come out for that."

"They wouldn't let him out," said Rose.

"Is he coming here now?" asked Mary.

"I wired to him when I wired to you and Jenny. But I don't know whether he'll come or not, and anyhow he can't be here for some time."

"What time is it?"

"Nearly twelve."

The three women shivered. The fire had gone out.

§22

The night wore on, and Sir John was still alive. Nobody thought of going to bed, but after a time Doris, Mary and Rose went upstairs to the greater warmth of their father's dressing-room. Here through the open door they could see the firelight leaping on the bedroom ceiling, and hear the occasional hushed voices of the nurse and Dr. Mount. Lady Alard sat by the fire, mute and exhausted. For the first time that they could remember she gave her family the impression of being really ill. Speller made tea, cocoa and soup on the gas-ring in the dressing-room. Hot drinks were at once a distraction and a stimulant. The night seemed incredibly long—nobody spoke above whispers, though every now and then Rose would say—"There's no good whispering—he wouldn't hear us even if we shouted."

"I do hope he really is unconscious," said Doris.

"Dr. Mount says he is."

"But how can he know? He knows Father can't speak, but he doesn't know he can't hear us."

"I expect there are signs he can tell by."

"The last words he ever spoke were said to me. That'll be something comforting to remember.... But oh, it was dreadful finding him like that! I do hope it hadn't lasted long ... that he hadn't been like that for a long time, all alone...."

Doris bowed her head into her hands and sobbed loudly. As she sat there, crouched over the fire, her face with the merciful powder and colour washed off by tears, all haggard and blotched, and the make-up of her eyes running down her cheeks, her hair tumbling on her ears, and revealing the dingy brown roots of its chestnut undulations—she looked by far the most stricken of the party, more even than the sick man, who but for his terrible breathing lay now in ordered calm.

A clock in the house struck three.

"I wonder when we'll hear about Peter," whispered Rose.

"I'm surprised we haven't heard already," said Mary.—"They must have gone all over the Starvecrow land by now."

"Um...." said Rose, "that seems to point to his not being anywhere about the place." Then she added—"I wonder if Gervase will come. I shouldn't be at all surprised if he didn't."

"I should. They'd never keep him back when his father's dying."

"Well—why isn't he here? He's known about it for over six hours."

"I shouldn't think there were any trains running now. It's not so easy as all that to come from Brighton."

Rose relapsed into silence. After a time she said—

"Religion is a great consolation at a time like this."

"Do you think we ought to send for Mr. Williams to come and see Father?" choked Doris.

"No—of course not. What good could he do? Poor Sir John's quite unconscious."

"But he may be able to hear. How do you know he can't? Perhaps he would like to hear Mr. Williams say a prayer or a hymn."

"My dear Doris, I tell you he doesn't know a thing, so what's the good of dragging poor Mr. Williams out of his bed at three o'clock in the morning? I had no patience with the people who did that sort of thing to George. Sir John couldn't understand anything, and if he did he'd be furious, so it doesn't seem much good either way. When I said religion was a consolation I was thinking of Mary."

"And why of me?" asked Mary.

"Well, I often think you'd be happier if you had some sort of religion. You seem to me to lead such an aimless life."

"Of course I'd be happier. Most people are happier when they believe in something. Unfortunately I never was taught anything I could or cared to believe."

"Mary! How can you say that, when poor George...."

She broke off as the door opened and Jenny suddenly appeared.

"Hullo, Jenny!" cried Doris—"have you come back? Have they found Peter?"

Jenny did not speak. She shut the door behind her, and stood with her back against it. Her face was white and damp. It was evidently raining, and wet strands of hair were plastered on her cheeks.

"Is Dr. Mount in there?" she asked.

"Yes—but Jenny ... Peter!..."

"I must see Dr. Mount first."

"Who's that asking for me?"

The doctor came in from the next room; at the sight of Jenny he shut the communicating door.

"I want to speak to you, Dr. Mount. Will you come with me?"

"Jenny, you really can't treat us like this," cried Mary, "you must tell us what's happened. Is Peter hurt?"

"Yes—he's downstairs."

"Is he dead?" cried Doris, springing to her feet.

Again Jenny did not speak. She bowed her head into her hands and wept silently.

A dreadful silence filled the little room. Even Doris was perfectly quiet.

"I'll come down," said Dr. Mount.

"So'll I," said Doris.

"No," said Jenny, "you mustn't see him."

"Why not?"

"He's—he's been dreadfully injured—part of his head...."

She stopped and shuddered. Dr. Mount pushed quietly past her to the door.

"I think I'd better go down alone. Your husband and the

men are down there—I can get all the information I want from them."

Jenny came forward to the fire and flopped into the chair Doris had left. Her clothes were wet and her boots muddy—it must be raining hard.

"I'd better tell you what happened," she said brokenly—"The men—some from here and some from Starvecrow—found Peter lying on the Tillingham marshes about half a mile below the Mocksteeple. His dog was watching beside him, and he'd been shot through the head."

"Murdered," gasped Doris.

"No—I don't think so for a moment."

"It was an accident, of course," said Mary.

"I wish I could think that. But the men seemed to think—my husband too—that it was his own doing."

"His own doing! Suicide!" cried Doris—"How could they imagine such a thing?"

"From the way he was lying, and the position of the gun, and the nature of the injuries. That's why I was so anxious for Dr. Mount to see him and give an expert opinion."

"Is there any chance of his being still alive?"

"Not the slightest. His head is nearly entirely blown away."

"Oh, Jenny, don't!—It's dreadful!"

"Yes it's dreadful, but I'm afraid it's true."

"But whatever could have made him kill himself?" moaned Doris—"He'd nothing on his mind—he was perfectly happy ... it couldn't have been because the baby was a girl."

"Peter may have had troubles that we don't know of," said Rose.

"He must have," said Jenny, "though I don't think for a minute they were of the kind you've been suspecting."

"I don't see what other kind they could be."

"It may have been something to do with the estate."

"He'd never have killed himself for that. If anything had gone wrong there, it was more than ever his duty to keep alive."

"Well, there's no good us arguing here about what he did it for—if he really did do it. The question is—who is going to tell Mother?"

"Oh, Jenny...."

They looked at each other in consternation.

§23

But Lady Alard, for all her frailty, belonged to a tougher generation than her children. In times of prosperity she might languish, but in times of adversity her spirit seemed to stiffen in proportion to the attacks upon it. If her cook had given notice she would have taken to her bed, but now when catastrophe trod on catastrophe and the fatal illness of her husband was followed by the death of her first-born son she armed herself with a courage in which her children, careless of kitchen tragedies, seemed to fail when they met the bigger assaults of life. She was less shattered by the news of Peter's death than was the daughter who broke it to her, and rising up out of her chair, independent of arm or stick, she insisted on going downstairs into the dark, whispering house.

The others followed her, except Doris, who stayed huddled and motionless in her chair in her father's dressing-room, like a stricken dog at its master's door. The dining-room was lighted up and seemed full of men. They were gathered round the table on which, with a sense of futility and pathos Jenny caught sight of a pair of stiff legs in muddy boots.

At the sound of footsteps Dr. Mount came out of the room.

"What! Lady Alard!" he exclaimed, quite unprepared for such a visit.

"Yes, I want to see him."

"You can't—yet!"

"Are you quite sure he's dead?"

"Quite sure."

Dr. Mount looked shaken—his face was grey. But all faces were grey in the light of the hall, where the first livid rays of morning were mixing with the electric lamps that had burned all night.

"How did it happen, Doctor? Does anyone know?"

"Nobody knows. He was found on the Tillingham marshes. His gun may have gone off accidentally."

"May have...." repeated Jenny.

"Will there have to be an inquest?"

"I'm afraid so. There always is in these cases."

"Well, Sir John has been spared something."

Her voice broke for the first time, and she turned back to the stairs. Rose and Mary went with her but Jenny lingered in the hall, where she had the comfort of seeing her husband through the dining-room door. Dr. Mount stopped as he was going back into the room.

"Has anyone told his wife?"

"Yes—one of the men came to Starvecrow at once.... I told her.... They thought it best not to take him there."

"Of course—quite right. How did she bear it?—Perhaps I ought to go and see her."

"Her mother's with her, but I'm sure they'd be glad if you went there."

"I've got the car—I could run round in a few minutes. I must go home too ... one or two things to see to ... I don't think I'm wanted here just now."

The doctor seemed terribly shaken by Peter's death, but that was very natural, considering he had known him from a child. Also, Jenny reflected, being a religious man, the idea of suicide would particularly appall him.

"Doctor—do you—do you think he did it himself?"

"I'm sorely afraid he did."

"But what can have made him?... I mean, why should he? I always thought he was so happy—too happy, even. I sometimes thought him self-satisfied and over-fed."

"We all have our secrets, Jenny, and your brother must have had a heavier one than most of us."

"But why should you be so sure he did it? Couldn't his gun have gone off by accident?"

"Of course it could. But the wounds would hardly have been of such a nature if it had. However, the matter will probably be cleared up in the Coroner's court."

Jenny shuddered.

"I wonder if he's had any trouble—anything worse than usual about the land...." Then she remembered Rose's suspicions of Stella Mount. Her colour deepened as she stood before Stella's father. Could that possibly be the reason, after all? She had never imagined such a thing, but Peter certainly had been fond of Stella once, and Rose's gossip was seldom quite baseless. She did not believe for a moment in any intrigue, but Peter might have turned back too late to his early love ... and of course Stella was going away ... it might have been that. Since undoubtedly Peter had had a secret buried under the outward fatness of his life, that secret may just as well have been Stella....

"Your husband tells me he came to see you this afternoon," the doctor was saying, "what was he like then?"

"He seemed rather queer and silent, but afterwards I put it down to its being his first visit since my marriage. He wouldn't forgive me for a long time, as you know, so it was only to be expected that he should feel a little awkward. But he said some rather queer things about Starvecrow—said he wished it was more like Fourhouses, said he'd spoilt it with his improvements, and seemed much more upset about it than you'd think natural."

"Um."

The doctor was silent a moment, then he said—

"Well, I think I'll run over to Starvecrow in a minute or two when I've finished with poor Peter, then I might as well go home and have an early breakfast, and see if there are any messages for me. I'll be back in a couple of hours."

He moved away from her, and was going into the dining-room when Rose's frightened voice suddenly shuddered down the stairs.

"Dr. Mount—will you please come up at once. There's a change in Sir John."

§24

Sir John Alard died when the cocks were crowing on Starve-crow and Glasseye and Doucegrove, and on other farms of his wide-flung estate too far away for the sound to come to Conster. His wife and daughters and daughter-in-law were with him when he died, but he knew no one. His mind did not come out of its retreat for any farewells, and if it had, would have found a body stiffened, struggling, intractable, and disobedient to the commands of speech and motion it had obeyed mechanically for nearly eighty years. Death came and brought the gift of dignity—a dignity he had never quite achieved in all his life-time of rule. When his family came in for a last look, after the doctor and the nurse had performed their offices, they saw that the querulous, irascible old man of the last few months was gone, and in his place lay some-thing he had never been of stillness and marble beauty. When Dr. Mount had invited them in to the death-chamber, the daughters had at first refused, and changed their minds only when they found that Lady Alard was unexpectedly ready to go. Now Jenny at least was glad. It was her first sight of death (for she had not seen George's body and would never see Peter's) and she was surprised to find how peaceful and triumphant the body looked when set free from the long tyr-anny of the soul. It comforted her to know that in its last fatal encounter with terror, pain and woe, humanity was allowed to achieve at least the appearance of victory. Her father lying there looked like one against whom all the forces of evil had done their worst in vain.

Nobody cried except Doris, who cried a great deal. She

had not cried for Peter, but when her father's spirit had slipped out after a sigh, she had burst into a storm of noisy weeping. She was sobbing still, kneeling beside the body of the father who had bullied and humiliated her all her life, the only one of his children who really regretted him.

There was the sound of wheels in the drive below.

"Is that Gervase?" asked Jenny, going to the window.

"No," said Mary, "It's Dr. Mount going away."

"He seems in a great hurry to get off," said Rose—"he didn't wait a minute longer than he could possibly help."

"I don't wonder," said Jenny.

"I expect he's gone home to break it to Stella," whispered Rose.

"He told me he was going to Starvecrow to see Vera," said Jenny icily. She hated Rose's conjectures all the more that she now shared them herself.

"It will be dreadful for some people at the inquest," continued her sister-in-law.

"Dreadful! How dreadful?—You don't mean Stella's to blame, do you?"

"Oh, of course, I don't mean she's really done anything wicked—but she let poor Peter go on loving her when she knew it was wrong."

"How could she have stopped him?—supposing it's true that he did love her."

"Any girl can stop a man loving her," said Rose mysteriously.

"Oh, can she?—it's obvious you've never had to try."

Jenny was surprised at her own vindictiveness, but she felt all nerves after such a night. Rose was plunged into silence, uncertain whether she had been complimented or insulted, and the next minute there was another sound of wheels in the drive.

"That must be Gervase."

A taxi had stopped outside the door, and out of it climbed, not Gervase but Brother Joseph of the Order of Sacred Pity, with close-cropped hair, a rough, grey cassock and the thickest boots man ever saw. As she watched him from the window, Jenny felt a lump rise in her throat.

She was going down to meet him when suddenly Doris started up from the bedside.

"Let me go first."

She brushed past her sister and ran downstairs before anyone could stop her. Jenny hurried after her, for she felt that Doris in her present condition was not a reassuring object to meet the home-comer. But she was too late. Doris flung open the door almost at the same instant as the bell rang.

"Welcome !" she cried hysterically—"Welcome—Sir Gervase Alard!"

§25

If Gervase was taken aback at his sister's appearance, he did not show it by more than a sudden blink.

"My dear Doris," he said, and taking both her hands he kissed her poor cheek where rouge and tears were mingled— "I met Dr. Mount—and he's told me," he said.

"About Peter?"

"Yes."

He came into the hall and stood there a quaint, incongruous figure in his cloak and cassock.

"Hullo, Wills," as the butler came forward.

"How do you do, Mr. Gervase—I mean Sir Ger—or rather I should say—"

He remembered that his young master was now Brother Something-or-other, having crowned an unsquirelike existence, much deplored in the servants' hall, by entering a Home for Carthlicks. He compromised with—

"Can I have your luggage, Sir?"

"Here it is," said Gervase, holding out on one finger a small bundle tied up in a spotted handkerchief, and Wills who was going to have added "and your keys, Sir," retired in confusion.

"Where's Peter?" asked Brother Joseph.

"In there," Jenny pointed into the dining-room where Peter still lay, now no longer pathetic and futile in booted and muddy death, but dignified as his father upstairs under his white sheet.

Young Alard went in, and standing at the head of the table, crossed himself and said the first prayer that had been said yet for Peter. His sisters watched him from the doorway. Doris seemed calmer, her tears came more quietly.

"How's Mother?" he asked as he came out.

"She's been wonderful," said Jenny, "but I think she's breaking a bit now."

"And Vera?"

Vera had not been wonderful. It is difficult to be wonderful when your husband has killed himself because he loved another woman and you did not die in childbirth to let him marry her.

"It's dreadful," moaned Jenny. Then suddenly she wondered if Gervase knew the worst. There was a look of bright peace in his eyes which seemed to show that he was facing sorrow without humiliation or fear.

"Did Dr. Mount tell you that—tell you exactly how Peter died?"

"He told me he had been killed accidentally out shooting. He gave me no details—he couldn't wait more than a minute."

"Oh, my dear, it was much worse than that...."

She saw that once again she would have to "break it" to somebody. It was easier telling Gervase than it had been to tell the others, for he did not cry out or protest, but when she had finished she saw that his eyes had lost their bright peace.

Doris was sobbing again, uncontrollably.

"The two of them gone—first Peter and then Father. To think that Peter should have gone first.... Thank God Father didn't know! He didn't know anybody, Gervase—the last person he recognised was me. That will always be a comfort to me, though it was so dreadful.... I went into the library, and found him all huddled there, alone ... and I said 'Are you ill, Father?'—and he said 'Get out'—and now, Gervase, you're the head of the family—you're Sir Gervase Alard."

"We'll talk that over later. At present I must go and see Mother."

"But you're not going to back out of it—you're not going to leave us in the lurch."

"I hope I shan't leave anybody in the lurch," he replied rather irritably, "but there are lots of more important things than that to settle now. Where is Mother, Jenny?"

"She's upstairs in Father's dressing-room."

She noticed that he looked very white and tired, and realised that he must have been travelling for the greater part of the night.

"Are you hungry, dear? Won't you eat something before you go up?"

"No thank you—I don't want anything to eat. But might I have a cup of tea?"

"Speller's making that upstairs, so come along."

They were halfway up, and had drawn a little ahead of Doris, when he bent to her and whispered—

"Does Stella know?"

"Yes—Dr. Mount was on his way home when you met him."

"Oh, I'm glad."

So he, too, perhaps thought Stella might be the reason....

The little dressing-room was full of people. Ben Godfrey was there, the son-in-law and the man of the house till Gervase came. Mr. Williams was there too, summoned by Rose at a seasonable hour. He was sitting beside Lady Alard, who had now begun to look old and broken, and was trying to comfort her with a picture of her husband and son in some nebulous Paradisaical state exclusive to Anglican theology. He looked up rather protestingly at the sight of Gervase, whose habit suggested rival consolations and a less good-natured eschatology. But young Alard had not come to his mother as a religious, but as her son. He went up to her, and apparently oblivious of everyone else, knelt down beside her and hid his face in her lap. "Oh, Mummy—it's too terrible—comfort me."

His sisters were surprised, Ben Godfrey was embarrassed,

Rose and Mr. Williams tactfully looked another way. But Lady Alard's face lit up with almost a look of happiness. She put her arms round him, hugging his dark cropped head against her bosom, and for the first time seemed comforted.

§26

The Mounts' little servant had gone to bed by the time Stella came home from church, so she did not hear till the next morning of the message from Starvecrow. Her father had rung her up earlier in the evening to say that he would probably not be home that night; and she was not to sit up for him. So she carefully bolted both the doors, looked to see if the kitchen fire was raked out, pulled down a blind or two, and went upstairs.

She was not sorry to be alone, for her mind was still wandering in the dark church she had left ... coal black, without one glimmer of light, except the candle which had shown for a moment behind the altar and then flickered out in the draughts of the sanctuary. Spring by spring the drama of the Passion searched the deep places of her heart. The office of Tenebrae seemed to stand mysteriously apart from the other offices and rites of the church, being less a showing forth of the outward events of man's redemption than of the thoughts of the Redeemer's heart.... "He came, a man, to a deep heart, that is to a secret heart, exposing His manhood to human view." Throughout those sad nocturnes she seemed to have been looking down into that Deep Heart, watching its agony in its betrayal and its forsaking, watching it brood on the scriptures its anguish had fulfilled.... "From the lamentations of Jeremiah the Prophet" ... watching it comfort itself with

the human songs of God's human lovers, psalms of steadfast-
ness and praise—then in the Responds breaking once more
into its woe—a sorrowful dialogue with itself—"Judas, that
wicked trader, sold his Lord with a kiss"—"It had been good
for that man if he had not been born" ... "O my choicest vine,
I have planted thee. How art thou turned to bitterness" ...
"Are ye come out against a thief with swords and staves for
to take me?" ... "I have delivered my beloved into the hand of
the wicked, and my inheritance is become unto me as a lion
in the wood"—"My pleasant portion is desolate, and being
desolate it crieth after me."

Through psalm and lesson, antiphon and response, the
Deep Heart went down into the final darkness. It was swallowed up, all but its last, inmost point of light—and that too
was hidden for a time ... "keeping His divinity hidden within, concealing the form of God." In the darkness His family
knelt and prayed Him to behold them; then for a few brief
moments came the showing of the light, the light which had
not been extinguished but hidden, and now for a few moments gleamed again.

It was all to the credit of Stella's imagination that she
could make a spiritual adventure out of Tenebrae as sung
in Vinehall church. The choir of eight small boys and three
hoarse young men was rather a hindrance than an aid to devotion, nor was there anything particularly inspiring in the
congregation itself, sitting on and on through the long-drawn
nocturnes in unflagging patience, for the final reward of seeing the lights go out. Even this was an uncertain rite, for old
Mr. Bream, the sacristan, occasionally dozed at the end of a
psalm with the result that he once had three candles over at

the Benedictus; and another time he had let the Christ candle go out in the draught at the back of the Altar and was unable to show it at the end, though his hoarse entreaties for a match were audible at the bottom of the church. But Stella loved the feeling of this His family sitting down and watching Him there in stolid wonder. She loved their broad backs, the shoulders of man and girl touching over a book, the children sleeping against their mothers, to be roused for the final thrill of darkness. She was conscious also of an indefinable atmosphere of sympathy, as of the poor sharing the sorrows of the Poor, and drawn terribly close to this suffering human Heart, whose sorrows they could perhaps understand better than the well-educated and well-to-do. She felt herself more at ease in such surroundings than in others of more sophisticated devotion, and on leaving the church was indignant with an unknown lady who breathed into her ear that she'd seen it better done at St. John Lateran.

Up in her bedroom, taking the pins out of her hair, her mind still lingered over the office. Perhaps Gervase was singing it now, far away at Thunders Abbey.... She must write to Gervase soon, and tell him how much happier she had been of late. During the last few weeks a kind of tranquillity had come, she had lost that sense of being in the wrong with Peter, of having failed him by going away. She saw that she was right, and that she had hated herself for that very reason of being in the right when poor Peter whom she loved was in the wrong. But her being in the right would probably be more help to him at the last than if she had put herself in the wrong for his dear sake.

Judas the wicked trader
Sold his Lord with a kiss.
It had been good for that man
If he had not been born.

She too might have sold her Lord with a kiss. She wondered how often kisses were given as His price—kisses which
should have been His joy given as the token of His betrayal.
She might have given such a token if He had not preserved
her, delivered her from the snare of Peter's arms ... oh, that
Peter's arms should be a snare ... but such he himself had
made them. She had not seen him for a long time now—a
whole fortnight at least; and in less than another fortnight
she would be gone.... He was keeping away from her, and
would probably keep away until the end. Then once more he
would see Vera, his wife, holding their child in her arms ...
and surely then he would go back. Probably in a few days too
he would be Sir Peter Alard, Squire of Conster, head of the
house ... then he would be thankful that he had not entan-
gled himself with Stella Mount—he would be grateful to her,
perhaps....

For I have delivered my beloved into the hand of the
wicked,
And my inheritance is become unto me as a lion in the
wood
My pleasant portion is desolate—
And, being desolate,—it crieth after me.

How the words would ring in her head!—breaking up her
thoughts. She felt very tired and sleepy and she would have to

be up early the next morning. "My inheritance is as a lion in the wood."...Those words had made her think of Starvecrow. She had always thought of Starvecrow as her inheritance, the inheritance of which Peter had robbed her.... Starvycrow ... oh, if only Peter had been true they might now be waiting to enter their inheritance together. Sir John Alard could not have kept them out of it for more than a few years. But Peter had cut her off, and Starvecrow was strange to her—she dared not go near it ... strange and fierce—a lion in the wood.

She was sorry for Sir John Alard, lying at the point of death. She viewed his share in her tragedy with the utmost tolerance. He had belonged to the old order, the toppling, changing order, and it was not he who had failed the spirit of life, but Peter, who belonged to the new but had stood by the old. Poor Peter who had inherited only the things which are shaken, when he was the heir of the kingdom which cannot be moved....

§27

Only her sudden waking showed her that she had been asleep. She started up and looked at the time. This was Good Friday morning, and it was now half-past six. She jumped out of bed, hurried on her clothes, tumbled up her hair, and was rather sleepily saying her prayers when she heard the sound of her father's car at the door. He was back, then—all was over—Peter was now Sir Peter Alard, and would not think of her again. Tears of mingled pity and relief filled her closed eyes till the end of her bedside office—

"May the souls of the faithful departed, through the mercy of God, rest in peace. Amen."

She rose from her knees and ran downstairs to meet her father. He was standing in the hall, pulling off his furry driving gloves.

"Hullo, darling"—kissing his cold face—"Come in to the surgery, and I'll light the fire and get you some tea."

"Were you going to church?"

"Yes, but I shall have to be late, that's all."

"I have something to tell you, my dear."

His grave face sent a sudden chill into her heart.

"Father!—what is it?—has anything happened to—"

"Sir John Alard is dead—"

"Well—"

She knew that was not what he had to tell her.

"And Peter doesn't inherit Conster."

She stared at him—she could not understand. Was Peter illegitimate? Her heart sickened at the monstrous irony of such a thought.... But it was impossible. She was conceiving the preposterous in self-defence—in frantic hope that Peter was not ... dead.

"Is he dead?" she asked her father.

He bowed his head silently.

She could not speak. She was kneeling on the floor in front of the unlighted fire. In one hand she held some sticks, and for a time she could not move, but knelt there, holding out the unkindled sticks towards the back hearth.

"I felt I must come home and tell you before the rumour reached you. He was found on the Tillingham marshes, with his gun...."

"How?—an accident?" she mumbled vaguely.

"I don't know, my dear—I'm afraid not."

"You mean...."

"I mean that from the way they tell me he was lying and from the nature of the wounds, I feel nearly sure that it was his own act. I am telling you this, poor darling, because you would be sure to hear it some time, and I would rather you heard it from me."...

"Will there be an inquest?" she heard herself asking calmly.

"Yes, there's sure to be an inquest. But of course I don't know what the findings will be, or if the Coroner will want to question you."

"I don't mind if he does—I can answer."

She did not quite know what she was saying. She went over and stood by the window, looking out. A mist was rising from the garden, giving her an eastward vista of fields in a far-off sunshine. The air was full of an austere sense of spring, ice-cold, and pierced with the rods of the blossomed fruit-trees, standing erect against the frigid sky.

Her father came and put his arm around her.

"Perhaps you would like to be alone, my dear—and I must go and see poor Mrs. Peter. I came here first, because I wanted to tell you ... but now I must go to Starvecrow."

(Starvycrow ... being desolate it crieth after me.)

He stooped and kissed her averted face.

"My darling ... I'm so sorry."

She felt a lump rise in her throat as if it would choke her—it broke into a great sob.

"Cry, dearest—it will do you good."

She gently pushed him from her—but when he was gone, she did not cry.

§28

The little shrill bell of Vinehall church, the last of a large family of pre-Reformation bells, was still smiting the cold air, but Stella could not pray any more than she could weep.

Neither could she remain indoors. She put on her furs and went out. She wished she had the car—to rush herself out of the parish, out of the county, over the reedy Kentish border, up the steep white roads of the weald, away and away to Staplehurst and Marden, to the country of the hops and the orchards.... But even so she knew she could not escape. What she wanted to leave behind was not Vinehall or Leasan or Conster or even Starvecrow, but herself. Herself and her own thoughts made up the burden she found too heavy to bear.

She walked aimlessly down Vinehall Street, and out beyond the village. The roads were black with dew, and the grass and primrose-tufts of the hedgerow were tangled and wet. There was nowhere for her to sit down and rest, though she felt extraordinarily tired at the end of two furlongs. She turned off into a field path, running beside the stacks of a waking farm, and finally entering a little wood.

It was a typical Sussex spinney. The oaks were scattered among an underwood of hazel, beech and ash; the ground was thick with dead leaves, sodden together into a soft, sweet-smelling mass out of which here and there rose the trails of the creeping ivy, with the starry beds of wood-anemones; while round the moss-grown stumps the primrose plants were set, with the first, occasional violets. A faint budding of green was on the branches of the underwood, so backward yet as to appear scarcely more than a mist, but on the oaks above, the first leaves were already uncurling in bunches of rose and brown. Then at the bend of the path she saw a wild cherry tree standing white like Aaron's rod against the sky. The whiteness and the beauty smote her through, and sinking down upon one of the stumps, she burst into a flood of tears.

She cried because her pain had at last reached the soft emotions of her heart. Hitherto it had been set in the hard places, in self-reproach, in horror, in a sense of betrayal, both of her and by her.... But now she thought of Peter, shut out from all the soft beauty of the spring, cut off from life and love, never more to smell the primroses, or hear the cry of the plovers on the marsh, never more to watch over the lands he loved, or see the chimney-smoke of his hearth go up from Starvecrow.... She had robbed Peter of all this—she did not think of him as cut off by his own act but by hers. It was she who had killed him—her righteousness. So that she might be right, she had made him eternally wrong—her Peter. She had been the wicked trader, selling her lover for gain. It had been well for her if she had not been born.

The softer emotions had passed, and with them her tears. She clenched her hands upon her lap, and hated herself. She saw herself as a cold, calculating being. She had said "I will get over it," and she had said "Peter will get over it." No doubt she was right about herself—she would have got over it—people like her always did; but about Peter she had been hopelessly wrong. He had deeper feelings than she, and at the same time was without her "consolations." Her "consolations"!—how thankful she had been that she had not forfeited them, that she had not given them in exchange for poor

Peter. At first they had not seemed to weigh much against his loss, but later on she had been glad and grateful; and while she had been finding comfort in these things, building up her life again out of them, Peter had been going more and more hungry, more and more forlorn, till at last he had died rather than live on in starvation.

She hated herself, but there was something worse than just self-hatred in the misery of that hour. If she had betrayed Peter it was that she, too, had been betrayed. She had been given the preposterous task of saving her soul at the expense of his. If she had not fled from the temptation of his presence—if she had given way to his entreaties and promised not to leave him without the only comfort he had left, Peter would still be alive. She would have done what she knew to be wrong, but Peter would not be dead in his sins. Why should her right have been his wrong? Why should his dear soul have been sacrificed for hers? He had died by his own hand—unfaithful to his wife and child in all but the actual deed. Why should she be forced to bear the guilt of that?

The pillars of her universe seemed to crumble. Either heaven had betrayed her or there was no heaven. She almost preferred to believe the latter. Better ascribe the preposterous happenings of the night to chance than to a providence which was either malignant or careless of souls. Perhaps God was like nature, recklessly casting away the imperfect that the fittest might survive. Poor Peter's starved, undeveloped soul had been sacrificed to her own better-nourished organism, just as in the kingdom of nature the weakest go to the wall.... She looked round her at the budding wood. How many of these leaves would come to perfection? How many of these buds would serve only as nourishment to more powerful existences, which in their turn would fall a prey to others. She would rather not believe in God at all than believe in a Kingdom of Heaven ruled by the same remorseless laws as the bloody Kingdom of Nature....

But she could not find the easy relief of doubt, though something in her heart was saying "I will doubt His being rather than His love." After all, what was there to prove the assertion that God is love?—surely it was the most monstrous, ultramontane, obscurantist dogma that had ever been formulated. The Real Presence, the Virgin Birth, the physical Resurrection were nothing to it. It was entirely outside human knowledge—it ran directly contrary to human experience ... and yet it was preached by those who looked upon the creeds as fetters of the intellect and the whole ecclesiastical philosophy as absurd. Fools and blind!—straining at a gnat and swallowing a camel! She laughed out loud in the wood.

Her laughter brought her to her senses—yes, she knew she would always be sensible. She would either have to be sensible or go mad. It is the sensible people who fill the asylums, for they cannot rest in the halfway house of eccentricity. To Stella it was a dreadful thing to have laughed out loud in a wood. She was terrified, and jumped up at once to go home. By the watch on her wrist it was half-past eight; her father would be home from Starvecrow and wanting his breakfast. Breakfast, dinner and tea ... people like herself could never forget breakfast, dinner and tea.

§29

"Well, my dear, did you go to church?"

"No, I went for a walk instead."

Her tone was perfectly calm, if a little flat. She was really being splendid, poor little girl.

"Gervase is back—I forget whether I told you. I met him on my way home early this morning."

"Oh—how does he look?"

"Very well—though changed, of course, with his hair cut so short. I'm glad he's there. He'll take Lady Alard out of herself."

"How is Lady Alard?"

"She's much better than I could have thought possible."

"And Mrs. Peter?"

"She's different, of course ... Jewish temperament, you know. But I left her calmer. I think she'll try and keep calm for the sake of the child—she adores that."

The doctor had had rather a rough time at Starvecrow, but he would not tell Stella about it. Vera was in no doubt as to the cause of her husband's death, and as soon as Stella was out of hearing, Dr. Mount was going to telephone to a Rye practitioner to take charge of the case. Mrs. Peter was nearly well, and really he could not go near her again after what she had said....

"When is the inquest going to be?" asked Stella abruptly.

"Tomorrow afternoon, my dear. Godfrey was at Conster, and he says he's seen the Coroner."

"And shall I have to go?"

"I fear so. But no doubt you'll get an official intimation. You aren't afraid, are you, sweetheart?"

"No, I'm not afraid."

"Will you drive me out this morning? I must go over to Benenden, and take Pipsden on the way back."

"Yes, I should like to drive you."

So the day passed. In the morning she drove her father on his rounds, in the afternoon she dispensed in the Surgery, and in the evening there was church again. Church was black.... "And they laid him there, sealing the stone and setting a watch.... Thou hast laid me in the lowest pit, in the place of darkness, and in the deep—free among the dead, like unto those who are wounded and lie in the grave, who are out of remembrance.... And they laid him there, sealing a stone and setting a watch."

The great three-days drama was over. For the last time the Tenebrae hearse had stood a triangle of sinister light in the glooms of the sanctuary. Tomorrow's services would be the services of Easter, in a church stuffed with primroses and gay with daisy chains. What a mockery it all would be! How she wished the black hangings could stay up and the extinguished lamp before the unveiled tabernacle proclaim an everlasting emptiness. She shuddered at the thought of her Easter duties. It would be mere hypocrisy to perform them—she who wished that she had mortal sin to confess so that Peter need not have died in mortal sin.

She thought of Gervase, so near her now at Conster, and yet spiritually so very far away, in peaceful enjoyment of a Kingdom from which she had been cast out. She had half expected to see him in church that evening, but he had not been there, and she had felt an added pang of loneliness. The sight of him, a few words from him, might have comforted her.

She thought of Gervase as he used to be in the old days when he first learned the faith from her. She almost laughed—she saw another mockery there. She had taught him, she had brought him to the fold—he himself had said that but for her he would not have been where he was now—and now he was comforted and she was tormented.

Then as she thought of him, it struck her that perhaps he might have written—that there might be a letter waiting for her at home. Surely Gervase, who must guess what she was suffering, would take some notice of her, try to do something for her. Obsessed by the thought, she hurried home from church—and found nothing.

Though the expectation had not lasted half an hour, she was bitterly disappointed. It was callous of him to ignore her like this—he must know her position, he must guess her anguish. She felt deserted by everyone, obscure and forsaken. It is true that her father was near her and loved her and shared her sorrow, but he did not know the full depths of it—he was satisfied that she had done right, and thought that she, too, was satisfied. She could not thrust her burden of doubt upon his simple soul. She was becoming rapidly convinced that only Gervase could share her burden with her, and if he stood away … could she bear it alone?

That night she scarcely slept at all. Her mind went round and round on its treadmill, its sterile walk of questions and regrets. In the small hours she must have dozed a little, for she dreamed she had gone to a Mass for Peter's soul, and Gervase was the Priest. The server had just carried the Book to the north end of the Altar, and she stood waiting to hear the grail—"The righteous shall be held in everlasting remem-

brance: he shall not be afraid of any evil tidings." But instead
a terrible voice rang out: "I have delivered my beloved into
the hand of the wicked, and my heritage is become unto me
as a lion in the wood.".... Trembling and panting, she awoke
to the realisation that no Mass could be said for Peter, no office read; that he was not one of "the Faithful Departed"—
that good company of many prayers....

She lay motionless, her face buried in the pillow, without
struggles or tears. She was aware, without sight of the dawn
breaking round her, of the cold white light which filled the
room, of the grey sky lying like a weight upon the trees. She
heard the wind come up and rustle round the house, and the
cocks begin to crow, some near, some far away—Padgeham
answering Dixter, and Wildings echoing Brickwall. The new
day had come—Holy Saturday, the day of peace, the last and
greatest of the Sabbaths, the seventh day on which God rested from the six days' labour of His new creation.

She was roused by a clock striking eight, and again her
abominable sense asserted itself. She had never lain in bed so
long in her life—she must get up quickly, and give her father
his breakfast before he started on his rounds.

With as it were leaden weights in her head and limbs,
she rose, dressed and went down. As she was going down
the stairs a kind of hope revived. Perhaps this morning there
would be a letter from Gervase....

Yes, there was. It was lying in the letter box with a lot of
others. She eagerly tore it open and read—

"Stella, dear—this is just to tell you how I feel for you and
am praying for you.—Gervase."

That was all.

A sick and silly feeling of disappointment seized her. She knew now that for some unaccountable reason she had been banking her hopes on that letter. She had been expecting Gervase to resolve her doubts, to reconcile her conflicts. But instead he seemed ridiculously to think she could do all that for herself. Her heart warmed against him—perhaps he shrank from coming to grips with the problem. His faith recoiled from the raw disillusion which he must know she was feeling. He would keep away from her rather than be mixed up in her dust.... Well, he should not. His aloofness should not save him. She would go over to Conster and see him, since he would not come to her. With a growing resentment she told herself it was the least he could do for her. She had given him his faith—he might at least make an effort to save hers.

"Father," she said when they were at breakfast—"do you mind driving yourself out this morning? I'm going to Conster to see Gervase."

"Certainly, my dear. I'm glad you're going to see him—I thought perhaps he might be coming here."

"So did I—but he's asked me to go there instead."

Something in her detached and dispassionate said—"that lie was quite well told."

§30

As soon as her father had gone, she set out for Conster. She went by the road, for the field way ran near Starvecrow, and she had not the courage to go by Starvecrow.

She did not get to Conster till nearly eleven, and as she walked up the drive she asked herself what she would do if Gervase was out. She would have to wait, that was all. She must see him—he was the only person on earth who could help her.

However, he was not out. Wills let her in very solemnly. He did not attach any importance to the gossip in the servants' hall—but ... she looked ill enough, anyway, poor creature.

"Yes, Miss, Sir Gervase is in. I will tell him you're here."

Stella started a little—Sir Gervase! She had asked for Mr. Gervase. She had forgotten. In her absorption in the main stream of the tragedy she had ignored its side issues, but now she began to realise the tempests that must be raging in Gervase's life. Would he have to leave his community, she wondered—after all, he could easily come out, and great responsibilities awaited him. The next minute she gave another start—as she caught her first sight of Brother Joseph.

He seemed very far away from her as he shut the door behind him. Between them lay all the chairs and tables, rugs and plants of the huge, overcrowded drawing-room. For the first time she became aware of a portrait of Peter on the wall—a portrait of him as a child, with masses of curly hair and wide-open, pale blue eyes. She stared at it silently as Gervase came towards her across the room.

"Stella, my dear."

He took both her hands in his firm, kind clasp, and looked into her eyes. His own seemed larger than usual, for his hair was cut very close, almost shorn. That, and his rough grey cassock buttoned collarless to his chin, altered his appearance completely. Except for his touch and voice, he seemed almost a stranger.

"Gervase...." she sank into a chair—"Help me, Gervase."

"Of course I will. Did you get my note?"

"Yes—but, oh, Gervase...."

She could say no more. Her breath seemed gone. She held her handkerchief to her mouth, and trembled.

"I should have written more—but I've had such a time, Stella, with my family and the lawyers. Perhaps you can understand what a business it all is when I tell you that I've no intention of coming out of the Order, which means I've got to make up my mind what to do with this place. I've been at it hard all yesterday afternoon and this morning with my father's London solicitors, but I've managed to keep the family quiet till after the funeral, by which time I shall have the details settled. Otherwise I should have come to see you.... But I knew you were safe."

"Gervase, I'm not safe."

"My dear—"

He held out his hand and she took it.

"I'm not safe, Gervase. You think I'm stronger than I am. And you don't know what's happened."

"I know all about Peter."

"Yes, but you don't know the details. You don't know that Peter killed himself because I insisted, in spite of all his entreaties, on going away. He told me that my presence was the only comfort he had left, but I wouldn't stay, because if I stayed I knew that I should be tempted, and I was afraid.... I thought it was my duty to run away from temptation. So I ran. I never thought that perhaps Peter couldn't live without me— that I was saving my soul at the expense of his. I wish now that I'd stayed even if it had meant everything.... I'd far rather sin through loving too much than through loving too little."

"So would I. But have you loved too little?"

"Yes—because I thought of myself first. I thought only of saving my own soul ... and I thought I could forget Peter if only I didn't ever see him again, and I thought he could forget me. But he couldn't—and I can't."

"In other words, you did right and behaved very sensibly, but the results were not what you expected."

"Gervase—if you tell me again that I've been 'right' and 'sensible,' I—oh, I'll get up and go, because you're being just like everyone else. Father says I've been 'right' and 'sensible'—and I know Father Luce would say it—and the Coroner will say it this afternoon. And it'll be true—true—true! I have been right and sensible, and my right has put Peter in the wrong, and my sense has driven him mad."

"And what would your wrong have done for Peter?"

"He'd still be alive."

"With your guilt upon him as well as his own. Stella, my dear, listen to me. When I talk about your being 'right' I don't mean what most people would mean by right. If it's any comfort to you, I think that most people who have intelligence and are not merely conventional would think you had done wrong. You loved Peter and yet refused to have him, with the result that his life is over and yours is emptied. I know, and you know, that you did this because of an allegiance you owed beyond Peter. But most people wouldn't see that. They'd think you had refused him because you were afraid, because you dared not risk all for love. They'd never see that all the daring, all the risk, lay in your refusing him. Now be candid—isn't part of your unhappiness due to your feeling that it would have been braver and more splendid to have done what Peter wanted, and let everything else go hang?"

"Yes," said Stella faintly.

"Well, I'll tell you what I think would have happened—if you'd stayed—stayed under the only conditions that would have satisfied Peter. Vera would have, of course, found out—she has found out already a great deal more than has happened; she's not the sort of woman who endures these things; she would have divorced Peter, and he would have married you. Nowadays these scandals are very easily lived down, and you'd have been Lady Alard. After a time the past would have been wiped out—for the neighbourhood and for you. You would probably have become extremely respectable and a little censorious. You would have gone to Leasan church on Sundays at eleven. You would have forgotten that you ever weren't respectable—and you would have forgotten that you ever used to live close to heaven and earth in the Sacraments, that you ever were your Father's child.... In other words, Stella, you would be in Hell."

Stella did not speak. She stared at him almost uncomprehendingly.

"I know what you think, my dear—you think you would have undergone agonies of regret, and you tell yourself you should have borne them for Peter's sake. But I don't think that. I think you would have been perfectly happy. Remember, you would have been living on a natural level, and though we're made so that the supernatural in us may regret the natural, I doubt if the natural in us so easily regrets the supernatural. Your tragedy would have been *that you would have regretted nothing.* You would have been perfectly happy, contented, comfortable, respectable, and damned."

"But Peter—he—"

"Would probably have been the same. He isn't likely to have turned to good things after seeing how lightly they weighed with you. But the point is that you haven't the charge of Peter's soul—only the charge of your own—'Man cannot deliver his brother from death or enter into agreement with God for him.' It cost very much more to redeem their souls than you could ever pay."

"But, Gervase, isn't Peter's soul lost through what he did—through what I drove him to—"

"My dear, how do we know what Peter did? What do we really know about his death? Can't you take comfort in the thought that perfect knowledge belongs only to Perfect Love? As for your own share—your refusal to love your love for him unto the death, your refusal to make it the occasion for treachery to a greater love—that refusal may now be standing between Peter's soul and judgment. You did your best for him by acting so—far better than if you had put him in the wrong by making his love for you—probably the best thing in his life—an occasion for sin. He takes your love out of the world unspoilt by sin. Your love is with him now, pleading for him, striving for him, because it is part of a much greater Love, which holds him infinitely dearer than even you can hold him. Stella, don't you believe this?"

She was crying now, but he heard her whisper "Yes."

"Then don't go regretting the past, and thinking you would have saved a man by betraying God."

"I'll try not...."

"And suppose as the result of your refusing to stay, Peter had turned back to Vera, and been happy in his wife and child again, you wouldn't have regretted your action or thought you'd done wrong. Well, the rightness of your choice isn't any less because it didn't turn out the way you hoped."

"I know—I know—but ... I was so cold and calculating—one reason I wanted to go away was that though I couldn't have Peter I didn't want to go without love ... for ever...."

"I scarcely call that 'cold and calculating.' I hope you will love again, Stella, and not waste your life over has-beens and might-have-beens. It's merely putting Peter further in the wrong if you spoil your life for his sake."

"You think I ought to get married?"

"I certainly do. I think you ought to have married years ago, and Peter was to blame for holding that up and damming your life out of its proper course. He kept you from marrying the right man—for Peter wasn't the right man for you, Stella, though probably you loved him more than ever you will love the right man when he comes. But I hope he will come soon, my dear, and find you—for you'll never be really happy till he does."

"I know, Gervase, I know—oh, do help me to be sensible again, for I feel that after what's happened, I couldn't ever."

"My dear, you don't really want help from me."

"I do. Oh, Gervase ... I wish I weren't going to Canada—I don't feel now as if I could possibly go away from you. You're the only person that can help me."

"You know I'm not the only one."

"You are. You're the only one that understands ... and we've always been such friends.... I feel I don't want to go away from you—even if you're still at Thunders...."

She spoke at random, urged by some helpless importunity of her heart. He coloured, but answered her quite steadily.

"I shall never leave Thunders, my dear. It's too late for that now. I shall always be there to help you if you want me. But I don't think you really want me—I think you will be able to go through this alone."

"Alone...."

A few tears slid over her lashes. It seemed as if already she had gone through too much alone.

"Yes, for you want to go through it the best way—the way Love Himself went through it—alone. Think of Him, Stella—in the garden, on the cross, in the grave—alone. 'I am he that treadeth the wine-press—alone.'"

"But, Gervase, I can't—I'm not strong enough. Oh ... oh, my dear, don't misunderstand me—but you say you owe your faith to me ... can't the faith I gave you help me now that I've lost mine?"

"You haven't lost it—it's only hidden for a time behind the Altar ... you must go and look for it there. If you look for it in me you may never find it."

She rose slowly to her feet.

"I see," she said, as a blind man might say it.

He, too, rose, and held out his hand to her.

"You'll know where I am—where I'll always be—my life given to help you, Stella, your brother, your priest. I will be helping you with my thoughts, my prayers, my offices—with my Masses some day, because, but for you I should never say them. In that way I shall pay back all you've given me. But to the human 'me' you've given nothing, so don't ask anything back. If I gave you anything in that way I might also take—take what I must not, Stella. So goodbye."

She put her hand into his outstretched one.

"Goodbye, Gervase."

"Goodbye."

She wondered if he would give her another of those free kisses which had shown her so much when first he went away.

But he did not. They walked silently to the door, and in the silence both of that moment and her long walk home she saw that he had paid his debt to her in the only possible way—by refusing to part with anything that she had given him.

§31

That afternoon the Coroner's inquest was held on Peter Alard, and twelve good men and true brought in a verdict of "accidental death." The Coroner directed them with the conscientiousness of his kind—he pointed out that, according to medical opinion, the dead man's wounds must almost certainly have been self-inflicted; but on the other hand they had rather conflicting evidence as to how the body was lying when found, and the doctor could not speak positively without this. He would point out to the witnesses the desirability of leaving the body untouched until either a doctor or the police had been summoned. No doubt they had thought they were doing right in carrying him to his father's house, but such action had made it difficult to speak positively on a highly important point. As to the motives for suicide— they had heard Miss Mount's evidence, which he thought had been very creditably given—indeed, he considered Miss Mount's conduct to have been throughout irreproachable, and whatever the findings of the jury she must not blame herself for having acted as any right-minded young lady would have done under the circumstances. Feeling herself attracted by the deceased, a married man, and realising that he was also attracted by her, she had very properly decided to leave the neighbourhood, and but for her father's professional engagements would have done so at once. The meeting at which she had made this decision known to Mr. Alard had taken place two months ago, and it was for the Jury to decide whether it was likely to have driven him to take his life so long after the event. The deceased's sister, Mrs. Benjamin Godfrey, had told them of a conversation she had had with him on the afternoon of his death. He seemed then to have been preoccupied about his farm of Starvecrow, and other evidence had shown that the estate was much encumbered, like most big properties at the present time, though the position was no more serious than it had been a year ago. The Jury must decide if any of these considerations offered sufficient motive for self-destruction, if the deceased's manner on the day of his death had been that of a man on the verge of such desperate conduct, and if the medical evidence pointed conclusively to a self-inflicted death. There were alternatives—he enlarged on the nature of gun accidents, dismissed the possibilities of murder—but the evidence for these hung on the thread of mere conjecture, and was not borne out by medical opinion.

The verdict was a surprise to the family. The loophole left by the Coroner had been so small that no one had expected even a local Jury to squeeze through it. But these men had all known Peter, many of them had done business with him, all had liked him. No one of them would have him buried with a slur upon his memory—no one of them would have his widow's mourning weighted with dishonour, or his child grow up to an inheritance of even temporary insanity—and incidentally they all liked Miss Stella Mount, and had no intention she should bear the burden of his death if they could help it. So they brought in their verdict, and stuck to it, in spite of some rather searching questions by the Coroner. They wouldn't even bring in an open verdict—they would do the thing properly for the kindly Squire who had for so long stood to them for all that was best in the falling aristocracy of the land.

Peter was buried with his father in Leasan churchyard, in the great vault of the Alards, where all of them lay who had not been buried at Winchelsea. He and Sir John mingled their dust with Sir William the land-grabber, whose appetite for farms lay at the bottom of all the later difficulties of the estate, with Gervase the Non-Juror, with Giles who met his casual loves at the Mocksteeple—with all the great company of Squires who had lived at Conster, lorded Leasan, built and farmed and played politics for nearly five hundred years. Perhaps as they stood round the grave in the late April sunshine, some of the family wondered if these were the last Alards for whom the vault would be opened.

Everyone went back to Conster after the funeral. Sir John's will had already been read by the solicitors. It presented no difficulties—the whole estate went to Peter Alard and his heirs; in the event of his dying without male issue, to Gervase. The will had been made shortly after the death of George.

Gervase knew that now the time had come when he must face his family. They were all there at tea, except Vera—who was still unable to leave her room—and he could tell by a certain furtive expectancy in some and uneasiness in others that a crisis was impending. Doris was the head of the expectant group, Jenny of the uneasy ones. Doris had never looked more unlike the hysterical, dishevelled woman who had wept for Sir John. In her new black frock, and her hat with the plumes that swept down to her shoulders—powdered, rouged, salved, pencilled and henna'd into elegance if not into beauty, she seemed to have gathered up in herself all the pomp and circumstance of the Alards. There was not much of it to be seen in Lady Alard's weary preoccupation with the burnt scones, in Rose's glancing survey of the other women's clothes, in Mary's rather colourless smartness, in Jenny's restlessness or her husband's awkwardness—he had carried his first top-hat into the drawing-room, and put it, with his gloves inside it, on the floor between his large feet—and there was certainly nothing of it in the present holder of the title, sitting with his arms folded and thrust up the sleeves of his habit, his shoulders hunched as with a sense of battles to come.

Gervase considered that the sooner the row was over the better; so, as no one seemed inclined to begin it, he decided to start it himself.

"Mother, dear, do you think you could lend me five shillings?—At least I'd better say give it to me, for I don't suppose there's the slightest chance of your ever seeing it again."

"Yes, dear—but why … I don't understand."

"Well, I've only got eighteenpence left from the money Father Peter gave me to come here, and the third class fare to Brighton is six and six."

"Gervase," shrieked Doris—"you're not going back to that place!"

"My dear, what else did you expect?"

"But you won't stay there—you won't go on being a monk—you won't refuse to be Sir Gervase Alard!"

"I haven't even begun to be a monk, and, according to the solicitors, I'll have to go on being Sir Gervase Alard to the end of my days—but I'm going to stay there."

"But what's to become of us? Gervase, you can't be Squire and not live here."

"Let me explain myself. I'm not thinking of being Squire. I forfeit all my rights absolutely, except the title, which I'm told I can't get rid of. But I shall sell the estate."

The silence that fell was almost terrifying. Doris sank back in her chair as if fainting, Lady Alard covered her face, Rose sat with her mouth open, Jenny and Godfrey stared at each other.

Lady Alard was the first to speak.

"You mean that you're going to turn us out—your mother and sisters—not even leave us a roof over our heads? And what becomes of the furniture?"

"I shall of course consult your wishes about the house. If you want to go on living here, the house and grounds are yours."

"But Gervase," cried Doris hoarsely—"what good will the house be to us without the land? Do you think we're going to live on here and see all the estate pieced out and flung to smallholders and contractors?—I'd rather go and live in a slum."

"If Gervase doesn't mean to live here, I'm by no means sure that I care to stay on," said Lady Alard. "The morning-room chimney smokes abominably, and the bedrooms are extremely inconvenient—also, with my illness, I really think I ought to live in a town. We might move into Hastings."

"But Gervase doesn't know what he's talking about," cried Doris—"he can't desert us and fling away his responsibilities like this. Sell the estate! Oh, God—poor Father!" and she burst into tears.

Rose sprang to her feet with an indignant look at Gervase, and put her arm round Doris's heaving shoulders, but her sister-in-law ungratefully pushed her away.

"I'm dreadfully sorry," said Gervase, "but I really don't think I'm letting anyone down. I've gone into things pretty thoroughly during the last few days, and really it would have been extremely difficult for us to carry on."

"Difficult—but not impossible."

"Not impossible. But possible only in the way we've been doing for the last ten years, and, honestly, do you think that's good enough?"

"It's better than throwing everything overboard, anyhow."

"I don't think it is. By 'throwing everything overboard,' as you call it, we can at least save the land."

"How?"

"For the last ten years we've been doing hardly anything for the land. We've been unable to introduce up-to-date methods; we can't even keep our farms in decent repair. If we hung on now, still further crippled by death-duties, the land would simply go to pot. By selling, we can save it, because it will pass into the hands of men who will be able to afford it what it needs. Possibly one or two of the tenants will buy their farms. Anyhow, there won't any longer be a great, big, unwieldy, poverty-stricken estate, paying more in taxes than it actually brings in profits and deteriorating every year for lack of money spent on it."

"But I'm perfectly sure that if you pulled yourself together you could save the estate without cutting it in pieces. A conservative government is sure to improve matters for us and reduce taxation. I know Peter could have saved us."

"I'm not Peter."

"But you could save us if you wanted to. You've only to put yourself at the head of things, and get a really good bailiff, and perhaps sell an outlying farm or two to bring in a little ready money.... But you won't. That's what you mean. You don't want to come out of your monastery and face the world again. You could save us. But you won't."

"You're quite right—I won't."

The discussion had somehow become a dialogue between Gervase and Doris. Why Doris should appoint herself as Alard's spokesman no one exactly knew, but none of the rest made any effort to join in. Lady Alard was too deeply preoccupied with the house and its impending changes to worry about the land, Rose was angry with Doris for having repulsed her, so would give her no support, Mary was indifferent, Godfrey diffident, and Jenny, though revolting deeply from her brother's choice, was too loyal to him to take anyone else's part.

"I won't because I can't," continued Gervase; "I can't leave the Abbey, even if I knew that by doing so I could save Conster. I went there long before I'd the slightest notion I should ever succeed to this place, but even if I'd known I should have gone just the same. The only other thing I could do now would be to appoint a trustee to administer the estate for me, but in that way I should only be adding to the difficulties all round. By selling the place I'm doing the best possible thing for the land and for everyone else. The land will run a chance of being developed to its fullest value, instead of being neglected and allowed to deteriorate, and I'll be making a fairly decent provision for Mother and all the rest of you—you'll be far better off than if we'd stuck to the old arrangement; you'll have ready money for about the first time in your lives. Mother and Doris and Mary can live on here if they like, or they can go and live in Hastings or in town. I think the sale ought to realise enough to make everyone fairly comfortable—anyhow, much more comfortable than they are in the present state of things."

"But, Gervase," sobbed Doris—"you don't seem to think of the family."

"What else am I thinking of? I'm just telling you that you and Mary and Mother—"

"But we're not the family. I mean the whole thing—the house of Alard. What's to become of it if you go and sell the estate, and shut yourself up in an Abbey, instead of coming here and looking after the place, and marrying and having children to succeed you? Don't you realise that if you don't marry, the whole thing comes to an end?"

"I'm afraid it will have to come to an end, Doris. I can't save it that way."

Doris sprang to her feet. She looked wild.

"But you must save it—you must. Oh, Gervase, you don't understand. I've given up my life to it—to the family. I've given up everything. I could have married—but I wouldn't—because he wasn't the sort of man for our family—he wasn't well-connected and he wasn't rich—it would have been a come-down for an Alard, so I wouldn't have him—though I loved him. I loved him ... but I wouldn't have him, because I thought of the family first and myself afterwards. And now you come along, undoing all my work—making my sacrifice worthless. You don't care twopence about the family, so you're going to let it be sold up and die out. We're going to lose our house, our land, our position, our very name.... I gave up my happiness for Alard, and you go and make my sacrifice useless. Gervase, for God's sake save us. You can—if only you'll come away from those monks and be Squire here. I'm sure God can't wish you to desert us. Gervase, I beg you, I pray you to save the family—I pray you on my knees...."

And suiting the action to the word, she went down on her knees before him.

The others sat rooted to their chairs—partly at the sight of Doris's frenzy, partly of her humiliation, partly to hear the multitudinous lovers she had always hinted at reduced in a moment of devastating candour to one only. Gervase had sprung to his feet. He trembled and had turned very white. Then for a moment he, too, seemed to turn to stone.

"I pray you," repeated Doris hoarsely—"I pray you on my knees...."

Her brother recovered himself and, taking both her hands, pulled her to her feet.

"Don't, Doris...."

"Then, will you?"

"My dear, is the family worth saving?"

"What d'you mean?"

"Listen, Doris. You've just told me that you've given up your life's love and happiness to the family. Peter ... I know ...

gave up his. Mary gave up part of hers, but saved a little. Jenny alone has refused to give up anything, and is happy. Is our family worth such sacrifices?"

Her head drooped unexpectedly to his shoulder, and she collapsed in weeping.

"No," he continued—"it isn't worth it. The family's taken enough. For five hundred years it has sat on the land, and at first it did good—it cared for the poor, it worked its farms to the best advantage, and the estate prospered. But it's outlived those days—it's only an encumbrance now, it's holding back the land from proper development, it's keeping the yeoman and small land-owner out of their rights, it can't afford to care for the poor. It can barely keep its hold on the land by dint of raising mortgages and marrying for money. It can only be kept up by continual sacrifices—of the land, of the tenants, of its own children. It's like a wicked old dying god, that can only be kept alive by sacrifices—human sacrifices. And I tell you, it shan't be any more."

There was another pause, noisy with Doris's weeping. The other members of the family began to feel that they ought to take their share in the argument. They none of them felt for Alard what Doris so surprisingly felt, but after all they could not sit round and watch Gervase turn the world upside down without some protest.

"You know I want to be reasonable," said Jenny in rather an uncertain voice, "and I don't want to push you into a way you don't want to go. But from your own point of view, don't you think that all this that's happened just shows—that—that this religious life isn't, after all, the right life for you—the life you were meant for?"

"I always said it was very silly of Gervase to become a monk," said Lady Alard. "He could do quite a lot of good in the parish if he lived at home. Mr. Williams said he was looking for someone to manage the Boy Scouts."

"Yes, that was what poor George was always saying," said Rose—"'Charity begins at home.'"

"Oh, don't think I haven't prayed over this," cried Gervase—"that I haven't tried hard to see if, after all, my duty didn't lie in taking my place here and trying to save the property. But I'm quite sure that isn't my duty now. As I've tried to show Doris, Conster simply isn't worth saving. It's lost its power for good—it can only do harm, to the district and to us. It had much better come to an end."

"But even if you feel like that about the estate," said Mary—"there's the family apart from the land. It's rather dreadful to think that a fine old family like ours should be deliberately allowed to die out—the name become quite extinct. And it's not only for the family's sake, but for yours. You're a young man—scarcely more than a boy. I think it's dreadful that you should already have made up your mind to live without marriage and die without children."

"So do I!" cried Jenny, fierce at last.

"I've gone into all that," said Gervase with a touch of weariness, "and you know how I've decided."

"But these new circumstances hadn't arisen."

"I shouldn't have decided differently if they had."

"I'm not sure," said Mary—"that even that other plan you spoke of wouldn't be best—better than selling everything, I mean. Couldn't you administer the estate through a bailiff or trustee?"

"If my father and Peter couldn't make it pay, what would be the result of an absentee landlord?—the place wouldn't stand it. We'd bust. No, in fairness to the land it ought to go back to the small landlords—that's its only chance of recovery. I'm not doing this only for our own sakes, but for the sake of the land and the people it ought to belong to."

"I think you're a traitor," said Rose—"a traitor to your house."

"I wish I was dead," cried Doris. "First Father—then everything else.... I've nothing to live for now."

"Why, you've got me," said Lady Alard—"You'll come with me, Doris. I think I shall go to Worthing—it's more bracing than the coast here. Gervase, do you think the dining-room sideboard would fit into a smaller house?"

"Oh, Father," sobbed Doris—"Oh, Father—oh, Peter.... What would you have done if you had known how it was going to end?"

THE END

The End of the House of Alard was designed in Adobe Caslon and
Mr. Eaves and composed by Kachergis Book Design of Pittsboro,
North Carolina. It was printed on 55-pound Maple Antique
Cream and bound by Mape Press of York, Pennsylvania.